HOSTILE HOSPITAL

By

John Avanzato

KCM PUBLISHING
A DIVISION OF KCM DIGITAL MEDIA, LLC

CREDITS

Hostile Hospital by John Avanzato

ISBN-13: 978-1-939961-16-7
ISBN-10: 1939961165

Second Edition
Publisher: Michael Fabiano
KCM Publishing www.kcmpublishing.com

Other Novels in the John Cesari Series

Acknowledgements

First and foremost, I would like to thank my beautiful wife, Cheryl, for her endless support editing, re-editing, and acting as a sounding board for ideas. Her input and attention to detail were invaluable as the manuscript progressed. It is not an exaggeration to say that I would have been lost without her.

I would also like like to thank my family, friends and beta readers for their time and effort on my behalf but especially Paul Kisatsky, Salvatore Montagna, Karen Deacon MD, Michele Keith, Mark Rego MD, Amy Secor FNP, Michael Fabiano and Bill Greanleaf whose sage advice and calm encouragement kept me grounded throughout the project.

We are all the products of our experiences, our environment and our relationships with teachers, mentors and role models. This is particularly true in medical education where as a young man, I spent a full ten years in training before they unleashed me on society. I am grateful and fortunate to have studied under some of the greatest names in my profession in both internal medicine and gastroenterology. They instilled in me an undying passion for the pursuit of truth and an unwavering devotion to my patients. Thank you all.

Finally, and most importantly a special thanks to my mother Isabelle, who always encouraged me to be the best I could be, never to fear criticism and to always stand for what is right. She was the most courageous person I have ever known. Words could never express my appreciation for having such an amazing woman in my life. It was like winning the lottery every single day and twice on Sundays.

Table of Contents

Dedication

In loving memory of my father, Joseph, who passed away at too young an age, and before I even had a chance to say goodbye. Thank you for all the sacrifices you made and the example you set. If I raise my children half as well as you raised yours, it will be said that I did a fantastic job.

I swear by apollo the healer to keep the following oath:

I will prescribe regimens for the good of my patients according to my ability and my judgment

AND NEVER DO HARM TO ANYONE...

--Excerpts from the Hippocratic Oath

Chapter 1

The Bronx, a long time ago.

It was Saturday night in mid-August and the humidity was stifling. The air was so thick with moisture, he could barely breathe, and his cotton shirt clung to him like a second skin drenched with perspiration. The heat wave blistering the city for the last two weeks had shown no signs of letting up. That was for sure. It was ninety-five degrees in the shade earlier in the day and maybe eighty-five now that the sun was down. Tempers were running short everywhere. This was the kind of weather that could turn a minor disagreement over a parking space into bloody combat. Heat like this caused people to run out of patience quickly. John Cesari had run out of patience about four hours ago and now he was angry. He was beyond angry. He was irate, but mostly at himself. He had been keeping an eye on this guy for nearly a week when the opportunity finally presented itself.

And he couldn't do it.

And he didn't understand why he couldn't do it. That annoyed him even more. He should have put a bullet in this guy's forehead an hour ago, but he didn't. The man sat opposite Cesari on a wooden folding chair, a strip of red duct tape across his mouth and his hands bound behind him. They were in the guy's two-car garage away from the central air of his living room. A silver Mercedes sedan was parked in the bay next to them. The guy was sweating too but for a different reason. He knew that any moment now all his religious beliefs about what lay beyond this earthly existence were about to be put to the test. He was probably a little more than surprised that he was still among the living.

He was a thirty-five-year-old, quick-talking financial guy named Lenny something or other. Married with one child, he was about to lose it all because of greed. It was always that way it seemed. He had scammed a boatload of money from Cesari's boss using a white-collar three-card monte scheme involving not so clever phony investments and dummy corporations with the help of a not so loyal accomplice in the legal profession whose stripper girlfriend was at this very moment probably wondering why he hadn't called her all day. Nor would he ever again. He took a nasty fall coming out of the shower that morning. Wet tiled floors were dangerous things. People were always banging their heads against them and the edge of porcelain bathtubs. Cesari had almost slipped and fallen himself while he helped the lawyer bang his head. Today was a big day for Cesari. His first doubleheader. After he finished with the lawyer, Cesari had come straight up to Riverdale to take care of Lenny. If he pulled this off, he would be legendary in his circles and certainly in the eyes of his boss.

Cesari's boss was Mr. Frank Dellatesta aka Frankie D. to his friends, associates and the FBI. Lenny knew Frankie D. both professionally and personally so he also knew that this day of reckoning was as inevitable as the turning of the planet on its axis and its revolution around the big star called the sun. He knew all right, which is why Cesari was a little perplexed at how poorly he was handling it, sniveling and weeping like a little girl. He had no pride in himself. That was easy to see.

Still, Cesari inexplicably procrastinated. He sighed, leaned over and ripped the duct tape off the guy's mouth. "Lenny, Lenny, Lenny," he said slowly. "What did you think was going to happen? Did you really think he wasn't going to find out?"

"I'm sorry. I'm sorry. I really am. Tell Frankie D. I'll give the money back…with interest. I swear."

"I think it's too late for that, Lenny. Mr. Dellatesta's taking this personally. He said you were like family. He trusted you."

He bowed his head and pissed himself. "I know. I know. I know," he sobbed.

Cesari pushed his chair back. "Lenny c'mon. Look what you're doing."

Lenny pleaded, "Look… Let me give *you* the money." He perked up suddenly as if he just had a great idea. "You let me go and I'll give you the money. No one has to know. I'll leave town. You'll never see me again. You tell Frankie D. you couldn't find me. That'll work."

"Lenny, you know I can't do that. Now stop making noise. I'm trying to think."

Cesari slapped the tape across Lenny's mouth again and reflected on his conflicted emotions trying to decipher the meaning behind his reticence. Beneath his calm exterior was a seething caldron of confusion. He started out his day cool as a cucumber and was now ending it like a head of wilting lettuce. What happened in between? He didn't know. This guy didn't deserve to live. That was as plain as the nose on his face.

John Cesari was the product of life on the streets of the Bronx, New York. He was an only child and his father was not a significant part of his upbringing. His mother tried her best to keep him in tow, but was swamped, working two and some-times three jobs all the while trying to stay on top of a rebellious teenager who hadn't yet matured enough to appreciate all she was doing for him. To say that she had her hands full with him was a major understatement. He was the mother lode of prob-lematic children. He was the reason women gave up their kids for adoption, but she loved him and he knew it. He just couldn't help being who he was.

To her dismay, he moved out on his seventeenth birthday. Partly because living with his mother was cramping his style and partly because he knew she would disapprove of the fast and furious path he had chosen for himself. But he didn't move far. He loved her too much for that. He dropped by once a week to see her and to give her an envelope stuffed with ill-gotten cash to help her out.

He wasn't lonely and had found common ground with street thugs and the like that lurked on every corner and in every dark alley of every inner city. He worked his way up quickly from the runners, the wannabes, the bag men and hangers on to the soldiers to the lieutenants, onwards and upwards until even the neighborhood capos had taken notice. He was smart and fast and could back it up with muscle and ruthlessness when he had to.

These were his teachers and they had nurtured and educated him according to the rules of the concrete jungle. Full of piss and vinegar, he had learned all the wrong things from all the wrong people, and he had learned well. He was the end result of some type of primitive zoological experiment gone terribly awry and now this guy sitting in front of him was going to pay the price for all of the misguided values instilled in him.

They had been sitting like that for almost an hour. A Smith & Wesson lay in Cesari's lap as he watched the tears stream down the guy's face. The gun was a snub-nosed hammerless .38 special loaded with five hollow point rounds. It had no silencer, but Cesari wasn't worried. It wasn't a particularly powerful weapon in the universe of handguns, but it was light and easily concealed and up close like this would get the job done as well as a .50 caliber machine gun. If he pressed the muzzle hard enough into the guys body or face, his internal organs would muffle the sound and further increase the lethality of the shot as the explosive force of the gases would take place inside the guy's own tissues, not that a hollow point round up close would need any help. It would flatten out on impact, possibly fragment like a hand grenade and rip and tear at vital organs and blood vessels and in seconds, the guy would be no more than a foot-note in history.

A shot to the head would be the most merciful thing of course and it was entirely up to Cesari's discretion how to carry out the guy's sentence. The only instruction that had been given to him was that it was to be obvious when he was found what had happened to serve as a lesson to anyone else who might be thinking of putting his hand in the till. Suffocating him with a plastic bag or strangling him with a rope would serve that pur-pose too and were the preferred methods in a family neighbor-hood like this because they were quieter but Cesari liked the challenge. The idea that someone might hear and that someone might call the police sent a rush of excitement through him as if he was a secret agent or something similar as he raced away down narrow streets. He was like that.

Cesari gazed at Lenny's blubbering face and wanted to slap it. He had no sympathy for him. You did something wrong and you had to own it like a man. Even worse, Lenny had a weak chin. Not that it mattered but Cesari didn't like weak chins. He imagined what a bullet hole in Lenny's left eye would look like. He should just do it now. Just raise the gun, point and shoot.

But he couldn't do it.

It wasn't like him to hesitate with anything. He was gener-ally a very decisive person, full of the confidence that came with youth. He had arrived from the lawyer's apartment at around 10:00 a.m. and had been camped out comfortably all afternoon watching Lenny mow his lawn, water his vegetable garden and do all the usual things normal people do on the weekend. Lenny lived in a modest split-level, white ranch with a decent sized, well-tended front lawn in a very nice section of the Bronx. The house was only a quarter of a mile from the entrance to the Henry Hudson Parkway, which led directly into Manhattan. It was in a prime location. He had taken his wife and kid to a mall in Westchester around noon. They'd had lunch in the food court.

His wife, Cathy, was an attractive thirty-year-old brunette with a nice figure, about five-feet-four inches tall. She would marry again. In Cesari's limited experience, the pretty ones always did. The boy was about six or seven years old and looked like Lenny.

The family had gone into a sporting goods store and came out with new baseball gloves for each of them. They all seemed so happy. This fascinated and upset Cesari for reasons that he couldn't easily explain. When they returned home, they formed a triangle on the front lawn and played catch for about an hour in the shadow of a large oak tree while Cesari watched from across the street.

Cesari had listened to the Giants-Eagles game on the radio to pass the time while they played. It hadn't gone well for Big Blue. They had blown a fourth quarter lead and lost. Picking up right where they left off last year, Cesari had mused. He never understood Saturday football or Friday night and nowadays Thursday night football. Monday night made sense. It was traditional, but now we faced five days of football a week. How much of a demand for three and half hour-long incessant beer commercials could there possibly be? The games weren't even fun anymore what with the narcissistic self-serving droning of know-nothing announcers and steady stream of penalties, time-outs, and play-reviews leading to more beer commercials. And yet if he had been home in his apartment, he was sure he'd have watched also. Go figure.

Sitting in the driver's seat of his new Saleen, 550 horsepower Mustang, he had tried to look ordinary. He wore nondescript clothes, blue jeans, sneakers and a short sleeve pull over cotton shirt and sun-glasses. He was suntanned and had thick, dark brown neatly cut hair. He had no identifying tattoos or body-piercings. The car was black, shiny and gaudy with partially tinted windows. It screamed of testosterone and sex. It had everything but a sign on it that said, "Hey I'm a tough guy." Anywhere else, he might have stuck out like a sore thumb, but this was the Bronx, and no one even noticed. Muscle cars were the norm and so were tough guys.

He liked to joke with his pals that the only thing around with more muscle than that car was him, and he was right. At six feet even, he was a ripped two-hundred-and-twenty-pound specimen. In his free time, he lived in the gym. Pushing and lifting heavy objects made of iron was very therapeutic and kept him grounded. When he wasn't doing that he was usually in some girl's bedroom. He had no regrets. He liked his life and his bosses liked him. He was on the fast track upward in his circles and everyone had their eyes on him.

But something was wrong tonight. It didn't feel the same. He had become edgy and off balance as he staked out the house earlier. Why? He didn't think anyone had noticed him. He'd gotten good at his trade. Every now and then as he watched them playing on the lawn, he would pretend to make a call on his cellphone or drive around the block, parking in a different place so his surveillance wouldn't be too obvious. There were a couple of other muscle cars here and there and he blended in fairly well from that point of view. A bright yellow Charger with racing stripes down the center was parked on the other side of the street and a Cobalt blue Corvette in someone's driveway provided great cover for him. He was sure no one had suspected a thing.

It was the kid's birthday and a source close to Lenny had told him that the wife was going to take the boy and a group of his friends to a movie and pizza later in the day. In this heat, they'd probably wind up somewhere for ice cream as well. Lenny would be home alone. He was a Yankees fan and planned on watching the big Red Sox game on TV. There was a chance of course that he might go out and celebrate with his family, but Cesari doubted it. Pizza and a Disney movie versus the Yankees? The movie didn't stand a chance and they could always bring him home some pizza. No, he'd stay home.

Something happened when they were tossing the ball around on the front lawn that bothered Cesari. There was something about the scene that nagged at the back of his brain. It was like an itch that he couldn't reach to scratch. It disturbed him and compelled him. He'd gotten out of the Saleen to stretch his legs, and as he opened the door, Cesari heard all three of them call out at once. He looked over at them and realized that the boy had missed his throw. The ball had gone over his head into the street and was rolling toward Cesari.

By the time it reached him, it had slowed enough that all he had to do was put his foot out to stop it. He held the ball under his sneaker for a few seconds before he reached down and picked it up. Inspecting it, he saw that it was a Rawlings brand. Aside from a few grass stains, it was pretty new. They waited to see what he would do, and as the clock ticked, he could sense their concern beginning to mount as he hesitated. When Lenny took a step in his direction, Cesari wound up and lobbed the ball to him. He stopped and caught it gracefully.

Cesari smiled disarmingly at him and said, "Strike three, you're out of here."

They all laughed and thanked him, but this triggered something in Cesari. He had hustled back into the driver's seat and to his dismay, started to hyperventilate. He willed himself to calm down but his head throbbed and a wave of nausea had swept over him. Not good, he'd thought but over time regained his composure. That was the turning point in his day, and he hadn't felt right since. His heart continued to pound in his chest, but he managed to soldier on.

Parents started dropping their kids off at around 5:00 p.m. At six, they had all piled into the wife's Bronco and headed toward the movie theatre. The nearest one was a multiplex at least a half hour's drive away, which meant the show probably started around seven. Two hours for the movie, two more hours for pizza and ice cream and the drive home. Cesari figured he had until about eleven to do the deed and clear out of there.

It would be a terrible thing to find when they got home, especially with all those kids excited about a sleepover, but Cesari didn't make the rules. Besides, it wouldn't be nearly as bad as it could be. The order had been to take out Lenny only and not his entire family. Cesari had never been given an order for total annihilation like that and wasn't sure what he would do if an order like that ever came. There were some lines that he knew he could never cross.

The wife had left the attached two-car garage door open. So around 8:00 p.m., just as the Yankee game was starting, Cesari put on a pair of latex surgical gloves and entered the open garage, found the switch that controlled the door and closed it behind him. He walked up to the house entrance and tested the door knob. It wasn't locked.

Cesari couldn't believe how stupid some people could be. The idea that someone would steal from a guy like Frankie D. and not even be smart enough to lock his doors was simply unfathomable to him. On the other hand if Lenny had any real brains, he never would have done anything this dumb in the first place. Entering the house quietly, he drew the revolver out from his pocket and found Lenny watching the ball game with a bowl of popcorn in his lap. And now here they were staring at each other. Defying all odds, Lenny was still breathing.

The ball and gloves that he and his family had played with sat on the garage floor a few feet away. They caught Cesari's eye and he ripped the duct tape off Lenny's mouth again.

"How old's your kid?"

Lenny gasped and breathed deeply before saying, "Ricky's seven."

"Do you play with him a lot? You know, catch?" Cesari asked, nodding in the direction of the gloves.

He nodded. His eyes were red and swollen. "Yeah, as often as I can. He's in little league. He really likes it."

It was well after 9:00 p.m. and he needed to make a decision. He felt it deep inside that for whatever reason this just wasn't going to happen. He said, "Lenny, do you have relatives or people you can stay with in an emergency?"

Lenny stared blankly at him, confused and then got hopeful. "You changed your mind. You want the money? I'll need a few days."

"No, Lenny I don't want the money, but you need to understand something. If I don't do this, someone else will. You made a big mistake and there's no going back on it. My advice to you is that when your wife comes home, you take her and your boy for a long ride and don't come back. I mean leave tonight, not tomorrow. Call the parents and tell them to come get their kids. Tell them that you have a family emergency. Tell them anything you want. Just get the hell out of here tonight. Understand? Whatever you do don't try to talk your way out of it with Mr. Dellatesta. It won't work."

Lenny nodded, "I understand."

"And forget you ever saw me."

"I will. I promise."

Cesari stood up and walked to the gloves. He picked up the biggest one from the floor and asked, "This one yours?"

He nodded.

Cesari put it on over the latex glove he was already wearing. It fit perfectly although like any new glove, it was a little stiff and needed some glove oil. He had always loved the smell of new leather. Picking up the ball, he tossed it into the glove a few times. It felt good. Real good. Why?

He let out a deep breath and his voice cracked a little. "I think it's great that you play with your kid, Lenny."

"Thanks... Why are you doing this?"

"I don't know. I really don't know. Just get out of town and don't look back." Cesari turned to leave but hesitated and said, "One more thing, Lenny..."

Lenny looked at him, eyes wide open.

"Would you please lock your damn doors."

Cesari tossed the glove and ball back onto the floor and exited into the night.

Chapter 2

Disturbed by something he couldn't name, Cesari drove around for hours trying to relax, weaving his way slowly in and out of side streets making endless loops stretching from Allerton Avenue all the way down to Pelham Parkway and back again. He knew these roads well and the car practically drove itself. He had managed to keep it together in front of Lenny, but he was pretty shaken up. What the hell was bugging him? It wasn't like this was his first time. In fact, it wasn't even his second time or third time. He was pretty seasoned. Not the most experienced guy on the roster by far but five full years had made him trusted and reliable. Until tonight anyway.

Frankie D. wasn't going to be thrilled when he heard the news. He wasn't the most understanding man to work for. Still, Cesari thought, Mr. Dellatesta had known him since he was a kid and would probably cut him more slack than some of the other guys. Nonetheless, whatever he told him would have to be creative, because he was definitely going to be livid. Lenny was on the short list for extinction and if he managed to escape his fate, there had better be a damned good reason. If Lenny returned the money, it might ease Frankie. D.'s disappointment, but Cesari doubted that Lenny would do that. He'd need it to get him and his family out of town and carry him through for an unspecified period of time. He suspected Lenny was going to be unemployable for a while.

As midnight approached, Cesari wasn't any closer to resolving his problem. His heart was still racing, and his head felt like it was going to explode. He pulled over and parked his car at the corner of Eastchester Road and Mace Avenue, a few blocks from where he lived. This was his neighborhood, and he was its de facto king. He looked down at his fists and thought about all the guys he had pummeled right here or somewhere nearby. He was getting a real reputation and deservedly so.

Sitting there under the glare of the streetlights, his brain spinning on its axis he decided to do something he hadn't done in quite a while. He pulled out his cellphone and dialed Mark Greenberg, his psychiatrist. On the third ring, Mark answered, his voice sleepy.

"Cesari."

"Hello Mark...Dr. Greenberg. I'm sorry to bother you so late."

"It's okay. I told you to call me anytime, and I meant it. And cut the formality, all right? We've known each other too long. Mark is just fine. Are you all right? I haven't heard from you in a while."

"I'm sorry about that, and no, I'm not all right," Cesari answered truthfully, practically gasping into the phone. "Something happened tonight that's sent me into a tailspin. I haven't felt this way in a long time, and I'm having trouble breathing."

"Take it easy, Cesari. Take it easy. We've been down this road before and we'll get through it just like we always have. Breathe slowly and deliberately. In and out. The way we used to practice. Remember? There you go. That's it. Can you tell me about it? Where are you, by the way?" he asked, genuinely concerned.

Cesari had been going to Mark for counseling on and off since early adolescence when his mother noticed he had under-developed coping skills. He tended to solve problems with his fists, and if fists didn't work, then chairs and baseball bats. Mark said he was manifesting subconscious anger at not having his father around. Cesari felt his anger wasn't subconscious at all. He felt it was very conscious in his opinion and very delib-erate. His ability to channel his anger had made him a lot of money so far. Mark knew Cesari about as well as anyone did.

He knew about the monsters under his bed, and he knew what made him tick.

"I'm in the Bronx, parked on the street near my apartment. Long story short, some guy was playing catch with his kid, and the kid missed his throw. The ball rolled toward me, so I picked it up and threw it back to them. No biggie, but something about the scene sent shivers up my spine. For a minute, I thought I was going to pass out." He paused to catch his breath. His voice trembled as he continued, "I was on a job, and I couldn't even finish what I was supposed to do. I've been driving around for hours hoping to shake the feeling off, but it just keeps getting worse and..."

"And what?"

"I've been crying, Mark. Like a baby."

"All right, Cesari. Calm down. Take a slow, deep, cleansing breath and let it out. Have you been taking your medications?" he asked patiently.

There was silence as Cesari hesitated.

"Okay, need I ask why?"

"You already know why," he replied. "I've told you before what they do to me."

"Sexual side effects?"

"Yes."

He didn't reprimand him like he deserved, but instead asked, "All right, fine. So until tonight, how were you doing?"

"Pretty well, I thought. Then this happened, and now I feel like I'm falling apart."

As they talked, a couple in their twenties came out of a bar arguing loudly on the sidewalk. The guy waved his hands all over the place while she pouted. They were about two car lengths from where Cesari sat.

"Look Cesari, you said you were on a job when this happened. You've never told me what kind of work you do. Don't you think it might help if I knew?" he prompted gently.

"Maybe, but probably not," he answered evasively. "What should I do, Mark? I need to calm down. I don't have any of the pills left. I'll try taking them again if I have to."

"It's too late to call in a prescription for you, but I'll do that first thing in the morning... I could probably lose my license for this, but why don't you go to your apartment and have a drink or two, and I don't mean Bud Light if you get my drift. A couple of shots of vodka or tequila might settle you right down. Or better yet, do you have any pot?"

Cesari smiled at that one. When he was fourteen, Mark had spent hours scolding him about his marijuana use. The guy from the bar yelled at the girl so loudly that he could hear him with the windows all the way up and the air conditioner on high. She yelled back. He was about five-ten or eleven, two hundred pounds, thick chested with big muscular arms and slicked-back hair. A braided gold chain dangled around his brawny neck. She was slim and short, wearing spiked heels and had shoulder-length brown hair. Her jeans appeared to be painted on. They were for all intent and purpose two typical Bronx guineas in love.

"John, are you still there?" Mark asked when he hadn't answered his last question about pot.

"Yeah, I'm still here, Mark. I got distracted. Sorry. There's a situation going on not too far from me. Some guy and his girl are arguing outside a bar." He still hadn't answered the question.

"Well try to get through tonight as best you can, and I'd like to see you as soon as you can make it in. Please call me tomorrow and let me know how you are doing, okay? And Cesari, it's after midnight. Go home and get some rest."

Too late for that. The guy, who was turning to walk back into the bar, swung around suddenly and savagely backhanded the girl. She fell across the front end of the Camaro she was standing next to, her head bouncing on the hood.

"He just hit her, Mark," Cesari said flatly without emotion, without passion. *He just hit her, Mark.* A statement of fact, almost like he was commenting on the weather. *Boy, it's a hot one.*

Cesari watched as the girl got up, holding her face. She was clearly dazed from the blow and staggered slowly back to face the guy. Cesari felt a gallon of adrenalin suddenly get injected into his blood stream. It was like he had stuck his finger into an electrical socket. He snapped to attention and his senses sharpened. Whatever doldrums he was feeling before suddenly resolved and his world came dramatically back into focus.

His tone had changed, and Mark picked up on it. He was smart and knew Cesari too well. "Cesari, don't get involved, all right? This isn't your fight."

"The hell it ain't." He took a deep breath and zeroed in on the guy like a hawk, searching for weaknesses and assessing strengths.

"Just hang up and call the police," Mark implored.

"You know I can't do that, Doc. It's not in my nature." Cesari always called him Doc when the conversation was over and he wasn't listening anymore.

"Think it through. You know how you get in these situations. Self-control, I beg you. Use self-control," he urged.

"Self-control. Got it. I'll use self-control. I promise. I gotta run now, Mark. He just hit her again."

Cesari clicked off the call and looked up and down the block for potential witnesses or anyone who might feel compelled to intervene. He felt good again. Real good. He cut the Saleen's engine, reached down into the space next to the driver's seat and grabbed the crowbar he always kept there. He studied it briefly and said to no one, "From this day forward you shall be known as self-control."

He wasn't a violent man by nature, but violence had become a way of life for him, and he was good at it. He embraced it and accepted its reality. As he approached, the guy was facing away. He had smacked her two more times since the opening salvo which made it a total of three blows and he was now clutching her roughly by the hair. Her heels made her naturally unsteady and she had fallen to her knees in front of him losing one shoe in the process. He was about to unload a fourth blow on her but it didn't happen.

The guy brought his right hand up, exposing his right side. It was as good a spot as any and Cesari whipped the crowbar around forcefully like a baseball bat. Not with all his might. He didn't want to kill the guy. Instead of swinging for a homerun he was trying for a double. The blow struck and one, probably two ribs cracked loudly. The guy groaned, instantly letting go of the girl who fell backward on her ass. Up close, her face was all red and her mascara was running. She was undeniably pretty.

The guy spun around awkwardly clutching his side in pain and gritting his teeth. He sucked wind trying to speak but couldn't. Rib fractures were like that so Cesari waited. He wanted him to know what was happening. Cesari counted to five and walked the guy back not unsympathetically to lean against the Camaro.

Oddly enough, the guy said, "Thank you."

Then Cesari helped the girl up. "Are you okay?" he asked.

She didn't say anything. She had a distant, unfocused look in her eyes and Cesari guessed she was in shock or maybe had a slight concussion. She'd be okay with a couple of aspirin and a good night's sleep. He leaned her against a different car and turned back to the guy who was still doubled over, gasping.

His health status was going to be a different matter. Cesari didn't like it when men hurt women. It triggered something primitive deep inside. All sorts of ancient genetic codes were firing all at once like the sixteen cylinders of a Bugatti sports car. He became instinctively protective and explosive and very, very dangerous. Right now, he was seeing the world through a veil of red.

The guy grimaced and hissed, "Who are you?"

He was a little confused and didn't seem to understand what was about to happen. Pain did that sometimes. Cesari looked at him and said, "Just a guy. That's all you need to know. Now give me your right hand."

The guy looked at him puzzled by the request, like he thought Cesari wanted to shake hands. Like they were going to be friends or something. His right arm was cradled tightly against right side in an instinctive splinting position because of the intense pain he was experiencing.

He studied Cesari warily, but Cesari didn't appear to be threatening him at the moment. Maybe he wanted to help, so he limply extended the hand afraid to move it completely outward. Cesari grabbed him quickly by the wrist, extended the hand over the hood of the Camaro and in one smooth motion smashed it hard with the crowbar. The guy screamed in agony for real as at least three or four bones broke maybe more. It was a solid blow. Full force. He hadn't held anything back on that one. The guy yanked his hand back and started bobbing around the sidewalk in distress.

Cesari grabbed him by the shoulder and tapped him under the chin with the curved end of the piece of steel known as self-control. Enough to slam his teeth together. It brought him back to the here and now. Cesari said, "You hit her three times. That means you have one more coming your way to even the score and then one more as a penalty. I'll let you pick where but I get to decide how hard."

"Oh Jesus, please."

Cesari smiled. "He's not going to help you, brother. It's just you and me."

Chapter 3

Atlantic City, New Jersey. Not quite as long ago.

Vito Gianelli sat at his desk in the security office of the biggest hotel in town, the El Paradiso. A large, powerfully built man in his late thirties, he had jet-black hair and hard, chiseled features. This office was the nerve center for all activities, legal or otherwise, that took place within the confines of the hotel and casino. This was the place where all the real decisions were made. Sitting across from him on a plush leather couch were his trusted friend Pinky and the casino boss. It was 10:00 p.m.

Row upon row of computer monitors filled the room, feeding Gianelli views of every corner of the casino floor from every angle. For the last thirty minutes, he had been focused on one of the customers at the craps table.

"So who's the runt, Pinky?" Gianelli asked in a raspy voice that screamed of having smoked too many unfiltered cigarettes. As if to accentuate the point, he picked up a pack of Camels and lit one up.

Gianelli looked at Pinky and noted the broad-shouldered man's muscles bulging and rippling beneath his awkwardly fitting clothing. His left hand revealed a grotesquely deformed pinky, the result of a hostile interview by a rival gang with a hammer and a pair of pliers.

Pinky read dispassionately from a manila folder in front of him, "Theodore P. Snell, age fifty-three, checked into the two-bedroom Governor's Suite last night with a younger male companion, his son. He used an American Express Gold card in his name. We found the usual accoutrements in his bedroom in addition to a handful of condoms, including a used one in the trash by his nightstand. According to the hooker he was with last night, he likes to be called Teddy."

The casino boss sat meekly next to Pinky. He was fiftyish with perfectly coiffed salt-and-pepper hair. He wore a hand-tailored suit and imported, thousand-dollar Italian shoes. As the face of the casino for public consumption, he looked and acted the part. In reality, he worked for Gianelli, who in turn worked for his own boss, Big Lou Barazza.

Gianelli ran the casino for Big Lou. Gianelli did not answer to the board of directors or give press conferences. His decisions were absolute and not open for discussion, whether they involved life, death, or which color chips to use.

"What about the son?" Gianelli asked.

"His name is William Raymond Robert Snell. He goes by Billy Ray Bob, and he's thirty years old. In his room, we found a small quantity of coke, a loaded 9mm Glock, and a badge from the Genesee Police Department."

Pinky paused politely to allow Gianelli to digest the information. Gianelli raised his eyebrows a little and after a moment, asked, "Is it real?"

"The badge?"

"Yes, Pinky, the badge."

"We're running it, but I think so. Internet search shows that our guy Snell is the CEO of the Genesee General Hospital in upstate New York in the town of the same name. He's been in charge for the last ten years. No priors. No red flags. That's all we got so far, Vito."

Pinky closed the folder and Gianelli zoomed in on Snell using one of the many cameras at his disposal, studying him carefully. He observed a man of unusually short stature, middle-aged and flabby. He wore an off-the-rack suit, had a thick mustache and dark wavy hair, graying at the sides. Gianelli appraised him quickly, concluding that he was weak, both physically and intellectually.

The pit boss had called about thirty minutes ago to see if he could extend Snell's credit. The guy had already dropped two hundred grand of his own money and wanted to extend his credit another two hundred thousand.

Gianelli asked, "What do you think, Pinky?"

"I don't like his face, Vito. I'd like to smash it for him and then piss on his grave."

The casino boss squirmed uncomfortably and Gianelli glared at him harshly. "Did Pinky say something that offended you?" The man shook his head no and Gianelli turned back to Pinky. "Aside from that brilliant analysis Pinky, what's your professional opinion?"

"That was my professional opinion. This guy Snell is a loser. He's drinking like a fish. He's sucked down three large martinis in the last half hour that we've been watching him and now he wants to play with our money. No one drinking at that rate is making great decisions, Vito. I don't think he can back up his markers. I wouldn't lend him a penny. His son is even worse. Look at him on camera ten. He's boozing just as hard and hitting on every cocktail waitress that walks by. I would escort them both back to their room and tell them to sleep it off."

They all looked at camera ten and saw a well-built, clean-shaven man in his early thirties grabbing a waitress's ass. The younger man bore a striking resemblance to his father, except taller and fitter. He too struck Gianelli as being exceedingly deficient in the character development department of life.

"All right, they're degenerates without doubt," Gianelli assessed. "I think we can all agree on that. Father runs a small hospital upstate, and the son is a cop. They came down to party hard for the weekend and they got no control. They're not poor but they're not rich either, which means this can't possibly be their money they're throwing away. People like that don't burn two hundred grand in a night and then double down on it. What do you think, Pinky?"

"I agree. There's no way they can afford to drop coin like this."

"So it begs the question; whose money is it? Either way, they're in way over their heads now."

The casino boss waited quietly for his marching orders, hands clasped in front of him. Gianelli's brows furrowed in thought as he glanced at the special phone on his desk, which made and received calls from only one number. The person at the other end of the line was Big Lou Barazza. Big Lou was the only one Gianelli cared about making happy, and he thought about making a call now that might make Big Lou very happy.

Finally, he turned to the casino boss and said, "Call the craps table and tell them to extend the guy's credit another two hundred grand."

Pinky cleared his throat. "You sure you want to do that, Vito? What if he gets lucky?"

Vito smiled, something he didn't do often. He said to the casino boss, "You make sure he doesn't get lucky. Replace the stickman with Ernie and give him a chance to swap the dice out. Nobody does sleight of hand like that guy. He should have been a magician, and you tell the waitresses to stick to this guy Snell like glue. I want someone handing him a fresh drink every ten minutes whether he needs it or not."

The casino boss nodded and stood up to leave. "Yes, Mr. Gianelli."

"Also, send a bottle of champagne and a couple of girls to their room later tonight. Tell them it's our way of thanking them for their business. I want them to feel like royalty. And make sure at least one of the girls isn't old enough to vote. Got that?"

"Loud and clear, Mr. Gianelli."

"Pinky, get me as much information as you can on this hospital in upstate. I want to have its financial sheets on my desk in an hour."

"Consider it done, Vito."

"Also, Pinky, set up some cameras in their suite before the girls get there. I got an idea but I want to run it by Big Lou first. Before I make that call, I want to know everything there is to know about these guys. I want to know when they wake up and when they go to sleep. I want to know what they dream about, Pinky."

"Understood, Vito."

Later, after reviewing all the information that had been brought to him concerning Snell and the Genesee General Hospital, Gianelli came to a conclusion. He picked up the special phone on his desk and called Big Lou in New York to discuss the situation and all its potential.

Big Lou Barazza was the not-so-silent majority partner in the El Paradiso Hotel and Casino, although his name could not be found on even one legal document involving the business. It was midnight and Big Lou was on his third serving of scungilli in marinara when the phone rang.

Gianelli asked, "Are you interested in owning another hospital, Lou?"

"I'm interested in anything that makes me wealthier than I already am," Big Lou answered in the deep baritone that only men of great size have. "Tell me more."

While he laid out his idea, Gianelli gently stroked the head of the large black English Mastiff that had been lying beside him. The dog was so large, in fact, that even lying down, its head easily reached over the armrest of his chair.

Chapter 4

Present Day

Seated on the edge of the elderly woman's bed, Cesari fluffed her pillow and gazed into her clear blue eyes. He thought they must have been beautiful when she was younger. Even now in the twilight of her life, they captivated him. He held her bony hands and waited for her to speak. She was as pale as a ghost, her features gaunt and drawn beneath thinning white hair. She was dying, and they both knew that there was nothing more to be done.

"You're awfully quiet, John. What are you thinking about?"

"Nothing in particular, Maggie," he replied. What he was thinking about was how sad she seemed. He had picked up Maggie as a patient when he first arrived in town a few months back and had diagnosed her with metastatic colon cancer. Because of her age and the advanced stage of her disease there weren't many options available in terms of therapy, so she had opted for supportive care, palliation and pain control. They were now in the pain control stage.

"Thank you for coming John," she said in a frail, barely audible voice. "Not many physicians make house calls like this anymore."

He could feel himself melt. She was such a sweet old lady. "You're one of my favorite patients, Maggie," he said softly. "Did you know that?" He squeezed her hands gently. "I wish there was more that I could do for you. Besides, I don't consider this a house call. I think I'd be within my right to say that we're friends now. So I'm just visiting a friend, aren't I?"

She liked that and nodded. She had fought her cancer bravely and the end was in sight. The anorexia had caused her to waste down to nothing and she was totally exhausted. He had been impressed by her spirit along the way, but like most people with terminal diseases something clicked inside at the end telling them further effort was futile.

"Thank you and you are a friend, a very good friend. You've done more than enough and I am very grateful. I'm eighty-two years old, and I've lived a very long and fulfilling life. My time has come and I'm ready to go, I really am."

"You have a great attitude… Any interest in a game of checkers?" he asked. She kept a small board with pieces under her night table and it had been their ritual to play one or two games when he came to visit.

"Not today, thank you. I have enjoyed our little matches although I know you've been cheating."

"Cheating? Me? I never cheat…not at checkers anyway."

"You cheat by letting me win all the time," she giggled. "I have cancer not Alzheimer's. Cheating is cheating."

He laughed. "You got me."

A teacup with a flowered pattern and matching pot sat on a serving tray next to her bed. Cesari peeked around the room and saw that the furniture was old, and the carpet as faded and worn as she was. The room had a musty odor to it. The curtains were drawn letting in the late morning light.

He smiled. "You know, Maggie, I'm very proud of you. I hope that I'm as brave as you when my turn comes, and it will come one day."

Cesari poured some tea into her cup, and they both watched the steam rise into the air. She shrugged her shoulders. "Thank you, I couldn't have done it without you. It's been so nice having a shoulder like yours to lean on. You've given me lots of comfort. It's tough being old and sick without any family."

Her husband had died from a stroke less than a year ago, and her only son had died in a motorcycle accident as a young man. Her wedding picture rested on the night table next to her, and she looked at it now. There was no one else.

He nodded at the photo. He commented, "You and your husband were quite a handsome couple."

"Yes, we were, weren't we? Thank you. I was very lucky. He was very good to me."

"I'll bet you were very good to him too."

"I like to think so. We were devoted to each other."

"How long were you married."

"It would have been sixty-one years next May."

"Wow, that's quite an accomplishment. You don't hear that much anymore...people being married for sixty plus years."

"Young people today don't realize that you're supposed to work at it. It doesn't just happen. He wasn't perfect and neither was I. You learn to be strong where your spouse is weak and vice versa, but most of all you learn to compromise...to give a little and always remember why you got married in the first place... because you loved each other like crazy."

"Very sound advice right there... Maggie, you remind me very much of my mother. If she were alive, I think she would have liked you a whole lot."

She coughed feebly and wiped her face with a cloth towel she kept nearby. As she lay the towel down across her lap, he could see blood on it. The cancer had metastasized to her lungs, and the constant hacking made her miserable. When she coughed, she had displaced the oxygen tubing that ran to her nose, so he gently replaced it for her.

"Thank you. What happened to your mother?" she asked.

Cesari sighed. "She had breast cancer. She was only forty-five years old when she passed. She suffered a great deal unfortunately, and I wouldn't wish that on anyone."

She nodded sympathetically. "Do you think that's the reason you went into the medical profession?"

"I *know* it's the reason, Maggie. Her suffering inspired me to help people, people like you. Until then I was just kind of living for the moment, if you know what I mean. It may be hard to believe, but I was a bit of a ne'er-do-well back in the day. When my mother became ill and passed, I reassessed my life and saw it from a different perspective. It didn't happen overnight mind you, but in stages. Gradually, over time I started to see the world in a different light. I guess in a way, her death gave me a sense of purpose that was missing, and I firmly believe that I became a physician to honor her memory."

"I'm sorry that your mother suffered John, but it is so nice to hear that she had such a positive influence on you. You must have loved her very much and I know she would have been very proud of you." She pressed his hand lightly. She had almost no strength left and had not eaten anything solid in two days. "What of your father? Where is he?"

"I don't know where my father is. He disappeared when I was a small boy. He went off to work one day and never returned. Nobody knows what happened to him. I was seven years old."

"How awful. I'm so sorry to hear that."

Her features registered true concern and sadness for him. He said, "It hurt a lot at the time for sure, but you learn to accept certain realities, even as a child. Fortunately, what memories I have of him are only good ones, and I guess in a sense my desire to help people now is also a way of honoring him."

Cesari didn't have the heart to tell her that he had violent dreams about his father almost every night. Dreams he didn't understand. Dreams his therapists and counselors didn't understand. Terrifying night terrors that just wouldn't go away and which he fully expected to haunt him all the rest of his life.

She gently squeezed his hand again to comfort him and said, "I know wherever he is, he would also be proud of the man you have become... So tell me, is there anyone special in your life?"

"Absolutely. I'm sitting right next to her." She smiled and he checked her IV tubing to make sure it was running well. He had three syringes of narcotics in his pocket, ten milligrams of morphine sulfate in each one. He was ready when she was.

"Are you comfortable, Maggie?" he asked sincerely.

"I am, thank you. The pain medications have helped a great deal. I don't think that I could have managed without them."

It was her wish to die at home, so he had set up things in her bedroom as if she were in hospice. Bedridden and terminal, she didn't need much, just an IV for pain management, oxygen, an emesis basin and a bedpan. He had arranged for a twenty-four-hour nurse and alerted the funeral home to the severity of her condition. She was severely malnourished, and he knew it wouldn't be much longer with or without his help. The room already smelled of death. She had asked him to be with her at the end and he was honored to do so. She wanted to go out with grace and dignity and on her own terms.

"How did such a handsome boy from the Bronx wind up in this little town?" she asked out of curiosity.

"You really are nosy today, aren't you? And quite the flatterer," he said, watching her.

She struggled to smile again.

"I was recruited by the Genesee General Hospital to be a staff physician. I guess they needed a gastroenterologist and I needed a job. No great mystery there. And Genesee isn't that small of a town, Maggie. It has a population of almost fifty thousand and there's a twenty-four-hour Walmart. What more could anybody want?"

She laughed weakly at that. "Oh yes, how could I forget about the Walmart?" She laid her head back on her pillow and glanced at him poignantly. "I never told you this but my son was about your age when he died, John."

A solitary tear ran down her face. She had told him that but forgot. A forgivable minor lapse under the circumstances. He started to choke up and said, "I'm sorry, Maggie."

She nodded and looked out the window. It was October and the leaves of a nearby sugar maple dazzled vibrantly. She could see her church steeple two blocks away.

"It's a beautiful fall day out, isn't it?"

"Yes, it is," he agreed.

She was quiet for a while before she said, "Do you believe there's a Heaven?"

"I do, Maggie, and I believe that good people like you will find peace there."

"And what about bad people?"

He didn't say anything.

"The man upstairs will fix their wagon?" she asked.

He nodded. "Something like that."

"What do you hope to find there, John?"

He thought about that and then said, "I hope that I'll be reunited with my parents, and that things will be just as they were when I was a little boy. I would like to see them together and happy again the way I remember."

"That's so sweet. I think I'd like that too. It would be so nice to see my son and husband again." She sighed deeply as the memories overwhelmed her. "I think I'm ready now, John.

Would you say the Lord's Prayer with me one last time, please? And John...?" She closed her eyes.

"Yes, Maggie?"

"If I can't finish, will you finish it for me?"

"Of course I will."

After she passed, he walked over to the window and looked outside. It really was a beautiful day.

Chapter 5

Cesari arrived at the office an hour late, and his secretary Linda was already fit to be tied. With short blonde hair and blue eyes, Linda was still very attractive at fifty and could easily pass for forty. She kept herself in great shape and liked to wear tight-fitting clothing to show off her figure. Today she wore a white blouse, and in his opinion, an inappropriately short blue skirt. With funky imported red eyeglasses, she resembled a sexy schoolteacher. He shook himself knowing he needed to stop having thoughts like that.

"The Indians are on the warpath," she said in reference to the waiting room full of impatient patients. He was at least four appointments behind by the time he arrived and could already hear the grumbling.

"I'm sorry," he said. "I got here as fast as I could."

"How'd it go with Maggie?" she asked sympathetically.

"It went about as well as things like that can. She's in a better place now. More importantly, her ordeal is finally over. I got tied up with the funeral home director. He had all sorts of paperwork I had to fill out and sign. That's why I'm late."

"It's okay and I'm sorry. I know she meant a lot to you."

He nodded. "She did. She was a nice lady."

"I know she was."

"Okay, give me a second to get myself organized and then start bringing them in."

"I hate to give you bad news, but Snell is waiting for you in your office, and he has a binder with him."

Cesari groaned and rolled his eyes. Great. Just what he needed right now, another lecture on hospital finances from the CEO. The guy had been leaning on him almost since day one.

"Did Teddy happen to say what he wanted this time, Linda?"

"No, he didn't say, but I think you already know." She saw the depressed look on his face and added, "Sorry, Doc."

Cesari's office was located on the second floor of the Medical Office Building, which was owned by and attached to the Genesee General Hospital by way of a long corridor. All the hospital-employed physicians shared office space here. The Medical Office Building was affectionately referred to as the MOB by the rest of the staff. He found that ironic, and just about everyone else thought it was hysterical to tell people that they worked in the MOB.

When he entered his office, the CEO stood up to greet him. At least Cesari thought he stood up. The CEO was pretty short. In fact, he was very short, like a large child. Attempting to compensate for his height, he wore specially made platform dress shoes which gave him an extra inch or two of self-confidence but only made him seem more ridiculous when people caught on. His thick mustache seemed to crawl across his face like a black caterpillar and presumably made him feel more masculine. Like many guys his size who reached positions of importance, he bully-boyed his way through life trying to force others to respect him. He had a gigantic chip on his shoulder and was constantly daring people to knock it off. So far Cesari had avoided taking the bait, but that could change at any time.

"Hello Cesari," he said in a high-pitched voice.

They shook hands. "Hey Snell, what can I do for you?"

Cesari sat behind his desk and Snell sat in one of the two consultation chairs across from him. The office was a functional twelve-foot square with a dark green carpet and off-white walls.

Patient charts, a laptop, and multiple coffee mugs cluttered the desk. He kept framed copies of the United States Constitution and the Declaration of Independence on the wall behind him. They had cost him three dollars each at the old North Church in Boston. He found the documents inspiring.

"I know you're busy Cesari, so I'll get right to the point. I've accumulated some stats that I wanted to share with you. You're way behind the national average in billings for your specialty, and you're only utilizing the operating room at fifty percent of what we budgeted for you." He spread several graphs out on the desk for Cesari to examine which he didn't.

"So what's your point?" Cesari asked as if he didn't know.

"My point is that we brought you here to do colonoscopies... and lots of them. Not to hold little old ladies' hands while they croak. That's what hospice is for."

"Her name was Maggie," Cesari hissed through his teeth.

"Who?"

"The old lady whose hand I held while she croaked just an hour ago."

"Well that's great. Now look at this particular graph Cesari," he said and held up a piece of paper for him.

Getting angry, Cesari asked impatiently, "Okay, what am I looking at?"

"It's a graph of your productivity compared to other gastroenterologists in New York State. In the last three months, you've only performed two hundred colonoscopies. That's less than a hundred a month. At that rate, we'll go broke on our investment in you and the OR equipment. We anticipated that you'd be doing at least twice that many cases."

He stared at the graph and then at Snell.

"Well Cesari?" he prompted. "Do you have anything to say?"

Snell believed that everyone who walked into the office should have a colonoscopy whether they need one or not and had told him so several times before. He was also under the impression that, as the new kid on the block, Cesari should kiss his ass. He had been profoundly misled on both points.

"I'm sorry to have turned out to be such a disappointment," he replied with an edge in his voice, "but I was recruited to be a gastroenterologist, not a scope jockey. My job is to take care of people not just shove tubes into them... Look Snell, I'm working as hard as I can, but I'm a physician first and foremost. If I think my patient needs a procedure, then I'll do it, but if I don't, I won't. That's all there is to it. You can bring all the charts, graphs and comparative data you want in here, but nothing is going to influence the way I treat the person in front of me. And no amount of coercion from you is going to change a thing."

"I'm not trying to pressure you into doing anything you don't think is necessary or in the best interest of your patients..."

"The hell you ain't," Cesari growled. He had enough of the bullshit and was already running behind schedule. "That's exactly what you're trying to do. Now take your graphs back to your bean counter friends and explain to them that they forgot to take into account the Cesari anomaly. Tell them they can read all about it on page 54 of the you-can-kiss-my-ass manual. I'm sure they'll be grateful to you for pointing it out to them. Now maybe you didn't notice, but I have a waiting room full of people out there."

Snell stood up, red in the face, shaking with anger at having been dressed down and then summarily dismissed. "Just remember Cesari, this is my hospital. I pay you, not the other way around. You got that?"

He had raised his voice, which only made it sound shriller, and Cesari was sure Linda had heard everything. Cesari stood up as well and spoke slowly with self-control. "Listen carefully Snell, because I am only going to say this once. You hired me, and you can fire me, but don't tell me how to practice medicine. Now I think you should leave before I decide that you need an urgent prostate exam, right here, right now."

Snell stood there a moment paralyzed and at a loss for words. Abruptly he stormed out without saying goodbye. What a loser, Cesari thought. Guys like that were infecting the entire healthcare system like a rapidly spreading virus. Cesari sat back down, booted up his laptop and logged onto the electronic medical records.

When he looked up again, he saw Linda, tsk-tsking him from the doorway. She had worked as a medical secretary for twenty-five years, which was why the hospital had assigned her to him. She was supposed to be the mama bear keeping her cub out of trouble. In that regard, she was having no more success than his own mother did. She was now definitely eyeing him in mama bear capacity.

Here we go.

She said, "Do you have a death wish, Seezari?" Much to his chagrin, she insisted on mispronouncing his name, but he liked her and she was a great secretary.

Chuckling, he chided her. "First of all, I may have mentioned this to you once or twice perhaps even three times before, but it's chez-ar`-ee not seez-ar`-ee. Second, if you're going to mangle my name and eavesdrop on me at the same time, you might want to at least address me as doctor."

"I'm sorry. Do you have a death wish, Dr. Seezari?"

So much for that. "No I don't, Linda. But I won't be bullied or intimidated into submission by him or anybody else. Trying to practice medicine these days is like swimming in a pool of caramel. Nobody wants me to think anymore. They only want me to do things. The hospital wants me to do procedures on people who don't need them. The patients want procedures they don't need. Even worse is that the insurance companies will pay for procedures no one needed in the first place as long as you tweak the billing codes properly. It's getting to the point that if I tell someone they don't need a procedure, I'll be accused of being a quack."

She laughed at that. "Maybe you are a quack, Dr. Seezari, but you're a good-looking quack, and I would hate to see you get fired."

"Are you trying to seduce me, Linda?"

"Why, do you need seducing?" she asked, batting her lashes.

He laughed out loud. "Maybe we should get back to work before the little guy decides to come back and supervise me some more."

"Sure thing, Doc. By the way, before I forget. The OR called to remind you that you have a colonoscopy to do when you're finished here in the office. It's a Mr. Grafton in room 331 over at the hospital. They said you knew all about it."

"I do, Linda. Thanks for the reminder."

Chapter 6

The room was dark and Kelly stood just a little too close. He could smell the fragrant soaps, shampoos and body splashes she used. She was the nurse who assisted him during colonoscopy. She was also the nurse who distracted him during colonoscopy and had been doing so quite effectively since his arrival in town.

Cesari gave her his best don't-be-naughty look and said, "Kelly, would you hand me the biopsy forceps, please?"

"Yes, Doctor," she replied, smiling mischievously.

"What are you taking a biopsy of and where are we in the colon?" Michele asked. She was the other, older, more mature nurse in the room, in charge of monitoring the patient's status and recording all the operative data during the procedure. She stood on the other side of the stretcher from Kelly and Cesari. She either didn't notice the goings on just a few feet from where she sat or didn't care. Nurses were like that.

"It's a five-millimeter flat polyp in the rectum, Michele." They all stared at the video monitor. "Thank you, Kelly," he said as she handed him the forceps.

He manipulated the colonoscope until the polyp was directly in view. "Okay, open the forceps," he instructed. "That's it. Now close them... Good." He tugged on the forceps and removed the polyp. "Thank you, Kel."

Kelly placed the tissue in a specimen jar, and Cesari withdrew the colonoscope from the patient. Michele turned on the lights. "Good job, everyone," he said. "We've saved another life."

The patient looked up at him with bleary eyes already starting to wake up. That was the beauty of modern sedatives. One minute you were down for the count and the next was like nothing had happened. "That's it? You're done already?" he asked, his speech just a little slow.

Cesari replied, "Yep, that's all she wrote, Mr. Grafton. How'd it go?"

"I didn't feel a thing, Doc. I can't believe it. The last time I had one of these, I screamed in pain the whole time."

"You didn't feel anything this time because I am one of the three best gastroenterologists on the planet."

"Oh, really? Who are the other two?"

"I don't know. They haven't been born yet." Kelly and Michele rolled their eyes as he made a drum roll sound. He'd used that joke once or twice before and it was rapidly becoming his trademark.

The patient chuckled. "Wise guy."

"Okay, Mr. Grafton." Cesari glanced at the man's vital signs on the display monitor. "I'm going to do my paperwork now, and then I'll speak to you and your wife after you've recovered a little more from the sedation. All right?"

"See you later, Doc. I'm going back to sleep." He closed his groggy eyes and in seconds started snoring.

As Cesari washed his hands at the sink, Kelly touched his arm lightly sending a gentle shock of electricity through him. He turned to her and smiled.

"We're still on for tonight, right?" she whispered so Michele couldn't hear. It was Friday and tonight was the big night.

Office romance was a tricky business. After only several months of timid flirting, Kelly had finally suggested they meet for a drink one night after work and enjoy a local band. He'd been laboriously working his way up to asking her out, but became tongue tied at all the wrong moments. Frustrated at his glacial advances, she'd mercifully put him out of his misery and made the first move.

"Wild horses couldn't keep me away," he whispered back and bumped her gently with his hip, causing her to giggle.

Kelly assisted him with all of his endoscopic procedures at the hospital. She had been assigned specifically and exclusively to him and for that he was exceedingly grateful. She was black, thirty years old, five-feet-three inches tall, with big green eyes and an absolutely adorable smile. She was gorgeous and as if that wasn't enough, she also happened to be the best endoscopy nurse Genesee General Hospital had to offer.

They had met at the Starbucks in the hospital lobby on his first day. In between orientation meetings, he had rushed down for quick cup. Standing ahead of him in line, wearing tight, navy-blue surgical scrubs, he couldn't keep his eyes off her. She had the cutest nose and most luscious lips, but that wasn't the best part.

She noticed him admiring her and said, "If I buy you a cup of coffee, will you stop staring at my ass?"

Embarrassed he had said, "I'm sorry, was I that obvious?"

"You're about as subtle as the iceberg that sank the *Titanic*."

"That's not necessarily fair," he countered. "That iceberg was minding its own business when the Titanic invaded its personal space."

She stood her ground and smiled and with a slightly snarky purr said, "Are you implying that my butt is so big it's invading your personal space?"

He had no adequate response to that and they both laughed. She had enjoyed dressing him down and he had enjoyed being dressed down. She bought him a large French roast and although Cesari was in heaven, he made a mental note to review the hospital's policy on sexual harassment as soon as possible.

When she asked him how he liked his coffee, he replied, "Black and sweet, like my..."

He didn't get to finish. She interrupted him with a stern look. "Please don't say it. You're trying too hard."

"Forgive me. I don't get out much."

She shook her head. "Are you always this corny?"

"Sadly, yes."

She extended her hand. "Hi, I'm Kelly Kingston, and you must be Dr. Cesari."

He hadn't been issued an ID badge yet and must have look puzzled, so she explained, "There was an article with a picture of you in the hospital newsletter last week introducing you to the staff, and I never forget a pretty face."

And neither do I, he thought as they shook hands politely. He said, "Well, it's nice to know I'm famous. My name is John Cesari, but people I like just call me Cesari."

She thought about that and said, "So what do people you don't like call you?"

"Violent, ill-tempered, dangerous, unhinged and stuff like that," he grinned.

She glared at him hard and then laughed. As they got to know each other over coffee, Cesari was pleasantly surprised to find they had a fair number of things in common. He liked to tell jokes and she liked to laugh. He liked women and she liked men who liked women. She liked pizza and so on and so forth. It only took an additional three months and there they were whispering secretively and exchanging glances in anxious anticipation of their first date.

The rest of his afternoon was spent doing in-patient consults, checking labs and x-rays, and completing the never-ending grind of paperwork. Being relatively new, he was still a little slow with the electronic documentation process and because of that, he got out late and therefore was running a little behind schedule.

They'd agreed to meet in the outdoor bar at the Ramada around 8:30 p.m. By the time he arrived and pulled his blue Camry into the hotel's parking lot, it was almost 9:00 p.m. and the sky was very dark. He was moving as quickly as possible. He was perturbed at the idea of leaving a woman as attractive as Kelly all alone in a bar and had texted her twice to hang on.

He quickly spruced up his hair in the rearview mirror, popped a breath mint, and headed over to where he heard loud music and voices. The Ramada was located at the northernmost tip of the Genesee Lake for which the town was named. There was a large marina filled with small boats rocking lazily back and forth in the water. Long strands of colorful Chinese lanterns lit up a very crowded outdoor-patio and bar. A middle-aged, five-piece band was banging out a classic rock tune as he walked up searching for her. The dance floor was jumping with raunchy, very near to drunk party animals. God, it wasn't even that late, and many people were already trashed.

He spotted Kelly at the far end of the bar sitting on a wicker stool. Never having seen her outside the hospital in civilian dress, he held his breath. She was stunning, wearing a sleeveless, low-cut black dress with gold hoop earrings and a matching chain necklace. From the amount of thigh he could see, he guessed the dress had a very short hemline. Black heels finished off the ensemble. He was already having trouble focusing.

In jeans and a dress shirt, he felt a little underdressed for the occasion. Thank God he'd worn dress shoes and not sneakers. That would have been embarrassing and possibly a deal killer. Everything would have been perfect, except that some guy he didn't know had grabbed her wrist and wouldn't let go. Apparently, the guy was having trouble reading her body language because she seemed plenty annoyed from where he was standing.

Cesari drew nearer and heard her say, "Let go. You're hurting me. I have nothing more to say to you."

He jerked her wrist harder. "It's not over unless I say it's over. Got that?"

His voice was a little slurred and Cesari saw his eyes were red and glazed. Preoccupied, neither one had noticed his presence yet, so Cesari cleared his throat and said, "Hi, Kel."

She looked irritated and uncomfortable and said, "Hi."

"This is a really cool place. Thanks for inviting me," Cesari continued, ignoring the other guy's presence and hand on Kelly. He forced himself to act nonchalant and non-threatening since his goal was to defuse the situation, not make it worse. What he hoped was that the guy would simply get the hint and walk away now that he was no longer alone with Kelly. And to some degree it worked.

He stopped yanking on her wrist and sized Cesari up, but he didn't walk away. Maybe a hair taller and ten pounds heavier than Cesari, the guy seemed to be in reasonably good shape. Physically he had the advantage. He saw it too. It was written all over the smug expression on his face.

But it wouldn't be a fair fight. No way, no how. He was stoned or drunk or possibly both and he was angry and there was a woman involved. In addition, he couldn't know that Cesari had spent much of a misguided youth kicking the teeth out of guys like him in the back alleys of the Bronx. Even worse for him right now was that Cesari didn't like his face. He had a weak chin. The fact that he didn't like the way he was treating Kelly sealed his fate. Cesari felt a primitive stirring deep inside.

The guy snarled at him, "Are you brain damaged? The bitch is taken, so keep moving before you get hurt."

The guy took a step closer and from three feet away Cesari was overwhelmed by the alcohol on his breath. If he got too close to a flame he'd ignite. Machismo and booze. There was nothing like it. Cesari let out a deep sigh. He didn't want to spoil his first date with Kelly, so he decided to give the guy one more opportunity to do the right thing.

"I'm not interested in the girl," he said.

He glared at Cesari, momentarily confused. "Then what the hell do you want?"

Cesari smiled. "The bartender told me you were the biggest man-whore in this town, and I was hoping that we could have a dance... maybe a tango or a rhumba? You know, something close and intimate."

Kelly's eyes widened in dismay, but she couldn't help herself and started to laugh. The guy didn't think he was nearly that funny. He released her wrist, let out a roar, and charged like a bull, leading with an all-out, clumsy right cross, which Cesari easily sidestepped. As his momentum carried him past, Cesari seized his arm and flung him forcefully over his outstretched leg. He stumbled and went down hard, face first onto the cement floor. Cesari bent down quickly next to him, as if he was going to help him get up. Instead, he grabbed his hair and smashed his face a second time into the concrete slab. The ugly crunching sound of his nose breaking could be heard above the background din of the music.

He went limp, and Cesari could already see blood trickling out from his injuries. He glanced around quickly. The room was noisy, dark, and crowded, and no one seemed to have noticed. So he punched him hard in the left kidney, a short powerful jab guaranteed to send him to a urologist.

Cesari leaned in close and whispered, "Are you still with me?" The guy groaned in response nearly but not quite unconscious so Cesari added, "The name's Bond...James Bond."

He stood up and smiled. He'd always wanted to do that. He turned to find Kelly staring at him, slack-jawed. She said excitedly, "Oh my God, are you crazy? Who do you think you are?"

"I think we should leave now, Kelly," he said with some urgency. "This night isn't going quite the way I had planned."

She grabbed her bag and stood up. "I agree. The quicker we get out of here the better."

People had noticed the commotion and started to form a circle around the guy on the floor. One stepped in close and asked, "Is everything okay? Can I help?"

Cesari said, "My friend had a little too much to drink and tripped." He gestured to the fallen man. "He hit his head pretty hard. Could you call an ambulance for us, please?"

"Sure will," he replied, happy to help, and whipped out his cellphone.

Cesari took Kelly by the hand, and they hustled out through the nearest exit not speaking again until they were well away from the crowd.

"Thanks." She rubbed her hurt wrist. "But I think you just got yourself in a lot of trouble."

Cesari studied her under one of the lights in the parking lot. She had gotten all dolled up for the big night and looked beautiful. She had the most amazing hair. It was soft brown and shoulder length with gentle waves. It complemented her green eyes and dark skin perfectly. A gentle breeze brought the scent of her perfume his way. Chanel No.5 maybe.

He replied, "Maybe, but I doubt that a drunk guy falling and busting his nose is going to get a whole lot of sympathy from anyone, but just the same, I'd rather not be here when the police arrive. I'm sure they'll want a statement."

"That's the problem."

"What's the problem?"

"That drunk guy who just fell and broke his nose was the police."

Cesari caught his breath and gave his best effort to pretend not to be bothered by that bit of news. He said, "Still want to have that drink? I have a great bottle of Chianti in my apartment."

"That doesn't bother you?"

"I didn't say that, but there's not whole lot I can do about it now, and I don't see why I should let him ruin my evening."

She laughed. "You are certainly an interesting guy."

"What about that wine?"

"Sure, why not. By the way, what did you say to him when he was on the floor?"

"Oh that. I told him I was sorry and that I hoped one day we could put this ugly episode behind us and be friends."

She looked at him suspiciously and said, "Yeah, right."

Chapter 7

Kelly followed him to his apartment in her white Civic and parked behind his Camry on the street. They walked into his building together, deep in thought. He had a small, first-floor, one-bedroom apartment in a low-rent building in a quiet residential neighborhood. It was actually an old two-story Victorian home that had been subdivided into five apartments, two on the first floor and three on the second.

All the homes on the block were similar: large, old houses built on big lots at the turn of the last century during a period of thriving economy and low taxation. At one point, it must have been an affluent and desirable neighborhood to live in, but one by one, the gracious homes had fallen like dominoes and kings of old. Reversal of fortunes, high taxes, and a slumping economy had resulted in most of the buildings falling into disrepair.

His apartment had a small living room with an old sofa and an even smaller kitchen with a breakfast nook. The refrigerator held a dozen eggs, some bologna, and bottled water. An imported Pavoni espresso machine and a package of biscotti rested on the kitchen counter. Three full cases of Ruffino Chianti Classico gold label sat in their wood crates on the floor. All in all, Cesari thought it was perfectly satisfactory domicile for a single guy.

She examined the apartment, sizing him up by proxie, and when she saw the three cases of wine in an otherwise bare apartment, she smiled. "I see you've got your priorities straight."

He reached into an overhead cabinet for two wine glasses and uncorked a bottle of Chianti with a Laguiole wine opener. "I could live without a lot of things Kelly, but not wine and espresso... So who was that guy?"

He poured them both a glass of Chianti and joined her on the sofa, not too close but not too far. She explained, "That was Billy Ray Bob, my ex-boyfriend. We broke up a few months ago, just before you arrived in town in fact. Needless to say, he didn't take the breakup very well."

"I'll say. He seemed very needy, if you ask me."

"I wouldn't joke too much," she said. "This isn't funny and you shouldn't have done that to him. He's a cop, and he's not going to let go of this."

She seemed a little depressed as she sipped her wine. He said consolingly, "I'm sorry. I know this is serious, but I didn't do anything. It appeared to me that he fell on his nose. By the way, how's the wine?"

"Oh, please." Her exasperation showed for a moment. "The wine is nice."

"So what, he's a cop? He was being an asshole, and besides, he was pretty wasted. Between that and the concussion, he may not even remember anything at all," he said, trying to cheer her up.

"First of all, I saw what really happened, and if I saw, then somebody else probably did too."

She had a valid point. She placed her glass down next to his on the coffee table and he topped them off. "Well let's hope that when tomorrow comes, he'll be so ashamed of his bad behavior that he'll change his life around. He may even want to thank me for the wakeup call. In fact, I fully expect that he will do just that."

She gave him a severe look and without warning punched him in the arm, laughing. "You're being such a jerk, I can't believe you. This is serious. He is definitely going to remember. He wasn't that wasted. He and his friends are going to start asking questions, and you haven't even heard the worst part yet."

"Go ahead. What could be worse than assaulting a police officer in a small town?" he asked seriously, but she hesitated and he prompted her again, "I'm waiting."

"His father is the CEO of the hospital."

Silence, as that one just hung around waiting to land. This was what the English would call a sticky wicket. "Snell is his father?"

She nodded, "Yes."

"Shit," was all he could think to say. He picked up his wine glass and took a long slug.

She added with deep concern. "Exactly."

"Okay, well you've got my attention now."

"It's about time."

"Is that really his name, Billy Ray Bob? Sounds like he should be running moonshine in the deep south," he said, trying to change the mood.

"Oh, he's from around here all right, born and bred. His full name is William Raymond Robert Snell. Either his dad or grandfather, or possibly both, were big New York Yankees fans. He was named after three of their favorite players. Give me a second, and I'll remember which ones. He told me enough times." She furrowed her brow in thought as she tried to recollect the names and then said, "I remember now. He was named after Billy Martin, Ray Scarborough, and Bobby Murcer."

"You're kidding, right? I don't think I ever heard of anything that ridiculous. Billy Martin I get, maybe even Bobby Murcer, but who on earth ever heard of Ray Scarborough? Did he even play for the Yankees? I'm as big a Yankees fan as anybody, and I've never heard of Ray Scarborough." For some reason, he took umbrage at this.

She giggled at his irritation. "Don't shoot the messenger, *Mr. I'm from New York.* All right? I'm just telling you what he told me. You don't have to like it. Boy, you're a piece of work, aren't you? You beat up a cop and make jokes, but now you're offended because he's named after some baseball player you never heard of."

"I'm not offended," he huffed. "I'm just skeptical as to the validity of the story."

"Yeah, yeah."

She lifted her glass for more wine. He refilled their glasses and put his arm around her, bringing her in close. Receptive, she snuggled into him. They were both starting to feel the effects of the wine and the stress.

"I got a little side-tracked tonight, Kelly. Did I mention how beautiful you look?" he asked.

She put her glass down on the table and he did the same.

"No, you didn't, and I spent hours getting ready for you. Then you showed up late, started a fight, and didn't even mention my appearance." She pouted and was a bit flushed.

He leaned in close to her and gazed longingly into her gorgeous green eyes. She sensed his yearning and responded by nestling in even closer. His breathing came in short shallow bursts and his pulse quickened. He reminded himself to keep control as he caressed her face and brushed her ear with his lips.

"You smell nice," he whispered softly, nibbling on her exposed neck.

"Thank you, and so do you. What are you wearing?"

"Black Polo briefs. The kind that hug snugly. You know, they keep everything in place."

She giggled. "I meant what kind of aftershave, silly. But that's good to know."

"It's called Drakar Noir. I get it at Walmart." he turned serious. "I have something I need to say to you Kelly."

They were nose to nose, studying each other now, and holding each other tight. She said, "I'm listening."

He cleared his throat and with his voice hoarse and dripping with sexual desire declared, "Kelly, I think you are the most beautiful woman I have ever known."

"That's better," she teased. "See? You're not that hard to train."

His need for her was overwhelming and he was at the breaking point. She put her hands up to his face and pulled him close, kissing him passionately. When they came up for air, panting and staring at each other with glazed eyes, they could barely speak.

He confessed, "I've wanted you ever since the first day I met you. It's all I've been able to think about, day in and day out."

He was starting to ache and she could tell he had fallen overboard. She smiled playfully and whispered, "Well what are you waiting for, cowboy?"

He didn't need a second invitation. They began to explore each other in earnest, and after a while, he scooped her up off the couch and carried her into the bedroom, where they allowed their passions to consume them until they fell asleep in tender embrace.

Hours later, Cesari heard a voice from far away speaking urgently, "John, wake up. You're having a bad dream."

Kelly was shaking him and his eyes opened slowly gradually getting oriented. The clock said it was almost 3:00 a.m.

"Are you all right?" she asked. "You were yelling in your sleep."

His heart was pounding, and he was perspiring. Taking a deep breath, he gathered himself. His voice trembled. "I'm okay, thank you. I'll be all right."

"What were you dreaming about? You were tossing and turning, and you kept shouting, 'No! No! No!' I was really worried for you."

Cesari sat up and turned on the lamp on his night table. "I was dreaming about my father. I always dream about him as far back as I can remember. He disappeared when I was seven years old," he explained.

She hugged him and said, "I'm sorry, John. That's so awful. Do you know what happened to him?"

He shook his head. "No, he worked for the post office in Manhattan, and one day he just didn't come home. No goodbye notes, no phone calls. Just gone into thin air like a magic trick."

"Do you mind talking about it?" she asked gently.

"I don't mind talking about it at all. In fact, I've talked to many counselors and a psychiatrist about it already. They've all told me that the dreams are just a stress reaction and should go away with time, but they seem to be getting worse. They're becoming increasingly more intense, violent and disturbing."

He paused, struggling to clear his head and then went on, "They started shortly after my last job in the Bronx, about ten years ago. I watched some guy playing catch with his kid, and for some reason, this triggered a subconscious reaction in me, which I can't seem to shake. What's even stranger is that, when I'm awake, I can barely remember anything about my father, yet in my dreams, I see him vividly, down to the last detail, and the dreams always end the same way...with him covered in blood and me holding a knife."

Kelly regarded him with sympathy. "That's terrible. I wish there was something I could do."

"Listening helps, Kel. Thank you. I have a psychiatrist friend Mark, who I haven't spoken to since I left New York a few months ago. I think I should give him a call. He's a good guy and really cares."

"That sounds like a really good idea," she said as she lay her head on his chest studying his physique and musculature up close. She ran a hand over his torso and noticed several scars. "What are these?"

He nodded his head, reluctant to talk about his street brawling days. Her hand came to rest on an area that he had been stabbed over a routine discussion about who owed who how much money. Since he'd shot the guy as a response to the knifing, he didn't feel comfortable going to the hospital to have it stitched. It eventually healed on its own but left an irregular, unsightly blemish.

He said, "Well back in the day, I would have considered them badges of honor. I used to be real proud of them, but now they're just reminders of all the dumb things I did."

She looked up at him. "You're not like other doctors."

"What are other doctors like?"

"Not like you."

Chapter 8

Cesari woke Saturday morning and found himself alone in bed. The clock said 10:00 a.m., and he heard the shower running. He went over to the bathroom, and through the door, listened to Kelly humming. He knocked lightly to announce his presence.

"Good morning, sleepyhead," she called out. "It's about time you woke up. You can come in. I'm almost done."

He entered the room as she stepped out of the shower and began toweling herself. He watched her and she said, "See anything you like?"

"How did I get so lucky?"

She smiled and he said, "Give me a minute to shower, and I'll make us some espresso."

She secured the towel around her body and gave him a kiss. "Sounds like a plan. Do you have an extra toothbrush for me to use?"

"You're pretty chipper this morning, and yes, there should be one in the overhead cabinet, and if not there, then in one of the drawers below the sink."

"Thanks."

He quickly cleaned up, threw on a cotton shirt and jeans, and caught up with her in the kitchen. He fired up the espresso machine and laid out some almond biscotti on a plate for them.

"So what's on the agenda for today?" she asked, inhaling the aroma of the liquid delight.

"Not much," he replied. "I was going to work out at the gym and then head over to the office to finish up paperwork. What about you?"

"Well, first I'm going to go home and put on some fresh clothes. It looks like it's going to be a beautiful day. I need to do some grocery shopping, and then I might take a walk by the lake. It's really nice there this time of year. There's a tree-lined walking path with a magnificent view of the water. Would you like to come with me after you finish your paperwork?"

He didn't hesitate. "I would like that very much. It sounds very relaxing, as long as we don't run into any more ex-boyfriends."

She smirked. "Yeah, right. I almost forgot about him."

They finished their espressos, and he pulled them another couple of shots from the Pavoni. "This is really very good coffee," she added before taking another sip. "The cookies are delicious too, but they're a little hard. Are they stale?"

He shook his head. "Espresso is one of my people's greatest contributions to world culture, and the cookies are made deliberately like that to be dunked in coffee."

"You're supposed to dunk them?"

"Unless you want to crack a tooth."

His cellphone went off in the bedroom, and he went to answer it. When he returned, his expression had changed. She asked, "What's the matter? Did something happen?"

He sighed. "That was Snell. The boss wants to meet with me in his office at noon. He didn't say what about."

Kelly sighed, suddenly apprehensive. "That's not good."

Cesari glanced at his watch. He had about half an hour. "Well, if it means anything, he didn't sound angry."

She thought about that. "That's something," she said encouragingly.

"Maybe he just wants to yell at me again for not scheduling enough colonoscopies. We had quite the exchange yesterday in my office."

Kelly laughed. "Yeah, Linda told me all about it."

He looked at her suspiciously. "I didn't know that you and Linda were tight."

She smiled. "Word gets around fast when there's a man involved."

"It's nice to know that I don't have any secrets. What else did she say about me?"

"Take it easy. Girls always talk about guys. She said you were hysterical and that you handled yourself very well. She also said I should bag you while I have the chance because you're probably going to get yourself fired."

He stared at her hard, relented and chuckled. "Bag me?"

"Yeah, that was a quote."

"Okay. Look, I might as well go over there and find out what Snell wants. Why don't you do your grocery shopping and we can meet later and take that walk by the lake? Who knows? After this meeting, I may want to throw myself in."

"Stop. It's probably no big deal... And John?"

"Yes, Kel?"

"You might want to call your psychiatrist friend Mark, sooner rather than later, about those dreams."

"I will."

Chapter 9

Cesari walked through the main entrance of the hospital to meet with Snell hoping that all he wanted to do was dress him down for the way he had spoke to him yesterday. He could deal with that. Upon honest reflection, he may have teed off on the little guy a little too hard. He couldn't help it. Snell rubbed him the wrong way on so many levels. Sometimes he felt like he just wanted to use the guy as a punching bag.

He let out a deep breath as he approached the office. He didn't want to be overly pessimistic, but felt he should brace himself for the possibility that he was about to join the ranks of the newly unemployed. It also occurred to him that waiting in Snell's office might be his son, Billy Ray Bob, and several other Genesee policemen all armed with metal batons and tasers.

He knocked politely and entered Snell's office. Hs secretary looked up and he said, "Hi, Elizabeth. I'm here to meet with Mr. Snell."

She glanced at him with disdain. Tall and blonde, she thought that because she worked directly for his boss that to some degree she was also his boss. It's funny how contagious arrogance can be, he mused. She said, "I'll let him know you're here, Dr. Cesari. Why don't you have a seat, and for future reference, it's Dr. Snell, not Mr. Snell. He's a board certified internist."

She was referring to the fact that the CEO had actually attended and graduated medical school. But Snell had realized early on that he didn't have the chops to practice medicine, so right after finishing his training, he jumped ship and went straight for his MBA, fast-tracking it into hospital administration. Now he got to piss on the rest of them.

"I'll try to remember that," he said and sat down.

He flipped through a magazine and glanced around while he waited in the outer office. He didn't like Snell, but he had to admit that the guy worked hard, including a full day every Saturday. His office was on the first floor of the hospital and designed to convey importance to all who entered. The outer office was spacious and bright with tall ceilings and a small but elegant crystal chandelier. Elizabeth's desk appeared to be Italianate with a marble top and hand-carved oak legs. Hell, even the waiting room chair he was sitting in was a nineteenth century Queen Ann wingback.

After a minute or two, Elizabeth returned. "He said to come right in, Dr. Cesari."

He entered the CEO's inner sanctum for only the second time since he had arrived in town and was again awed by its palatial elegance. It was four hundred square feet with a gigantic picture window overlooking the Genesee Lake. The hospital had been built on the city's highest point. The view from almost any window was impressive, but that of the lake from Snell's office was simply spectacular.

He'd selected his office décor to impress, with two Persian rugs, a leather couch, Brazilian cherry hardwood floors, a wet bar, multiple oil paintings on the walls, and a ten-foot-long mahogany desk. With the five-foot-two-inch CEO seated behind it in a high-back leather chair, the décor only served to accentuate his diminutive stature. On the wall directly behind him was a sixteen-foot replica of *The Coronation of Napoleon* by Jacques-Louis David. Man, did this guy have a pair.

Two plush leather chairs sat in front of his desk, and Snell signaled Cesari toward one of them. In the other chair sat Vito Gianelli, a homicidal maniac from the Bronx. He stopped and blinked, wondering if Gianelli was some kind of apparition or if this was just another bad dream. Then Snell and Gianelli both stood up to greet him, and he knew this was really happening.

"Good afternoon, Cesari," said Snell full of cheer. "Thank you for coming by. I knew you'd want to see your old friend from the Bronx."

Gianelli turned to Cesari. "Long time no see, Cesari. How the hell have you been?"

He extended his hand, and Cesari hesitated just long enough to ensure that Snell's heart skipped a beat before he reached out and took it. Gianelli's hand was huge and strong, and it gripped Cesari's like a vise. They stood there for a moment testing each other's tolerance for pain before separating.

Gianelli was impeccably dressed in Armani, sporting alligator shoes and a diamond-studded Rolex. He was a large man with an imposing physical presence. Standing well over six feet and weighing close to 250 pounds, he was all muscle, hardened on the streets of New York City. He had a face like chiseled granite and hawk-like gray eyes that underscored his predatory nature. Vito Gianelli was the most sadistic human being he had ever known, and he hated Cesari.

Great.

"I'm fine Vito, and you? What brings you to this part of the world?"

Gianelli grinned. "I had business with Snell that required my personal attention, and he happened to mention that there was a new physician on staff from New York City, from the Bronx of all places. Imagine my surprise when he told me your name."

Snell said, "Mr. Gianelli suggested I give you a call so you two could catch up."

Gianelli turned to the CEO. "Hey, Snell, how about we all have a drink to celebrate this little reunion?"

With that cue, the CEO jumped to attention. "Certainly, Mr. Gianelli. I agree wholeheartedly. What'll it be, boys, scotch or whiskey?"

Gianelli said, "Scotch, neat, and make it the good stuff. What about you, Cesari?"

Cesari glanced at his watch. A little early, but he thought he should go with the flow. "Scotch will be fine, some ice if you have any."

Snell scurried from around his desk to the bar and poured a round of scotch for everyone. Cesari saw the bottle he was pouring from. It was thirty-year-old Fine Oak Macallan. Not bad, it goes for about four thousand dollars a bottle. Snell was doing okay. The hospital was understaffed and under supplied, nurses were living paycheck to paycheck, there was a physician shortage and patients couldn't afford their medications but it was nice to know somebody was prospering from healthcare.

Cesari sized up Gianelli and said, "Nice suit, Vito. You seem to be doing very well."

He returned the compliment. "I wish I could say the same for you, Cesari. What's with the jeans and sneakers? Hey Snell, don't you pay your doctors?"

The CEO chuckled from the credenza where he was pouring the drinks. "I pay them what they're worth."

Snell and Gianelli laughed. Everybody was a regular riot today. Snell returned with the drinks and they all sat down. As Vito adjusted himself, his suit jacket opened a little, and Cesari caught a glimpse of a large handgun in a shoulder holster. Not good. He swirled the Waterford crystal tumbler and sniffed the amber liquid before taking a sip. Nice and smooth.

Vito said, "So are you really a doctor, Cesari? When Snell told me, I could hardly believe my ears."

"It's true, Vito. I'm really a doctor. I'm a gastroenterologist."

"And what exactly does that mean?"

"I take care of digestive disorders and do procedures such as a colonoscopy."

He thought about that for a moment. "Colonoscopy, huh? I know what that is. Well that makes sense, that you would specialize in giving it to people in the ass," he said with an edge in his voice. It was almost as if he were talking out loud to no one in particular.

Cesari let the unpleasant insinuation slide, but reminded himself to stay alert. Snell sensed an unpleasant breeze enter the room and started to twirl the edge of his mustache nervously. He seemed to be fascinated by the relationship of the two men and asked, "How exactly did you two know each other in the Bronx?"

Bad move, Snell. You just threw gasoline on the fire.

Gianelli jumped at the question like a shark at chum. "I'm glad you asked, Snell. Before he became a doctor, Cesari and I worked together for a couple of years for a guy named Frankie D. Remember those days, Cesari?" He crossed his legs and sipped his scotch. He made no attempt to cover the exposed weapon. If Snell saw it too, he didn't let on.

Cesari said, "I remember."

Frankie D. was the capo who ran most of the rackets in the Bronx. He was also Cesari's father's friend and ergo, Cesari's friend. Vito and Cesari had run Frankie D.'s collections department together for a couple of years. Frankie D. would give them the name of someone who owed him money and they would go and get it. Insufficient funds on the other end generally resulted in a certain amount of unpleasantness.

Cesari was getting edgy. Strolling down this kind of memory lane couldn't possibly end well. There was a lot of bad blood between Gianelli and him. Much of it had never been resolved. To complicate matters, Vito was armed and he wasn't. But would he really try something here? Cesari suddenly felt naked and exposed.

"Great times. Weren't they, Cesari?" Vito said.

Cesari tried to sound sentimental. "Sure were, Vito. The best."

Gianelli nodded his approval and turned to Snell. "You know Snell, Cesari and I were raking in the dough hand over fist back then. We were doing pretty well until that nasty car accident on Pelham Parkway. Do you remember that accident, Cesari?"

"Yeah, I remember it. That was a shame," Cesari said with as much feigned sympathy as he could muster, but his heart skipped a beat. He felt like he was on a runaway train and just realized the conductor had jumped over the side and there were no emergency brakes.

"What happened?" Snell asked naively, and I resisted the urge to squirm.

"That's a very good question, Snell. I've asked myself the same question a thousand times," said Vito. "Cesari and I were returning from dinner at Patsy's Restaurant in Manhattan one night. You know the one? Sinatra used to eat there all time. Stuffed calamari in marinara to die for. Anyway, we were on our way back to the Bronx. It was about one in the morning and we had stopped at a red light. Cesari was driving, and I had fallen asleep on the passenger side when a drunk rammed us from behind at about eighty miles an hour. I woke up a month later in the neurosurgical intensive care unit at Jacobi Hospital with multiple broken bones and a headache that still hasn't gone away. Cesari, on the other hand, walked away with barely a scratch on him."

Snell's eyes went wide. He looked at Cesari and said, "Unbelievable."

"It was a Goddamn miracle is what it was," added Vito.

Cesari said, "Vito, I hope you're not still upset about that. I mean, the guy was drunk and hit us from behind. What was I supposed to do?"

Snell nodded his head in agreement and Gianelli continued, "Here's the thing, Cesari. I went through the windshield and wound up on the street with a ruptured spleen, a cracked skull, and God knows how many fractures. The doctors told me that if I'd had my seat belt on like you, I could have spared myself six months' worth of rehab and physical therapy. For about a year, I couldn't remember anything from the day of the accident because of the head trauma, but gradually things started to come back to me. Fuzzy things, vague at first but eventually they became clearer. You were long gone by then, but guess what I eventually remembered?"

He looked first at Snell and then at Cesari who fought the urge to bolt from the room. Snell stared mouth gaping as if he were watching an Alfred Hitchcock thriller. He leaned forward on the edge of his seat and asked, "What did you remember?"

Thanks for nothing Snell.

"I remembered very clearly buckling my seat belt."

Cesari didn't respond immediately and Vito let him chew on that for a minute as they sat there sipping scotch and studying each other. Cesari's thoughts drifted back to another time and another place, when Vito and Frankie D. were at the center of his universe. Snell pulled out a box of Cuban cigars and started passing them out. It was that kind of a morning. Old friends getting together, telling old stories. Reminiscing about the good old times or not so good old times as the case might be. Cesari declined the smoke, but Snell and Gianelli lit up a couple of big fat ones, filling the air with the robust scent of illicit tobacco. Snell really was living large.

Cesari remained unfazed by the not so subtle implication and eventually said, "Look Vito, I'm not sure what you're getting at. Seat belts malfunction all the time. Even the car insurance guys said so."

But that was especially true when the guy sitting next to you deliberately disengages the mechanism while you're sleeping. Cesari was only trying to do the world a favor. Who would have thought anyone could possibly survive something like that. Aside from internal bleeding, fractures and blood clots, Vito had hemorrhaged into his brain and required no less than three separate neurosurgical operations to save his life. He had clung to life support for more than month and a half even after he had regained consciousness.

"That's true Cesari, that's very true. But I became curious anyway about the events of that night. It was a peace of mind kind of thing. So I got the police report about the accident, and guess what?"

"What, Vito?" But he already knew.

"The guy in the other car swore up and down and on his mother's grave that you rammed him and not the other way around. He said that he was the one who stopped at the red light and that you slammed him with your car in reverse. He saw you coming from across the intersection at a million miles an hour but couldn't do anything about it. He was drunk all right, but he only blew a 0.9. That's barely over the limit."

"Oh please, Vito. Of course the guy would say something crazy like that. He was just trying to save his own skin."

He studied Cesari hard and blew a smoke ring in his direction. "That's exactly what Frankie D. said when I brought it to his attention. You had vanished by then, so I couldn't discuss the matter with you personally."

"Vito, what possible reason could I have had to do something like that?" he asked reasonably.

Gianelli thought about it for a while and said, "That's the one thing I was never able to figure out."

"See?" Cesari said. "It makes no sense."

"Maybe." Gianelli concluded and reclined into a more comfortable position in his chair, signaling an end to the hostilities for the moment. Cesari could see Snell relax as well, as the tension eased.

Cesari took another sip of scotch, breathed a bit more easily and decided it was time to change the subject. "So Vito, you said you had some sort of business here. What kind of business are we talking about?" It seemed like a natural question.

"The medical supply business. You know…"

"No, I don't know. Why don't you tell me."

He waved his hand. "People need medical stuff, so I supply it." He grinned as if he had said something clever and Cesari stared at him. He continued, "By the way Cesari, have you heard the news?"

"Heard what news?"

Snell was watching us both so intently that he didn't notice the ash from his cigar fall onto his desk top. Vito seemed amused by what he was about to say. "Your pal Frankie D. retired about a month ago. I was at his going away party. You should have been there. It was a real blast."

"No, I hadn't heard," he said. "Good for him."

"That's funny you didn't know. I always thought you two used to be real close," he snickered.

"Frankie D. and I were close for many years, but times change and people change. I will always consider Frankie D. a good friend. I owe him a lot."

"You know Cesari, everybody wondered what happened to you. Some guys even speculated that you had left this world permanently, if you know what I mean. I was of that opinion myself. It seemed like one day you were there, and then one day you weren't. Why is that, I wonder?" Vito eyed him carefully and the tension in the room started to gradually rise again.

Cesari put his scotch glass down gently on a coaster Snell had provided. "I've always been a very private person, Vito. You know that. I always kept a low profile even when we worked together," Cesari responded, choosing his words carefully.

Vito's eyes narrowed. "That's funny because I saw a nature show once about rats. The narrator said they liked to keep a low profile too."

Cesari had enough of his crap. Gun or no gun, he made up his mind that they were going to settle this once and for all. Vito was bigger, but he was quicker and had taken on guys as big and bigger. He scanned the room looking for something to use as a weapon, and had settled in on a large glass paper weight sitting on the edge of Snell's desk near to him when the CEO's phone rang.

"Snell here," he announced still watching Cesari and Vito. There was a pause while he listened and then he became noticeably upset. "What happened? Where is he now? Is he okay?" He glanced at his watch and said, "I can be there in fifteen minutes. Try to find out who did it and get back to me immediately... No, there's no need to involve the police. Thanks."

The CEO was upset. He slammed the receiver down and said to Gianelli, worry etched in his features, "We've got a problem. Billy Ray Bob was assaulted in a bar last night. He's got a broken nose, a concussion, and a badly bruised kidney. He's in the emergency room right now peeing blood. There were lots of witnesses, but no one saw anything."

"Why didn't they call you last night?" Gianelli asked in alarm.

"Because his idiot friends didn't take him to the emergency room last night. Somebody called an ambulance, but they insisted on taking him home. I assume a fair amount of alcohol was involved and probably other stuff as well. They were just trying to protect him and at the time he was too out of it to call me. This morning he wasn't much better so they had to bring him to the ER."

Gianelli was definitely disturbed by this turn of events and growled, "This better not affect anything, Snell."

"He wasn't able to make his appointment," Snell said meekly.

"Shit." Gianelli banged his scotch glass on the mahogany desk, splashing some of its contents onto the wood.

Snell glared straight at Cesari and made it clear that he was no longer welcome. "Look Cesari, Mr. Gianelli and I need to conclude our business. Maybe you two can finish catching up some other time. I took the liberty of giving him your address and cellphone number while we were waiting for you. I knew you wouldn't mind."

Great. He stood up to leave.

"Yeah, now that I know where I can find you, we'll have to finish this later," Gianelli sneered.

As he walked toward the hospital parking lot, Cesari thought about Frankie D. and all he had meant to him. He'd stepped in as father figure when his own father disappeared and had treated him very well over the years. When he went to medical school, they had both agreed that it was time to part ways. Nonetheless, he felt a twinge of guilt over not staying in touch with him over the years. He made a mental note to give him a call sometime soon.

Cesari also made a mental note to find out why Vito Gianelli, the biggest jerk on the planet, was in town and palling around with Snell, the biggest jerk in upstate New York. What could those two possibly have in common? Maybe there was some sort of convention for assholes being held somewhere and they were the masters of ceremony. In any event, things had just changed. Gianelli's presence had all sorts of unpleasant implications for his future health and he couldn't afford to be passive about it.

Chapter 10

Cesari's cellphone went off as he was driving back to his apartment. It was Kelly.

"Where are you?" she asked, sounding very anxious.

"I just got out of my meeting with Snell. Why? Are you okay? You sound upset."

"I am upset, very upset."

"What happened?"

"When I returned home from the grocery store, I spotted an unmarked police car parked in front of my apartment. The car was facing away from me, so I doubled back. I don't think he saw me."

"Okay, slow down. Let's not be paranoid, Kel. First of all, are you sure it was an unmarked police car?"

Most people wouldn't be astute enough to notice that sort of thing. At least not until the lights started flashing behind them. She said, "I'm very sure. I used to date a cop remember? It was a full-sized, four door sedan, a black Crown Victoria, and who drives Crown Victorias? Do they even sell them to anyone but law enforcement?"

She had a point. It was pretty much a police thing. Maybe a taxi thing too in some places. They weren't in production anymore but there were still a lot of them in circulation. "Okay, so maybe it was an unmarked car. It's probably just a coincidence. It doesn't necessarily mean that it was there looking for you," he reassured her, but didn't like the vibe he was getting.

"Get real," she said. "I live in a nice neighborhood. We never see cop cars, marked or unmarked. I rent an apartment in a small house and the only crime my landlady ever committed was overfeeding her cats. Besides, I recognized the guy sitting in the car. It was one of Billy Ray Bob's cop friends, a guy named Ozzie."

"Fair enough. I agree, he may have been looking for you, but you didn't do anything wrong, so try to stay calm," he said soothingly.

"Whether I did anything wrong or not is irrelevant to Billy Ray Bob and his friends. Can I meet you back at your place? I need to talk this over with somebody, and I don't feel safe right now."

"Of course. I'll meet you there in ten minutes."

When he arrived, Kelly stood waiting for him on the sidewalk in front of his apartment. She was trembling, so he put his arm around her and they entered. Inside, she sat on the sofa while he got her a glass of water.

"Take a deep breath, Kel. It's going to be okay," he said, trying to comfort her. She was still shaking.

"I'm really scared, John. You don't know Billy Ray Bob. He has an awful temper. He's capable of anything, and his friends are just as bad."

"I believe you, but I find it hard to accept that the Genesee police don't have anything better to do than to stalk their ex-girlfriends. Although I have to admit, stranger things have happened."

She took a sip of water and seemed better. She was wearing blue jeans and a white top. "How did your meeting go with Snell?" she asked.

"It went okay. He didn't know anything about Billy Ray Bob's adventure last night until halfway through the meeting when the emergency room called, and even then, he didn't seem to know that I was involved in any way. He was pretty irritated when he heard the news as you can imagine. Apparently I caused your ex to miss an important appointment last night. That seemed to concern him the most, not that he was peeing blood with a concussion. Regardless, I think we have a bigger problem on our hands now or at least I do."

He gave her a synopsis of his recent encounter and past relationship with Gianelli, including a highly redacted version of the car accident. She asked, "So who is this guy anyway?"

"Just one of the many animals I used to frolic with back in the day. I had the misfortune of working with him for a couple of years before I saw the light."

She seemed puzzled and asked, "So what do you think the real reason is for his being here?"

"I haven't a clue, but it can't be good for anyone, especially not me. He made it clear he's still holding a grudge. He said that he was involved in some type of medical supply business. God only knows what that means because he was carrying a gun. He found out about me accidentally from Snell, but now that he knows I'm here, all bets are off."

Kelly sat there and was justifiably confused. "I guess I don't understand. You seem to think this guy Gianelli, might try to hurt you, but why? The car accident happened so many years ago, and it wasn't even your fault. Why would he hold a grudge?"

He looked at her for a long moment. "It's hard to explain Kel, but he would definitely want to hurt me because of that. That's just the way guys like him are. He was less than subtle about it."

She studied his face and wasn't buying it. Not all of it anyway. She said, "What are you hiding from me? I can see it in your face. Was the accident your fault or not?"

"It's complicated, Kelly... In my pre-doctor life, I was involved with some very nasty characters, like Gianelli. We did things together...things I'm not proud of. Long story short is that some guy owed my boss money, and he couldn't afford to pay. He was a nice guy, a family guy, nice wife, nice kids. They owned a little mom and pop restaurant in the Bronx. Gianelli was planning on terrorizing them. He was going to hurt the guy pretty bad and the wife too. There were some lines I wouldn't cross and I couldn't let that happen. I had to act quickly and didn't have a whole lot of time to think it through..."

"And...?"

"I sort of acted on impulse."

"So you did do it. You deliberately caused the accident."

He nodded. "I unhooked his seat belt first. I didn't think he'd survive. He wasn't supposed to. Well he eventually pieced together what happened, and although he probably still isn't absolutely certain, he doesn't need to be. He'll be coming after me all right. The only reason he never tried to get back at me before is that he presumed I was dead already. When I left the Bronx and guys like him behind, I didn't leave a forwarding address for this exact reason."

Kelly was quiet for a long time. She had never heard anything like this before. This was stuff of movies. She didn't know what to say or how to react. All sorts of things were running through her mind.

She asked, "What was he going to do to them?"

"The guy he was going to beat with a baseball bat, not enough to kill him but to hospitalize him for a few weeks, maybe months."

"And the wife?"

"Probably the same. He hadn't worked it out completely in his mind whether to use a bat on her or his fists or his belt. He was also thinking maybe it would be better to beat the wife in front of the guy. This way he would suffer more or maybe he would miraculously come up with the money if he saw what was happening to her. His logic was all twisted. When he told me that, I realized I had to do something to stop him."

She was horrified. "What kind of a monster is he?"

"The kind that doesn't forget minor transgressions apparently."

"You call that a minor transgression? I need to know something, John. Gianelli's clearly a bad man and maybe you were justified, but I want to know about you."

"What would you like to know?"

"You were okay with beating the guy but not his wife?"

He nodded. "I can't hurt women. It's a DNA thing. I just can't."

She took in a deep breath and let it out slowly. "Well this has certainly been an interesting morning. Any more surprises for me?"

"Wait here."

He went into the bedroom and came out with a small metal box which he placed on the coffee table in front of them. He opened it with a key, reached in and came out with his Smith & Wesson .38 special and a box of hollow-point bullets. Kelly's eyes widened as he loaded the weapon.

"What are you going to do with that?" she asked, alarmed.

"Nothing, I hope."

"Let me see if I got this right," she said slowly. "You were a gangster or something like that before becoming a doctor? Is that what you're telling me?"

"Something like that. Like I said, I'm not proud of some of the things I've done but that's all in the past for me now."

"Except the past has caught up with you, and some guy you tried to kill is now in town and wants revenge."

"As a working premise that pretty much covers it."

Chapter 11

Snell closed the door behind him. He, Gianelli, and Billy Ray Bob were now alone in one of the trauma rooms in the emergency department. Snell then drew the curtains closed so that none of the staff could see them.

Half sedated, Billy Ray Bob lay on a gurney with an intravenous line in place. He had two black eyes. The ear, nose, and throat surgeon had set his broken nose in an aluminum splint. The urologist said that he had a mild contusion of the left kidney, and there was nothing to do about the blood in the urine but wait it out. The neurologist advised him that he would have a headache for a few days, but should recover fully from the concussion. His head CT and other x-rays were normal. No broken bones. Billy Ray Bob was a little groggy, but coherent.

Gianelli leaned over him menacingly and growled, "You better not have screwed this up. Do you understand me, Billy Ray Dickhead?"

Billy Ray Bob glanced up at him meekly and nodded and Gianelli continued, "Now tell me what happened, and don't leave anything out...and I mean anything."

Billy Ray Bob glanced at his father for support but got none. His head throbbed and he was queasy. He spoke slowly, "The shipment was supposed to arrive at midnight and I had plenty of time, so I thought I'd go have a drink at the Ramada with some of the guys. You know, just one or two, to unwind a little. It was still early, only about eight. I ran into Kelly, and we were hanging out, shooting the bull and catching up when this psycho comes out of nowhere and attacks me. The guy was crazy.

I was just standing there and he sucker-punched me. It felt like he had a brick in his hand. My head hit the cement floor and it was light's out."

Gianelli grunted. "Some psycho comes from out of nowhere and for no reason decides to beat up on you, a cop? And no one knows who he is or who he might be working for? What kind of bullshit is this? There's a rumor going around that you were shitfaced and passed out without any help from some psycho."

Billy Ray Bob was visibly distressed and vehemently defend-ed himself, "No, that's not true. I only had a few drinks and maybe a couple of hits too, but I was fine. I swear I'm telling the truth." He again looked to his father for support and again was disappointed. As families went, theirs wasn't the most closely knit.

"Tell me about this girl, Kelly," Gianelli demanded impatiently.

"She's a friend of mine, a nurse at the hospital. I'm pretty sure she knew the guy. Everything happened so quickly and then I got hit on the head. I've got my friend Ozzie out looking for her. He's a cop too. He rides shotgun with me during pick-ups. You met him once after a delivery. When we find her, we'll find out who this guy is."

Gianelli's suspicions were on the rise. "Yeah, I remember Ozzie. Big fat guy, right? So this girl's a friend of yours, huh? How good a friend is she, and how much does she know about what's going on?"

"She's just some girl I used to date. She doesn't know any-thing, I swear. We were just hanging out catching up, when this guy showed up."

"Yeah, I got that part. He came out of nowhere and for no reason put you in the hospital. I'm not sure I like what I'm see-ing and hearing Snell, and if I don't like it, Big Lou sure ain't gonna like it either." Gianelli leaned in close. "And where's the Goddamn truck?"

Billy Ray Bob shrugged his shoulders. "I don't know. I never missed a pickup before."

Snell maneuvered uncomfortably and cleared his throat. "I know this isn't good, but I think we can still salvage the situation. The truck can't be too far from here. The driver wouldn't take off without payment. No one could be that stupid. He would probably hang around for at least a day or so is my guess. If we can find it in a hurry, we'll be at worst a day behind schedule."

Gianelli glared at them both harshly through slitted eyes, his height and physical bulk seeming to grow with his anger. "Maybe the truck's gone Snell, as in hijacked. Maybe someone sent that guy to beat the crap out of your son on purpose. Maybe that guy knew little Billy's routine, took him out, and then grabbed the goods. It's possible, isn't it? You two had better hope not. That was about ten million dollars' worth of merchandise."

Snell and Billy Ray Bob appeared dismayed. The older Snell asked, "Big Lou won't hold us responsible, will he? We've always carried out our end without any problems. This wasn't our fault. You have to explain that to him."

"Big Lou ain't the forgiving type, Snell." Gianelli was in a foul mood and felt one of his famous headaches coming on. He turned to them and said, "Let's think this through. The shipment arrives at around midnight last night. The driver is told to get off the New York State Thruway at the Genesee exit, pull into the rest stop there and wait. The driver doesn't know the final destination, so it's not like he can make the delivery himself. All he knows is that a squad car with two uniformed officers, Billy Ray Bob and Ozzie, is supposed to show up with the payment in cash.

Okay, so the driver gets a cup of coffee, and Billy Ray Bob is supposed to drive the truck to the hospital while Ozzie rides shotgun. The boys unload the truck and take it back to the driver at the rest stop, who then returns from whence he came. Now what the hell would he do if no one shows up? By the time he realizes you're a no-show, it's got to be at least one or two in the morning, right? He's been driving all day, so he's got to be exhausted."

"There's a motel at the rest stop he might have crashed in," Billy Ray Bob offered, trying to be helpful.

Gianelli sneered. "You mean, if we assume the truck wasn't already hijacked?"

Billy Ray Bob didn't say anything. His cellphone buzzed. It was Ozzie. Gianelli glared at him. "Well, aren't you going to answer it?"

Billy Ray Bob put the phone to his ear. "Yeah Ozzie, what have you got?" He listened and then gave Gianelli and his father a thumbs-up. "Good work, Oz. We'll be right over. Don't do anything until we get there. You might need help." He clicked off the phone and turned to Gianelli. "Ozzie found Kelly and the guy. She led him right to the guy's apartment. He's sitting outside right now in an unmarked Crown Vic."

Gianelli nodded. "Good. Let's get moving. Now we'll find out who this guy is and what he's up to. We'll go pick him up quick and then go search for the truck."

Billy Ray Bob wasn't sure what to do. He still had an IV sticking in his arm. Gianelli gazed down at him in disgust and suddenly slapped him hard in the face, "You waiting for an invitation? Get your ass out of that stretcher."

Snell cringed, but stepped forward to help his son remove his IV as Billy Ray Bob rose unsteadily to his feet. Gianelli took out his cellphone as they walked toward the parking lot.

"Pinky, we have a problem up here in Genesee," he barked into the receiver. "These yokels have misplaced the shipment, and there's even a chance that it may have been hijacked. I don't have any way of reaching the driver of the truck to find out what's going on. For all I know, the guy might be dead. Previous contact has always been directly from Big Lou to his boss to keep everything compartmentalized, and I don't want to get Big Lou involved yet."

"What can I do, Vito?" Pinky asked.

"I need backup. There's a distinct chance we might be under attack, and I don't have a handle yet on who from. Our friend Billy Ray Bob got the crap knocked out of him last night by persons unknown, causing him to miss the pickup. I don't know who did it or how many friends he might have with him. We think we may have found at least one of the guys, and we're on our way to pick him up."

"Are you sure it wasn't Billy Ray Bob himself who hijacked the truck, Vito?"

Gianelli eyed Billy Ray Bob and Snell suspiciously. "It was the first thought that crossed my mind Pinky, and it's still a possibility, but I just don't think so. I'm with Billy Ray Bob right now, and he looks like shit. Whoever took him out practically disabled him for life. He's peeing blood, for Chrissake. No, I think he's probably telling the truth. Besides, I think Billy Ray Bob and his father share one testicle between the two of them, if you know what I mean. It would take quite a pair to do something like this."

"That makes sense, Vito. You're probably right. Okay, what now?"

"I want you to grab Tony and maybe two other guys and haul ass up here. That should give us enough boots on the ground to discourage whoever it is that's messing with us. If all goes well, we'll all be back in New York by Monday at the latest. If something changes, I'll give you a call back."

"You got it, Vito."

Gianelli glanced at his Rolex. "All right then, it's just past two p.m. Get moving, and one more thing…"

"What's that, Vito?"

"Bring the dog."

Chapter 12

Kelly and Cesari sat on the sofa, mapping out their next move. He said, "I need to find out why Gianelli is here and what his relationship is with Snell. They seem to fit together about as well as a killer whale and a baby seal. If somehow I interfered with their plans last night, then I'm afraid things are going to start getting nasty around here real quick. I think we have to assume that it won't be long before they figure out that I'm the one who put Billy Ray Bob in the hospital. And when that happens, I'm certain Gianelli will blow a gasket."

She nodded, trying to digest what was happening. He asked, "Did Billy Ray Bob ever talk about anything that seemed odd to you, like maybe he was boasting about something? It might have seemed stupid at the time."

She thought about it a little and said, "Yeah, sure. He liked to brag about how he knew important people and how he was too big for this town. He also loved to flash money around, trying to impress people. That's one of the reasons I left him, his constant bragging...and his temper. He was always losing control over little things. Once, we were coming out of a movie and some kid was leaning against his Porsche. The kid didn't mean any harm, but Billy Ray Bob nearly killed him. Knocked him down and started kicking him. God, it was awful."

"Billy Ray Bob owns a Porsche?" he asked, surprised.

"Oh yeah, that's his baby. Souped up black 911 GT3, 475 horsepower," she said, smiling.

Cesari smiled back at her. "I bet you looked great in it."

"Damn right about that," she laughed playfully and performed a perfect head bob at him, flipping her hair from one side of her face to the other. A woman couldn't get much sexier than that, he thought.

He said, "I guess it's true what they say."

"What's that?"

"The Vette makes them wet."

She squinted at him suspiciously. "What's that supposed to mean?"

"You never heard that before?"

"No."

"It means that hot chicks and hot cars go together like apple pie and the Fourth of July."

"You think I'm hot?"

"Kelly, if you were any hotter, they'd blame you for global warming."

She liked that one. "Thanks. You're not so bad yourself."

He thought about the Porsche. "A car like that easily goes for over a hundred thousand dollars base price, and souped up, probably comes close to a buck and a half. I think it's safe to say that it's well out of the price range of your average police officer. Did he get in trouble for beating on that kid?"

She laughed bitterly. "No, the kid didn't even report the incident. There were plenty of witnesses but no one saw anything, if you know what I mean. That's just the way it is around here."

"I don't mean to pry, but why exactly did you end it with him?" He regretted the question immediately.

Regarding him crossly, she said, "In case you haven't been listening, he's a total asshole."

He didn't say anything.

She paused and turned her head away. Something was bothering her that she wanted to get off her chest. "I mean, he wasn't like that at first, you know? In fact, he was even a little charming and kind of funny. He's got a great body too, but he drinks too much and does coke. Anyway, his temper and mood swings kept getting worse and worse. He pushed me around a couple of times when he was high and threatened me once or twice, but he never really did anything terrible until a couple of months ago. It finally came to a head when he had a couple of his friends over one night to watch a football game."

He waited patiently as she hesitated. "God, I can't believe I'm telling you this."

"Look, Kel, if you don't feel comfortable talking about it, I'll understand."

He put his arm around her and drew her near. She took a deep breath and went on, "By halftime, they were pretty tanked up on beer, pot, and whiskey... I was sitting on the couch in between Billy Ray Bob and his friend Ozzie... Ozzie put his arm around me and tried to kiss me. I pushed him away and laughed it off, you know. I turned to Billy Ray Bob for help, but all he did was grab my wrists and slap his handcuffs on them..."

Cesari caught his breath and raised his eyebrows at the revelation. Tears welled up in her eyes as she recalled the lurid details of that night. He didn't say anything and just held her tightly while she spoke. To say that he was shocked and angry would have been the understatement of the year. He knew that Billy Ray Bob was a top-of-the-line prick but this was beyond belief.

"I'm sorry for bringing it up," he offered gently, when she had concluded. "I don't know what to say. I feel so bad. No woman should have to go through something like that. My God, he's even worse than I had thought." Cesari felt his blood pressure rising.

She didn't say anything for a while, and they sat there like that. Finally, she exhaled slowly and whispered with a trembling voice, "It's okay. I really should talk about it with someone. I've been bottling it up, and that may not be the best thing for me.

I don't have family here, and I didn't think going to the police would help since they were the police. Anyway, the next day I left him, and he's been wild ever since. He calls me every day and harasses me whenever he sees me in public, like at the Ramada last night. In his mind all he has to do is say he's sorry and then everything should go back to the way it was before."

"A lot of abusive guys are like that. Most of them are simply incapable of taking responsibility for their actions... You said his friend's name was Ozzie? Was that the same Ozzie you saw in the unmarked car outside your apartment?"

She nodded. "Yes, which is why I got so upset. There were two of them that night besides Billy Ray Bob. One was Ozzie, a nickname for Oswald...Oswald Pennington...and the other was Dave Culpepper, who goes by Pepper."

"Is Pepper a cop too?"

"Even better, he's a detective," she said with disgust.

He kissed her lightly on the forehead. "I am so sorry for what happened to you. Men can be such assholes."

What else could he say?

She snuggled closer to him, arched her head back, and pulled him down closer for a real kiss. Her lips were moist from her tears, and her nearness sent ripples of excitement through his body, but Cesari was distracted. He felt something deep inside snap like a twig of a branch. It was a strand of primitive, unevolved DNA. Ozzie and Pepper didn't know it, but they had just made it onto the same list as Billy Ray Bob. It was a list of who was going to get hurt. The only question that remained was how badly he was going to hurt them.

Chapter 13

"Feel like talking?" he asked. They had been sitting quietly on the sofa in silence, the atmosphere a bit down since she opened up to him about her sexual assault at the hands of Billy Ray Bob and his friends. He was seething on the inside and wanted to smash the walls in but he knew that wouldn't help and certainly not what she needed at the moment, so he just sat there and held her. He figured she'd snap out of it sooner or later, and she did.

She said, "Sure,"

"I don't mean to change the subject, but I'd like to ask a few more questions about Billy Ray Bob if it's okay with you? If you'd rather not think or talk about him anymore, I'll understand."

"No, it'll be fine. What would you like to know?"

"Aside from his flashing green around, was there anything else you might have seen or heard that seemed unusual to you?"

She thought long and hard and finally said, "Well, about a year ago, there was a huge construction project at the hospital. There was a major renovation of certain parts, particularly in the basement where the pharmacy area is. Billy Ray Bob was unusually interested in it, always talking about it, which I thought was a little odd because he's a cop, right? Why should he care about a construction project at the hospital, but then I figured he was just getting pumped up about it because his dad runs the place."

"Interesting, but not that unusual, not really. Hospitals are always renovating and expanding. And you're right about Billy Ray Bob's enthusiasm. It may simply have reflected conversations he may have had with his father about it. It's almost routine these days to see construction going on at healthcare facilities. A project like you just described is actually kind of ordinary."

"I know that. On the face of it yes, but they also installed high-tech security cameras everywhere in the basement with signs warning people that certain areas are restricted. When you're down there, it's really kind of creepy. I'm surprised you haven't noticed, but then again, you haven't been here that long and probably haven't had much reason to go down there."

"You're right about that. In fact, I've only been down there once or twice since I started working here, and I didn't notice anything. The pharmacy is on one side of the basement, and the cafeteria is on the other, right? I don't go to the cafeteria much, since food trucks pull up to the front of the MOB every day, and they're more convenient for me. I only have a few minutes between the time I finish my last colonoscopy and the time I have to start seeing patients in the office."

She was starting to perk up and giggled, "Are you sure it's not because you prefer a fresh, hot Gyro to a lukewarm burger that's been kept in a water bath to keep it moist, like they serve in the cafeteria?"

He was about to respond when suddenly she snapped her fingers and said, "Now I remember. About six months ago, I was sent down to the pharmacy by the nursing supervisor to pick up some medication for a patient. Something happened that struck me as very strange at the time, but I put it out of mind.

Most of the construction took place at the pharmacy end of the basement. Well, a long corridor leads past the pharmacy to a set of double doors. There are security cameras on either side of those doors. We were told that's where all the computers, servers, and other electrical equipment for the hospital are kept. There are warning signs about high voltage everywhere, and we were told that for our own safety we should stay away from there, but now that I think about it, I don't believe it."

"I agree it seems a bit odd, but not that odd. Why don't you believe it?" he asked, trying to think it through.

She beamed at him triumphantly and said, "Because when I was down there, the doors opened, and a group of doctors came out arguing about something in a foreign language. They saw me looking their way, shut up, and went back in."

"Now that is interesting," Cesari said. "So I gather the docs weren't anyone you knew or had seen before?'

"No, definitely not. I've been working there for more than two years, and I know all the doctors on staff by sight, but I never saw these guys before. They were thin and very dark skinned, but not African. At the time, I thought they might be Indian or Pakistani. The hallway is pretty long, so I really couldn't swear to what I saw or heard, but it definitely caught my attention. I was in a hurry and didn't give it a whole lot of thought until now. The whole encounter was fairly brief."

"If you didn't know them, how do you know they were doctors?" he asked.

She furrowed her brow in concentration. "Well, I guess I never really asked myself that question before. They sure seemed like doctors. For one thing, they were wearing white lab coats."

He thought about foreign docs in a restricted area of the basement that housed computers and other electrical equipment. "Maybe they were scientists whose job required them to wear lab coats, like engineers. Maybe they were servicing the computers and other equipment kept there."

She closed her eyes, trying to remember more clearly. "Shhh, let me think. They were wearing white coats and were well dressed with ties, and there was something else..."

He interrupted her, "A white lab coat and a tie don't necessarily mean you're a medical doctor. Lots of professionals wear white lab coats and ties."

"Which part of shhh didn't you understand, Cesari?"

He shut up and smiled. She went from calling him John to Cesari after only one night together. She said, "They were medical doctors, all right. It's coming back to me. I'm sure of it, because I remember now that they all had stethoscopes in the outer pockets of their lab coats or around their necks. I remember that clearly now. Engineers don't use stethoscopes, right?"

"That is true. Only members of the medical profession used stethoscopes with a few rare exceptions, such as veterinarians."

"And now that I think about it, that's another thing that struck me as odd about Billy Ray Bob. He kept asking me if I noticed anything unusual going on at the hospital or if I saw anybody I didn't know. To be honest, at the time I didn't make too much of it."

"Did you ever ask him why he was asking those questions?"

"I did, and he said that as a cop he was just being vigilant. Like he was working for homeland security or something."

Cesari thought about that. "That is interesting."

"Isn't it though?"

So who were these doctors, and what were they doing in a restricted area of the hospital? Why was Billy Ray Bob asking so many questions and what on earth did any of this have to do with Gianelli? Cesari was starting to feel out of the loop which in turn made him feel very exposed.

He said, "Kelly, I want you to stay here while I go out and grab us some supplies. I don't have much here, and I wasn't expecting any houseguests. I don't want you to feel like you're under house arrest, but I don't think you should be out in public right now if Billy Ray Bob and his friends are looking for you."

She sighed wistfully but saw the wisdom of it. "You're right, although I would feel better if I wasn't alone so don't take too long, and we'll need food. We can't live on biscotti and bologna.

Pick up a few things like shampoo, body lotion and bubble bath. A scented candle would be nice. Maybe I should make a list?"

"A list would be great."

He found a notepad and a pen for her, and she quickly jotted down her honey-do list. He read it and mentally added shotgun, shells, duct tape and a crowbar. He'd never regretted having a crowbar handy. They stood up together and she threw her arms around him, pressing her face into his chest.

"Hurry back, all right?"

"I will."

It was late afternoon, and he felt his temperature rising. He went flying out the door and in his haste, forgot the .38 on the coffee table.

Chapter 14

They all sat in Ozzie's unmarked Crown Victoria about half a block away from Cesari's rental house. Two in the front and two in the back. Gianelli's Cadillac was parked directly behind them and Billy Ray Bob's Buick behind that.

Ozzie who was in the driver's seat explained, "She thought she was real clever. She spotted my car in front of her apartment and doubled back around, but I caught her in the side mirror. I gave her plenty of lead-time, so I don't think she saw me tailing her. I really hung back and almost lost her a couple of times."

"So who's the guy, Oz? Ever see him before?" Billy Ray Bob asked.

"Nope, I ain't never seen him before. He's about six feet, clean shaven, brown hair, looks like he spends a lot of time in the gym."

Billy Ray Bob touched the splint over his nose. "That's the guy. I'd bet everything on it."

Sitting in the back with Snell, Gianelli asked, "When did he leave?"

"About ten minutes before you arrived. He's driving a blue Camry, but I couldn't make out the plates from here."

"Why would he have left the girl here all alone?" Gianelli asked no one in particular.

"Probably went out for condoms," Ozzie offered, grinning.

Irritated, Billy Ray Bob snapped, "Is that supposed to be helpful?"

"Sorry. It's just that…"

"Spit it out, Oz. I'm already having a bad day."

"When she greeted the guy, they kissed, long and slow. You know what I mean? Long and slow."

"Shut up, Oz."

"Knock it off, you two," ordered Gianelli.

"I'm sorry I let him go, Mr. Gianelli." Ozzie glanced in the rearview mirror. "Billy Ray Bob told me not to move in until you got here. Besides, I figured we still got Kelly in there, and if we got her, then we'll get him."

Gianelli thought about that and said, "You did the right thing, Oz. Besides, it's his apartment so he's going to have to come back sooner or later, right? It might even work out better this way, because it'll be a lot easier to snatch them one at a time." He paused for a moment contemplating strategy and then continued, "Billy Ray Bob, you grab Kelly now and be quick about it. Take her back to your house, where we can take our time questioning her. We'll stand guard out here in case the guy comes back. Think you can handle her by yourself?"

Billy Ray Bob ignored the sarcasm in Gianelli's tone. "Yeah, I think I can handle her."

"Then, what are you waiting for? Get moving."

As Billy Ray Bob got out of the car, Ozzie chuckled. "Billy Ray Bob, make sure you don't tire her out too much before I get my turn to question her."

Gianelli spoke to Snell. "At least now we'll know who this guy is. Once Billy Ray Bob gets the girl, you and I will head over to that thruway rest stop to search for the truck. Ozzie, you stay here and keep an eye out for the guy. If you think you can bring him in by yourself, go for it and take him to Billy Ray Bob's place. If not give us a call and we'll take him down together."

"He won't be any problem," Ozzie said self-assuredly.

"Don't get overconfident, all right? He made a real mess out of your pal last night," Gianelli cautioned.

"I know he did a number on Billy Ray Bob, but he was stoned at the time and got caught off guard. This prick's going to find out that the situation's a little different tonight. I'm the one with the element of surprise on his side this time. He doesn't even know who I am. I'll just walk up to him and nail him with the stun gun. Once he's down and cuffed, I'll teach him the real meaning of police brutality." Ozzie smirked.

"You're my kind of guy, Oz," Gianelli replied. "Well be careful and don't give him brain damage. I need to talk to him."

They watched as Billy Ray Bob put on a pair of black leather gloves and walked up to the house where Kelly was.

Gianelli said, "It's show time."

Chapter 15

Kelly sat on the sofa, sipping a glass of wine and staring at the .38 on the coffee table thinking things over. She didn't like or know anything about guns and was afraid to touch it. But she liked Cesari. Good-looking, muscular and charming, he was magnetic in an animal way. He was a good doctor and everyone at the hospital liked him except for Snell, but now she was seeing his personal side. There were dark undertones that she found a little disturbing. His past was something she was sure she didn't want to dive too deeply into but was sure she would have to at some point. He'd already told her more than she wanted to know. But he's not like that anymore she told herself. That was him then, not now. Everybody deserves a second chance. It wasn't his fault this guy Gianelli was in town and it wasn't his fault Billy Ray Bob had attacked him in the bar. Her cellphone rang. It was her friend Linda, Cesari's secretary.

"Hi Linda, how are you?"

"I'm great, Kel. How'd your date with the doc go last night?"

"It went okay," she answered coyly.

"C'mon, Kel, I want details."

Kelly laughed. "Well, it didn't start off great because Billy Ray Bob was there and in rare form, but things ended well, if you know what I mean."

"Did Billy Ray Bob make a scene again?" Linda asked.

"Did he ever. He started a fight with Dr. Cesari."

"Oh no. What happened?"

"Dr. Cesari cleaned his clock is what happened."

"Really? Well good for him. It's about time somebody set that ex of yours straight. I knew I liked the doc. I'm sorry to hear about all the drama, but I'm glad that you and the doc hit it off, Kel. I really am. He's nice and you're nice, and I was getting tired of you two flirting all the time. So what are you doing tonight? Got any plans?"

"Actually, I'm sitting in his apartment having a glass of wine. He went to pick up a few things. I think we're going to hang out here tonight."

Linda laughed. "A twofer? Girl, you move fast. You better take it easy on him. I have to work with him Monday, and I don't want to hear him whining about how tired he is."

Kelly laughed. "He's really nice, Linda. I don't think I've ever met anyone quite like him. He's a little rough around the edges though, and his apartment is an absolute disaster. There's nothing in it. I can't tell if he just moved in or is about to move out."

"That's why God made women, honey, to tame the savage beasts. I've tamed three of them already myself and am close to subduing a fourth," Linda explained wisely.

Kelly lowered her voice as if there was someone else in the room listening. "He has a gun, Linda…and a past. I don't want to go into it right now but he told me things about himself that are shocking. I'm still not sure I heard right. It was that bad."

Linda snorted, "A past? Boy, you really did fall off the turnip truck, didn't you? No one talks like that anymore. So he has a past, who doesn't? And all that the gun means is that he believes in the second amendment. I have one too, darling."

"You own a gun? I didn't know that."

"Sure I do. It's a little thing but it'll get the job done. I'll take you out to the range some time. We'll have fun."

"I'll have to think about that. Guns kind of scare me."

"And rightly so. We'll talk about it more some other time. So tell me about the doc. Was he a real gentleman?"

Kelly smiled into the phone. "Yeah, he was. I've got to tell you, Linda, I think he's got real potential, but I don't want to get ahead of myself here."

"Do I hear wedding bells already?"

"Oh stop, that's not what I meant." She started blushing even though she was by herself. "Although Kelly Cesari has got a nice ring to it."

They both laughed mischievously. When the door buzzer sounded, Kelly jumped as if she thought Cesari had heard her last comment.

"I got to run, Linda. He's at the door and probably got his hands full of groceries."

"Ain't that sweet. Bye."

Kelly ran to the door and opened it with a big smile on her face, but then froze, speechless with horror, as she gazed upon Billy Ray Bob's frightful appearance. She hadn't seen him since the Ramada incident, and was stunned by the physical damage that Cesari had inflicted upon him. Both his eyes were black and puffy. A metal splint covered his nose, which had swollen to twice its normal size.

He was wearing the most malicious grin she had ever seen. "Expecting someone else?"

Without warning, he dealt a savage blow to her face, knocking her into the wall behind. She crumpled to the floor stunned, her lower lip bleeding and already starting to swell. Billy Ray Bob stepped over her into the apartment and closed the door behind him. He immediately knelt down beside her and cuffed her hands behind her back. Then he proceeded to perform a quick search of the small apartment while she lay there dazed. Within seconds, he spotted the gun lying on the coffee table and placed it in a plastic lunch bag he found in the kitchen. He turned to Kelly, who remained disoriented from the blow.

"Hope your boyfriend's got a permit for this." he snickered and held up the bagged pistol.

She heard him but could only moan in response. He concluded his search of the apartment and found nothing else of interest, so he grabbed Kelly roughly under one arm and hoisted her up to a standing position. She was a little wobbly, but starting to come around.

He said callously, "C'mon, you can stand. You're all right. I barely touched you. Now let's get something straight. We're going to walk out to my car. If you make any noise or try to get away, I'll smack the snot right out of you. Do you understand?" To make sure she understood, he squeezed her arm hard enough to elicit a yelp of pain from her.

She whimpered, "I understand."

Chapter 16

It took Cesari a little longer than he had anticipated to collect everything he needed. The mandatory background check for the shotgun seemed to take forever. One terrorist attack and all of sudden an honest American couldn't buy a lethal firearm without everyone staring at him like he belonged to Al Qaeda. But eventually he passed muster which was ridiculous anyway because he shouldn't have passed any background check. He had an arrest record as long as a human arm including aggravated assault and extortion. Nonetheless, the process ended in his favor and he purchased a 12-gauge, pump-action Mossberg 500 with a pistol grip and five-round capacity. A small flashlight, duct tape, hunting knife, and crowbar completed his armament.

Maybe he was over-reacting, but he thought it prudent to be safe. He threw everything in the car along with the groceries and a DVD he found for one dollar. He thought Kelly would like *Under the Tuscan Sun*. The back cover blurb said it was a light-hearted romantic story set in Italy. Nothing wrong with that. He never tired of reading about Italy or watching stories set there.

By the time he got back to his place, it was almost 6:00 p.m., and the sun still glowed brightly in the autumn sky. He spotted the unmarked police car from about half a block away as he turned onto his street. Fortunately, he was approaching from the rear of the Crown Vic which was facing east. The glare of the sun coming from the west and behind rendered its mirrors useless.

From his limited vantage point, Cesari thought the driver appeared just as fat and stupid as Kelly had described. He stared raptly in the direction of the apartment, and Cesari had no doubt in his mind that this was the now infamous Ozzie.

Cesari parked the Camry on the same side of the street about five cars back and thought through his options. He had attacked enough police officers in his life to know he was walking on thin ice. Smacking Billy Ray Bob around in a bar was bad enough but possibly excusable in the minds of the blue brotherhood. He was drunk and getting out of line with an ex-girlfriend. They might even think it was funny, like he deserved it.

But this was different. Ozzie hadn't done anything to him. Two battered cops in one weekend would be a crisis. There would be pride on the line. There might be an all-out manhunt for him. They might even call in the state boys to help out. He had this vision of retired officers being recalled to duty, oiling up their rusty old pistols and racking up their shotguns for one last rodeo. Not good. On the other hand, this was Ozzie and he had hurt Kelly. In the final analysis, that was all Cesari needed to know. The only questions he had now were how long had Ozzie been watching the apartment and whether he knew what he looked like.

He was a cop and no doubt confident in his skills. They always were. He was Billy Ray Bob's friend and probably considered himself above the law. They always did. Right now, Ozzie's greatest weakness was his overconfidence. In Cesari's mind, dirty cops were no different from guys like Gianelli. They all thought that the world was their oyster and that they were smarter, faster, and stronger than the other guy. So it always came as a surprise to them when a bullet unexpectedly entered their gray matter at a thousand feet per second or in this case, a crowbar came smashing through the driver's side window.

He got out of the Camry and glanced down at his packages. Two paper bags full of groceries were on the passenger seat. The shotgun and shells were on the floor. The crowbar was in the space between the seat and center console. He picked the crowbar up and hid it along the length of his right arm. Then he picked up one of the grocery bags and shut the door. There was no one else on the street.

Adrenaline surging, he walked slowly and casually toward Ozzie along the driver's side of the row of parked cars. He was counting on the sun shining in his mirrors to obscure his view, and in case that didn't work, he cradled the grocery bag high in the crook of his left arm, blocking his face from view. He was merely a citizen returning home with dinner.

Thirty feet, twenty feet...

The driver's side window of the car unexpectedly opened, and Cesari froze in place, expecting Ozzie to jump out pointing a gun at him. He held his breath and waited. Instead, Ozzie's left arm came out with a cigarette attached, which he tapped lightly to discard its ash onto the street. Then he rested his arm on the car door with his elbow jutting out. He continued to stare down the block toward the apartment. Cesari could hear music coming from the car radio. Satisfied, he began to creep forward again.

Ten feet, five feet...

He was squarely in the blind spot of the Vic's mirrors now and he took a deep breath. Gently laying the grocery bag down onto the street, he brought the crowbar into position. His initial thought was to hit him in the head, but without the window to diffuse some of the force, a direct blow from a crowbar would probably kill him, and he wasn't in that kind of mood just yet.

Then a better idea came to him. He raised the twenty-two inch, six-pound, steel crowbar over his head and slammed it as hard as he could onto Ozzie's exposed elbow. It broke with an awful sound, and he howled in pain and shock. Cesari leaned through the open window and popped him forcefully in the side of the head with the curved end of the crowbar. It was enough to stun him but leave him conscious. He moaned but Cesari knew the real pain hadn't registered yet.

He quickly opened the door and relieved Ozzie of his pistol and stun gun. The pistol was a Glock 17, standard issue for many police departments. It was loaded but not chambered. Ozzie was starting to focus again, and Cesari shoved him across the bench seat toward the passenger side as he whimpered in pain. Cesari leaned across him and secured his good arm to the passenger door with his own handcuffs. He was still groaning and gasping, barely aware of what was happening. The sleeve of his white shirt was staining red with blood suggesting a displaced fracture or laceration from the blow.

He was about forty, ruddy complexion, and looked like he ate too much, drank too much, and smoked too much. Cesari guessed he probably had undiagnosed hypertension and the beginnings of diabetes. He was a heart attack waiting to happen. In one of his pockets Cesari found his ID which read, *Oswald Pennington, Genesee Police Department.*

"Hello, Ozzie," he said. "Funny meeting you here."

Surprised recognition filled his eyes as he gritted his teeth and spat at him, hissing, "You're a dead man walking. I hope you know that."

Cesari wiped saliva off his face and was a little surprised at the man's defiance considering the situation. He gave Ozzie's broken elbow a short, sharp admonishing rap with the crowbar causing him to wail in distress.

"I'm glad we're getting to know each other, Oz. I've heard a lot about you from Kelly."

He was perspiring and gasping, but still thought he was in charge. "You're going to regret this big time."

Cesari shook his head. Cops were the worst prisoners. They were so used to being on the other end of the abuse, it took forever for it to sink in. He said reasonably, "Ozzie, you're not getting it. I'm the one with the crowbar and you're the one trying not to get hit again. Let's start over. Why don't you tell me what's going on around here, and you can spare yourself another broken bone."

"What's going on is that you're playing with fire, and you don't even know it. We already got the girl, and you're next."

The news hit Cesari like an electric shock, causing alarm to race through his body. He whipped out his cellphone and called Kelly. The call went to voice mail. He tried again with the same result and then left a voice message for her to call him. He was getting nervous.

Ozzie laughed. "I told you, but don't worry. She's probably giving Billy Ray Bob a blowjob right now. I'm sure she'll call you when she's done."

Just for that, Cesari pressed the stun gun against his chest and unloaded fifty thousand volts into him. He went into a spasm, his eyes rolled up in their sockets and he passed out. He propped him up against the window, hoping to give any casual passersby the appearance that he was taking a little nap. After he took the keys from the ignition, he ripped the wires from the police radio out from under the dashboard. Then he found Ozzie's cellphone and threw it out the window onto the street.

Cesari got out of the car and ran to his apartment, his heart racing. Someone had left the door cracked open, and he had a sinking feeling in his stomach. Running from room to room, he called out frantically for Kelly. On the coffee table he saw the open lockbox, but the .38 was gone. Even worse, next to the lockbox was her cellphone showing the two missed calls from a moment ago. Women don't go anywhere without their cellphones these days. That had to be bad. Other than that, nothing else seemed out of place. As he was leaving to discuss the situation with Ozzie, he noticed it. There were several small spatterings of red on the entranceway wall. Blood.

He was starting to get angry.

Chapter 17

Cesari transferred the rest of the stuff from his shopping spree to the back seat of Ozzie's cruiser, and drove to the Genesee State Park by the lake. It was dark by the time he arrived and the park was mostly deserted. The few people he saw were heading toward the exit. The lake was serene and he drove the car right onto the small beach to within several feet of the water's edge. Stately old poplars and willows ruled the shoreline, some of them with trunks three and four feet in diameter. The moon shimmered on the gently rolling waves and Cesari was at peace with what he had to do. The water felt cold as it rushed up against his lower legs and this exhilarated him. He had taken his socks and sneakers off and rolled his jeans up.

"It's beautiful here, Ozzie. Don't you think?"

Ozzie was on his knees in the water and Cesari held him tightly by the hair with his left hand. He held the crowbar in his right hand. Ozzie didn't answer him right away but twisted his head awkwardly to look up at him.

After a few seconds he sputtered, "I guess so."

Cesari glanced down at him. Blood dripped down his lip onto his chin. He was talking a little clumsily because he was now missing two teeth from where Cesari had hit him with the crowbar. His broken left arm dangled uselessly. The bravado was gone and he was way past any sort of real resistance. The only thing left was complete and total capitulation.

"I'm only going to say it one more time, Ozzie. Tell me where Kelly is and then the healing can begin."

He hesitated and Cesari slammed the crowbar onto his shoulder. Ozzie moaned in pain. Cesari let go of his hair and he collapsed face forward into the water. With his good arm, he raised himself, coughing and gasping for air.

Cesari grabbed him roughly by the hair again, pulled him up and snarled into his face, "I can do this all night long, Officer Pennington."

"No, please. No more, please," he begged. "I'll tell you where she is. Billy Ray Bob took her to his place out in the country. It's an old white farmhouse about five miles straight out of town on Route 96. You can't miss it. There's an old barn and a detached garage."

"Now you're being reasonable, Ozzie. Keep talking."

He would have, too, except he started to vomit. Eventually he settled down, and Cesari assisted him to his feet. He said, "Take a deep breath, Ozzie. There you go. All better now? How many others are there with Billy Ray Bob?"

"Okay, okay," he groaned in resignation but didn't answer the question.

He didn't look too good, and Cesari hoped he wasn't going into shock. He shook him hard. "Ozzie, stay focused. How many others are there?"

"Billy Ray Bob was by himself when he snatched Kelly, so I don't know who else might be there."

Cesari struggled with that but eventually accepted it. "Okay, I believe you... All right then, we're making good progress here. Don't you agree?"

Ozzie nodded and asked very reasonably, "Aren't you even going to tell me your name?"

"No Oz, it's not germane to the process here. I hope that doesn't present a problem for you."

He grunted and shook his head no.

"Next subject, Oz. What's going on at the hospital with the Snells and that mob guy Gianelli?"

"I don't know," he said, and Cesari swung the crowbar into his left knee, causing him to buckle and fall into the water again. From his knees, he wailed, "Wait, wait, please! I meant I don't know everything. I just help Billy Ray Bob from time to time. He doesn't tell me everything. Once a month or sometimes every other month, we drive to the thruway rest stop. Usually at midnight or thereabouts. We meet a truck there. Billy Ray Bob pays the driver, and we take the truck. That's all I know. I never look in the truck. I don't want to know. He pays me a grand for a couple of hours of my time."

"Where do you take the truck?" Cesari asked, now very curious. The crowbar was in the raised position.

"To the back of the hospital where the loading dock is. I follow in the car and act as lookout while Billy Ray Bob unloads the truck. Sometimes his dad is there helping him. I never see anything."

"What's your best guess about the cargo?"

"Drugs of course. That's why I don't want to know." His words had the ring of truth. Interesting. "What's so important about Kelly that you guys are willing to risk kidnapping charges?"

"It's not just Kelly. They want you too. Billy Ray Bob and I were supposed to pick up the truck last night, but you kicked his ass and he missed the rendezvous. That greaser Gianelli is pissed and thinks you took Billy Ray Bob out on purpose and maybe hijacked the truck. They think Kelly may have been in on it, like maybe she set up Billy Ray Bob for you."

I thought about that one. "What kind of vehicle is Billy Ray Bob driving tonight?"

"A green Buick LaCrosse."

"Okay, Ozzie, we're going for a ride. You be good, and you might get through the night without any more unpleasantness. Understand?"

He nodded. "Where are we going?"

"We're going to Billy Ray Bob's house to see if you're telling the truth and if we can resolve this unfortunate business."

Cesari led him to the back of the car. He was in no shape mentally or physically to try anything. His left arm was useless, and he was limping badly from the blow to the kneecap. Emotionally, he was toast.

He opened the trunk and ordered Ozzie to climb in. It wasn't easy, but he managed it without too much difficulty. Cesari thought about handcuffing his wrists behind his back but didn't want to hear him scream from the manipulation of his wrecked arm. He considered breaking the other arm and giving him a matching pair but discarded the idea on the grounds of unnecessary cruelty. Although if he did break the other arm, he wouldn't have to restrain him at all. In the end, he did neither and wound up cuffing his ankles together. Even though he wasn't much of a flight risk, Cesari wasn't into taking chances. Once Ozzie was secured in the trunk, Cesari slapped a strip of duct tape over his mouth.

"Are you going to make any noise?" he asked.

He shook his head no.

"If you take the duct tape off, I'll have no choice but to break the other arm. Understand?" he showed him the crowbar again. Ozzie's eyes went wide and he nodded comprehension.

Cesari slammed the trunk shut on him and glanced up at the moon. He hoped he wasn't going soft. In his younger days he would have broken Ozzie's other arm and maybe both his legs. He sighed and got in the driver's seat.

Chapter 18

"**A**re you sure you heard right?" Snell was speaking to Billy Ray Bob on his cellphone. "Okay, we'll deal with him later. Did the girl say anything else? Does she know anything?" He listened intently some more before adding, "Good work. Keep her under wraps until we can talk to her. Now I have good news for you too."

He paused a beat for effect and then continued, "You got lucky Billy Ray Bob. We found the truck. When no one showed, the driver used his head, got back on the thruway, drove to the next rest stop and waited there. He was hanging out, not sure what to do. He was too scared to return home without the money, so he slept in the truck. He was just thinking about giving up and heading back when we found him there eating lunch. We're driving the truck back to the hospital as we speak. Meet us there to help us unload and secure the cargo. When we're done, you can bring the truck back to the rest stop and pick up Mr. Gianelli's Cadillac, and make sure Ozzie stays with that guy."

He concluded the call and Gianelli said, "I don't like surprises, Snell. What's going on?"

Gianelli drove the ten-wheel cargo like a pro, and they were nearly at the hospital's rear entrance.

"Billy Ray Bob's got the girl at his place. So far, she doesn't seem to know much about anything, but the night's still young. When he last checked in with Ozzie, the guy hadn't returned yet. Kelly said that he went out for groceries and stuff, but that's not the best part."

He savored the next tidbit and Gianelli became impatient. "Spit it out, Snell. I'm not in a good mood."

Snell's mood however, had elevated considerably. "She had to be slapped around a little naturally, but eventually she gave up the name of the guy who beat up Billy Ray Bob. It's John Cesari... Dr. John Cesari, the newest member of our medical staff... and your good friend from the Bronx."

He added that last to emphasize the shared guilt should things fall apart. Gianelli exhaled slowly. "Shit! And we had him right in our hands this morning. He was probably laughing at us the whole time."

Gianelli knew perfectly well what Snell was hinting at and thought the little weasel was correct in his logic. If Big Lou heard that Cesari had risen from the grave to tear him a new one and got away with it, Gianelli would be no better than dog meat...literally. In this business shit generally rolled downhill but very occasionally it went the other way. He'd have to be careful. On the other hand, the only people who really knew what was going on were Snell and his son, and what was that expression? *Dead men tell no tales.* That was it. *Dead men tell no tales.* He grinned at Snell. "Good work, Snell. I may have to make you a full partner some day."

Snell smiled appreciatively and started thinking aloud. "I wonder why though. It doesn't make sense to me. Not really. Cesari just finished ten years of medical training. He's got a good job and he's making decent money. He's got a lot going for him and a lucrative future in front of him. Why would he throw it all away?"

Gianelli chuckled sarcastically and pontificated a perverse street logic. "Don't think too hard, Snell. You'll hurt your brain. People throw their lives away all the time over things like greed and lust. Look at you and your son. One drug-and-booze-filled weekend in Atlantic City, and you and your whole damn hospital are now the property of Big Lou Barazza. It's that easy. And with this guy Cesari, it's in his blood. Just remember, a leopard can't change its spots."

Snell bowed his head at the memory of that weekend in Atlantic City. He said, "I know it's that easy, but Billy Ray Bob said the girl swears that she didn't set him up. He thinks the whole thing was random and that Cesari didn't know anything about the shipment. He thinks Cesari just happened to be there to have a drink with Kelly and lost it because she was paying more attention to Billy Ray Bob than to him."

"You've got to be kidding. She's just telling him what he wants to hear, Snell. Don't you get it? No guy wants to believe his girlfriend or ex-girlfriend would betray him like that. She knows she's screwed and is just trying to wiggle out of it. I know this guy, Cesari. He's involved, all right. I feel it. We got lucky because the driver used his head and changed his location. The only thing I can't figure out is who Cesari is working for. Or more to the point, who would have the balls to take on Big Lou and me. I can't believe he would do this as a rogue operation. Not possible." Gianelli was quiet for a few moments while he thought it over and then asked, "How many guys really know what's going on here, Snell?"

Snell was still thinking about Atlantic City but replied, "No one that I know of. We've kept it real quiet as we were told. Obviously, there's Billy Ray Bob, who knows everything. Ozzie knows a little, but I'm not sure how much. I doubt that he knows the full extent of what's going on. Billy Ray Bob swore to me that he never told him anything. Then there are the doctors of course, but who are they going to tell? They barely speak English. That's about it from my end. Various people know bits and pieces like the truck driver, but very few know everything. It's been kept very compartmentalized."

Gianelli glared at Snell accusingly. "Well I think it's possible that Billy Ray Bob might have let slip what's been going on to this girl Kelly. Guys say lots of things they shouldn't when their shorts are down around their ankles. Then maybe this Kelly girl told Cesari. He in turn, maybe told someone else higher up the food chain who might have given him the go-ahead to snatch the truck."

Snell squirmed in his seat as he saw where the conversation was heading. "Billy Ray Bob is a lot of things, some not so nice, but he is not that stupid. We are both well aware of what would happen to us if we ever betrayed Mr. Barazza or you either purposefully or accidentally."

They were stopped at a red light. Gianelli pinned Snell with his gaze. "You had better keep that thought uppermost in your mind at all times, Snell. Now make yourself useful and call those Pakistani doctors. Tell them to sober up. We've got patients for them."

As he drove, Gianelli thought back to the night he had met the Snells. It was almost two years ago in Atlantic City at three a.m. He and Pinky had burst into their room at the El Paradiso Hotel and chased all the hookers out. They dragged father and son, naked and hung over, down to the basement of the casino where Gianelli showed them videos of themselves snorting cocaine and engaging in assorted acts of perversion with teenage girls. He had made them sit side by side on wooden chairs in a bare room with a cement floor and no windows. They sat there perfectly still for hours.

Every time they moved even slightly, the two English Mastiffs that were lying down in front of them jumped to their feet, snarling savagely. The big dogs weighed over two hundred pounds each and looked hungry.

There was blood all over the floor because an hour before, Gianelli had given them a demonstration of what the dogs were capable of. He had brought in a full-grown Rottweiler on a leash. The Rottweiler weighed about a hundred pounds and moved like a predator until it saw the Mastiffs. Then he started whimpering like a baby. When Gianelli unleashed him, he ran to the far corner of the room, crying. The two Mastiffs watched him quietly, unconcerned, until Gianelli had pointed his finger at the Rottweiler and said, "Dinner."

He knew that it was the most horrible thing the Snells had ever witnessed, worse by far than any nature show they had ever seen on television. Body parts and blood flew in every direction as the Rottweiler screamed and the Snells cringed. When it was over, Gianelli commanded the Mastiffs to lie down in front of the Snells. Billy Ray Bob had vomited.

Gianelli told the naked men, "You two guys sit here for a while and think about Mr. Barazza's proposal, okay? I wouldn't move if I were you. Marc Antony and Cleopatra are very suspicious about strangers." He'd grinned, and then he and Pinky left them there to marinate in their fear.

Later, they had happily agreed to everything that Big Lou had wanted, and within a month, the construction crews were furiously remodeling the Genesee General Hospital basement to Big Lou's specifications.

Gianelli oversaw the remodeling effort and had been amused by the CEO's growing consternation. The little guy was up to his eyeballs in guineas with guns. Hell, there were probably more armed Italians in the town of Genesee back then than there were in the entire Goddamn Italian army. He knew that Snell was shaken up by what he'd gotten himself into, but he had wanted to play with the big boys, and now he was.

Welcome to the jungle, Snell.

Chapter 19

At ten minutes after nine, Cesari reached Billy Ray Bob's farmhouse. He drove slowly along the winding one lane country road with the headlights turned off, guided by the light of a half moon. Ozzie had kept quiet in the trunk of the car like he had promised, and Cesari made a mental note to reward him by not hitting him so hard the next time he required it.

He stopped the Crown Vic roughly fifty yards from the gravel driveway leading up to a detached garage and looked around. Way out in the country now, there were no other homes in sight and he was hidden from view of the house by a clump of mature birch trees. He cut the engine and stepped outside to reconnoiter. It was a balmy, cloudless night, the kind of night where people ought to be in their backyards sitting by a campfire roasting marshmallows and telling jokes or kidnapping pretty girls depending on which part of the country you were from.

From the cover of the trees, he studied the foreboding house carefully. It was an old two-story white farmhouse with a wraparound porch probably built in the mid-nineteenth century. A brick chimney rose high in the air. There was an old barn and silo in disrepair another fifty yards to the rear of the house and a relatively new two-car detached garage just ahead. The grass had been mown but not recently.

No vehicles sat in the driveway or on the side of the road, but Billy Ray Bob could have parked in the garage. He would have to check. There were no streetlights and no lights shone in or near the house, not even a porch light. He wondered what that meant.

Ozzie might have lied and this wasn't the house at all. Except so far, it was exactly as he had described it, a lonely old white farmhouse on an isolated country road with an old barn and a detached garage. What were the odds that he could have described the wrong house? On the other hand, it could be a trap, but would Ozzie really have been that foolish when his very existence at this point depended on Cesari's good will? There was only one way to find out.

He returned to the car, retrieved the Mossberg shotgun and loaded it with five rounds of buckshot, one in the chamber, four in the magazine and put another five shells in his pocket. He duct-taped the small flashlight toward the end of the muzzle and tucked the hunting knife into his waistband. It was a tactical and somewhat fatalistic decision to leave Ozzie's Glock in the car. He had too much to carry and he figured if he needed more than ten shotgun shells and a ten-inch-long hunting knife, he would probably be in full retreat or dead.

He took a deep breath and let it out. Then he flipped the shotgun safety off and crept up to the garage as warily as possible, keeping it between him and the house for cover. The shotgun could deliver devastating firepower, but he derived little comfort from that and hoped only to use it as a last resort. He definitely did not want lead flying around if Kelly was inside the house and he cautioned himself to not overreact.

Reaching the garage without detection, he made his way around to the back of it, hoping there were no motion detectors or dogs. Fortunately, there weren't. He found the entrance and tested the handle. It wasn't locked and he stepped inside. There were no windows, and it was much too dark inside to see anything, so he closed the door and turned on the flashlight attached to the end of the barrel. Using the shotgun as a pointer, he panned around the room.

The garage held only one vehicle in it, the black Porsche that Kelly had described. She was right. It was beautiful. He tested the door handle but it was locked. The green LaCrosse wasn't here. It could be in the barn, but why would he have done that? That didn't seem to make sense. Except for the usual items you might find in a garage, there was nothing else of interest, so he turned the flashlight off and headed over to the barn.

He maneuvered around the back of the house in the darkness, managing somehow not to fall into groundhog holes or trip over thick viny things that seemed to have taken over the property. Glancing around at the unkempt landscape, he guessed Billy Ray Bob wasn't much of a gardening enthusiast. Proceeding cautiously, he eventually made it to the barn unscathed as an owl hooted from a nearby perch. The structure was very old and dilapidated with rotting and missing boards and a sagging roof. The two large sliding doors on rusty tracks were partially open, so he slid in between them and pulled them shut. Once inside, he turned the flashlight on again, illuminating an old, out of commission tractor and assorted other farm equipment but no Buick. He turned the flashlight off and left.

Okay, the green LaCrosse wasn't here. Then where was Billy Ray Bob? It seemed unlikely that Ozzie would have lied given his predicament, but people did stupider things. The Porsche was here, so this was definitely the right house, but maybe Billy Ray Bob had changed his plans and taken Kelly somewhere else. Maybe Ozzie wasn't in the loop about that or maybe it was a spur of the moment change in plans? That wouldn't be good for Kelly and definitely not good for Ozzie. He would need somebody to vent his frustrations on and there wasn't any other candidate available at the moment.

Cesari sighed. There was nothing left to do but search the house and hope for the best, so he walked up to the back porch as stealthily as possible and gingerly climbed the four steps leading to the entrance. Standing at the door, he held his breath and listened carefully for any sounds, such as water running, a television blaring, or a girl screaming but there were none.

Either Billy Ray Bob went to bed early, or he wasn't here. Or maybe he was busy entertaining Kelly in the dark. Cesari didn't like that thought, but it galvanized him to action.

The back door was ancient, wooden and covered in aged, chipping paint. The old-fashioned skeleton key lock mechanism would easily break if he weren't concerned about the noise. The window next to the door on the back porch slid open freely however, so he lifted it quietly and squirmed through into Billy Ray Bob's kitchen. He stood there, anxiously fingering the Mossberg and waiting for the flashing lights and screaming sirens of an alarm system but there were none. Apparently Billy Ray Bob wasn't very concerned with home security. That kind of made sense. Billy Ray Bob was a cop in a small town. He grew up here and everybody knew him and who would knowingly break into a cop's home? Not many people, probably.

His eyes slowly adjusted to the moonlight filtering in from the windows, and he didn't have to bother with the flashlight. The first thing he noticed was that the kitchen was quite large and probably served as the main dining room which was typical for many old farmhouses. He saw a familiar cluster of furniture and other accessories. There was a long rectangular table, chairs, a refrigerator, a pantry and a door that he presumed led to the cellar. On the countertop he spotted a coffee maker and cups.

Making his way through a short hallway into the living room, he found a large couch, a couple of reclining chairs and a large-screen television. He searched around and determined that there was nobody hiding behind the couch or underneath. A staircase led up to the second floor and he hesitated at the foot. Deciding it would be better to search the cellar first, he returned to the kitchen.

The cellar door opened quietly, and he peered down into the blackness but couldn't see anything. He was starting to feel tense and a little jumpy. It was crunch time. Walking around a dark kitchen with some partial light wasn't the same thing as entering a pitch-black basement where he couldn't see his hand in front of his face. He hesitated only momentarily however, gripped the shotgun tightly and stepped onto the first tread of the staircase, closing the door behind him.

Darkness enveloped him and he forced himself to control his breathing. For Kelly's sake, allowing his nerves to fray wasn't an option, so he pointed the Mossberg straight ahead and blindly made his way down the staircase. The gentle creaking of the old steps seemed loud to him, like the blaring of a bullhorn. He felt like the steps were trying their best to announce his presence to anyone who might be lying in wait.

But nothing happened and eventually he reached the bottom and decided he had no choice but to turn on the flashlight. He crouched and braced himself before reaching out and pressing the button. He pressed and an explosion of light flooded the room, revealing a macabre and ominous scene.

The cellar was spacious with field stone and mortar walls. The aged mortar had cracked and crumbled in multiple places from water damage. The room was cold and damp, and Cesari surmised that it was probably a root cellar long ago when it was first built. Now, there was a furnace, a hot water heater, and a large chest-style freezer off to one side. The low ceiling revealed exposed wood beams, electrical wires, and water pipes. Along one wall was a series of painted wood shelves which housed tools, cans of varnish, a couple of large cardboard boxes, and a row of glass jars of various sizes with...human body parts in them.

Stunned and sickened by the grisly discovery, he walked up to the shelves to get a better look, hoping his eyes were playing tricks on him. They weren't and he counted ten jars. One had an ear in it, another a hand. Several of the jars contained parts of internal organs. There was a heart in one and a set of eyes in another. The room reeked of formaldehyde.

Whatever Billy Ray Bob was into didn't bode well for Kelly. He suddenly got a sickening feeling about the freezer and walked over to it. Lifting the door open, he found multiple plastic and paper wrapped packages. They were labeled *beef*, *venison*, and a few *lamb*, but none said *Kelly*.

He breathed a sigh of relief for that small victory and was about to close the door when something caught his eye. It was a deep freezer and he thought he saw something odd under a few layers of meat packages. He pointed the flashlight directly into the freezer. He did see something.

Shoving meat parcels out of the way, he reached in and eventually came out with a man's head wrapped in cellophane. Severed cleanly at the neck, the eyes were gone and frost covered the guy's face and beard. He used to be Caucasian but now he was just plain paper white. There was a small icicle dangling off one of the ears. Cesari nearly lost it at the sight. What the hell was going on here?

There were a lot of questions being raised but right now he needed to keep moving, so he replaced the gruesome finding and closed the freezer. He returned to the jars with the pickled body parts and again noticed the two cardboard boxes on the lower shelf. They were big enough to hold a case of wine and he thought that at one time they probably did. One box had nothing in it but a couple of screwdrivers, a roll of electrical tape and some rope. In the other, he found a collection of porn magazines, DVDs, and sex toys. One of the DVDs had Kelly's name written on it in magic marker. He pocketed that one and concluded his search.

He turned off the flashlight and tiptoed back up the stairs, holding his breath, on the lookout for a trap. There was none and he reentered the kitchen, greatly relieved. Now he could search the upstairs knowing there were no threats from the rear. He went into the living room and found the staircase leading to the second floor. It was another old set of wooden steps and was bound to make noise but it was carpeted which would help muffle the sound. He placed his feet as far apart as he could to the side of each step to minimize the stress on the center and then slowly and deliberately, ascended to the upper level with the Mossberg in the lead. Creeping around someone else's home in the dark was risky business, and he imagined an old woman suddenly turning on the lights and getting her head blown off. Or maybe an old woman would suddenly appear holding her own Mossberg and blow his head off. Anything was possible.

After what seemed like an eternity, he reached the top of the staircase. There were four rooms on the second floor, including a bathroom at the far end of the hallway whose door was ajar. Moonlight from a window in the bathroom shone in illuminating that room and the corridor enough for him to see that he was alone. The three other rooms were behind a series of closed doors along the hallway. They were probably bedrooms.

He crept up to the room nearest him and tested the doorknob. It turned silently, and he gently nudged the door open. Peering in, he saw the outline of a bed and some furniture. It didn't seem like there was anyone in there, so he entered and closed the door behind him. A quick search of the closet and under the bed revealed nothing, so he moved on to the next room.

In the middle of the hallway, he stood in front of the next door for a few seconds listening but didn't hear anything. So he turned the knob ever so gently and pushed the door inward an inch at a time.

Moonlight filtered into the room from a window, and he could make out a four-post bed and the silhouette of a person lying on their back. Cesari froze in place, heart racing, fight or flight hormones surging through his body, as he tried to understand what exactly he was seeing in the gloom. He let go of the doorknob and aimed the shotgun at the figure on the bed who was now just one sudden move away from joining the ranks of the dearly departed.

Chapter 20

The person lying there became aware of his presence and turned toward him. It was Kelly. Her wrists were bound to the bedposts. She had duct tape across her mouth, and her eyes were wide open, watching him. She appeared very frightened. In the dark, she probably thought he was Billy Ray Bob.

He swung the door inward another foot and entered the room carefully, crouching and ready to fire at anything that moved. He saw no one else there and stepped into the moonlight so she could see his face better. She became excited when she recognized him, but he put an index finger across his lips to caution her to silence.

Sitting down on the bed next to her, he untied the ropes restraining her and then gently helped her pull the duct tape off her mouth. From her swollen lip, he surmised Billy Ray Bob had gotten nasty, but otherwise she seemed okay. Without speaking, they held each other briefly and he pointed to the door to let her know her know he still had one more room to clear.

She nodded her comprehension and a few minutes later, he returned and said, "We're all good."

She threw her arms around him, and he could feel her trembling.

He said, "I'm so sorry."

"For rescuing me?" she asked, puzzled, holding him as if she would never let go.

"No, but if I had backed off with Billy Ray Bob last night, none of this would be happening."

She shook her head. "I don't believe that for a minute. He's not a nice guy and eventually this would have come to a head. I've been feeling it ever since we split up. Besides, he got what he deserved. I have no regrets and neither should you."

He nodded. "How badly are you hurt? I was a nervous wreck because I saw blood on the wall in my apartment and I can see he gave you quite a shot."

"Yeah, he hit me pretty hard, and I was dazed for a while. But I'm okay now. He caught me by surprise. He rang your doorbell, and I answered, thinking it was you. You really should have a peephole put in that door."

He grinned, "I'll speak to the landlord asap. What was the point of all this? Did he say?"

She shifted uncomfortably. "I'm afraid that you were the point. It's you he's interested in mostly or so it seemed. He asked an awful lot of questions about you, who you were, what did you want. That kind of stuff. When he got me here, he slapped me a couple of times, and I told him your name. I'm sorry. I thought I'd be tougher than that."

"It's okay," he told her. "They would have figured it out anyway. They're cops. All they would have to do is run my plates or ask my landlord. Besides, considering what you've been through, I think you're very tough."

"Thanks, but I don't feel very tough."

"Why did Billy Ray Bob leave you here alone?" he asked.

"His father called him. I overheard part of the conversation. Something about finding a truck. It sounded very important. They needed Billy Ray Bob there in a hurry to help unload it. He told his father about you. I think you're about to be unemployed. Billy Ray Bob said that when he got back, me, him, and Ozzie were going to have another party." She shuddered as she spoke.

He looked at her and for the first time in his adult life tried to put himself in the shoes of a woman who had just been threatened with sexual violence. It was hard for him. He was big, strong and mean when he wanted to be. Many guys were afraid of him not the other way around. He felt bad.

He said, "That's not going to happen on my watch, Kelly. C'mon, let's go. I have an idea."

They walked out the front door, and as they headed toward the Crown Vic, he brought her up to speed on all that Ozzie had told him about the truck's possible contents, Snell, Gianelli, and Billy Ray Bob.

She was astounded. "Drugs? The mob? I can't believe it."

"Ozzie wasn't certain about the drugs but what else?"

"Speaking of Ozzie. Where is he?"

"He's in the trunk of his cruiser."

"He's in the trunk?" she asked incredulously. "Like right now, as we speak?"

Cesari nodded.

They got into the Crown Vic and drove it into the garage, parking next to the Porsche. They shut the garage door and he turned on the overhead light. He regarded her carefully before speaking.

She sensed something amiss and asked, "Is something wrong?"

"Yes, everything is wrong. Things are spiraling out of control, and I feel like I've dragged you into this mess without your permission. What's going on right now could get us both into a lot of trouble and my actions have already placed you in harm's way. You don't have to be involved in this anymore if you don't want to. I could drive you to a friend's house or even to the next town if you want. I would understand. You could even go to the police. You were kidnapped, after all."

She looked at him as if he was crazy. She said, "I want to see this through to the end. These guys are bad and I want to help take them down so they can't hurt anyone again. And you can't be serious about going to the police. What would I tell them? That my ex-boyfriend who's a cop, got beat up by my new boy-friend who's a gangster. So my ex-boyfriend, the cop, kidnapped me. Then my new boyfriend, the gangster, beats up a different cop so he could rescue me. You have got to be kidding with that story. No thanks. I'll take my chances here with you."

He considered her reasoning and thought she was right, at least about going to the police. To even vaguely hint that he had assaulted a police officer would only get him thrown into a holding cell pending a massively biased investigation. It would be impossible to guess how many flights of stairs he might accidentally fall down before he got released. With any luck, he might come out of police custody with only minor brain damage.

Looking at her sympathetically, he said, "I know what you're saying, and I understand where you're coming from. It's just that things are about to get dicey around here, and I don't want you to get hurt any more than you've already been."

She took a deep breath. "Thanks for caring about what happens to me, but I'm not a baby. I've been taking care of myself for a long time. I know what I'm getting into, all right? I'm the one who was tied to the bed up there, remember?"

She glared at him defiantly, daring him to try to dissuade her. He said, "Welcome aboard this train wreck known as my life,"

He thought about what his psychiatrist friend Mark would have said about this situation. He was sure he would not have approved of him recruiting Kelly into his dysfunctional lifestyle. As they talked, they had moved to the back of the cruiser.

"Brace yourself, Kelly. Ozzie doesn't look too good."

She nodded and he popped the trunk open. Ozzie was staring at them, wide eyed and frightened. Kelly shrunk back at the sight of him all bruised and battered.

"Hi, Ozzie," Cesari said. "Remember Kelly?"

Ozzie nodded but didn't speak because the duct tape was still in place. Cesari saw that and was pleased. "Good boy, Ozzie. You're well on your way to rehabilitation."

Because of his injuries, Cesari had to help him out of the trunk. Together, Kelly and Cesari walked him up to the house where they put him in the same bedroom Kelly had been in.

Cesari ordered, "Take your clothes off, Ozzie."

Without arguing, he tried but with his injuries, it proved to be too much for him and they had to help him. Once he was naked, Cesari had him lie on the bed in much the same position that Kelly had been in when he found her. He used the same rope to tie Ozzie's right arm to the bedpost. He had mercy on him and left the broken arm alone. With the rest of the rope, he tied his ankles tightly to their respective bedposts. The knee that Cesari struck with the crowbar earlier had swollen up pretty badly. Ozzie wasn't going anywhere.

"What do you think?" he asked Kelly. "There's a certain amount of karma here."

She glared at Ozzie's naked form with loathing and her voice dripped with venom when she said, "You don't want to know what I think. Can we go now?"

"Yes, but there's one thing left to do before we leave."

He leaned over Ozzie and ripped the duct tape off his mouth none too gently, causing him to grimace. He said, "Ozzie, is there something you would like to say to Kelly?"

Ozzie nodded in fear and turned his head to Kelly. In a weak and hoarse voice, he choked out, "I'm very sorry for what I did."

Kelly turned her back and left the room without a word and Cesari put the duct tape back over his mouth. Downstairs, they searched for a spare set of Porsche keys and found them in the kitchen on a hook inside the pantry door. Leaving the house dark, they went out to the garage. After they transferred the grocery bags and weapons from Ozzie's car to the trunk of the Porsche, they got in and buckled up. Cesari turned the ignition and the engine roared. He glanced over at Kelly. She was wolfing down chips she found in one of the grocery bags.

He said, "If you don't mind my saying. You look damn hot sitting in a Porsche."

She smiled, "Why would I mind that?"

Chapter 21

The Pakistani doctors were busy at work in the basement of the hospital while Snell and his son unloaded boxes of oxycodone from the back of the truck. Gianelli's crew had finally arrived from New York and were busily engaged. Gianelli and Pinky sat on folding chairs contemplating Cesari's .38, which rested on the desk in front of them in a clear plastic bag.

"Billy Ray Bob isn't as stupid as he looks, Pinky. He saw the handgun at Cesari's apartment and had the smarts not only to pick it up and effectively disarm Cesari, but also to place it in a protective bag so that despite all its recent travels, it still only has Cesari's prints on it."

"Billy Ray Bob thought like a true cop, Vito. Most guys would have just pocketed it and ruined all the prints. You want some more coffee?" Pinky leaned over with a thermos and filled Gianelli's cup without waiting for a response.

"Thanks. Yeah, I have to give him credit for that, and then he brings the gun to me as some sort of peace offering like, 'I know I screwed up, but I'll make it good.' He doesn't seem to understand that's not how it works in this business, Pinky. Still, it was definitely a strong move that has possibilities."

"Definitely has possibilities," Pinky affirmed, sipping from a mug.

"Johnny Cesari," Gianelli mused. "Who would have thought it? The guy disappeared from sight years ago. Everyone assumed he'd either been whacked or was on the run because he did something no one wanted to talk about. And it's funny that no one ever did talk about it, at least no one important, anyway."

"Well I'll tell you something, Vito. The guy has moxie to walk right into Snell's office with you there and act like nothing happened. Man, think about what a pair it takes to do something like that."

"You hit that one on the head Pinky, but I already knew what kind of guy he is. The headaches I've had every day for the last ten years remind me constantly about what kind of guy John Cesari is. I have a score to settle with him and I never thought I'd get the chance. Then just like that, there he was. When Snell mentioned his name, I couldn't believe it. I almost fell out of my chair. So I made him call Cesari in to make visual confirmation."

Pinky echoed the sentiment, "And there he was... It's a sign, Vito. Definitely a sign."

Gianelli winced as he sipped his coffee. "This is awful, Pinky. Are you trying to poison me?"

"Sorry about that. It's been sitting around all day. You know Vito, maybe he's not even a real doctor. I mean, would they really let a guy like that into medical school? They must really be lowering their standards if they did, or maybe he's got a fake degree." Gianelli listened intently while Pinky talked. "Yeah, I bet that's it. I've heard about stuff like that. He probably forged all his paperwork so he could get on staff. That way he could get close to the operation and keep an eye on things until he was ready to make his move."

Gianelli chortled, "Oh c'mon, Pinky. You don't think he could really fake being a doctor, do you? Wouldn't someone notice? On the other hand, Cesari always thought he was smarter than everyone else, so maybe..."

"Alls I'm saying is it's a possibility."

"Understood. Real doctor or not, I need to find out exactly what Cesari knows and who he's working for. So even though I'd like to put a bullet in him and be done with it, I need him in one piece for a while longer."

Pinky asked, "Do you think there's a chance he's working by himself, Vito?"

"There's no freakin' way he's by himself. Think about it. It's way too complicated."

"Fair enough. Do we have any other assets up here besides the Snells?"

Gianelli thought for a moment. "Billy Ray Bob has a cop friend, Ozzie, who's on our side and hunting Cesari as we speak. There's another guy, Dave Culpepper. He's a detective, a black guy. He's tight with Billy Ray Bob and might be available for the right price."

"That's good to know, Vito."

"Excuse me a minute, Pinky."

Gianelli stepped out into the hallway and saw Snell and Billy Ray Bob toiling with their loads. He called out to Billy Ray Bob. "Any word from your pal Ozzie?"

"Not yet. I called him twice and both calls went directly to voicemail, so I left a message. I'm not sure what it means."

"It means he doesn't have Cesari, because if he did, then he would have called you, right?" Gianelli turned slightly and addressed Snell, who was standing near his son. "How much longer are those doctors going to need? We can't stay here all night."

"I just asked them. They said it shouldn't take more than another hour. I'm glad they were able to get here as quickly as they did. We were lucky they didn't skip out on us."

"All right, keep me posted. I want to wrap things up and get out of here." Gianelli went back to talk with Pinky.

Chapter 22

After leaving Billy Ray Bob's house, Kelly and Cesari stopped at a coffee shop about a mile from the hospital to settle themselves down and get something to eat. She had a latte and a panini and he ordered a coffee with a croissant.

"That's all you're going to have?" she asked, eyeing his croissant.

"I'm not that hungry," he said. "Besides, I'm trying to watch my weight."

She laughed. "You're too funny. That's something a girl would say."

"I'm glad to see you still have your sense of humor," he said and then added. "I'm not trying to make you angry by being repetitive but are you sure you want to see this through?"

He was hoping she would change her mind and had probably asked her the same questions ten times while they drove around looking for quiet place to stop.

She replied, "I'm sure, and don't ask again. I'm a big girl. I get it. They're dangerous people. I think I already figured that part out. Now let's move on already."

"You're kind of feisty. I think I like that." He smiled and resigned himself to her decision.

She ignored that. "So where do we begin with something like this?"

"Good question. For starters, I think we should go to the basement of the hospital and snoop around a little. If they're unloading some type of contraband, we may find evidence of it and figure out what's really going on. I don't think we can just call the authorities to investigate without any hard evidence. According to Ozzie, the whole process of unloading the truck usually only took about an hour or two. I would think that they'd be finished by eleven at the latest."

"You want to go there tonight?"

"There's no time like the present and we don't want to give them the opportunity to move it to another location."

"What if they decide to linger there."

"It's a risk but I doubt they will dillydally when they're done. By now they've probably noticed Ozzie hasn't reported in and I'm sure that will be making them edgy. They'll want to go so somewhere safe to discuss strategy just like we did. Sitting in the basement of a community hospital with a truck load of illegal drugs for very long is not the smartest thing to do. I think they'll want to secure the load and get out of there as quickly as possible. Billy Ray Bob's house is the most logical place and if I know Gianelli, he will want to talk to you personally."

Kelly took a sip of her latte and chuckled. "Billy Ray Bob is really going to be upset about his Porsche. That's his baby. I wish I could see the look on his face when he finds out it's missing."

"I'm sure he will be, but probably he'll be more upset about finding Ozzie tied to his bed."

"It'll be a toss-up for sure. He's such a jerk. I can't believe I wasted time with him," she added.

"Forget about him for now. We have to focus on how we're going to get into the basement of the hospital. I know of two entrances. One is from the rear of the hospital where the loading dock is and the other is down that newly built corridor where you saw those foreign doctors. I'm sure all the doors are going to be locked tight and you mentioned that there are security cameras."

As they ate and talked, Cesari noticed Kelly wincing from time to time because of her bruised and swollen lip. Billy Ray Bob had hit her very hard. He commented, "You have a pretty fat lip, Kel."

She paused a beat and replied, "That's a heck of a racist thing to say."

He was quiet for a second, trying to digest the accusation and responded apologetically, "I didn't mean it that way."

"That's what racists always say."

"Look, I'm sorry. Can we get back on point here?"

She laughed. "I was just busting on you. God, that was too easy."

He laughed with her, relieved. "I can't believe you're making jokes."

"Lighten up, Cesari. I'm the one with the fat lip."

"Good point. Look Kel, there's something else we have to talk about. When I came looking for you at Billy Ray Bob's house, I searched his cellar first and then worked my way up to the bedroom... Well, I found a box with porn magazines in the cellar."

She stared at him curiously. "So? He's a pig. I thought we already established that."

I took a deep breath. "There were also a bunch of DVDs in the same box." He reached into his pocket, took out the one marked *Kelly* and slid it over to her, adding, "Including this one."

She looked at it but didn't touch it. Then she studied him for what seemed like forever. Eventually she whispered, "It's probably from that night at Billy Ray Bob's house... They filmed the whole thing. Dave Culpepper, the third guy there, was really into it. He was the cameraman until it was his turn, and then Billy Ray Bob took over. I guess I blocked it out of my mind."

He was speechless. What could you say at a time like this? After a time, he let out a deep breath and said, "I'm sorry. I was hoping that it was just vacation pictures or something along those lines."

"Yeah, right. Well, at least now we can destroy it."

"Unfortunately, it's not that simple. We don't know how many copies there are or where they are. This could already be all over the internet," he explained.

"Great," she groaned.

"Tell me about this guy Culpepper. Do you think he might be involved with Billy Ray Bob's business at the hospital?"

She thought it over and said, "Well, I only met him a few times. He's a little taller than you, black, about forty years old. He's a heavy guy but in decent shape. He's a detective and likes to be called Pepper because his partner on the force is a blonde guy named Reynolds. He thinks it's cool that people call them Salt and Pepper. You know, like Starsky and Hutch, that sort of thing. That's about all I can tell you about him, other than he's a sadistic pervert like his pals."

She watched him put the DVD back in his pocket and asked, "What are you going to do with it?"

"I don't know yet, but it's evidence of a felonious sexual assault and it probably would be a good idea to hang onto it, at least until we have a firm strategy on how to proceed."

She nodded reluctantly in agreement and, then asked with sudden worry, "You're not going to watch it, are you?"

"Absolutely not," he reassured her. "But I will need you to take a look at it at some point, to confirm its contents... Would you do that for me?"

"Yeah, I guess. If it will help," she said reluctantly.

She had only eaten half of her panini with the rest sitting on her plate. He stared at a piece of prosciutto hanging out of her sandwich and asked, "Are you going to finish that?"

"No, I've lost my appetite. Let's pay the bill and go."

"Do you mind if I take a bite? I consider myself a bit of a panini connoisseur."

"By all means, connoisseur away." After he ate the whole thing and wiped his face with a napkin, she laughed. "I thought you were watching your weight."

"You shouldn't laugh at people, Kelly. It makes them feel bad. All sorts of negative things happen to their self-esteem."

"I was laughing with you, not at you. There's a difference."

"All right then. All is forgiven." He looked at her seriously and said, "The DVD wasn't the only thing I found in his basement..."

"What else did you find? I think I can handle anything at this point."

He told her about the body parts, and she nearly sprayed latte across the table at him. "Oh my God, are you serious?"

"I'm very serious."

"I think I'm going to be sick."

Chapter 23

"**G**oddamn mercenaries, that's what they are, Pinky. I'm paying them a fortune, and these freaking doctors show up for work drunk and stoned."

"It's disgraceful, Vito."

"I thought doctors took some sort of oath or something."

"That's why the world's going to hell in a hand basket, Vito. You can't rely on anyone anymore."

"Did you know that one of them even had the balls to ask if he could bring some hooker named Tina with him to show her what he does? You know, like bring-your-whore-to-work day, that kind of thing. I was so mad I almost threw them all in the lake."

Pinky laughed. "Very unprofessional."

"Still, I have to admit, they came through when I needed them. They were very open minded about this whole bomber thing."

"Didn't even blink at the idea?"

"Didn't even blink, Pinky."

"How'd you bring it up with them?"

"Okay, so you know the deal. I fly them in every month from Pakistan to remove the organs, right? Then one day I call them up and tell them I want to try something different, like planting explosives in suicide bombers. There was silence on the phone and I'm waiting for the guy to tell me to go jump in the ocean, but you know what he says? You ready for this one, Pinky."

"I'm ready, Vito?"

"It's a deal if I can get him tickets to a Lady Gaga concert while he's in the country. He's been dying to see her perform live forever. Can you believe that? Is that the funniest thing you ever heard or what?"

They both sat there chuckling. Gianelli crossed his legs, took a sip of coffee, and grimaced. "You know, Pinky, if I didn't know better, I'd swear you were trying to poison me."

Chapter 24

Cesari paid the bill and they left the coffee shop. As they approached the Porsche, he was again struck at what a beast it was, sleek and feline. It seemed that if he stroked it just right, it might purr.

He opened the passenger side door for Kelly and said, "Milady."

She said, "Thank you... So gallant. I could get used to this kind of treatment."

And he could get used to treating her special. It gave him a rush. That's the way it's supposed to be, he thought. But deep down, he desperately hoped he didn't get her killed. He closed her door and went to the driver's side. A minute later, they were heading south on Route 14 toward the Genesee General Hospital.

The Porsche handled like a dream. The nineteen-inch tires and low center of gravity hugged the road tightly making for smooth and efficient turns with no effort and barely any need for deceleration. After a few minutes, they pulled into the hospital's nearly empty parking lot and he parked the car in a poorly lit area about fifty yards from the main entrance. It was well after eleven by that time and he doubted that Gianelli would expect them to be running around the hospital after the night they'd had. Any normal person would be in hiding or on the highway, driving as fast as they possibly could to get the hell out of here.

"I need to make a call," he said to Kelly and took out his cellphone.

He dialed and waited. Two rings, three rings, four rings. Then she picked up.

"Well hello, Cesari. It's been a long time," said a woman's icy voice, dripping with sarcasm.

"Hello, Cheryl. Yes it has been a long time, and I'm sorry I haven't called, but... you know how it is," he said lamely.

"No, I don't know how it is. How dare you call me in the middle of the night after the way you treated me?" she barked angrily into the receiver.

"I'm sorry, Cheryl. You're absolutely right to be angry with me but to be honest, it's not really the middle of the night."

"Save it for someone who cares, Cesari. You better not be calling to ask for a date."

He cringed from her onslaught and tried to lighten the mood with an ill-timed joke. "Out of curiosity, if I was asking for a date, what would the answer be?"

Kelly frowned as she listened to this exchange. She didn't know who he was talking to, but it sounded an awful lot like he was flirting which would have been a bit impolite given their circumstances.

"I hate you, Cesari. do you hear me?" Cheryl continued to berate him. "Every red blood cell in my body hates you. You make me fall in love with you, and the minute I mention the word 'marriage' casually in conversation, you disappear and I never hear from you again. I cried myself to sleep every night for a month, and then a year later, you have the nerve to call me in the middle of the night making jokes. Are you aware that I own a gun?"

This wasn't going well. "I'm sorry, Cheryl. I really am. I get crazy when I hear the M word. I should have warned you about that. To be honest, I didn't even know how badly I would react. I have all sorts of psychological baggage that even my psychiatrist doesn't know how to handle. He says that I have problems with intimacy." He knew how weak that sounded.

"Oh, shut up. What do you want? And make it quick." He could practically feel her finger next to the *end call* button on her phone.

"Cheryl, I just stepped into something big and bad. I need help and I don't know where to turn."

"You've got one minute, Cesari."

"Thank you. I really…"

"Fifty-eight seconds."

He gave her a fifty-eight second synopsis of the events of the last twenty-four hours as well as the major players involved. He left out the part where he was about to break into a restricted area of the hospital.

"Wow," she said, the edge gone from her voice. "It sounds like you've been busy as usual. I wish you hadn't told me about assaulting the police officers, although I agree that based on what you've said they probably deserved it. Now, the body part stuff is interesting, but can you be sure that they weren't just Halloween gags? I mean, is anyone up there actually missing a head? Regardless, we've been trying to nail Gianelli and his boss Lou Barazza for years, so I'm sure my people will be interested."

"Does that mean you'll help us?" he asked, suddenly feeling like the cavalry was on the way.

She thought about it for a while and said, "I don't know how much I can do other than pass the information up the chain of command to my boss the D.A. I'll call him right now. He loves tips like this. I'm sure just mentioning Gianelli's name will get a rise out of him. Is that it?"

"That's it. Thanks for listening."

"Try to not get yourself killed before the night's over. Can I go now?"

"Do you still have those cowboy boots?"

She hung up.

He had met Cheryl at a dinner party in Manhattan. A mutual friend fancied himself a matchmaker and had arranged a soirée for various unattached members of his circle to socialize and hopefully develop lasting relationships. Sitting there all by herself, Cheryl was wearing the tightest blue jeans and of all things, full-length leather cowboy boots. Boys from the Bronx don't get to see gorgeous blondes in cowboy boots very often and he couldn't keep his eyes off her. But the joke was on him if he thought he was chasing her. She had reeled him in like a marlin off the coast of Florida, except he didn't have nearly as much of a chance. Before he knew what was happening, she was discussing what church she wanted to get married in and he lit out of there like an Apollo rocket on takeoff.

"Who was that, and why are you still smiling?" Kelly interrupted his daydreaming.

He'd nearly forgotten she was there. "Her name is Cheryl Kowalcik and she's the assistant district attorney for lower Manhattan. For the last two years, she's worked as the liaison to the FBI's organized crime task force. They catch the bad guys and she helps decide if they have a solid case or not," he replied. "We became acquainted during my medical training down in the city. She's a friend."

"Is she a blonde friend or a brunette friend?" Kelly asked half-joking, half-serious.

He knew that questions posed like that, in that tone, were never really jokes. They were always serious. It seemed like an odd time to have a lover's quarrel but Cesari's experience with women told him that there was no such thing as a wrong time for an argument.

He said, "To be perfectly honest, Kel. I can't remember. She wore a lot of broad-brimmed hats and I didn't like to look directly at her face because her complexion was so bad. She practically lived at the dermatologist's office. It was really a tough time for me."

She gave him a wry look. "Very funny. You're being evasive, Cesari. You know what I'm getting at. Were you good friends or ordinary friends? It sounded like you were good friends."

He didn't like where this was going. "What's the point of all this? We got along."

"The point is that if you're going to flirt with old girlfriends while I'm sitting right next to you then I think I have the right to ask a few questions."

He thought that over. She had a point. "You're right. I'm sorry. I didn't mean to do that. It was inconsiderate... I hadn't spoken to her in a long time and I felt a little awkward. I was just trying to break the ice."

"Better. Now how is she going to help us?"

"She's hardwired in to law enforcement and is going to pass the information I gave her to the New York District Attorney. From there I'm sure it will find its way to the desk of the local branch of the FBI. Gianelli and his boss, Lou Barazza, are on a perennial watch list, so this may cause a stir down there. There's no guarantee they'll react in our favor but you never know."

"Okay, what now?"

"I think we should get going."

It was midnight.

Chapter 25

Directly in front of them, the main entrance to the hospital housed a large automatic door controlled by a motion sensor. At a small desk in the lobby sat a middle-aged, unarmed security guard named Bill, who was busy flipping through a magazine. Bill knew Cesari and Kelly from their comings and goings during normal work hours. Cesari knew he wouldn't raise an eyebrow at them entering the hospital even at such a late hour. He would assume they were on their way to the OR to do an emergency case. But Kelly's facial injury would certainly arouse his curiosity and that of anyone else they ran into. Bill would no doubt feel compelled to say something and he would remember. He was that kind of guy. By morning, everyone in the hospital would know they had been there and that Kelly looked like she had walked into a wall.

"What should we do?" she whispered. "We can't walk in there armed to the teeth like this." She was referring to the shotgun he held in one hand and the crowbar in the other. He offered her Ozzie's Glock but she declined. She had no experience with handguns and didn't want any.

"No, we can't," he agreed.

"Do we really need a gun with us anyway?"

He thought that one over. "Maybe not, but knowing the kind of people we're dealing with, it would make me feel better."

"I thought you said there won't be anyone down there."

"Are you willing to bet you're life on that?"

"I guess you're right, but I don't like guns."

"I understand and I don't disagree. They're unpleasant tools but sometimes they're the only ones that will work in certain situations."

Setting the weapons down, he reached into the trunk of the Porsche to retrieve the two plastic grocery bags. He emptied their contents into the small trunk and put the business end of the Mossberg into one of the bags along with the crowbar. The crowbar fit pretty well, but the pistol grip of the shotgun stuck out a little so he covered the protruding end with the remaining bag.

He said, "That should do it. There's a side door about fifty yards from here. It's off to the right and around the corner from the main entrance. I've seen the maintenance guys use it. Let's go over there and give it a try."

They kept well out of sight from Bill, who never lifted his head from his magazine, and walked over to the side door. Away from the well-lit parking lot, several very large evergreen bushes hid them from casual view. An examination of the door revealed that the bottom half was made of metal and the top half was made of reinforced glass. It was self-locking and designed to open from the inside by pressing against a horizontal metal bar.

Cesari assessed the situation in his mind. This was a relatively small town. Most local crime consisted of petty burglaries, bar fights, minor drug busts, and the like. His instincts told him that the door wasn't wired to a security system. Why would it be? More to the point, why would someone break into a hospital from a side entrance when they could simply enter through the front door a short distance away?

He took the crowbar out of the grocery bag and laid the shotgun down. After signaling Kelly to stand clear, he raised the curved end of the crowbar like a club and struck the glass pane in its center. It cracked without making too much noise but did not shatter. However, its strength was compromised, and he was sure the window would give with enough time and effort.

Kelly peeked over her shoulder nervously. "Hurry up. I don't like being out here like this."

He beat on the glass repetitively and with each blow, glass fragments flew in all directions and the pane sagged inward. When he felt the time was right, he jabbed at the center of the glass with the straight end of the crowbar. He did this hard several times and on the third try, the glass gave way and started to spill larger pieces of itself onto the floor behind the door. He chipped out an opening large enough for his arm to pass through and delicately snaked his hand into the hole. He reached down and pressed on the bar opening the door.

As Kelly walked through, he said, "Milady."

"Enough with that," she said.

Inside, they found themselves on a large square landing with cement steps leading up to the second and third floors of the hospital and another set of steps leading down to the basement. There was a door directly in front of them with a placard reading, *Medical Staff Only.*

Kelly asked, "What's in there?"

"It's a lounge area for the surgeons and medical guys who spend the night here. It's got beds, showers, stuff like that. I've been in there a couple of times but I've never gone out this way. There's another entrance on the other side."

They took the stairs down and went through the door at the bottom, which opened into the main corridor of the basement. Opposite them were two elevators and a sign on the wall indicating that the cafeteria was to the left and the pharmacy to the right.

The lighting was very dim at this hour to conserve energy, and every other overhead fluorescent light was off. The cafeteria closed at 8:00 p.m., so hungry employees had to depend on vending machines and delivery after hours. Late on a Saturday night, it would be very unlikely that they would accidentally bump into anyone down there.

"Damn, it's dark down here," Kelly whispered as they reached the pharmacy.

"Yeah and deserted too. That's good, I suppose. It would be kind of hard to explain what we're doing here and why I have a crowbar and a loaded shotgun in a grocery bag."

"Out of curiosity, what would you say if someone did see the gun?" Kelly asked.

"That I spotted a ten-pointer in the parking lot and chased it down here."

She laughed and shook her head at me. "I have a serious question for you. When you were a kid, did somebody make the mistake of telling you that you were funny?"

"All the time, Kel. All the time."

"Well they were lying."

"You mean prophetic. I wasn't half as funny then as I am now."

Beyond the pharmacy, all the overhead lights were out and the double doors at the far end of the hallway were not visible. The door to the pharmacy itself was half wood and half glass but the lights were off inside and they couldn't see anything. Out of curiosity, he tried the door but it was locked. They stood there and peered into the darkness of the corridor ahead.

He asked in a hushed tone, "Is this where you were standing when you saw those foreign doctors arguing?"

Kelly was getting jittery. "Yes. I was sent to pick up a bag of Remicade for one of our patients with Crohn's disease. It wasn't ready when I arrived, so I had to wait here while the pharmacist reconstituted it. I was here a solid fifteen minutes with nothing to do but stare at the walls. They came bursting through the doors jabbering at a mile a minute. It really startled me. They came about halfway down the corridor before they noticed me and turned back."

"How far away do you think the doors are from here? I can't see anything in this lighting."

Kelly stared down the dark hallway. "Maybe a hundred feet, give or take. I'm not sure. Boy, it really is scary down here with the lights off. I feel my heart racing already."

"That was probably the idea. Fear is the best security," he said. "Think about it. Employees who accidentally wandered down here would automatically turn around and get out as quickly as they could. Hell, I want to get out as quickly as I can right now. Did it feel like this when you were here that time?"

"Well no, not really. It was the middle of the day, so all the lights were on. Everything seemed more or less normal. I could easily see the doors from where we're standing. What do you think? Maybe we should use the flashlight?"

He thought about that. The shotgun in the grocery bag still had the small flashlight attached. "No, I don't think that would be a good idea just yet. We can't be sure if the video cameras are on or not. They might be recording in the dark. I doubt that there's a guard monitoring the cameras full time but why take a chance? It's a straight hallway, right? We should be able to make it to the doors without too much fuss." He caught a glimpse of her and added, "Are you frightened?"

She nodded. "Yeah."

"Me too. Okay, stay close."

They stepped cautiously into the blackness beyond the pharmacy. He touched the wall with his right hand for guidance and held the weapons in his left. Kelly held on to the waistband of his pants to keep from getting separated, and they slowly crept along the wall in the dark.

He didn't know what to expect. This caused him to be excited and concerned. Men like Cesari were programmed for combat and were thrilled by the prospect, drawn to the conflict like a moth to the flame. With each step, he braced himself for some unexpected calamity. After what seemed like an eternity, they made it to the end of the corridor and he could feel the form of the double doors Kelly had described. He tested the handles just to be sure, but they were locked. Too bad but it never hurt to try.

He estimated the hallway to be about twelve feet wide, and the doors occupied about six feet of that space. Using the crowbar, he probed the corners above the doors and found a video camera on each side. They were only about eight feet off the floor, and he was able to reach them easily. He readjusted their angles so that rather than focusing on the corridor in front of the door, they were pointing away and up at the ceiling.

"Why didn't you pull the wires or smash them with the crowbar?" Kelly asked in a hushed voice.

"I thought about it, but if there is someone monitoring them, they would immediately notice a problem with the video feed and investigate. This isn't a perfect solution, but it will help."

He took the shotgun out and aimed it at the door handles.

"What are you doing?" she asked, hearing the rustling of the grocery bags but unable to see.

"Hold on." He clicked on the small flashlight, illuminating the doors in front of them.

There was no immediate adverse consequence to the sudden shining of the light which was reassuring to them both. The doors were made of solid oak and seemed to be industry standard. He didn't notice anything particularly special about them. There was a looped handle on each door and the door on the right had a key lock. Signs on both doors screamed warnings about high voltage and danger. He studied them for a minute, trying to decide how best to defeat them.

He murmured, "I should have spent more time learning how to pick locks."

"Wouldn't it have made more sense for them to have an armed security guard here?"

"Not really. That would only have raised everyone's suspicions about the nature of what was really going on down here. I mean, who places an armed guard outside a computer room? The Pentagon and CIA maybe, but that's about it. I bet even Microsoft doesn't have guards other than at its main entranceway."

"Well how are we going to get in?" She asked, staring at the doors.

He sighed deeply. "The old-fashioned way, I guess. Would you mind holding the shotgun for a minute? Shine the light at the handles and keep your finger outside the trigger guard, all right? The safety's on but it's good practice."

She took the gun from him and did as he asked. He wedged the end of the crowbar into the space between the doors by the lock mechanism and made himself ready.

He said, "You might want to cover your face with one hand, Kel. There might be splinters."

Chapter 26

Gianelli pulled up to Billy Ray Bob's house and parked his Cadillac on the street. He turned to Pinky. "Where's Snell and his kid? I thought they'd be here waiting for us, not the other way around."

"They'll be here soon. Billy Ray Bob was mopping up the OR after the mess those surgeons made. Remind me never to have an operation until after I check the blood alcohol level of my doctor."

"You know Pinky, I'm starting to feel good again. We got the bombers tucked away, the drugs are secured and we got the girl. Tony's guarding the rear of the hospital with the dog, and Sal's with Mike looking for Cesari. Man, it was a tough day at the office for sure, but things are looking up. It's times like this that I sometimes wonder what it would be like to have a nine to five job, an hour for lunch, a guaranteed paycheck, that kind of stuff. It must be nice not to have any stress in your life."

"Sure was a tough day Vito, but nine to five…never going to happen to me. I'd rather get a lethal injection than be an ordinary schlemiel. By the way, it was a good thing I brought Tony along. I had no idea how much the other guys were scared of the dog until the trip up here. They were shaking like a leaf the whole way and I don't blame them. If she wasn't crated, she might have done them some serious harm. But she likes Tony. She listens to him."

"Yeah, Tony helped me train her when she was a pup. She can't stand me though, that's for sure. I never understood why, either. I've always been nice to her. The other dog and I get along real well. Funny thing."

He took a pack of cigarettes out of his jacket, offered one to Pinky and lit them both with his lighter. Pinky said, "Thanks. Where did you get these guys from anyway? The bombers, I mean. If you don't mind my asking."

Gianelli took a drag on his cigarette and blew the smoke out the window. "Nah, I don't mind. If I can't trust you who can I trust? There's some fat-cat Arab who calls himself the Sheik. He flies in to the casino once a month, parties like an animal, and then disappears. He's connected back home with these religious lunatics. I guess he funds a lot of their activities and in return they overlook the fact that he's a degenerate."

"I know that guy. I mean, not personally but I've delivered girls to his room at the hotel. He likes them to dress up like cheerleaders."

"That's the guy, Pinky. Well one night he takes it hard on the chin and drops about ten million at the tables. So rather than make him pay up, I sit down with him privately and try to work things out. You know, quid pro quo. It turns out that some people over there have been very eager to take action against our federal government." Gianelli took another drag. "They're pissed off about some terrorist trial that's about to start in Manhattan this week and they'd love to make a statement, but they couldn't figure out how to get past the tight security. I ran my plan by them and they loved it. They supply the schleps, and I take care of everything else. It's win-win for the good guys, Pinky. Everybody in that courtroom goes up in smoke including that Goddamn D.A."

"You're a genius, Vito."

"Yeah, that's what I think."

The lights of another car shone brightly as it approached.

"Here they are, Pinky. C'mon, let's go meet this Kelly."

Chapter 27

Cesari applied the full force of his two hundred and twenty pounds against the crowbar and with a mighty heave, demonstrated to Kelly why this simplest of tools still thrived from prehistoric times well into modernity. The door groaned and the wood split and then splintered, but it did not completely give way. The lock mechanism had weakened considerably however, and the space widened between the two doors. He repositioned the crowbar, took a deep breath, and again pulled toward himself with as much force as he could muster. Every muscle in his body strained and he panted from the exertion, beads of perspiration beginning to form on his forehead. Again. More splinters, cracks, and space. Two more tries and the bolt abruptly disengaged from its receptacle, allowing the door to swing open.

"You made a lot of noise doing that," Kelly whispered anxiously.

"I know, but it couldn't be helped. Let's hope no one heard."

He took the shotgun from her and turned the flashlight off. Closing the doors behind them, they entered another long dark hallway. Some light filtered in from a window above a large metal garage door at the far end. Visibility was poor, but they could see the shadowy outlines of two doors on each side of the corridor.

Turning to Kelly, he said, "Well, this is what we came for, so let's get to it. Ready?"

She nodded uneasily.

"Are you going to be all right?"

"I'm not happy," she said.

"Me neither."

They started on the left side of the corridor. The first room had two large swinging doors which were unlocked and opened in both directions. He gently pushed one of the doors forward and walked in with Kelly close behind. It felt like a big room, but it was too dark to make out details. They let the door close behind them and he turned on the flashlight.

What they saw shocked and surprised them. It was a complete operating theatre. The room was approximately a twenty five-foot square with an operating table in its center and an overhead boom light source. There was anesthesia equipment off to one side, multiple cabinets, specialized sinks, oxygen tanks, medication carts, and so on. The walls were a light green and the cabinets white. It was like any other OR he had ever seen. They glanced at each other with confused expressions on their faces. Cesari noticed a familiar scent.

He said, "I don't get this at all. It's an operating room."

"Why on earth would they have gone through the trouble and expense of building an operating room down here and then keep it a state secret?" Kelly asked.

"I haven't the slightest idea." He panned around with the light. "Let's check it out." They walked around the room for a few minutes, opening and shutting cabinets and drawers, hoping to find a clue. He noticed that there were some wet areas here and there on the tiled floor and said, "This room has recently been mopped down."

"Yes, I noticed the smell of bleach when we entered. Why would anyone scrub the place down this late on a weekend?"

"I don't know Kel, but it begs the question of what just happened here that needed to be cleaned up. This doesn't make any sense. If they were bringing drugs in here like Ozzie suspected, they wouldn't just decide to start mopping the floors."

He turned the light off and they entered the hallway. He decided to risk turning the flashlight on only after they had fully entered each room and closed the door behind them. They elected to search the next room on this side of the corridor and then work their way back from the other side.

The next room was a generic storage area filled with unlabeled, nondescript brown boxes. The boxes were stacked neatly in twenty rows, eight high and eight deep, along the back wall of the room.

He wasn't great at math but Kelly read his mind and declared, "There are twelve hundred and eighty boxes, but what's in them? I don't see any labels."

"Let's find out."

He reached up and took one of the boxes off the top row. It was very light, and he placed it on the floor in front of them. Using his hands, he ripped through the tape on the top of the box and pulled the flaps apart. Inside were six rows of six by six deep smaller boxes for a total of two hundred and sixteen and each one was labeled *Oxycodone*. They each took one of the little boxes out and studied it. The label said each bottle inside contained ten, five-milligram pills. They were both thinking the same thing as they gazed around the room, trying to estimate the total street value.

"Wow," she said.

"Wow is right. No wonder everybody's getting bent out of shape," he said. They opened a few more boxes and they were all the same.

Kelly asked, "Where are they from?"

"I'm not sure. Maybe they hijacked a truck or a couple of trucks. It happens all the time, except you never hear about it. All you have to do is bribe the right person to find out the truck routes and delivery schedules. The drugs themselves look generic, so they could be from anywhere." He paused for a few seconds, thinking it over. "Who knows, maybe they're even scamming Medicare. That happens all the time too. The hospital submits false claims saying they used thousands of pills on thousands of patients that they never really did. That wouldn't be hard to do. Charge for a couple of extra pills per patient here and there. Medicare will overlook the nickel and dime stuff and over time, the sheer volume adds up. Medicare sends them a check, and they purchase thousands of real pills from their supplier and instead of sending them to the pharmacy, they divert the shipment here and sell them on the street. It's pure profit for them and the taxpayer foots the bill."

Kelly made a face, as if she had eaten something bitter. "Could they really do that?"

"If you've got brass ones, you could pretty much get away with anything in this business, at least for a short while. In this case, you cook the books in collusion with the billing department and financial officer of the hospital. It's not really that difficult. The health profession largely runs on the honor code and through self-policing. If you flash enough cash around, you can entice people to do lots of things they know they shouldn't."

"You're depressing me by how easy you make this seem. How do you know things like this?"

"Welcome to the jungle, Kelly."

Chapter 28

They came out of the narcotics room and crossed the hallway to the other side passing within several feet of the large metal garage door that opened to the loading dock at the rear of the hospital. As they crept along, they heard a muffled voice coming from outside the door causing them to freeze in place, listening.

Kelly tugged on his arm and he urged her to silence. They must have left someone to guard the rear of the hospital. A normal sized door was adjacent to the large one, but it had no window to see who it was. But that was good in a way because whoever it was couldn't see in either. He hoped the door wasn't locked. It was always a good idea to have a second escape route if necessary. He crept over to it and gently tested the handle. It wasn't locked. He then placed his ear against it to hear better.

"All's quiet here, Vito," a man's voice said. "We're doing just fine. No problems."

Cesari signaled Kelly that there was at least one guy outside, possibly more and that they needed to move as quickly and quietly as possible. She nodded anxiously and followed him to the next room which had a door made of heavy metal with a latch-type handle. As it opened, they were hit with a gust of cold air. The room was refrigerated and quite large. They entered and the door closed behind them with a click.

Cesari turned on the flashlight. In the center of the room was a large, rectangular metal table. A metal desk and file cabinet sat off to one side, and on the other side was a bank of twelve drawers built into the wall, four rows and three drawers high. Each drawer had a metal handle with a space underneath where cards could be placed with names and identifying information. It was a morgue.

"It's freezing in here," Kelly said, shivering as she spoke, her breath forming little clouds in front of her mouth. "What going on down here?"

"Looks like a morgue Kel, but why would they need to store bodies here? I know for a fact there's a perfectly fine morgue attached to the pathology department upstairs. I've been there, and you're right, it's freezing in here. Much colder than any morgue I've ever been in."

The thought crossed his mind that maybe they had taken a wrong turn somewhere and wound up in the wrong hospital, but he knew they hadn't. He didn't want to spend too much time in any one room, but this one showed some promise so they lingered.

He walked over to the metal drawers and examined them. They looked like standard morgue drawers from the outside. None of them had any names, birthdays or social security numbers on them. He pulled one open quietly and found nothing. He tried two more until he finally found one with a dead guy in it. As part of his medical education, he had been in many morgues, but he'd never seen anything like this. The deceased was fully dressed in an expensive silk suit, tie and a nice white shirt with cufflinks. Except for the bullet hole in his forehead, he didn't look too bad.

Damn it, they hadn't even bothered to clean the blood off him. As he looked down at the face of his friend Frankie D., a blood vessel on the side of Cesari's head started to throb with anger. He was furious. Somebody was going to have to pay and he knew who that someone was. This had just gotten personal.

Wide-eyed, Kelly said, "I don't know if I can take much more of this. I really want to go."

"I'm sorry Kel, but I can't leave yet. This guy was a friend of mine."

"You know this guy?" she asked incredulously.

He nodded. "His name is Frank Dellatesta but we called him Frankie D. He and my father were best friends growing up. It's complicated but when my dad disappeared, Frankie D. stepped in as a father figure for me. He deserved better than this."

He fought to control his rising emotions. He wanted to start punching the walls. "I'm so sorry, John," she whispered consolingly.

Moving down the row of drawers opening them one at a time, he wondered how many more of his friends he would find. Eventually, he came across another corpse. This one was in a plastic body bag, which he unzipped.

Kelly covered her mouth in horror. "Oh my God."

Cesari didn't know this guy. The corpse was that of a middle-aged white male. He was mottled and in the early stages of decomposition. His eyes were missing, and he had been cut open in the midline from the neck down to his pelvis. All his organs had been removed, and then he had apparently been shoved into the body bag without any attempt to put him back together.

"This is why it's so cold in here. They're trying to slow down the rate of decomposition as much as possible until they're good and ready to dispose of the bodies," he said. "These guys are almost frozen. Most morgues are chilly, but this is ridiculous. This guy's probably been here a lot longer than Frankie D."

Before concluding his search of the drawers, he found two more eyeless splayed open cadavers in plastic body bags. He closed the last drawer and walked over to the desk on the other side of the room. Only a penholder and a small lamp sat on the desktop. The file cabinet had two drawers, and he opened the top one first. He found a ledger book in it, which he opened.

Each page briefly described different people and what happened to them. The first page documented a fifty-year-old displaced white male from Toronto, Canada. He had organ-matched for liver, kidney, and heart. The organs were harvested successfully and delivered to the recipients. Electronic payments were made and verified in an offshore account to the tune of almost three million dollars.

Flipping through the pages quickly revealed similar entries throughout. They harvested different organs, such as corneas, pancreas, or lungs, but generally with the same result, a fat bankroll. The dates suggested that the organ harvesting took place monthly beginning about one year ago and usually involved at least three to four patients, sometimes more.

He noticed several common denominators in the records. One, none of the donors listed had any associated identifying information. They were listed numerically and by date of admission only. There were no names. Two, they were all displaced males from various large cities in Canada and three, it didn't say it, but he was certain that none of them had walked out of here alive. There were more than fifty entries in the book.

Kelly had been reading with him and asked, "Is this what I think it is?"

"Certainly looks like it."

Chapter 29

They put the ledger back in the file cabinet and left the morgue. Not knowing what new horror lay ahead, they tread along the dark hallway toward the last room. Kelly was holding up well, but the reality of human cruelty shook her to the core. She was out of her element, and he felt bad for allowing her to come with him.

The outline of the last door was in front of them, and as he gently turned the knob, his cellphone started ringing loudly. From outside the garage, a dog barked in response and the man out there shouted, "What the hell was that?"

Cesari hastily powered off his phone and shoved Kelly ahead of him into the room where they huddled in the corner behind the door. Kelly pressed tightly up against him, and he could feel her trembling. The sound of footsteps could be heard loudly as the man entered the corridor from outside. There was another sound too, an unpleasant, dangerous sound.

With a faint click, a sliver of light shone from under the door. Cesari held the shotgun and Kelly held the crowbar. They both held their breath. The deep, throaty growl of a large canine echoed in the hallway.

The man said in a low voice, "Easy, girl."

They heard him open the door to the room with the oxycodone first. Cesari looked around but couldn't see anything in the darkness.

"Not good," he whispered to Kelly. "He's searching the rooms."

Cesari turned the flashlight on. With the hallway lights already on, he figured it would be safe. This room had a set of bunk beds on either side with a bathroom at the far end. The room was bare otherwise. No desk, no chairs, no television. There was nothing here except for two guys sleeping in the set of bunk beds to their right. They froze in place and he quickly turned the flashlight off. They gave no sign that their slumber had been disturbed.

He leaned next to Kelly's ear. "The bathroom."

They tiptoed past the bunk beds and entered the bathroom, flicking the flashlight briefly on and then off to get their bearings. The room was large for a bathroom, with two urinals, two toilets, and a shower stall with a plastic curtain. They stepped into the shower stall and hid behind the curtain, waiting and praying. Cesari had left the bathroom door partially open, exactly as he had found it, to give the room a more natural, relaxed appearance. A closed door would have begged for a search.

Kelly was close to having a panic attack and he whispered softly to her, "Take a deep breath, Kel. That's it. Now let it out slowly. Good. It's going to be okay. I want you to sit down and cross your legs. There's plenty of room. You're shaking, and you're going to make noise if you don't calm down."

He worried that she was going to start crying but she didn't. Kelly sat down and crossed her legs. He could hear her trying to control her breathing and she slowly regained her composure. She was going to be okay. He flipped the shotgun's safety on and gently rested the shotgun in her lap. He had considered shooting the guy if he discovered them, but now there were two other men he had to contend with, and he really didn't want tonight's adventure to turn into a mass murder. So he took the crowbar from Kelly and waited anxiously.

He didn't have long to wait and soon the hallway door opened, allowing light to flood into the room. Then the overhead room light went on. There was a mirror over the bathroom sink facing the doorway, and peeking out from the edge of the curtain, he could see a man built like a truck. He easily weighed two hundred and seventy pounds. His head was shaved and he looked ridiculous in his ill-fitting tight suit. In his right hand, he held a .357 magnum revolver out in front of him. In his left, he held a leash attached to what appeared to be the largest dog on the planet. It was Cesari's impression that the dog weighed almost as much as the man if not more. Its head was as gigantic as it was ferocious. He was glad Kelly couldn't see from her position on the floor. The man and the dog entered the room together, and the dog let out a low, rumbling growl as it discovered the sleeping men.

Man and dog moved slowly, glancing around to see if anything was amiss. The dog snarled some more and began to pull at the leash as they got closer to the bunk beds. The man pulled the dog back and cooed, "Easy, Cleo girl. There's nothing to worry about. We don't want to hurt these guys."

But the dog wasn't that easily persuaded and started barking and straining in the direction of the bunk beds. She began to pull harder on the leash, and the man was having difficulty controlling her.

"Be a good girl, Cleopatra. I just want to check out the bathroom and then we'll be done. I promise."

Cesari looked down at Kelly, who was sitting there wide-eyed. She hadn't seen the dog, but she could hear it and seemed to intuitively sense its size. Afraid to blink, he nodded in agreement that he shared her fear. Five hundred pounds of terror headed their way, and all he had was a crowbar. He considered the shotgun again but was afraid to move lest he make even the slightest of sounds.

As the guy wrestled for control of the dog, a cellphone rang stridently from one of the bunk beds. The dog erupted, growling viciously and yanking violently on the leash. The guy was big and muscular but he was rapidly losing control of the situation. If that dog got loose, she'd tear those guys to shreds, and them next, Cesari thought. He calculated the risk of grabbing the shotgun while he still had the chance but thought that any untoward sounds at this point might attract the attention of the dog.

"Damn," the guy hissed. He grabbed the leash with both hands, and Cesari prayed that it wouldn't snap.

With great effort, he maneuvered the powerful dog back out into the hallway while it growled and barked savagely the whole way. Throughout all of this, the cellphone kept ringing and the men kept sleeping.

From the hallway, Cesari heard the man reprimand the dog. "Now I'm pissed, Cleo. No doggie treats tonight. Come with me." They walked down the hallway and the dog gradually calmed down. "Now stay here," the guy commanded.

Cesari peeked down at Kelly and shrugged. He whispered almost inaudibly, "I have no idea what he's doing."

The lights were still on and the door still open, so they dared not move. They dared not breathe.

The cellphone finally went quiet.

Chapter 30

The guy returned to their room a minute later. This time he was alone. He went directly over to the bunk beds and searched under the covers until he found the cellphone in question. He powered it off and placed it in his pocket.

He glared at the sleeping guy and said, "You have no idea how lucky you are."

The sleeping man showed no signs of arousal which Cesari thought strange. Lights going on and off, dogs barking, he just got frisked and nothing. No response whatsoever. What on earth had he been given?

Grumbling, the guy walked to the door and turned off the room light. He hesitated there a moment at the entrance as if he had forgotten something. He turned the light back on and stared in the direction of the bathroom. Cesari tried to make himself small behind the shower curtain. With a deep breath, the guy walked toward them. Cesari tensed and gripped the crowbar tightly as he approached. He was obviously used to being very thorough and it bothered him that he hadn't searched this last place.

He stopped at the bathroom door with the .357 magnum held out in front of him in his right hand. Cesari watched him in the mirror and Kelly buried her face in her hands listening to the approaching footsteps and sensing impending doom. The bathroom was still too dark for comfort and in order for him to search it properly, he would have to turn on the light. The panel was to the left of the doorjamb as he entered. Cesari stood behind the shower curtain about three feet from there.

With his left hand, the guy fumbled for the light switch, which he missed by inches. Cesari saw frustration on his face as he decided he was overreacting and being unnecessarily cautious. He took a step into the bathroom and turned to reach for the switch again, bringing him closer to Cesari who decided it was time to act while he still had the element of surprise. He had quietly raised the crowbar while he watched him and now he swung it down hard through the shower curtain onto the guy's right arm, breaking his wrist and causing him to drop the gun which clattered on the floor.

He howled in pain and Kelly screamed in fright. The dog barked like hell in the hallway as pandemonium ensued. Cesari raised the crowbar and again swung it down hard, but the guy had backed up a step, so instead of hitting him in the head as he'd hoped, the crowbar landed squarely on his massive pecs. He might have broken a rib or a clavicle. He wasn't sure. Thick, dense muscle like he had could very effectively cushion the blow, but he had no doubt that he had caused him a lot of pain. Though injured and distracted, he wasn't out of the fight. The shower curtain was down now and he could see them clearly as surprised registered in his eyes. His right arm was useless, but he was still much bigger and stronger than Cesari and...he had another arm.

Snarling, he hurled a gigantic left hook, which caught Cesari in the chest, knocking him backwards into the shower stall. The back of his head hit the tiled wall and he dropped the crowbar. He charged forward, pinning Cesari against the wall with his mass. Kelly yelped as he entered the shower stall with them, trampling her. Trapped against the wall, he dug his right elbow into Cesari's neck. He was pinned and couldn't move. The guy intended to pummel him with his ham hock-sized left fist, but Cesari managed to grab his wrist with his right hand just before the blow landed deflecting it upward. They started wrestling in a life and death struggle while the dog went nuts in the hallway and Kelly scrambled around on all fours crying.

Cesari glared into his savage eyes and could feel his hot breath and spittle on his face. He smelled like the bastard he was. Suddenly his left hand broke free, and he immediately gave Cesari a quick shot to the side of the head before he could defend himself. He saw stars and felt a sharp pain inside his temporal lobe. One more blow like that and he would be done.

There was a unexpected, deafening explosion as a shot was fired. It reverberated loudly in the small room, hurting his ears. The guy screamed again and collapsed to the floor. Kelly had picked up his .357 and shot him in the ankle.

Cesari jumped on him before he could react, grabbed his head, and smashed it repeatedly into the tiled floor until he stopped moving. Cesari lay on top of him panting, while Kelly sobbed, huddled in a corner.

Cesari went over and put his arm around her. She was quivering. He said soothingly, "It's okay, Kel. Everything's okay." He held her face in his hands and looked into her eyes. "Kelly, can you hear me?"

She was still crying, but nodded.

"We've got to get out of here," he said.

He helped her up, and they tiptoed over the guy. He was still breathing. Blood oozed out of his ankle and from the back of his head, pooling onto the floor. Cesari briefly studied the gunshot wound. It wasn't pretty. He'll probably be using a cane the rest of his life, he thought.

He picked up the weapons. "Let's go."

As they passed the bunk beds, they paused to study the two sleeping guys. Between twenty and twenty-five years old, thin and swarthy with jet-black hair, they wore blue surgical scrubs and despite everything, were still out cold. He shook one, then the other to no effect. He opened one guy's eyelids and noticed his pupils were constricted. The same for the other guy.

"Narcotics," he said. "They've been drugged."

We uncovered them to see if they had any identification and discovered that both men were restrained to their respective beds with thick leather straps wrapped around their wrists and ankles. The restraints were attached to the metal frames of the beds, and Cesari doubted that even a robust, conscious man could free himself. Certainly not doped up guys like this. Without help, they had no chance of escape. The restraints were quite simple, heavy belts with large metal clasps that could easily be done or undone by anyone except the person who was restrained. They held the ankles and wrists relatively taut with limited range of motion.

"What should we do? We can't leave them here like this," Kelly said, starting to recover from her shock.

"I agree with you. Start unbuckling them. There was a medication cart in the OR across the hall. There might be some Narcan on it. If they've been drugged with narcotics like I suspect, it will reverse the effects. I'll go check and come right back."

As he turned to leave, Kelly asked, "What about that guy in the bathroom? Do you think he'll die?"

"I sincerely hope so."

Crossing the hallway to the operating room, he saw the dog at the far end of the hallway by the garage door, growling and barking. The sight of me provoked her to even greater frenzy. The guy had tied the end of her leash to the garage door handle, and from the way she was frantically straining and pulling, he didn't think they had much time left. He hustled into the OR and found the medication cart. In one of the drawers, he found vials of Narcan and some syringes. He grabbed a handful of both and returned to Kelly.

It took less than a minute for them to draw up the Narcan, find a suitable vein, and inject them with it. The Narcan acted rapidly and within seconds, the two guys started to wake up.

They were groggy but aware that something unexpected had happened. One of them seemed to be in pain. He lifted his scrub shirt and they saw a bloodied gauze bandage taped over his abdomen. He pulled it down to inspect it, revealing a freshly stapled midline surgical scar. The other guy then lifted his shirt and found the exact same thing. Matching surgical scars...what did that mean? They both started jabbering at each other in a language neither Cesari nor Kelly understood.

He turned to Kelly. "Any idea what language they're speaking?"

She shook her head. "No. I speak some Spanish, and that wasn't it."

"It wasn't Italian either."

"They look Middle Eastern to me."

"Who they are will have to wait. We've got to move," he said with some urgency.

The guys were now fully awake and becoming increasingly distressed. They had gotten up and were gazing around. Soon they discovered the guy in the bathroom and started freaking out. I was sure that the sound of the dog barking in the hallway and the sight of the shotgun increased their level of anxiety.

Cesari tried smiling and using hand gestures to explain that they were trying to help them, but it was obvious they didn't trust him. The language barrier was insurmountable, and it seemed perfectly reasonable that they acted cautiously. Although uncertain of their intentions, they sensed the imminent danger they were all in and followed them into the hallway. When they saw the dog, they began to chatter excitedly. In turn, when the dog saw them, her ferocity went nuclear. Cesari heard the word 'Allah' repeatedly.

"Arabs?" Kelly asked.

"Probably. Muslim for sure," he replied.

They turned toward the double doors from which they had entered and headed back out. As they did, there was a snapping sound and the rush of padded feet. Cesari glanced over his shoulder and saw that the dog had broken the leash and was charging down the hallway at them.

"Run, run, run!" Cesari yelled, grabbing Kelly by the arm and dragging her along. The Arabs didn't need a translator for that. They were ahead of them in the hallway and barreled through the double doors first. Kelly and Cesari followed closely behind.

On the other side of the doors, Cesari tossed the weapons down, grabbed the edges of the doors and slammed them closed. He leaned against them with all his weight and braced himself for impact which came seconds later. The doors shuddered from the weight of the beast as she hurled herself against the barrier with reckless abandon. A shock wave of pain ran through Cesari's shoulder as the dog pounded against it over and over. The doors gave a little, but he was able to keep them closed as the dog bounced off time and again.

Their side of the hallway was dark, but not as dark as when they first arrived because of light filtering through from the dog's side.

"Kelly, get the crowbar. It's on the floor by my feet," he requested and braced for another impact as the dog again leapt at the door, barking and growling.

"I got it. What should I do?"

"Slip it through the handles, please."

She took the straight end of the crowbar and slid it through the looped handles, hooking the curved end on one side. He stepped away and watched as the dog crashed into the doors. They jiggled from the attack but did not give way. The crowbar stayed securely in position. Eventually the hound from hell gave up, settling for vicious growls and an occasional bark.

He turned to Kelly, and they both breathed a sigh of relief. But as he looked around, he realized they were alone.

"Where are those guys?" he asked.

She scanned around just as baffled. "I think they flew the coop."

He said, "All things considered, I can't say I blame them. That was a rough way to wake up from a nap."

He turned to leave, but Kelly paused. "Don't forget the guns," she reminded him pointing at the .357 and the shotgun on the floor.

"I thought you didn't like guns."

"I do now."

Chapter 31

Gianelli strummed his fingers on the kitchen table as he sat silently brooding across from the CEO in Billy Ray Bob's house. Billy Ray Bob had been tasked with the job of burying his friend Ozzie behind the barn.

An hour before, they had entered Billy Ray Bob's bedroom, expecting to find Kelly as Billy Ray Bob had promised. Instead, they discovered Ozzie's badly battered and bruised corpse tied to the bed, his lifeless eyes staring upward. He looked awful and smelled worse. In death, he had lost control of his bowels. Gianelli had finally lost it. Ten years of frustration over Cesari's transgressions had finally come to the boiling point.

"You stupid pissant hillbillies!" he shouted at the Snells. "Cesari is making fools out of all of us. I've had it with the both of you and this shithole town. I've had nothing but aggravation since I got here. If I didn't know better, I'd think you two were on his side."

Snell and Billy Ray Bob stood there quietly, looking down at their feet as expletive after colorful expletive was hurled at them. No one could know that in his struggle to free himself from his bindings, accentuated by his high stress state, blood loss and poor diet, Ozzie had managed to precipitate a massive heart attack. The crushing chest pain had been intense and he had known he was dying when it happened. His lungs had filled with fluid as his stunned heart muscle failed, causing him to drown in his own secretions.

Appearances being what they were, Gianelli assumed the worst. He turned to Pinky and said, "I told you this guy Cesari was trouble. He's trying to send us a message."

"He certainly is Vito," Pinky replied. "He's declaring war on us. That's what he's doing."

Gianelli nodded his agreement and continued his tirade. "Don't they teach you guys how to defend yourselves up here? What kind of a cop gets himself beaten to death by a Goddamn gastroenterologist?"

Pinky chuckled at that and Gianelli continued, "If I wasn't so pissed, I'd think it was funny too, Pinky. Billy Ray Bob, I want you to clean this mess up and I mean now. He stinks, and I don't like sleeping with dead guys next door to me. Take him out and bury him behind the barn. You and your dad can share this room tonight. Pinky and I will take the other two bedrooms. Snell, you come with Pinky and me. We need to talk."

"How am I supposed to get him out by myself?" Billy Ray Bob whined.

Gianelli snapped back, "Do I look like the fucking Encyclopedia Britannica? Figure it out."

They left Billy Ray Bob alone in the bedroom to tend to Ozzie. Billy Ray Bob stared at the corpse. Ozzie was much too big to carry by himself and he didn't want to drag his blood and excrement all over the house. So he cut Ozzie free from the bedposts, wrapped him up in the sheet, and secured that with rope. He then opened a window, dragged Ozzie over to it, and hoisted him up and through it.

Gianelli was sitting at the kitchen table with Pinky and Snell when he saw the body fall past the window. It landed with a loud thump in the bushes by the side of the house. Gianelli turned to Snell and asked in a thoroughly exasperated tone, "Is that kid of yours retarded or what?"

Chapter 32

Kelly and Cesari left the hospital and drove to a motel off Route 5, a small arteriole which ran around the perimeter of the city. They figured it was too risky to go back to her place or his, so they rented a room with a queen bed and hunkered down for the rest of the night. The guy at the desk was bored and tired but the room was clean and amply furnished. Nothing fancy but not a flea bag either.

It was past three in the morning. They were both exhausted and he said, "We need to get a couple hours of sleep or we'll be useless."

She seemed unhappy like something was bothering her.

"What's the matter, Kel?" he asked.

"I don't want to wear the same clothes and underwear again tomorrow, and you're ripe."

He nodded. His battle in the bathroom had left the guy's stench on him. He said, "You have a point. I'll take a shower right now. That should ease your pain. I don't have a solution for your wardrobe dilemma however, other than going to your apartment first thing in the morning or to a department store for new clothes for the both of us."

"I like a man who agrees with me."

"Then I'm your man."

She stood there smiling, then stepped in close and put her arms around him. "Kiss me," she said.

So he did, for a long time, fat lip notwithstanding. She pressed her body into his, and he felt himself falling off a cliff.

They held each other tightly swaying to the music in their heads. Her hand slid slowly around from his back, across the flat of his stomach, then down to his waistband and didn't stop there.

"Maybe I should take that shower now," he suggested.

"Maybe I should join you."

"Maybe you should."

For a while, they did nothing but look into each other's eyes. After they showered, they laid down on the bed staring at the ceiling.

"What's going on here, Cesari?" she asked.

"A lot. That's for sure. Prescription drug trafficking is obviously one part of the equation. Another part appears to be illegal organ harvesting, but I think it's much worse than that. When people talk about illegal organ donation, they're usually implying the selling of one's organs voluntarily for a price. Most countries have outlawed selling organs because it victimizes the poor and uneducated. Unfortunately, despite the fact that it's illegal, it still occurs commonly in third-world countries. I've read about villages in Asia where upward to fifty percent of the residents have only one kidney because they sold the other for the equivalent of a mere one hundred U.S. dollars."

"Why do you think this is worse?"

"Because I don't believe the donors are being paid for their organs. The basement isn't set up for the long-term, post-operative care or rehabilitation that people would need after big operations. I think they're luring homeless people here, probably with the promise of monetary compensation, and then selling whatever they can harvest to whoever they can match the organs with. When they're done, they dump the bodies."

"Like those guys in the morgue who had been hollowed out?"

"Exactly. You find some guy in a homeless shelter or on the street, give him a hot meal and promise him a fortune for one of his kidneys. You tell him it's a safe operation and that he only needs one to live anyway. Maybe you tell him that he'll be saving some kid's life. I noticed that in all of the files I read, the donors were from Canada. That's really clever, because even if somebody noticed they were missing up there which I doubt would happen anyway since they're homeless, it certainly wouldn't cause any noise here in the States."

"But who pays for these organs?"

"There's a long list of people on a national transplant registry waiting for various organs. Many will die long before they receive their livers or hearts. Some would pay almost any price to live just a little longer. If they become desperate enough and if they've got the means, they pay up. Neither they nor their doctors are going to care where the organs come from."

"That's awful." The hard lines of repulsion etched her features.

"Yes, but it's human nature."

"Aren't these very complicated operations? I mean, who would they get to do this properly?"

"If you mean, what kind of animals would do this to another human being, that's a good question. Only a trained surgeon could successfully harvest an organ and know how to prepare it for transport. Maybe it's those foreign doctors you saw down in the basement that time. You said that you thought they might be Pakistani. That would make sense. Pakistan has one of the highest rates of illegal organ harvesting in the world and the donors there aren't doing it by themselves. That means Pakistan would also have an abundance of highly skilled and ethically dubious surgeons."

"Ethically dubious? Don't they take oaths? Wouldn't they be bound by some sort of code of conduct as doctors here are?"

He turned to look at her better. "First of all, don't kid yourself too much about doctors here but yes, of course they take oaths like we do. But doctors are just people, Kel. It doesn't matter where they're from or what oath they took or what language they took it in. Some are more scrupulous and professional than others by nature, but they're all human which means they're subject to the same weaknesses and temptations as everybody else. Besides, any surgeon who would do this sort of thing would also be unlikely to question the morality of it. And if you're from the Punjab region of the world, the temptation would be incredible. The compensation in the U.S. for even one operation of this type would probably be close to or greater than what they would receive as a whole year's pay in Pakistan or India or anywhere over there."

"How do you know all this?"

"I was one of the few people in my class who stayed awake during our ethics course in medical school. The information is out there, Kel. All you have to do is let it in."

He yawned and closed his eyes for a few seconds. When he opened them again, he was staring into Kelly's smiling face. She had climbed on top of him.

"Can I help you?" he asked.

"Who said you could go to sleep?"

Chapter 33

Cesari slept fitfully, tormented again by dreams he didn't understand. His subconscious took over at night and dragged him kicking and screaming to the far recesses of his mind. It introduced him to persons and places he knew and some he had never heard of. It took real memories and mixed them up with pure fantasy. Was there a purpose? He didn't know and he didn't care. He just wanted the dreams to stop. They were too real and too painful and he couldn't take it much longer. He was reaching the breaking point. Living in his dreams was like having his eyes forced open while he watched his worst fears parade in front of him.

Tonight was no different as he dreamt he was in Rome, the eternal city. Italy, the land of his forebears. He was with his boss Frankie D., and they had chased some dirtbag named Nicolo Pesce aka Nicky the Fish into the mouth of a dark alley not too far from the Pantheon. Nicky was a rat and was about to get what he had coming to him, old-school style. Cesari carried a pair of brass knuckles in one pocket and a switchblade in the other.

"Where'd he go?" Frankie D. whispered in the blackness.

Cesari replied, "I don't know. I can barely see you and you're standing right next to me."

"I don't like this," he said ominously. "Nicky could be hiding in there waiting to ambush us."

"We have no choice but to go in there after him," Cesari said with some degree of apprehension.

They entered the dark narrow passage in tandem with Cesari behind, fingering the five-inch pearl handled blade. They had crept stealthily along the ancient cobble-stoned street for about fifty feet when a dark figure leapt out from a doorway and grabbed Frankie D. by the throat, hurling him to the ground.

The figure straddled Frankie D., who hit his head when he fell and was too stunned to fight back. His assailant was choking the life out of him with one hand and beating him mercilessly with the other using something that caused a loud slapping sound. From where he stood, Cesari couldn't see what was making the curious sound.

In a weakened voice, gasping for oxygen and only seconds away from death, Frankie D. managed to cry out, "Johnny, help me. Do something."

Initially Cesari was frozen with fear but recovered quickly and flicked his blade open. He grabbed the attacker from behind with his left arm around his neck and stabbed him in the back, not once, not twice, but repetitively until he felt him go limp and slump over Frankie D. who was panting and choking where he lay. He pushed the body to the side and stood up.

"Good job, Johnny. I owe you my life," Frankie D. exclaimed when his strength returned. He embraced Cesari warmly. "Thank you, kid."

A light went on in one of the windows above them and they could see the body of the dead guy lying face down, his shirt covered in blood from the many stab wounds.

"Turn him over, Johnny. I want to see his ugly mug."

Cesari bent down, rolled the guy over and recoiled in horror at what he saw. He started puking. Cesari's father lay there dead, wearing the same clothes he'd last seen him in. On his left hand he wore the baseball glove they used to play catch with, which had caused the slapping sound as he beat Frankie D. He stepped back in dismay and confusion.

Frankie D. came over to him and put an arm around him. He said, "You couldn't have known kid."

As they both stood there staring incredulously, the hand with the glove relaxed a little and a baseball rolled out onto the street toward Cesari. It slowed just before reaching him and came to a stop at his feet. He looked down at it and started screaming.

"No, no, no! Dad please. Dear God, no!"

"Cesari, wake up. You're having a nightmare again." Kelly shook him hard.

"Oh my God," he gasped.

His heart was pounding, he was perspiring and he realized he was hyperventilating. The intensity of this particular dream shook him to the core.

Kelly put her arms around him. "Your father again?"

"Yeah, only much worse. Now Frankie D. was there, too. It was so real."

She could see he was distraught, stroked his head gently and held him close. "I think you better call that psychiatrist friend of yours this morning."

He nodded and glanced at the clock. "Wow, it's eight already."

"I'm going to get cleaned up. Why don't you make that call?"

She walked off to the bathroom, and he heard the shower start running.

On the fourth ring, Mark answered. "Well, good morning, Dr. Cesari. How are you doing this fine Sunday?"

Mark had been one of several people who had given Cesari the necessary resolve to change his life. Throughout the rigors of medical school and residency, he had been there like a cheerleader on the sidelines. He had even shown up on graduation day and taken him out to dinner. Although he was still his psychiatrist and always would be as long as he had breath in him, he was now also Cesari's friend. After graduation, he had told him that they were peers but Cesari knew he would never be his equal.

"Hi, Mark. I'm doing well. How are you?"

"All's well here. How's the practice coming along? Are you enjoying being a real live doctor, or was it more fun play-pretending as a student?" he jibed.

He chuckled. "Yeah well, it has certainly been challenging in ways that they never prepared me for."

Mark laughed. "Welcome to the club, Cesari. Welcome to the club. Enough small talk. The meter's running and my wife is waiting for me to hold my new grandson."

"Mazel tov, Mark. I hadn't heard. What's his name?" he asked, sincerely happy for the guy.

"His name is Asher, which means 'happy' in Hebrew. He weighs seven pounds, six ounces and was born two minutes after midnight this morning. My daughter is doing well but we're all exhausted as you could imagine. You've got five minutes, starting now."

"Remember those dreams I used to tell you about?"

"Sure do. Go on."

"They were always violent and surreal and I could never make out exactly who, what, or where. Well over the last few months, things have been coming more clearly into focus. I'm starting to recognize people I know and situations I remember, and I don't like what I'm dreaming about. This latest one was a doozy."

"Tell me the dream." Mark listened while Cesari told him the details as succinctly as possible and then said, "Well, I must say that would have shaken me up too. However, as we've previously discussed, any dream can have multiple meanings or no meaning at all. They can simply represent your subconscious blowing off steam. I wouldn't read too much into it. For instance, when I was an undergrad at Fordham University, I used to routinely dream about killing my physics professor. All it really meant was that I was under a great deal of stress at the time, trying to get good grades in a course I found extremely difficult. Are you under any unusually severe stress right now?"

"No, everything's great," he lied. Kelly stepped out of the bathroom wearing nothing but a towel wrapped around her hair and he held his breath. "Look, I'll let you get back to your family. This is such a great time for you all. I can't even begin to tell you how happy I am for you."

"Thank you, Cesari. I appreciate you saying so. I'll think about the dream some more when things settle down around here, and then I'll give you a call. How's that sound?"

"Sounds great. I would appreciate it. Take care, Mark." he hung up.

Kelly asked, "So what did he have to say?"

"He said I'm crazy, and there's no cure."

"You'd better not pay him, because I could've told you that." she laughed but was happy that he had at least started the wheels in motion for help.

"He said he needs to think it over, and that he'll get back to me. Do you realize how beautiful you are?" he was ogling her as she dressed.

She laughed again. "Of course. I have a mirror, you know."

Chapter 34

They checked out of the motel and drove the Porsche a couple of miles sticking to the backroads until they found a small freestanding mom and pop diner. It was an old thing, silver and beaten down by time. It had probably prospered in the early days of roadside eateries when such things were springing up everywhere to accommodate the nations's new past time of travelling by car. But then the inevitable happened and traffic and business were diverted away by the large interstate highways built not so much in response to consumer demand but for the military to ready itself for the next war.

They seated themselves in a corner booth away from the other customers. The waitress poured them coffee without asking and he ordered scrambled eggs, bacon and toast. Kelly had a bowl of oatmeal with cinnamon and raisins.

"No espresso machine here?" he asked.

The waitress gave him a puzzled look. "What's that?"

"Espresso? It's a type of coffee."

"It sounds foreign."

"It is. It's Italian."

"I'll ask Alvin. He's the cook. He knows lots of things. He almost went to college," she said politely and walked away.

Kelly rolled her eyes and laughed, "Why did you do that?"

"I just asked a question."

"Please don't torment the waitstaff. We'll get better service if they don't hate us."

"Well I'm done anyway unless Alvin wants to find out what espresso is."

She shook her head. "Can we talk about important stuff?"

"Shoot."

"Okay, so the basement is being used as a transfer point for illegal prescription medications or so we think. That I got. And probably there is some type of organ harvesting scheme going on as well. You said last night that you didn't think anyone survived those operations, but then how do you explain those two guys we found down there? They seemed fine to me. And why would they have built an area for recovery like that in the first place if no one was supposed to get out alive?"

He pondered that for a moment and then said, "Good questions, and I don't quite see how those guys fit in with any of this. They were strapped in as if they were prisoners but didn't seem particularly grateful to us for saving them. In fact, if my ability to read people is even vaguely close to what I think it is, I would guess they were significantly annoyed that we woke them up."

"I agree, but maybe they were confused. After all, they were heavily sedated."

He shook his head. "Something doesn't fit. What about the surgery they had? Those scars weren't like any I've ever seen before and they both had identical scars. That's very strange too. And there's no way they could have just had an organ removed and jump out of bed like that. Removing an appendix is one thing. Removing an organ for transplant is another thing entirely. They were there for a different reason. I'm sure of it."

She nodded. "What about your friend Frankie D? How awful for his family. They don't even know where he is. All they know is that one day he didn't show up for dinner."

Cesari thought about that. "That's not as uncommon as it might sound, Kelly. Because of what happened to my father, I spent a lot of time researching the subject. Thousands of people are reported missing every single day in the United States alone. Many don't want to be found but for some, it's like Frankie D. and my father. One minute they're there and the next they're gone without a trace."

She reached across the table to hold his hand. "I'm sorry. I guess you understand what it feels like more than most."

"Unfortunately I do, but I've come to terms with it. By most standards, Frankie D. was a bad man, but he was there for me when I needed someone and he helped me get through a very difficult period. He also helped me pay for my education and I owe him a lot for that. He didn't have to do that. Nonetheless, I also recognize that he was a flawed man. My feelings toward him are complicated to say the least."

"I understand."

"Do you?" he gave her a hard look.

The waitress placed their breakfasts in front of them. Before taking her first bite, Kelly asked, "Why do you say that?"

"Because right now I feel like a pot that's about to boil over. I know who did that to Frankie D. and I intend on making him pay."

She looked at him as if he was a total stranger. "I know you're upset about your friend, but you can't seriously intend to handle this by yourself. We barely got out with our lives last night. It's time we called the police. Besides, you can't be sure who did that to your friend."

He swallowed a mouthful of eggs and washed it down with coffee. "All the reasons we chose not to go to the police yesterday still hold true today, Kelly. Only now we have to add breaking and entering and possibly murder, to the list of things we'd have to explain to a corrupt small-town police department. I understand if you want out. In fact, I would encourage you to disassociate from me as soon as possible, but I'm not going anywhere. And as far as who did that to my friend, believe me, I know who did it. As sure as rain I know."

"Gianelli?"

"Of course. He made a not-so-subtle joke about it when we were in Snell's office. He told me that he was at Frankie D.'s retirement party and that it was a real blast. I thought that there was something strange about the way he said it but there was so much else going on at the time, it went over my head."

"Why would he bring the body all the way up?"

"I don't know. Frankie D. was a pretty big guy in the Bronx and well-liked. I'm sure a lot of people are going to be upset when they hear about this. My guess is this was an unauthorized hit and Gianelli wasn't ready for the truth to come out. Believe it or not Kel, you can't just whack people without permission. Not even in the Bronx."

Kelly giggled. "Whack? Do people really talk like that?"

"Only in the movies."

"And in small town diners too apparently... So what now?"

"Well things are going to be heating up around here when Gianelli finds out what we did to his friend, so I'm advising you to leave town. I'll drop you off wherever you want."

She smiled in a joking way. "Traditionally, when a guy dumps the girl, he's the one who leaves town, not the other way around."

He liked her sense of humor. "I'd hardly call this a dumping. It's a temporary separation for health reasons. Think of yourself as being quarantined from a disease. Besides, we haven't been seeing each other long enough for it to be called dumping anyway. And just for the record, I would never dump you. You're too damn cute. I just don't want you to get hurt. I'll bring you to a hotel or a friend's place in the next town or wherever, until things blow over here."

"Good response, slick, but I think I'll stick around for a while. I find you kind of entertaining in a will-I-live-to-see-tomorrow kind of way."

Chapter 35

They paid the bill and were finishing their coffees. Kelly said, "So what's the whole story with you, Frankie D. and Vito? You and your friends have turned my life upside down. I think you owe me that much. It's not like I don't have my suspicions already. Why don't you just clear the air for me?"

He took a deep breath and said, "This is hard for me Kelly. I've never really opened up to anyone, and I've already told you more about myself in the last few days than I ever have anyone else including Mark."

"Only if you want to..."

"I do want to because it's you."

"Thank you."

He hesitated for a moment as he looked at her and then began slowly, "Kelly, try to understand and this might be hard for you because you're a nice person and nice people sometimes can't comprehend what really goes on. It's outside their breadth of experience. Certain things just can't compute for nice people... Where I grew up, life was cheap. Really cheap. Violence was everyday and everywhere. You were either the predator or the prey. Over time, I became numb to it all and accepted it and was part of it. It wasn't unusual to wake up and find out a good friend had just got killed the night before, a bullet between the eyes like Frankie D. and you know what I would do?"

She shook her head and said softly, "No. What would you do?"

"I'd pour myself a cup of coffee, read the newspaper and move on. No tears. No sentimentality. Just like that, because that's the way it was. Frankie D. was a family friend and a role model for me. When my father disappeared, I needed someone, a male figure in my life, so I clung to him. His world became my world. At the time, it was all I knew. Vito and I worked for him. Believe it or not we were sort of partners in a loose sense of the word and I tried to do the best I could. I was proud of who I was and I was good at it."

"I understand," she said.

"Unfortunately, doing the best you could in that business meant that someone else had to get hurt. Do you understand what I'm saying?"

She didn't say anything. She just watched him.

"My job...the thing that I got paid very well to do, was to hurt people and I did just that. Lots of people. I caused lots of pain. Now, many of the people I hurt wouldn't have hesitated to reciprocate if they had the chance but certainly not all of them. The thing is I didn't really care. You see, I was on top of the food chain and that was all that mattered."

He paused to take a breath and collect his thoughts. Kelly just sat there as he continued, "When my mother died, something happened inside me. It was like a chain reaction and once it started, I couldn't stop it. She suffered so much it broke me emotionally, and eventually I came to the realization that I couldn't go on the way I was. I was ashamed of what I had become. It was like waking up from a bad dream and I knew I had to get away from it. I told Frankie D. I wanted to go back to school and he one hundred percent supported my decision. He told me he was proud of me. He transferred a sizeable sum into an account for me to use for tuition, and then helped me drop off the map so people like Gianelli couldn't find me, couldn't hound me. Until yesterday, everyone who knew me then believed I was just another victim somewhere, maybe lying in a morgue drawer with a bullet hole in my head. But now everything I'd tried to get away from has somehow caught up with me and like it or not, I have to face it because it's not going to go away."

Kelly was pensive. He could see the inner conflict in her features as she digested all he had said. She put her coffee cup down but didn't seem to have anything to say which said it all, of course. She was probably thinking that compared to him, Billy Ray Bob wasn't so bad.

He said, "I know it's not much of an excuse, but it was what I saw and knew. It was my version of normal. I was just trying to survive. I'm sorry if that sounds harsh but I'm not like that anymore, if that helps."

She was staring.

He watched her, wondering what she was thinking. Maybe she didn't hear him. Was that possible? She looked like she was about to start crying.

Not good.

Her eyes welled up and reddened and a teardrop formed in one corner. Definitely not good. He wished he could take it all back. "I'm sorry, Kelly. Maybe I said too much or said it too bluntly. That was selfish of me."

She began to sob. Damn, you never knew what women were going to do. She said, "Excuse me."

She got up from her seat and headed toward the restrooms, sniffling into a napkin. He thought about following her but changed his mind, thinking it might be a good idea to let her have a few minutes to herself.

Moments after Kelly left the table, his cellphone rang. It was Cheryl. "Good morning, Cesari. How nice of you to finally answer your phone after I've been up all night trying to help you out."

He glanced at the phone and just then saw the missed calls. It was Cheryl's call when he was searching the basement that had alerted the guy and his dog. He had powered the phone off after that. "I'm sorry I missed your call last night, Cheryl. I was tied up. So how did it go with your D.A.?"

"He is very much interested in anything that concerns that slimeball, Gianelli. Obviously we have no authority where you are, but this morning he's going to talk to the FBI branch director here in Manhattan. He's probably having coffee with him right now in his office."

"On Sunday morning? They're in their offices? I'm impressed. I thought law enforcement was a nine-to-five kind of job."

"Do you live in a cave, Cesari? Don't you guys get the *New York Times* or CNN up there? There's a huge terrorist trial getting ready to start down here this week. Some mental case tried to blow up Saint Patrick's Cathedral on Easter morning last spring. Everybody's working double and triple-time to make sure every *i* is dotted and every *t* is crossed. If this guy gets off because of some technicality, heads are going to roll. I've never seen so many uptight lawyers and federal agents."

"I thought you were working with organized crime, not counter-terrorism. How does this trial affect you?"

"We all wear multiple hats around here, and we're all located in the same building with offices down the hall from each other. We share the same copy machines, coffee makers and bathrooms. I'm helping them out temporarily until the trial is over. Everybody is extremely on edge. To be honest, they're treating me a bit like a paralegal and I'm not happy about it. This business about Gianelli perked me up a bit. It certainly got Harry's attention."

"I apologize for doubting their work ethic. Who's Harry?"

"Harry McClellan is the new D.A. He got appointed about a year ago and is hot to make a name for himself. He'd prosecute his own mother for child abuse if he thought it would further his career. Get the picture?"

"Loud and clear," he answered. "By the way, I found out some more information for you that might be helpful. I did a little snooping around last night after we spoke and found a room in the basement of the hospital filled with oxycodone."

"So what?" she responded. "It's a hospital. I thought they had lots of rooms filled with stuff like that."

"Yes they do, but this wasn't locked in the pharmacy. It was in a different room and there was way too much of it for ordinary hospital use. It was more like a ten year supply for a hospital of this size."

"Are you telling me they have narcotics lying around for anybody to pick up and walk away with? This sounds more like a problem for the Joint Commission to deal with rather than law enforcement. Maybe you should give them a call."

"Well they weren't just lying around," he said. "There was a locked door to the hallway leading to the room with the narcotics."

Kelly returned to the table, sat down and seemed a little better. He mouthed the word *Cheryl* to her to indicate who he was talking to and she nodded.

Cheryl said, "If there was a locked door, how did you get past it at night, or don't I want to know? You don't seem to understand, Cesari. You can't break the law just because you're curious about whether someone else broke the law. And another thing, I'm the damn assistant D.A. for the city of New York. I'm sworn to uphold the law. You can't just casually inform me that you committed a felony. How do you know the oxycodone wasn't going to be moved to the pharmacy first thing tomorrow morning? By the way, did you relock the door after you left, or is there now a real reason for me to be worried about all those narcotics?"

She was very annoyed. Despite that, he told her about finding Frankie D. and the two Middle Eastern guys. She was equally unimpressed with that. He didn't think it would add much to tell her about the guy Kelly shot in the ankle, so he left that part out.

"So what?" she said. "You found a dead guy in a morgue. Isn't that where they live anyway? I agree, a bullet to the head is a strange way to retire for me and you, but not for guys like that. As for the two sleeping Arabs…"

He interrupted her, "I said they were drugged, not sleeping and I'm not sure they're Arabs although probably. They could be Pakistani or Iranian. They were dark-skinned and spoke a language I didn't understand. And they used the word Allah a lot so I'm presuming that part of the world."

"Fine, let's just say Middle Eastern for now. You said they weren't hurt, right?"

"They had some type of minor abdominal surgery. I saw the scar when one of them lifted his shirt."

"Okay, but you also said that they seemed a little irritated at you for waking them up and they ran as fast as they could to get away from you. That's a funny way to act when somebody just saved your life."

"True. That's what I thought."

"As far as being drugged is concerned, without a toxicology report that's pure speculation on your part. I don't mean to question your clinical skills but you're on thin ice with this stuff. Let me play it out for you in a way you can understand. Maybe they had some sort operation in the regular OR. Just because you've never seen a scar like they had doesn't mean anything because you're not a surgeon. Are you with me so far?"

"Yes," he said.

"Okay then. So they have their operations but now the doctors realize the regular recovery room is short of beds. It happens all the time is my understanding of the situation. Bear with me here, Cesari. So they place the guys down there in the basement which acts as an overflow recovery area. Someone notices them having seizures and decides that for their own protections they should be restrained and sedated. How are my post-operative medical skills so far?"

She was on a roll but she was wrong. "It doesn't make any sense. The lights were completely out down here and there weren't any nurses to care for them."

"And yet they were so happy you saved their lives, they didn't even say goodbye. By the way Cesari, did you know that it's a felony to inject a controlled substance into another human being without their consent?"

"You mean the Narcan I gave them? I was trying to help them."

"News flash. This is America. From a legal point of view, you have absolutely nothing here against Gianelli or your CEO. You on the other hand, have committed multiple crimes, such as aggravated assault, breaking and entering, and the administration of a controlled substance to an individual without his consent. You could get about ten years. I recommend you stop playing detective before you wake up in a cell next to a guy who thinks you're more attractive than I do. Understood?"

"But..."

She hung up.

"That didn't sound like it went very well."

"She seemed singularly underwhelmed with our nocturnal investigation last night. Her boss the D.A. however, is talking to the FBI today about Gianelli and any possible connections with Snell. Until we hear back, she wants us to stay out of it. She suggested I call the Joint Commission about the narcotics we found."

"You didn't tell her I shot that guy, did you?"

"No, it never happened anyway. He obviously fell and his gun went off. He shot himself. Just remember that."

"That seems to happen a lot to people you don't like. You know, falling and breaking their noses or shooting themselves."

"Yeah, I know. It's kind of a weird thing."

"So tell me about the Joint Commission. What exactly is it, and why does all hell break loose at the hospital whenever they come to visit?"

He explained, "The Joint Commission on Accreditation of Healthcare Organizations, JCAHO or JAKE-O as everyone calls it, is an organization that develops standards of quality for hospitals. JAKE-O accreditation is used by hospitals to indicate to the public that their institution meets certain quality standards."

She asked, "What happens if a hospital loses its JAKE-O accreditation or never bothered to get accredited in the first place?"

"According to most hospital administrators, the sky will fall and we will all descend into the fiery pits of hell."

"No, really."

"That's just it, Kel. Nothing will happen. JAKE-O has no official ties with the government or insurance companies. It has no legal power. It's strictly a voluntary program. But the fear is that if you lose your accreditation you will be viewed as a substandard medical facility. Cheryl was right of course, in that an unsecured room filled with narcotics would certainly be of interest to them although technically, the room wasn't unsecured. We broke in."

She was brooding and it wasn't about JAKE-O. She was still teary-eyed, and he could see that the elephant was back in the living room, so he decided to tackle it directly.

He said, "Are you okay, Kel? I know that what I told you about myself before has got to be troubling and I am very sorry.

I didn't want to lie to you. I realize that this probably changes things between us, and I understand completely why you wouldn't want to be with a guy like me."

"Wrong on all counts. I wasn't crying because of the things you said you did. What matters to me is the person you are now. I was crying because I had this image of a little boy whose father went off to work one day and never returned. I can't even imagine how painful that must have been for you at that age. It just made me feel so bad for you."

He nodded.

"Your life got turned upside down and inside out, and you tried to fill the void by turning to the nearest male role models for comfort. It's not your fault they were monsters. They in turn tried to turn you into a monster too, something that you were never meant to be and despite their best efforts, you were able to overcome their bad influences. Look how far you've come against all the odds. I know you are a kind and decent person and I'm glad we're friends."

He looked at her carefully, looking for a sign. He cleared his throat and asked meekly, "So just to clarify, you're not going to dump me?"

She smiled and shook her head no.

The waitress came up to the table and asked them if they wanted more coffee.

He looked at Kelly. "How did I get so lucky?"

The waitress beamed. "See, who needs espresso anyway?"

Chapter 36

Back at Billy Ray Bob's house, the smell of bacon frying in a cast iron skillet permeated the kitchen as Gianelli took report from his men over breakfast. It had been a quiet night. Sal and Mike reported no activity at Cesari's or Kelly's apartment.

Gianelli was annoyed, an almost chronic condition at this point. "Where on earth is Tony? It's after eight already. Doesn't he know how to tell time? I said I wanted everyone here at eight sharp."

"He's not answering his cellphone either, Vito. I wonder what that means," Pinky added.

"It means he fell asleep on the job, that's what it means. And it isn't the first time. Me and him are going to have a long talk about this after we're done up here. Hey Snell, get me some more coffee and Billy Ray Bob, are you almost done with the bacon? I said not too crispy."

"It's almost ready," replied Billy Ray Bob while his father topped off everyone's mugs.

Gianelli said, "All right Pinky, after breakfast we'll head over to the hospital to see what's going on with Tony and the dog. Billy Ray Bob, I want you to stay with us. Snell, you to go to your office and sit tight until you hear from me. By the way, nice aprons you two got on. You almost look good enough to bend over this table."

All the men burst into laughter.

Chapter 37

After they left the diner, Kelly and Cesari cruised by her apartment to get a change of clothes. Wearing the same things from the day before was really bugging her. They sat in the Porsche a block away for about twenty minutes, observing the area for any unusual activity or sights such as a stakeout vehicle. The coast was clear, so they went in. When she came out of her bedroom, she had on sneakers, jeans, a yellow blouse, and a light sweater. He still wore yesterday's clothes. He was standing by the sink drinking a glass of water, when his cellphone went off. He didn't recognize the number.

"Cesari here," he said.

"This is Vito. We should talk."

He recalled that Snell had given Vito his cellphone number. He said, "We are talking. What do you want?"

"We should talk face to face. It will be easier and then there'll be no need for the girl to get hurt."

"What girl?" Cesari said. Kelly was watching him and picked up on the conversation.

"Don't be stupid, Cesari. I know all about your girlfriend Kelly, and I know all about what you did to Billy Ray Bob and Ozzie. We were at Billy Ray Bob's house last night." He chuckled. "Not bad, Cesari. I have to admit, you still got what it takes but I have to ask you something."

"So ask."

"Was that absolutely necessary?"

"Was what absolutely necessary?"

"Killing that poor bastard, Ozzie. I mean seriously, wasn't that a bit of an overreaction?"

"For the sake of this discussion, let's pretend I don't know what you're talking about. What happened?"

"Ozzie was cold and blue when we got there. You did quite the job on him too. He was a mess. Broken bones, swollen all over, missing half his teeth. Covered in vomit and crap. It was disgusting. Nicely done though, I have to say. You put the fear of God into Snell that's for sure. And Billy Ray Bob's afraid to tell anyone because there's no good explanation for how Ozzie was found. It took Billy Ray Bob half the night to bury the poor slob behind his barn. If you were trying to send me a message, then consider it received but now I want to send you one. Let's talk about what's going to happen to your girlfriend if you don't give yourself up." Vito had always enjoyed this part of the job. "Are you listening, Cesari?"

"Kelly's not my girlfriend, Vito. Whoever told you that was misinformed. I barely know her. The night at the Ramada was the first time I'd ever seen her outside the hospital and now she blames me for everything that's happening. She's so upset about last night, she took off and I haven't seen or heard from her since. She didn't even thank me for rescuing her, so this is between me and you only. And let's face facts, it's always been between me and you only."

"Well that's too bad she doesn't appreciate you the way you deserve Cesari, but I hope you won't be offended if I tell you I don't believe a word of your bullshit except for maybe that last part about this being between me and you. You're right about that and that's why you're going to turn yourself in because you and I have unfinished business and you don't want Kelly to be part of the collateral damage. Now I'm going to read you something and you can stop me when I'm wrong."

Cesari heard him shuffle papers around and then say, "Here we are. Her full name is Kelly Karla Kingston, that's Karla with a

K, age thirty, black female, social security number 098-55-9978, drives a white Civic, license QVR-6709. She currently resides at 21 Holly Street, Genesee, originally from Ohio. Has two aunts in Kent, Ohio. Mother and father deceased, no siblings. Hey, did you know she's got a birthday coming up? How am I doing so far?"

"Okay, Vito, I get the point."

"Do you? Because I have a lot more. Aren't employment records a wonderful thing? Well I'm glad I finally got your attention, Cesari. Now listen carefully. I want you to come to the back of the hospital where the loading dock is at 10:00 p.m. tonight. Come alone, come unarmed and don't be late. In the meantime, my boys will keep searching for the girl and you better hope we don't find her before we find you."

"I'll be there Vito, but I'm telling you now that neither she nor I know anything."

"I'll decide that for myself, Cesari. If you're telling the truth, then you and the girl can go back to playing doctor, or Oreo cookie or whatever. Just remember, you had better show up."

He hung up.

"What was that about?" Kelly asked, worried. "It sounded a lot like you were going to meet him. Please tell me I misunderstood."

He turned to her and said, "He's using you as leverage, Kel. He knows everything there is about you from your employment file which he probably got from that rodent, Snell. He wants to meet with me at the rear of the hospital tonight. If I don't show up, he made it clear he's going to take it out on you. He's going to hunt you down. He has guys looking for you as we speak. He was letting me know that if he doesn't find you today or tomorrow, then it'll be next week or the week after. There won't be any place you can hide. I'm sorry... We need to get out of here right now and find a more secure location while we think."

Kelly looked horrified. "I understand and I'm not thrilled by that, but you can't possibly be thinking of going anywhere near him. That would be suicide. There has to be another way."

She was right, but he wasn't sure what his alternatives were. He supposed they could get in the Porsche and drive as far away as possible. Then they would be on the run, out of work, and broke as soon as the credit cards charged out. Assuming he didn't wind up in prison for grand theft auto, he certainly would have to find a new profession. Not many hospitals are going to hire a physician suspected of as many felonies as he was. Besides, it would be pure fantasy to think that Gianelli would let go of this. He's been waiting too long to get back at him. Definitely not good. One way or the other, he had to finish this.

He finally replied, "Unfortunately, I can't not meet with him either."

"Cesari, I'm not going to let you go there, so get the idea out of your head."

"Kelly, you don't understand people like Gianelli...They don't forget and they don't forgive...anything. He won't hesitate to hurt you to flush me out. Hell, he might hurt you just for being my friend. If I don't meet with him, he won't stop coming until either one or both of us is dead."

She sighed deeply and thought for a while. "Fine, I don't know what you hope to accomplish by going there but I'm coming with you."

"Whoa, stop right there, Kelly. I don't think you understand. The fun and games part has ended. This is going to be dangerous enough without you."

"I'm coming with you Cesari, and if you try to stop me, I'll go straight to the police and tell them that you kidnapped me and have been selling drugs out of the basement of the hospital." She stood in front of him, arms folded defiantly, all five feet three inches of her.

Silence.

"Did you just threaten to have me arrested and then make false accusations against me?"

"Damn right I did," she said proudly.

They stared at each other and he blinked first. "Ozzie's dead, Kel," he said flatly, changing the subject.

"What happened? He didn't look that bad when we left him."

"I don't know. Vito said they found him dead, but I wouldn't put it past him to have put Ozzie down like a lame animal if only to ease his own frustrations. He said Billy Ray Bob buried him somewhere behind the barn."

"This isn't good."

"No, it isn't. Although it's interesting that he didn't mention anything about what happened in the basement of the hospital last night. Either he doesn't know yet, or he hasn't connected it with us... Let's go. We really shouldn't stay here any longer. They're bound to swing by at some point. That's what I would do."

As they walked out to the car, he said, "By the way, Gianelli told me your full name was Kelly Karla Kingston. KKK? What's with that?"

"My grandmother's name was Karla. My mother liked the ring of it. That's all. No big joke, if that's what you're getting at."

He held the door to the Porsche open for her. "I'm not getting at anything. But it did make me wonder what you dressed up as for Halloween."

"Oh, shut up," she giggled. "Not as a ghost. That's for sure. Besides, if I had a dopey name like yours, I wouldn't be making comments."

He buckled up. "What's dopey about Cesari?"

"Please... It sounds like some kind of pizza topping."

"It's the Italian word for Caesar. You know, the emperors of ancient Rome."

"Spare me."

"I mean it. I might be related."

"To the salad dressing maybe."

Chapter 38

They stopped at a gas station, topped off the tank and drove to the Super Walmart on Main Street so he could get a new shirt. Kelly had complained that the one he was wearing reeked, and he didn't want to risk going back to his apartment now that they knew there was an all-out manhunt for them. He also picked up a dark nylon windbreaker, a duffel bag and a two-pound package of ground beef.

"You making burgers for dinner?" she asked as they approached the check out line.

"Maybe. I should have warned you that I'm a great cook."

"Really? I didn't know the emperors of ancient Rome did their own cooking. Well once things settle down around here, I'm going to put you to the test."

"You doubt me?"

"Just a lot. The last guy who told me he could cook nearly burned his house down showing me how to flambee Crêpes Suzette which he had never made before. It was a disaster. So what dish is your specialty?"

"His first mistake was preparing French food for you. He might as well have served you animal crackers. Beautiful women like you deserve better."

She smiled. "Really?"

"Italian food is like the Italian language. It's all about love. My specialty is spaghetti alla carbonara," he said. "I grate my parmagiano reggiano cheese fresh and use only the best pancetta. When I have the time, I even make home-made pasta."

"You sound like you know your stuff. I can't wait."

They reached the cashier and Kelly paid the bill while he changed into the clean shirt. The woman ringing them out was about fifty and stared shamelessly at his pecs. He didn't care and gave her a double pump. First the right pec and then the left. He was preparing for war and starting to feel very primitive.

When he finished adjusting himself, she winked at him and said, "Thanks for the show, honey."

As they walked away, Kelly pretended to be annoyed, "Out of curiosity, don't you have any rules at all about who you flirt with?"

"I didn't do anything."

"A guy like you could single-handedly cause the divorce rates to skyrocket in a small town like this."

"You think?"

There was a sandwich shop and an ATM in the Walmart, so they picked up lunch, a couple of sodas and two hundred in cash. They sat in the Porsche and talked things over while they ate.

"You know that expression, the best place to hide something is right under your nose?" he asked.

"Yes, what are you thinking?"

"Well obviously Gianelli wants to get me in the basement of the hospital, maybe to put me in one of those drawers next to Frankie D. Who knows? He definitely wants to know what I know, how I know it, and who else knows it. Which means that he's lying about you ever being safe whether I cooperate or not. You're with me and as far as he's concerned, that makes you a liability."

He paused, thinking it through and she said, "Thanks. You're making me feel real good about my future."

"I'm just assessing the situation as realistically as I can, Kel. Remember, I've known this guy a long time. On the other hand, he doesn't know that we know about the basement of the hospital. If I did, I'd be crazy to agree to meet him there. It would be way too risky for me."

"That makes sense, although I don't see how it helps."

"Well if the idea is to trap me in the basement of the hospital and leave me there forever, then maybe that would be the best place to hide in order to spring an ambush on them. Think about it. The last place they would expect me to be hiding would be in one of those rooms with Beyoncé by my side."

"You have completely lost your mind," Kelly said, peering at herself in the vanity mirror. "Do you really think I look like Beyoncé?"

"If she was a little prettier and a whole lot sexier, then yeah I think so. Am I making any sense?"

"I think we're both going to die tonight," she said very seriously.

He took out his cellphone and dialed Cheryl but it went to voicemail. "Too bad," he said. "I thought I'd bring the D.A.'s office up to speed in case no one ever sees us again."

She looked at him. "This is going to sound dumb but it kind of bothers me that you keep calling her. Are you sure you're over it?"

"I've been over it for a whole year Kelly, and it doesn't sound dumb. I don't usually make a habit of calling ex-girlfriends when I'm with another woman but we need her. The circumstances are a little unusual."

She sighed, "I guess."

They drove to the hospital and circled around the perimeter a couple of times, searching for anything unusual. They'd gotten into a vigilant rhythm of checking for surveillance vehicles. It was a good habit because the Porsche stuck out like a sore thumb but with a full tank of gas, he was confident no one was going to catch them if they needed to get away in a hurry. There were very few cars that could handle and accelerate like the 911.

The hospital parking lot was crowded with cars. Sunday afternoon was prime time for visiting the ill. He got lucky and parked close to the same spot as he had the night before. Then they noticed a familiar figure.

"Look," he said and they both watched Snell walk through the main entrance of the hospital. "I wonder what the pipsqueak is up to on a fine day like this."

"Why don't we go ask?" Kelly suggested.

"You know, that's not such a bad idea. I must say. I like your attitude."

"He sold me out and now he must die."

They both laughed and he said, "That's the spirit."

They got out and went to the back of the Porsche. He opened the trunk and took the shotgun out, inspecting it to make sure it was still loaded and the safety was on. The flashlight was still attached to the end. He put it in the duffel bag along with the duct tape and ground beef. He still had Ozzie's Glock which he also placed in the bag. Then he held the .357 magnum in his hand deciding whether to arm Kelly or not.

"Was last night the first time you ever used a handgun?" he asked her, indicating the revolver.

"Yes," she answered truthfully. "And I hope I never have to again."

"Me too."

He placed it in the duffel bag, and she said, "Are you sure you have enough guns?"

He replied seriously, "You can never have enough guns."

Chapter 39

They walked right through the main entrance of the hospital just moments after the CEO. They waved to the daytime security guard sitting at his desk, who nodded back. Thankfully he didn't try to engage them in the usual friendly banter. The main lobby was spacious and circular, tiled with black and white marble. There were potted plants and leather couches off to one side and flat screen TVs on the walls cycling endless advertisements promoting the hospital interspersed with a steady stream of images of Snell smiling at them.

"His office is down the main corridor and then off to the left," Cesari said.

"What if he's not in his office?"

He glanced at her, puzzled. "Where else would he be going?"

She shrugged. "I don't know."

"Well let's go find out."

They arrived at a solid oak door with a shiny brass placard that read *Theodore P. Snell, M.D. MBA, CEO & President, Genesee General Hospital*. Cesari opened the door to the waiting room and they entered. But no one was home. He scanned quickly for any sign that Elizabeth, Snell's secretary, was around but didn't see any. There was no coffee cup on her desk, no sweater around her chair and no open documents lying around. Her computer was turned off. He closed the door and locked it.

"Kelly, it might be better if you stayed out here in the waiting room while I talk to him."

"Sure, I'll just read a magazine while he fires you."

"That's a distinct possibility but let's not be negative."

He put the duffel bag down by her feet, opened it and took the .357 out. He placed it in his waistband and said, "How do I look?"

"How are you trying to look?"

"Scary."

"Maybe. Stop smiling for a second...much better."

He walked over to the inner door leading to Snell's office and quietly let himself in.

"Hi, Snell."

The CEO was staring at papers on his desk and practically jumped out of his skin with surprise when he saw Cesari. He said, "Hello, Cesari. What are you doing here?"

"We need to talk, Snell."

At first glance, Snell hadn't noticed the pistol tucked in Cesari's pants but his gaze soon picked it up and his eyes went wide. The color drained from him and he took on an even more pasty appearance than usual.

"What about?" he asked cautiously, not referencing the weapon.

"I thought maybe we could go over those colonoscopy statistics again. What do you think?"

"Look Cesari, there's no need to overreact."

"Me? Overreact? Wouldn't dream of it. By the way, I heard you were looking for me."

"I don't know what you heard. I was just doing some paperwork like I always do."

Cesari went over to the credenza and found what he needed, the bottle of thirty-year-old Macallan. "Want a snort with me, Snell? I would consider it friendly."

"Sure, that would be great. Whatever this is about, I'm sure we can work it out."

Cesari chuckled as he poured the scotch. "I wish I had your confidence."

Snell cleared his throat. "You probably know this already, but it's against the medical staff bylaws to bring firearms onto hospital property."

Cesari feigned surprise. "Is it really? I didn't know that. You'll have to bring it up at my next job performance review."

The CEO didn't say anything as Cesari placed the large glass filled to the top with scotch on the desk in front of him. He just stared at the crystal tumbler brimming with ten ounces of liquid gold.

A drop splashed over onto the fine wood of the desk and Cesari said, "I'm sorry Snell, but I didn't see any coasters."

Beginning to get nervous, the CEO said, "No problem... Aren't you going to have any?"

"Nah, I'm fine. It's a little early in the day for me."

He started to sit in one of the leather chairs opposite Snell, but made a big deal about the gun being in his way. So he took it out and held it in front of him with his right hand, casually pointing it in Snell's direction as he sat back.

He said, "There, that's much better. That was a little uncomfortable."

"Cesari, what is it you want? There's no reason for us to be enemies."

Sweat started to bead up on Snell's forehead. Cesari noticed and said, "Who said anything about us being enemies, Snell? Cheers."

Cesari raised his left hand, mimicking holding a glass. Snell stared at him and didn't raise his tumbler. Cesari raised the gun and pointed it directly at Snell's chest. He hissed, "Start drinking Snell, and don't stop until it's all gone. I want you nice and relaxed."

"I can't drink all of this. If I had the whole night I couldn't drink all of this."

"You can and you will."

Snell's hand trembled badly as he raised the glass to his lips. More drops spilled over the side as he took a first sip.

"More," Cesari ordered.

His eyes went wide, but he drank a little more. The little beads of sweat on his forehead were turning into large drops.

"More."

He put the glass down after about half. "I can't do it. I'll get sick."

Cesari stood up and aimed the weapon at his face. He got close enough so that Snell could see the round line up in the barrel when he cocked it.

"Be careful Snell. This kind of gun has a hair trigger."

Snell picked up the glass and downed the rest of the scotch in one long gulp.

"All right then, let's give that a minute or two to swish around," Cesari said and sat back down, crossing his legs and settling into the comfortable chair.

"What do you want, Cesari? What do you really want?"

Cesari could see that Snell was already reeling from the alcohol crossing his blood-brain barrier. Ten ounces of scotch in under five minutes would work really fast on almost anybody. In a shrimp like Snell, the effect would be almost instantaneous. In fact, he might have trouble keeping him awake.

"I want answers Snell, and you're going to give them to me."

Snell took a long, slow breath and then hiccupped loudly. "I don't know what you expect me to tell you."

"I expect you to tell me everything and keep in mind the image you have of Ozzie, all right? I know you saw him last night."

"Who are you, Cesari?"

"I'm just a wop from the Bronx. That's all."

Cesari glanced up at the painting of Napoleon on the wall behind Snell. He had never seen the real one in the Louvre but this seemed like a pretty good replica. Some people thought Napoleon was a great man but others thought he was a tyrant, a real megalomaniac. The only thing you could say for sure about him was that he was a little man with big dreams. It was funny that Snell identified with him. Maybe it wasn't that funny at all. Height challenged gnats like Snell were always causing misery for others because of their own insecurities.

The side wall displayed an impressive array of diplomas and awards. Harvard undergrad, Columbia School of Medicine, MBA from Dartmouth, the guy was no slouch. That was for sure. He'd won the New York State small hospital CEO of the year award for the last four years, and the hospital had won best hospital of its size for the last two years in a row. No small accomplishment. What a waste.

He looked back at Snell. His eyes were starting to glaze over, and he was having trouble focusing.

"Okay Snell, you ready?" he asked.

"Ready for what?" he slurred and hiccupped again.

"Tell me about the medical staff bylaws again."

"What are you talking about?" His tongue was thick and he was having trouble forming sentences.

"You said it's against the bylaws to bring firearms onto hospital property."

"That's right, it is."

"But it's okay to sell drugs and steal people's organs?"

"That's ridiculous."

"This is just water cooler stuff Snell, but people are starting to talk. You know what they're saying?"

"What?"

"That this is a hostile hospital."

Chapter 40

Gianelli and Pinky were in the basement of the hospital. They had found Tony unconscious but still alive, lying in a pool of his own blood. The dog was running wild and loose in the corridor, attacking anyone and everyone. She had charged them in a savage frenzy and Pinky had to use a stun gun to subdue her. If she hadn't gone down when she did, Gianelli had planned on shooting her.

"What happened here, Pinky?" Gianelli asked when he saw Tony's injuries.

"Not sure, boss. I know it sounds ridiculous but it seems like those Arabs got free and somehow managed to get the best of Tony."

"How could they get free? Have you seen those restraints? Even if they did, the two of them together weighed less than Tony. And what about the dog? You expect me to believe that she just stood around while they pistol-whipped Tony with his own gun? Man, look at that hole in his ankle and look at his skull. They went to town on him."

"Those Pakistani doctors were pretty high last night, Vito. Maybe they got sloppy and didn't restrain the Arabs properly. The Arabs might have been disoriented from all the drugs they'd been given and caught Tony by surprise."

Gianelli thought about that and let out a long, slow, frustrated breath. "I don't know if I like that explanation Pinky, although I guess anything's possible. But why? Why would they do that? Confused or not, you don't just attack a guy Tony's size, and for crying out loud, I thought we were all on the same side."

"Maybe they changed their minds about blowing themselves up."

"Well at least that makes sense, but these guys were handpicked. They were supposed to be the cream of the crop. Their handler assured me that they would jump at the opportunity to do something like this for Allah. It's a little hard to believe they would come all this way, have the bombs put in, and then back out at the last minute like this."

"Everything changes when the shooting starts, Vito."

Tony groaned and opened his eyes momentarily, and then closed them again. "Pinky, have Billy Ray Bob mop this place up and then drag that worthless mutt in here until I can figure out what to do with her. There's some rope and a muzzle in the trunk of the car. Have somebody secure her in case she wakes up wild. Who knows, maybe she got rabies? We'll come back later tonight to check on her. If she's not back to her old self by then, we'll put her down... And make sure to recharge that stun gun so it's ready for Cesari."

"Sure thing Vito, but what about Tony? He's lost a lot of blood and needs a doctor in a hurry. We could take him upstairs to the emergency room."

"Hell no, Pinky. Forget about him. We have bigger problems now. I got two Arabs running around this town loaded with plastic explosives. When Big Lou finds out we let them get away, Tony's going to seem like the lucky one. Just put him in one of those drawers in the morgue."

"But Vito, he's still breathing."

"So what?"

Chapter 41

Snell gazed at Cesari sleepily and groaned, "I need to lie down."

He rested his head on his desk in front of him and Cesari uncocked the revolver.

"Snell...?"

He lifted his head a little and watched Cesari through bleary eyes. "What now, Cesari?"

"You're in over your head, Snell. You're a mouse playing with lions. It's only a matter of time before Gianelli decides your services are no longer required and then you know what's going to happen?"

"What?"

"He's going to take you apart piece by piece and you know how I know this?"

Snell was managing to stay focused as he listened. "How?"

"Because I used to take guys apart with him. Guys like you... I don't like you, Snell. You're the worst kind of vermin there is. At least Gianelli's honest about who he is and what he does. But you...you're a parasite taking advantage of sick people, poor people and hard-working doctors and nurses. You're using this hospital like it's your personal piggy bank and I resent that. You should be ashamed of yourself. And your son's even worse. Last night he hurt Kelly. That was a big mistake. When you see him, tell him I'm coming for him too."

Snell looked at him long and hard before sniveling, "You're not going to kill me like you did Ozzie?"

"Hell no. I wouldn't waste the ammunition. It'll be a lot more fun seeing you go to prison or even better, watching what Gianelli's going to do to you."

"What can I do?"

"Nothing. It's time to get out of Dodge or turn yourself in to the police with a full confession. If I were you, I'd start thinking about going on a long vacation and I wouldn't tell Gianelli where."

Snell's head abruptly fell back down onto the desk and he started to snore. Cesari stood up and left him to find Kelly.

She glanced up from a magazine. "You were in there over an hour. That must have been quite the conversation."

He put the gun back in the duffel bag. "It was, that's for sure. C'mon, I'll fill you in while we walk. Let's go over to my office in the MOB. We need to kill a few hours anyway while we plan our strategy."

He glanced at his watch. It wasn't quite 2:30 p.m. His office was a short walk from the main hospital through a connecting passageway and they arrived five minutes later. He unlocked the door with his key and they entered. It was Sunday and the MOB was dark and deserted. He tossed the duffel bag down and sat behind his desk. Kelly took a chair opposite him looking around. She had never been in his office before.

"Did I ever tell you that you have great hair?" he said. He'd always loved women's hair but Kelly's especially. There was something about it. It was soft and wavy and long. The longer the better. He didn't know why he liked long hair on women. Conversely, he couldn't deal with men with long hair. Maybe it was wrong for him to feel this way but when he saw a guy with long hair, he just wanted to slap him. Cesari wasn't the most woke guy on the planet.

She grinned. "Pretty much every time you see me, but thanks again anyway. And you don't have to tell me about my eyes again. Not that I don't love hearing it."

"So I have mentioned that too?"

She laughed. "A couple of times, yeah."

She peeked around the office. "You could use some furnishings in here. You know, like a lamp. Maybe something for the walls. It's even worse here than your apartment. What's that on the wall behind you? The Constitution?"

He grinned. "Yes, and the other one is the Declaration of Independence. You're pretty funny, Kelly. We're about to die, and your last thoughts are about decorating my office?"

She found that amusing. "What should I be thinking about? What a stud you were in bed?"

"If you were unhappy with my performance, young lady, then maybe I should clean off my desk and we could try again."

"Is that all Italian men ever think about?"

"That's the most racist thing I've ever heard. If we're still alive tomorrow, I'm going to file charges against you for that."

"Bring it on. I would love the chance to tell my side of it."

"Besides, it's not all we think about. Sometimes we think about eating too."

She was having fun but decided it was time to get down to business. "Okay, enough with the games. I'm dying to know what happened with Snell. What did he say?"

He leaned back in his chair and swung his feet onto the edge of the desk, crossing them at the ankles. With hands clasped behind his head, he took a deep breath and said, "He said a lot so brace yourself... About two years ago, he incurred a huge gambling debt at one of the casinos in Atlantic City. The El Paradiso, I think it was. Apparently, he is a degenerate gambler and has been most of his life. But even better is that he was playing with the hospital's money. Nice guy, huh? Unfortunately for him, Big Lou Barazza owned the casino he picked to lose his shirt in. Our boy Vito Gianelli manages the place. When Snell couldn't pay up, they coerced him into going into business with them or else wind up with a third eye the size of a nine-millimeter bullet.

It started out with illegal prescription drugs, which are stored here and then eventually brought down to the casino for distribution. Soon it escalated to the harvesting of organs from homeless people, which they sold on the black market like we discussed. He confirmed my fears that no one ever leaves here alive. They duped the poor slobs by promising them easy wealth and a quick and safe journey back home. The minute they got these guys alone, they slammed them with narcotics to keep them quiet."

She scowled. "That's awful. I feel so bad for those people. What kind of person is Snell that he would agree to such a monstrous scheme? I don't care how much he was coerced. For God's sake, he runs a hospital. This is a place of healing. Plus, he's a doctor. Didn't he take the Hippocratic oath?"

"He may have taken some kind of oath, but not necessarily the Hippocratic oath and certainly not in its original form. Remember, it was written in the third century B.C. A lot has changed since then. It's mostly been abandoned in favor of more modern codes of ethics and relevant reiterations. It doesn't matter anyway because most medical school graduates today consider taking an oath an archaic ritual, something steeped in tradition but not necessarily to be taken seriously or verbatim."

"Well that's too bad. I think taking an oath is a good thing for certain types of professions. It sets the bar for expectations high and serves as a reference point for behavior."

"You're absolutely right and just for the record, I took a modernized version of the Hippocratic oath when I graduated. There was one particular line I really liked and pretty much sums it all up for me. It's straightforward, impossible to misconstrue and easy to remember. I'm paraphrasing but basically it says that as a physician you swear to always help the sick according to the best of your ability and judgment and never deliberately cause injury."

She said, "Above all else do no harm."

"Exactly. If every physician stuck to that simple rule the world would be a much better place."

"I agree. I guess Snell didn't take that particular oath."

"It wouldn't have mattered if he did because he's not a real doctor, Kelly. Don't kid yourself on that point. He only went to medical school to give himself enough street creds to become a hospital administrator. He has no loyalty to the ill. Snell's just another pencil-pushing, bean counting mercenary, the kind that have taken over almost every hospital in the country. Guys like him are breeding like rats."

"I don't get it. Just how do people like him get to be in positions of power like this?"

"Welcome to modern healthcare Kel, the kind of affordable care that we can't afford to have. As long as you agree to drink the Kool-Aid, you can do very well in this business. But if you raise your hand and disagree with the bureaucrats about what constitutes good healthcare, then you'd better have your parachute ready."

He paused to take a breath. "It's like this, Kelly. The ranks of the system are gradually filling with like-minded people. They dress alike, talk alike, and think alike. If you stand out, then you're an anomaly and anomalies don't last long. Guys like Snell do well because they say all the things that everyone wants to hear in this current political and social climate. And because he's a physician, his words carry weight."

"And what is it that everyone wants to hear?"

"I'm glad you asked. They want to hear that health care is a commodity, an exact science that can be regulated and legislated and therefore controlled. The bubbleheads that run this country have this vision that if you want a colonoscopy, then one day you'll look at a menu, much as you would when you enter a fast food restaurant. You can order it with a side of curly fries if you want. You agree to the price, get your colonoscopy, and go home. Nothing is more vexing to the bean counters than the elephant in the middle of their living room known as the doctor-patient relationship. All of healthcare begins and ends with this, and yet all this healthcare reform bullshit you've been hearing about has vehemently tried to pretend that it doesn't matter or even exist."

"And why is that?"

"It's because they can't quantify it and don't really understand it. All bureaucrats work on the principle that if you don't understand something and can't control it, then you must get rid of it. It makes their lives much too difficult otherwise. The practice of medicine is still ninety percent art and ten percent science, and this drives the bookkeeper types crazy.

Guys like Snell are doing their best to undermine the doctor-patient relationship so that the power resides in their hands and not the physicians. They've tried to make it so that the doctors are no different from the guys at the counter serving you the burger. This way they can control the price of your meal, the size of the portion you get and what condiments go on it. I hate them...all of them and the lawyers too. They're ruining the country."

He was red in the face by the time he was done. Kelly seemed depressed but abruptly started to giggle, then chuckle, and then laugh out loud. "So how do you really feel, Cesari?"

He settled down to a simmer and said, "I guess I got carried away. Sorry."

"No, don't be sorry. I think this is great, an ex-gangster scolding me about who's ruining the country. I wish I could have recorded it."

"So now you're laughing at me."

"Not at all. But if you ever become president, I would love for you to use that as your inauguration speech especially the part about how much you hate lawyers. That would be a riot as you address congress."

"You're making me angry."

"Too bad."

"In a minute I'm going to throw you on top of this desk and have my way with you."

"In a minute you'll be too late to do anything. Because in about five seconds, I'm going to throw *you* on top of this desk first. And by the time I'm done, you won't be in any shape to do anything to anybody."

They looked at each other for a moment and then started laughing. He said, "Man, you're my kind of woman."

Chapter 42

His cellphone went off. "Cesari here."

"Hello, Dr. Cesari. This is Gloria, the secretary in the emergency room. Dr. Morton would like to speak to you. Can you hold for a second?"

"Sure, Gloria."

He covered the receiver and said to Kelly, "It's the ER."

"Yeah hi, this is Dan Morton. Is that you, Cesari?"

"Hi, Dan. It's me. What's up?"

"We need a GI consult down here. I hope you're available."

He glanced at his watch. It was after three o'clock. "I'm not on call this weekend, Dan."

"I know, and I'm not trying to bother you. But the guy who covers you is such a pain in the ass to deal with. I figured it's early enough in the day, and if it's not too inconvenient, you might want in."

"I'm kind of tied up but go ahead, tell me what you got and I'll decide."

"Fair enough. Two unidentified males were brought in this morning with a narcotics over dosage. They responded to Narcan, but one of them is real sick. Temp of 102, white count's elevated, bad abdominal pain, bilious vomiting, the whole nine yards. We're not sure what's going on. The surgeon is here too."

"Can you tell me anything else about the guy? You know, age, past medical history? Is he on any medications?"

"Sorry, but we don't really know much except that he and his friend appear young, late teens, early twenties maybe. They were found in the medical staff lounge early this morning unresponsive and covered in their own vomit. They were wearing surgical scrubs like they were patients, but they didn't have any ID bracelets on them, and none of the wards are missing anybody. Both of these guys had some type of recent abdominal surgery. But it's a funny type of scar, one that I'd never seen before. I don't know what it means. Now here's the kicker. Are you ready?"

"I can't wait to hear, go ahead." he signaled Kelly and wrote on a piece of paper. *Those guys from last night are in the ER.*

She moved closer, interested and concerned.

"Okay, Cesari, get this. So we pump them full of Narcan, right? Now they're both awake. They both seem intelligent." He paused for effect.

"All right, Dan. No drama, please."

"You're going to love this." He paused again.

"Spit it out, already. I got things to do."

"Neither one of the guys will speak."

"What do you mean?"

"They just won't speak."

"Won't speak or won't speak to you?"

"Won't speak to anyone. Won't even try."

"Not even the sick guy?" Cesari asked, puzzled. Kelly had moved close enough now to share the cellphone.

"Especially the sick guy. He's clearly in agony and very weak. He'll groan and wince but won't form words, if you know what I mean. He won't even look me in the eye. They're both sort of on the dark and swarthy side. Half the ER thinks they're Arabs trying to go 9/11 on us all over again. We have an interpreter down here who speaks five different languages besides English.

She's tried French, Spanish, Farsi, Arabic, and Hindi, and they won't budge. She's Lebanese and swears they're Arabs."

"Well I have to say, this is interesting. What have you done for them so far?"

"We've got them both plugged in with large-bore IVs and oxygen. The sick guy's getting broad-spectrum antibiotics and has a nasogastric tube. They're both getting abdominal CAT scans as we speak and should be back soon. So what do you think, Cesari?"

"I think I'll be there in fifteen minutes."

"Thanks, I knew I could count on you."

He put his phone away. "Feel like walking down to the ER with me?" he asked Kelly.

"Sure, but what happened? I caught most of it but not all."

"Those guys from last night found their way into the medical staff lounge and passed out. The Narcan I gave them must have worn off. One of them is very sick with a fever and abdominal pain. Neither one of them will speak a word, not even to an interpreter. They want a GI consult to help sort things out."

"Thank God they weren't trying to cross the highway or something when they passed out," Kelly said. "But I don't understand. They were speaking fine last night. Why won't they speak today?"

"Your guess is as good as mine. They could simply be disoriented and scared. After all, they had a rough night and one of them it seems, is about to have an even rougher day. Are you sure you don't mind coming with me?"

She stood up and made sure the duffel bag was zipped tight. "I'll come. What else have I got to do? While we're on the subject, what did Snell have to say about those guys?"

"Ah, yes. I got distracted by my inauguration speech. I asked about them and he said he didn't know for sure. But he did say they were definitely Arabs and they weren't the only ones. Three others just like them came through last week for the same operation. What kind of operation he didn't know but it had nothing to do with organ donation. If it did, then he would have had to be involved. He's the one who has access to the transplant waiting list, and only he can authorize the appropriate testing necessary to determine a tissue match. Furthermore, he's the one who actually does all the electronic bookkeeping while Gianelli watches over his shoulder."

"Looks over his shoulder? Why is that?"

"Another layer of security for Gianelli I guess, in case this thing ever blew up in his face. He never touches anything and his name isn't on anything. The money eventually gets rerouted from the Cayman Islands to a Swiss bank. On paper, Snell is hanging out there all by himself. You gotta love Gianelli. It's almost like he was never here."

"Isn't he worried Snell might try to cheat him?"

He smiled. "That's always a risk, but I doubt Snell has the gumption for that. Gianelli probably figured the same thing."

"So if those guys aren't organ donors, what are they?"

"Good question. Snell doesn't know and doesn't want to. Apparently Gianelli was very closed-mouthed about them. Snell thought that maybe they were mules. You know, humans who smuggle drugs. But rather than the usual body cavity stuff, he thinks the drugs were implanted surgically."

Kelly thought about that. "That would be different, but then wherever your destination was, you would have to find a surgeon and have them removed. Kind of rough on the mule. And then there's the question of why you would go that route in the first place."

"Yeah, it doesn't make sense. C'mon, let's go to the ER. Those guys should be back from their CAT scans by now and then we will know all as they say."

"What are we going to do about Snell?"

"I don't know yet. We may have to do nothing. Minions for the mob like Snell generally don't have long life expectancies when things go sideways like they are right now. I mentioned that to Snell already and gave him some unsolicited advice, but I'll think about it some more after we resolve this situation with Gianelli. Speaking of whom, Snell told me that counting Billy Ray Bob, there are only five guys left to deal with."

"Only five? Hardly seems worth getting out of bed for," Kelly said jokingly.

"That's the way I see it."

"Are you sure you can believe him?"

"I think I do. Maybe I'm wrong, but I can't believe Gianelli had the foresight to bring too many guys with him up here. He had no way of knowing things were going to unravel and he's not exactly what you would call visionary. Besides, it would've attracted way too much attention if he'd brought a brigade of oversized guineas wearing silk suits with him. No, I think Snell got the number right."

"Five guys it is then. No sweat."

"Easy peasy."

Chapter 43

"What do you want, Vito? I'm on my way to church," Big Lou Barazza growled into the phone.

"Sorry for bothering you Lou," said Gianelli, "but we've got a situation up here in Genesee."

"What kind of a situation?"

After Gianelli brought him up to speed, Big Lou exhaled loudly into the phone. "Cesari? That kid from the Bronx? I thought he was gone, as in forever?"

"That's him, resurrected from the dead," Gianelli said.

"Isn't he the one that was driving the car when you had that bad accident?"

"Yup and now he's back for round 2 apparently."

"Well I'll be. Who would have thought it? John Cesari... Frankie D.'s pal from way back when. Where's he been?"

"Not sure but right now he's masquerading as a doctor."

"Unbelievable... All right, so where do we stand, Vito? The drugs are safe, right? What about the Arabs? Weren't they in the same truck?"

"The situation's contained and the drugs are secure. They'll be delivered to the casino on schedule. Cesari agreed to a sit-down tonight and then we'll know more about who he's working for and what his game is. But we've taken a couple of hits, Lou. We lost two guys this weekend. One was a cop named Ozzie who helped Billy Ray Bob with the deliveries. Cesari got to him. And Tony got taken out permanently in a separate incident."

"Cesari went after a cop? Is he nuts? And that's too bad about Tony. He was a good kid. What happened to him?"

"It's not clear, Lou. We think those Pakistani doctors were so trashed when they came to work last night that they failed to restrain the Arabs properly after they planted the bombs in them. My best guess is that the Arabs woke up confused and caught Tony by surprise, not realizing he was on their side. There's also the possibility that maybe the Arabs had a change of heart about becoming martyrs. They shot Tony with his own gun. We're searching for them as we speak."

"You mean they're gone? You can't be serious, Vito?" Lou said. "Tell me you're not serious."

"I'm serious, Lou."

Big Lou was becoming apoplectic as he ascended the steps to his church. "The Arabs shot Tony and are now running around loose up there? Is that what you're telling me? You better not be telling me that."

"That's what I'm telling you, Lou."

"I don't believe this. How incompetent can everyone be up there? And you got to tell me this just as I'm stepping into church?"

"I'm sorry, Lou. It couldn't be helped. I thought you'd want to know."

Lou took a seat in one of the back pews barking loudly into the phone. "You better fix this Vito, and you better fix it fast and I don't give a shit how you do it... Jesus Christ, did you hear that? You got me using profanity in church. I haven't done that since the ninth grade. That could be a mortal sin."

"I'm sorry Lou, but don't worry. Maybe you can receive communion twice or something while you're there?"

"Twice? Can you do that?"

"It's worth a shot."

"Enough with that. We need to get something straight, Vito. I bought and paid for those Arabs. I own them. They're my property and I want them back."

"I hear you Lou and don't worry. I'm sure we'll find them. I mean where can they go, for crying out loud. But if worse comes to worst, we still have the two bombers from last week. They're sitting in a hotel in Manhattan waiting for their marching orders. That's more than enough C4 to take out the entire courtroom and everyone in it, including that D.A., McClellan. He's going to get the surprise of his life when they show up at opening arguments. It will be like the fourth of July all over again. I promise," Gianelli reassured his boss.

"You better be right about that. It's a good thing we had the presence of mind to have a backup team of bombers. But I thought there were three bombers last week."

"There *were* three bombers last week Lou, but we only paid for two of them, remember? The Sheik wanted one for some side project he has going on."

"Yeah, I remember now... Look, I'm relieved we have a plan B, but we can't have loose ends like this. It's too risky. Suppose they get picked up by law enforcement. Who knows how much they know? I don't need another headache. You better find those guys in a hurry, Vito. Time is not my friend. That damn D.A. hates me and he's like a dog with a bone. With him around, I feel like I have a blowtorch up my ass. My source on the inside tells me that he's planning to ask the grand jury for my indictment as soon as this terrorist trial is over. The plan is to throw cuffs on me and then deny me bail on the grounds that I'm a flight risk. Once that happens, I'm toast. I'll never see the light of day again. If we can nail him there at the trial, it would be perfect. The Arabs will take all the blame and with McClellan gone, they'll forget about me."

"It's in the bag Lou, one way or the other."

"Is Frankie D. still on ice up there? A lot of people are asking uncomfortable questions about that. Half the New York families already suspect me. They're just waiting for a body to show up to start pointing fingers. The old guineas don't like it when one of their own gets it."

"He's still in the fridge, Lou. Once things settle down, I'll carve him up into little pieces and get rid of him. No one will ever know. It was an honest mistake. Somebody's been squealing to McClellan. I thought it was Frankie D., too."

"I know but we can't afford another mistake like that, Vito. Hey, I got to go. Mass is about to start and everybody's giving me dirty looks. Keep me posted and no more screw-ups. And one more thing..." He paused while he thought it over. "I hate to do this, but I think we ought to shut down operations up there. Things have gotten way too messy. I got other hospitals that aren't giving me nearly this much aggravation."

"When you say shut down operations, Lou..."

"Snell and his son, Vito. Make it happen."

"Understood."

Chapter 44

"**O**h my God, it's like a three-ring circus down here," Kelly commented as they walked into the ER and immediately noticed a crowd of people outside one of the patient rooms.

"Well, let's go find out what's going on. Don't let that duffel bag out of your sight, all right?"

She nodded. "Maybe I should take the shotgun out and fire a round at the ceiling just to get everyone's attention."

Cesari chuckled. "Pretty soon you'll be whacking people just for taking your parking space."

As they approached the group, the ER physician spotted them. "Thanks for coming, Cesari. Things are heating up down here. I know you're relatively new in town, so let me introduce you to everyone real quick." He turned to the group. "Everyone, this is Dr. John Cesari, our new gastroenterologist. Everyone say 'hi'."

Two surgeons, an anesthesiologist, a security guard, several nurses, a respiratory therapist, the interpreter, a social worker and a psychiatrist all said hello back at once.

Cesari nodded. "Hi everyone. Thanks, Dan. I've already met most of the people here before."

Alex, the senior of the two surgeons, was in the center of the action. He was tall and solid, an avid cyclist in his mid-fifties. He had spent four years in the army after college while he tried to find himself and he looked like he'd never left the service. He was the kind of guy you wanted on your side. He had been engaged in conversation with the psychiatrist when they arrived. He turned now to Cesari and stuck out his hand.

"Always a pleasure to see you Cesari," he said. "I doubt this guy needs your services as much as mine, but it's such a peculiar situation that I thought I would pick your brain if you don't mind."

"Not at all, Alex. Anything I can do to help, although I'm glad I don't have white coat syndrome. You think you've got enough people down here? By the way everyone, this is my endoscopy nurse, Kelly."

Kelly smiled politely and made a little wave with her free hand.

Alex said, "Hi Kelly, nice to meet you."

She nodded. "It's mutual."

Alex turned back to Cesari, "Yeah, I know what you mean about the white coats but things are little complicated."

"Bring me up to speed," Cesari said. "I got the basics from Dan, but what's your take?"

"I think they're mules. I don't know where they're from and I'm not sure that it matters. What matters is that one of them is quite ill. He might be obstructed or have peritonitis. He's pretty sick but not quite surgically sick yet, if you know what I mean, but he's very close. We just got the preliminary read on their CAT scans, and they both have foreign bodies in their abdominal cavities."

As they spoke, the crowd surrounded them to listen in. "What kind of foreign bodies?" Cesari asked, very interested.

"That's just it. The radiologist said he didn't know what they were. They have the density of soft tissue. They're oblong in shape about eight by six, and maybe two inches thick. It's got to be some type of drug, but what I don't know. Whoever put it in them didn't exactly care about being too neat, either. The wound's a mess. It's almost as if the guy who did it was drunk. If I ever saw one of my surgeons do something like that, I would have boxed his ears right there in the OR in front of everybody." Alex was old-school like that.

"So what's the problem? Take him to the OR and cut it out. Then we won't have to play guessing games."

He laughed. "You think like I do Cesari, but that makes you a dinosaur like me. You can't just do stuff like that anymore. You need something called informed consent. You ever heard of that?"

"And he won't sign consent?"

"He won't do anything. He won't talk to anyone, not even our interpreter. He won't even make eye contact. He just lies there and won't acknowledge that anyone else is in the room with him. Jazlyn tried talking to him in five different languages, including Arabic and Farsi."

A very attractive woman in her late twenties stepped forward. She had big beautiful, almond-shaped eyes with long dark lashes. She said, "That's right and I'd bet everything that those two speak Arabic. I'm Lebanese and they look like half of my family. It's my opinion, they simply don't want to talk. I also tried signing with them and got nowhere." She put her hand out. "Jazlyn Hadid, official interpreter for the hospital."

He took it. "John Cesari."

"Okay Cesari, enough with the guinea charm," said Alex. "Jazlyn is happily married, so keep your eyes in your head."

Jazlyn smiled and turned eight shades of scarlet. Cesari didn't think he'd acted inappropriately in any way and was about to defend himself but Kelly stepped in before he could respond. She said, "And I'm Kelly, his nurse."

Jazlyn and Kelly shook hands and Jazlyn politely stepped back into the crowd. Cesari turned to Alex. "All right, so he won't speak. What's that mean?"

"Cesari, I thought you were smart. It means that I can't take him up to the OR and cut him open," Alex said. "If he won't speak or acknowledge that he understands me through an interpreter, then legally he can't sign a consent form."

A little guy wearing a brown pullover sweater chimed in. "I'm Morty Stein, psychiatrist at large, at your service. I was about to go in there and assess this guy's competency. But so far, it sounds mostly like he's got a case of bad attitude."

"Okay, so what are our options?" Cesari asked.

Alex folded his arms. "Well, we're not quite there yet, but if it looks like he's going to die without surgery, then he'll need to sign an AMA form. You know, 'against medical advice.' Trouble is, if he can't sign a consent saying that he understands why he needs surgery, then for the same reason he can't sign an AMA form saying he understands that he'll die without surgery. Get it? That's where Morty comes in. If he declares the guy incompetent, then I can drag his ass upstairs and save his life whether he likes it or not."

"Okay, I got it. So you want me to take a look at the guy and render a second opinion as to the necessity and urgency of surgery in case the shit hits the fan. In other words, the more names on the chart, the more people there are to share the fallout."

Alex smiled. "Hallelujah. There is a God."

A new voice joined in from behind them. "And the quicker you get this guy out of here, the better. We don't need any more uninsured Mexicans dying in our ER. The press is still having a field day over the last one."

They all turned and saw a pasty looking, bald guy of about forty with horn-rimmed glasses and close-set eyes, wearing a two-piece navy suit. He carried a binder with him and had an air of authority. He wasn't wearing any ID.

"And just who are you?" Alex barked, signaling his alpha male status to the newcomer. "And why should I give a rat's ass about anything you say?"

Alex was definitely old-school and kind of fun to watch in action.

"I'm Seymour Schuster, the hospital attorney, and I think you should be getting the OR ready. I'd like this guy out of here as soon as possible. He can die anywhere he wants just as long as it's not in the ER. I'll even help you wheel him upstairs if you want."

Alex scowled darkly and Cesari was glad that he wasn't the lawyer. Had he been holding a scalpel, Alex surely would have stabbed Schuster in the heart, or possibly the neck. Tough call on that one.

Alex said drolly, "Would you excuse me a minute, Mr. Shyster? I need to finish up with Dr. Cesari and then you and I can talk about what is the best way to manage my patient."

"Sure, no problem. I'll wait here. And the name is Schuster not Shyster. No worries though, a lot of people get it wrong."

"Right. I'll remember that."

Alex put his arm around Cesari, and turning their backs on the attorney, they stepped away. He lowered his voice. "Look, Cesari. This kid needs surgery. You know it and I know it. I'm not going to let a twenty-year-old die just because he made a poor decision in whatever damn country he came from. It's also obvious that no matter what happens, some bureaucrat from the state is going to do a thorough and unpleasant examination of my anus."

Cesari nodded. "I understand. You want me to write a note supporting your decision to take him to the OR. Don't worry. I'll give you carte-blanche to do whatever you need to do."

"I appreciate it. Hopefully, the state will only cut off one of my testicles for doing the right thing."

"Don't worry, Alex. I got your back. I'll spit-shine the chart good. As far as I'm concerned, this guy needed surgery the minute he woke up this morning and should have been in the OR hours ago. I don't see how anyone could have handled these difficult and challenging circumstances any better than you. After they read my note, they're going to give you a medal."

"Thanks, Cesari. Now let me go deal with Mr. Shyster."

"I thought he said his name was Schuster."

"Right."

Chapter 45

By the time they left the ER, it was almost 6:00 p.m.

"Sorry it took so long, Kel."

"It's okay. While you were writing your note, I made myself comfortable in the lounge and had a cup of coffee. There was a football game on. It was kind of fun, even though I'm not much of a sports fan. The Giants were playing Dallas."

"Oh yeah? How were the Giants doing? That's my team."

"I think they were doing okay. Somebody hit a homerun or something as I was leaving. Everyone was cheering. It was very exciting."

He stopped and checked her face to see if she was serious. She was. He said, "Well let's go down to the basement and start scouting around. I'm supposed to meet them at ten. I doubt they'll show up much before nine."

"How can you be sure?"

"Why would they? How much preparation would they need? There are five of them and one of me, so I doubt they'll be overly concerned about their safety."

They walked out of the ER and down the same stairs they'd used the night before. The corridor beyond the pharmacy was just as dark. They retraced their steps until finally reaching the double doors. It was a lot easier and much less stressful the second time around.

He reached out and felt the handles. "The crowbar is still in place, so I don't think anyone from the hospital has been down here yet. You know, like maintenance."

"Do you notice anything?" Kelly asked, lowering her voice.

"Like what?"

"There's no light filtering from under the door or through the space between them. When we left last night, the lights in the hallway were still on."

"I see what you mean. So somebody turned off the lights in there. Which means Gianelli found that guy you shot, so he must also know the two Arabs are gone."

"It also means he could be in there waiting for us right now."

"That's a very good point." He paused, thinking about that and said, "You're pretty smart."

"Thanks."

"Maybe smarter than me."

She smiled. "Thanks again."

"I'm not sure I like girls who are smarter than me."

"Have you ever met one that wasn't?"

He laughed quietly. "Touché. Okay, let's think this through from Gianelli's mindset. He finds his guy and the dog but he doesn't know what happened. Would he think that I'm somehow involved? That's a possibility but whatever happened last night centered around those Arabs and what possible reason would I have to get involved with that? Then there's the room with millions of dollars of narcotics. It wouldn't make sense for me to come here, shoot the place up and then leave all the drugs behind. From his perspective, that wouldn't make sense at all. To him everything is about profit. So my guess is Gianelli probably thinks he now has two separate and unrelated problems on his hands. Despite what happened to his guy, he most likely doesn't think that I had anything to do with it or even that I know about the basement, so what would be the point of setting up a trap for me in there?"

Kelly digested his logic and said, "Makes sense, sort of. Unless he's an overly suspicious guy."

"Which he is but I doubt that a guy like him would sit around in the dark waiting for me to show up through the back door unless he was absolutely certain I was coming that way. It's not his style. Besides, he believes he's got me over a barrel because of his threat against you. He has very rightly come to the conclusion that I don't want to see you get hurt, so I think he's fully expecting me to behave."

"I don't want to see you get hurt either."

"And I appreciate that... Well, we can't stand here all night."

As he reached to pull the crowbar out from the handles, Kelly put her hand on his arm. "What about the dog?"

"Miss Gloom and Doom tonight, aren't you?"

"I'm just trying to stay alive."

"We just reasoned that Gianelli most likely doesn't believe I would be coming from this direction, right? So he and his men most likely are not in there and certainly wouldn't be this early anyway. And if they're not in there, then why would they leave the dog there by herself?"

"I don't know. I'm not a gangster."

He put his ear as close to the door as possible and listened intently for a minute. "I don't hear anything, Kel. I think it'll be okay."

He slid the crowbar out from the handles, and they entered the shadowy corridor for the second time. They both wore sneakers, which allowed them to move quietly along the tiled floor.

Kelly asked, "Okay, so what now?"

"I don't know yet. I need to scout around and hopefully get some sort of inspiration."

After placing the duffel bag on the floor, he reached in and took out the shotgun with the flashlight attached. He turned the light on and scanned the corridor. It was clear of enemy combatants, so he suggested, "Let's check the rooms again to see if we missed anything the first time around."

Kelly bent over to pick the duffel bag up and stopped. She reached in and came out with the package of meat he had bought at Walmart.

"Hey, you never told me what this ground beef was for. Are we planning on giving them E. coli?"

"It had crossed my mind to make little meatballs and stuff them with oxycodone and then scatter them on the floor for the dog to find in case they brought her back."

"I like that idea. She goes to sleep and we don't have to shoot her."

He raised his eyebrows. "I don't shoot animals, Kelly."

"Only people?"

"Only people that act like animals."

Chapter 46

"**I** want to check that room first," he whispered, nodding in the direction of last night's slugfest. "I'm kind of curious about the guy we left in the bathroom."

"You don't think he's still in there, do you?"

"I doubt it, but I don't know what to think anymore."

"Do you think he died?" she asked nervously. "Am I a murderer?"

"No, you're not a murderer. He was a young, physically fit guy. He may have survived. But if he didn't, then it was self-defense. Besides, I'm the only witness and I didn't see anything."

"Is that what they taught you in the mafia?"

"No, that's just common sense and I wasn't in the mafia. Not really. I was just a maladjusted street punk with anger management issues."

Cesari walked up to the door and turned the knob quietly. Using the tip of the shotgun, he gently pushed the door inward and looked around quickly. He then stepped in with Kelly close behind. Someone had been mopping up again. He smelled bleach.

Not much had changed since last night, except for the two-hundred-and-fifty-plus-pound dog named Cleopatra lying on its side in the center of the room. She was mostly black with occasional patches of brown. She watched us but didn't bother trying to move because she was muzzled and hogtied tightly with rope. Last night she had appeared to be ferocious but now her eyes were sad.

Cesari flipped on the overhead lights and put the shotgun down.

"Oh my," Kelly said. "What have we here?"

"I don't know what happened, but apparently Cleo and Gianelli had a bit of a falling out."

The dog let out a little whine and stretched her neck to get a better look at them. They were a solid ten feet from her and approached slowly, hands down by their sides, trying hard to be non-threatening. They stopped about three feet away and studied the situation. All four of her limbs were bound clumsily but securely. Judging from her expression, she was in a lot of pain. Even the muzzle seemed to have been tightened excessively and she was having some difficulty breathing.

Kelly said, "Damn. These friends of yours are real jerks, aren't they?"

"I agree, except they're not my friends. This is no way to treat man's best friend."

Cleo cried a little more and Cesari said, "I don't know about you Kel, but I think I'm ready to forgive her for trying to kill us last night."

Kelly nodded. "It was clearly a misunderstanding." She stepped closer to Cleo. "Do you think she knows we feel sorry for her?"

"I'm not sure, but probably. Animals are very intuitive about things like that. Especially dogs."

"What are we going to do?"

"Well she can't hurt us tied up like that... What the hell. Let's try something." He walked right up to the dog, knelt down behind her and gave her a long, slow gentle stroke down the length of her body. "Hi, Cleo. I see you've had a rough day."

He spoke very softly to her, letting her know he meant no harm. Kelly knelt beside him and gave Cleo a tummy rub causing her to stretch and whine even more. She turned her enormous head toward Kelly like she wanted to thank her. Apparently she was also ready to let bygones be bygones.

They massaged her and caressed her for a few minutes, gradually working their way up to her ears and head. They both took turns talking to her as soothingly as possible trying to get the message across that they were her friends. She responded with contented sighs and an occasional whimper to encourage more petting. She let Cesari hold her head, which he thought was a good sign. They were almost ready to take a chance.

In his best baby voice, he asked, "If Daddy sets you free, will you promise not to eat him and his friend? That's a good girl."

Kelly started laughing. "You're killing me, Cesari."

"Well what do you think? I don't know about you, but I can't leave her like this."

"I agree. She seems so sweet and sad right now. I can't imagine what happened that they did this to her."

"Animals generally respond to acts of kindness, so let's give her some food and water and see what happens. Would you mind getting a basin from the OR room for her water and I'll start untying her legs."

She said, "I'll be right back."

Kelly left the room and Cesari went over to the duffel bag to retrieve the ground beef and the .357 magnum. He was hoping for the best but saw no point in taking chances, so he put the gun in his waistband.

Kneeling by Cleo, he cooed, "Okay girl, let's see what we have here." They were simple knots and easily undone. He left the muzzle on her for the moment. She wiggled her legs and tried to stand but wobbled and flopped down.

Kelly returned and watched the scene for a few seconds as Cleo staggered to her feet a second time but collapsed down again. She then walked behind Cesari to the bathroom and filled the basin with water. She commented from inside, "Someone cleaned up in here pretty good. Is she going to be okay?"

"I think so. They tied her so tightly they cut off her circulation, but she'll be fine. She just needs a minute or two like you or I would."

They had used a single length of rope to tie her, so Cesari looped it through her collar and made a leash out of it. While he was doing that, she picked up one of her giant front paws and gently stroked him with it. Then she leaned forward with her head and tried to lick him through the muzzle.

Kelly put the water down next to Cleo, which immediately got her attention. She struggled to her feet but still wasn't quite ready and again fell down. Cesari opened the package of beef and set it down near the water.

"I'm sorry they did this to you, girl," he said. "Kelly, go over to the door and get ready to bolt. If she gets wild after I take the muzzle off, we'll need to make a hasty exit. Her legs are like jelly right now, but you never know."

Kelly went to the door and grabbed the shotgun and duffel bag. She positioned herself halfway in and halfway out of the room. "I'm ready."

He looked into Cleo's eyes. "Okay, girl. Be good."

Then he unfastened the leather muzzle and quickly stepped away toward Kelly. Cleo shook her head and wiped her face with her massive paws. Then she sneezed loudly and looked bewildered by it.

Cesari couldn't help himself and laughed.

Chapter 47

"What kind of dog is she? I've never seen one so big," Kelly asked as they watched Cleo wolf down the ground beef. She was hungry and very thirsty.

"She's an English Mastiff, one of the largest breeds in the world. I've seen them on nature shows. The males can be up to three feet high at the shoulder and weigh more than two-hundred-and-fifty pounds, but she's easily bigger than that. God only knows what they fed her as a pup."

"I don't get it. Right now she's so sweet, and yet last night it seemed like she was possessed. Her head is so big. She looks like a lion."

"Yeah, she does. From what I've read and heard, they're usually quite docile and friendly. Apparently, despite their ferocious appearance, they're great family dogs. The only thing I can think of is that she's been trained as an attack dog, but now that the guy who usually gives her orders isn't around, she's no different from any other big, friendly dog."

Cleo finished her meal and came over to them wagging her tail. Her head was higher than Cesari's waist. Kelly instinctively stepped back from the massive beast, and he didn't blame her. Cleo nuzzled into him and then, without warning, stood up on her hind legs and braced her front paws on his shoulders. Her weight and the surprise of the act caused him to step backwards until he was pinned against the wall.

Kelly laughed. "Oh my God. It looks like you're dancing."

He stood there face to face with her. She was actually a teeny bit taller than him. He joked, "I know what you're getting at Cleo, but interspecies dating never works."

"I don't think she agrees." Kelly thought this was a riot.

Cleo started licking his face affectionately, and he stroked her head with both hands until she eventually let him go.

"Okay," he said. "Let's leave her here for now. She'll be fine, but we on the other hand, still have to come up with a strategy."

When they left the room, Cleo cried.

Chapter 48

"Any luck, Pinky?" asked Gianelli.

"No, Vito. Sorry. Me and Sal even broke into Cesari's apartment to make sure he wasn't hiding under the bed. Same thing at the girl's place. No luck. We've swept the public parks and shelters for the Arabs, and they're nowhere in sight. Billy Ray Bob checked at the police station, and no one's heard anything. There aren't any mosques in this town either. I do have one piece of good news, though."

"And what's that?"

"Billy Ray Bob approached his detective friend Pepper about helping us, and the guy was agreeable to the idea. Seems he'd like to own a Porsche too."

"That is good news. We could use a little diversity on team Gianelli. Okay, it's almost seven. Let's regroup and talk about things over dinner. When we're done, we'll head over to the hospital to set up for Cesari."

Chapter 49

"Oh my God. I can't believe it. We murdered him. I murdered him."

They had found the guy from last night lying on the floor of the morgue near the wall of drawers. He was blue, unresponsive and clearly dead, stiff from rigor mortis and the near freezing temperature of the room.

"You didn't murder anyone, Kel. You shot him in the ankle. I'm the one who banged his head on the floor. Besides, he was trying to kill us, remember?"

He walked over to the corpse to inspect it. One of the morgue drawers near the body had dried blood on it. He opened it and saw more blood smeared on the sides.

He studied the guy carefully. "Neither one of us murdered him. He's got rope burns on his neck."

"Rope burns? Why?"

"I think he was still alive when they found him and they decided it would be too risky to get him medical attention, so they put him out of his misery. By appearances, they strangled him and tried to put him in one of these drawers but he was too big, so they just left him here."

"That's awful. How can you be sure that's what happened?"

"Because it's what I would have done."

"That's a terrible thing to say and I don't believe it."

"It is what it is, Kelly. He's dead."

"Don't you feel guilty?"

"Guilty? About what? Trying to stay alive? Not me." He thought about it a little and softened up. "That was a little harsh. I guess I wouldn't have strangled him."

"Thanks for that."

"You're welcome, but I still think stuffing him into one of these drawers was a pretty good idea. Okay, I'm getting a thought. They have all these bodies in here, right? They think they've got the upper hand too. As I mentioned earlier, my gut tells me they have no clue that I know about the basement. Therefore they most likely will not associate what happened down here with me."

"I would agree with that, but how does that help?"

"It gives us the element of surprise, that's how."

"I'm all ears, but can you speed it up a little? It's freezing in here." She was hugging herself.

"Well, they left the dog tied up there for some reason. I'm thinking this guy here was her handler. He was probably the main guy in her life, or at least the one she responded to the best. When he went down, they probably found they couldn't control her. However they left her alive, which means they haven't given up on her, and probably planned to return at some point to see how she's doing, or maybe to introduce me to her."

"How do you think they were able to tie her up like that? I'm sure she didn't volunteer."

"They probably either drugged her or tasered her. Yeah, I bet they tasered her. tasers and stun guns are very common these days, especially with law enforcement. Billy Ray Bob has one, I'm sure. I know Ozzie did because I used it on him yesterday. In any event, it's not that hard to get hold of one."

"You tasered Ozzie?"

"Technically, no. I used his stun gun. It's the same principle though, only with a stun gun you have to press it against the person. A taser has prongs attached to wires so you can shoot from a distance and disable your target without having to get too close."

"You're a regular fountain of dangerous information, aren't you?"

"If you want to run with the big dogs Kel, you have to learn how to bark."

"What the heck is that supposed to mean?"

"I don't know. I just made it up."

She made a face.

"All right," he continued. "If you killed a guy and hid his body somewhere, then you would be pretty surprised if it unexpectedly turned up somewhere else, right?"

She thought about his perverse logic. "Yeah, sure. That makes sense. You'd be very surprised, shocked even."

"Now if I found a body out of place like that, I would also naturally be curious as to what happened. So I think I would want to check the original hiding place. I think that's pretty sound reasoning so far. Are you still with me?"

"Unfortunately, yes. Please go on. Is this some sort of Bronx thing, knowing how to hide bodies and where to look for them?"

"It wasn't part of my formal education, but it was definitely part of my after-school training."

"I'm worried about the way you think. Is there a chance you'll outgrow this one day?"

"Not if I can help it and why would I? Some of the things I've learned have a habit of coming in handy at just the right times... Anyway, I'm thinking that if we relocate this guy's body, we might have a chance at luring one or two of the other men back into the morgue in a preset trap. It could reduce some of their numerical advantage, like at the Battle of Thermopylae."

She laughed and corrected him, "That's not what happened at Thermopylae. A few hundred Spartans were able to hold off thousands of Persians because of their geographical advantage. The Persians were funneled into a bottleneck, and the Greeks only had to face a small number at a time. It has nothing to do with what's going on here."

He looked at her. "Are you sure about that?"

"Very. Where did you go to school? And remind me not to let our kids go there."

Silence...

Followed by embarrassment...

He said, "Our kids? That was sort of a breach of first date protocol. Don't you think?"

"It's a figure of speech. Don't read into it."

"Then why are you blushing?"

"It's warm in here."

"Warm? It's freezing in here."

"Can we move on? So they see the dead guy's somewhere he's not supposed to be, and then they come back here out of curiosity. Then what? None of these rooms have any locks on them."

He walked over to inspect the inside of the morgue door. It was made of steel and had a latch-type handle on the inside as well as on the outside. From the inside, you lifted the handle and then pushed open the door.

"You're right. There's no lock but if we removed the handle, you would be unable to open the door. Plus, if we killed the lights, they'd really be up a creek without a paddle."

"Then maybe we should find a breaker box."

Chapter 50

A round 8:00 p.m., Gianelli and his men sat down at a corner table in a small Italian restaurant in downtown Genesee. It was the kind of place where people minded their own business. It was Sunday night in a small city, and the restaurant was nearly empty. The waiter took one look at the group and realized he'd better give them plenty of space.

Gianelli asked, "How's your linguini, Pinky?"

"Not bad, Vito. Not as good as Paulie's, though." The placed reeked from the overuse of garlic in every dish.

"You're right about that. When it comes to food, Paulie's a genius."

Three empty bottles of Barolo already sat on the table, and Gianelli signaled the waiter for a fourth. Gianelli wiped some clam sauce off the corner of his mouth. He addressed the table, "Okay, so does everybody understand what their role is?"

Everyone nodded or grunted their assent. Everyone but Billy Ray Bob that is, who looked like he was going to be sick as he sat there staring at his uneaten grilled veal chop with rosemary. It sat on top of a bed of creamy saffron infused risotto with porcini mushrooms.

Gianelli commented, "You going to eat that or just gawk at it all night, Billy Ray Bob? It looks delicious."

"I'm not that hungry."

"You know it's a sin to waste food, right? There are people who are starving." The inflection in Gianelli's voice caused everyone to stop eating. Everyone but Billy Ray Bob that is, who took the hint and dug in.

Gianelli turned back to the group, which had resumed dining. "One more time, just so there's no confusion. Pinky and I are going to Snell's office to discuss operational issues. We'll catch up with you guys when we're done. Sal, Mike, and Billy Ray Bob will set up at the rear of the hospital and wait for Cesari. When you get there, check on the dog. If she gives you any problems, put her in the freezer with Tony. And don't take any chances with Cesari, either. The minute he shows up, you hit him with Billy Ray Bob's stun gun and restrain him in one of those beds. I would like to interrogate him, but if he gives you any trouble, then he goes in the freezer too. Everybody understand? All right Billy Ray Bob, give me your cellphone and your piece. You won't be needing them tonight, and they might get in the way."

Billy Ray Bob slid his cellphone over the table to Gianelli and then did something unheard of in the annals of law enforcement. He voluntarily surrendered his service weapon to a civilian.

Chapter 51

Inside the operating room to the right of the doors, they found the breaker box. It had five labeled breakers, one for the lights in the main corridor, which they flipped off and one for each of the rooms. Then they went back to the morgue.

"Okay Kelly, you stay out here and I'll try to get the handle off with the crowbar. If things go well, I shouldn't be able to open the door, so I'll tap on it for you to let me out."

"I won't go anywhere, but I might leave you in there for a while to cool off," she said, smiling.

"Now that's an interesting thought."

"Why is that?"

"I don't remember seeing a thermostat in there. Do you?"

"No, but I wasn't looking for one."

"I'll be back in a minute."

He shut the door behind him and flipped on the long overhead fluorescent lights. The room with its white walls, slate-gray floor and central drain, had a strange antiseptic feel to it. He searched the walls but didn't find a thermostat. That meant the temperature of the room was controlled elsewhere. Good. It felt very cold and he guessed it was barely above freezing in there.

He went back to the door and studied the latch handle again. Sliding the crowbar underneath it and through to the other side, he braced himself and heaved backwards. The handle snapped off so easily that he almost fell onto the floor. Damn, he thought. They sink all this money into building this place and they cut corners on the door.

He felt around the sharp edges where the handle had snapped off. There didn't seem to be any way of working the mechanism now. He tried for a few minutes to open the door by putting his finger and even the crowbar into the space left by the dislodged handle and couldn't. Satisfied, he rapped on the door with the crowbar.

Kelly opened it. "How'd it go?"

"Good. I hope they brought winter clothing. Let's get the dog."

Chapter 52

Gianelli and Pinky let themselves into Snell's office and found him looking a little disheveled as he concentrated hard on the laptop in front of him. He looked up, surprised at the sight of the two large men. "Hello. I thought you were going to call me when Cesari got here."

"Change of plans, Snell. You know how that is. Say hello to Pinky, Snell."

"Hello, Mr. Pinky."

Pinky didn't say anything as he sat down in one of the large leather chairs.

Gianelli walked over to the liquor cabinet. "How about a scotch everyone?"

Snell said, "I'm good but help yourself."

Gianelli held up the nearly empty bottle of Macallan. "Damn, Snell, this bottle was almost full yesterday. No wonder you look like hell. You ought to think about AA."

He poured the remainder of the scotch into a glass tumbler and took a seat next to Pinky. Pulling a pack of Camels from his pocket, he shook one out, struck a match and lit it up. He took a long, slow drag and blew smoke in the direction of the CEO.

"Mind if I smoke, Snell?"

"Not at all," the CEO coughed.

"Are you okay, Snell? You look like you're going to be sick." Gianelli noted that the small man was sweating and a little pale.

"I ate something this afternoon that disagreed with me. I just need to splash some cold water on my face. Excuse me a minute." He discreetly closed his laptop, got up from his chair and disappeared into the private bathroom behind his desk.

"Who would have thought it?" Gianelli said to Pinky. "The guy's got a weak stomach."

"Did you see the way he slammed the laptop shut, Vito?"

"Yeah, I saw. He was probably watching porn. Go take a peek."

Pinky stood up and opened the laptop. He suppressed a laugh. "Even better, Vito. You've got to see this."

He turned the screen for Gianelli to view. They both grinned and Pinky replaced the laptop to its original position.

"Too funny, Pinky. You can't make this stuff up. He thinks he's going to Bermuda tomorrow morning."

"Too funny, Vito."

Gianelli glanced at his watch. He finished his scotch and snuffed out his cigarette on the leather arm of the chair before donning a pair of black leather gloves. "C'mon, Pinky. It's getting late and Cesari will be here soon. It's time to wrap things up."

He reached into his pocket and took out the plastic bag containing Cesari's Smith & Wesson .38 special that Billy Ray Bob had given him. He slid the gun out, put his cigarette butt in the baggie, and put the bag back in his pocket. He then concealed his hands below the surface of the desk so that Snell wouldn't see the weapon from the bathroom door.

Chapter 53

Cleopatra walked with them playfully from the recovery room over to the room with the prescription drugs. She was very happy to have company and they were startled by just how affectionate she really was.

"Are you going to be okay alone in here with her, Kel? She easily weighs more than twice as much as you."

"I think so. The biggest problem I have right now is that every time she nudges me to pet her, she practically knocks me over. I simply can't imagine her trying to hurt me."

"Okay then let me finish up, and I'll be right back. Keep the door closed. I don't want her to see what I'm doing. I'm not sure how she'll react."

He untied the rope he had used for a leash and crossed the hall to the morgue, propping the door open with the crowbar. The big guy was lying on his back with his feet toward him. He tied his ankles together with the rope and dragged him to the door. He was a big load. Grunting and sweating, Cesari slowly hauled him through the door and down the dark hallway back to the recovery room. By the time he got there, he was panting and drenched with perspiration.

He paused in front of the door with his hands on his knees, trying to catch his breath. A minute later, he pulled him into the middle of the room and hogtied him in much the same fashion they'd found Cleo but with his wrists behind his back and pulling his ankles up to meet them. It was difficult because the body was so stiff, but he eventually got the job done to his satisfaction. Then he put the muzzle tightly on his dead face and fastened it. That should get their attention, he thought. Talk about firing a shot across their bow. He left the light on and the door open a sliver to focus their attention immediately on that room when they arrived.

When he was done, he returned to Kelly. "Everything's all set up. Now let's hope they go for the bait."

"What if they don't come for Cleo?" Kelly asked.

"That's a possibility but then why tie her up? Why not just shoot her or whatever? No, I think they'll come for her. I can feel it. She's a valuable weapon for them if they can control her."

He opened the door a crack and could see the outline of the morgue door directly across the hall from him. The light shining through the recovery room doorway shone like a beacon in the blackness of the corridor. His cellphone vibrated in his pocket.

It was a text message from Alex, the surgeon. *We're taking this guy up to the OR for a laparotomy. He finally broke down, signed consent and is speaking to Jazlyn now. Thanks for your help.*

He powered the phone off just as he heard a car pull into the parking lot outside.

Let the games begin.

Chapter 54

Cesari stood by the door listening to the muffled voices coming from the loading dock. One, two, possibly three voices. They were doing something out there, but what? He thought he heard the scraping of a chair and then the sound of feet on cement. Then silence.

Kelly had seated herself on the floor in the center of the room just in front of the boxes of oxycodone. Cleo was lying down next to her with her gigantic head in Kelly's lap so she could stroke it. He heard a key unlock the door leading in from outside and held his breath as the door opened. He hoped that he would only have to deal with one guy at a time, and that the others would wait in the parking lot as planned. He got lucky. A lone man entered, fumbled for the light switch and flipped it several times unsuccessfully, swearing under his breath.

Cesari held the crowbar tightly. The man would surely see the light coming from the recovery room and head straight there. Wouldn't he? If he did anything but what Cesari had planned, he would have to act decisively to neutralize him. He had a bunch of weapons at his disposal and could always shoot the guy, but that would alert the others. No, this was crowbar territory. It was his favorite weapon anyway.

The guy's shadow passed by on the other side of the hallway as he made a beeline for the light source. So far so good. The breaker trick had worked. Cesari smiled. It was human nature. He walked right past two doors that he could easily have opened and turned on lights, but instead he took the path that had sparked his curiosity.

Reaching the room where Cleo had been tied up, he opened it more fully, flooding the hallway with its light. He cursed loudly from the doorway when he saw his bound colleague. He hesitated and then went into the room, shutting the door behind him. It took a minute or two for him to think about the situation, and then the light from under the door went out as it dawned on him that he might not be alone down there.

At this point, he must have been deciding what to do. He could call for help, but then he would seem weak to his friends, hiding in the recovery room like a little girl. After all, it's not like anyone had attacked him. If he started searching the rooms one by one, Cesari could wait for him to enter his and crush him with the crowbar. If the guy caved and called for backup, he would have to start shooting. He had the .357 in his waistband, the shotgun on the floor next to him and Ozzie's Glock in the duffel bag. He had plenty of firepower but not knowing how many more there were placed him at a significant disadvantage. Then there was the issue of collateral damage. He glanced over at Kelly. It was very dark but he could see she was hugging Cleo. A shootout would be very bad, he thought and resolved only to fire if fired upon.

"What's happening?" Kelly whispered, sensing his apprehension.

"Shh," he cautioned, praying the guy would head straight for the morgue like he had planned.

Moments later, they heard the door to the recovery room open stealthily. Unfortunately for the guy, he was wearing dress shoes and although he tried his best to be quiet, he could only do so much. This told Cesari he wasn't the brightest bulb in the box because if he were, he would have taken his shoes off.

Cesari made out his shadow hugging the opposite wall as he crept back toward the morgue. He could practically read his mind. If his dead friend had been dragged from the morgue and trussed up in the recovery room, then maybe the dog was in the morgue. His curiosity having gotten the better of him, he inched his way along to find out. Eventually he was close enough that Cesari could see his large shadowy silhouette moving slowly, his right hand out in front undoubtedly holding a pistol.

He reached the morgue door and hesitated and Cesari's heart skipped a beat. What the hell was he thinking? Probably what the downside would be of going back outside and telling his friends that he was too scared to search the rest of the rooms alone. Not a great admission for someone in his business. Gianelli might consider that grounds for termination. He made up his mind. Being labeled a coward in his world was the same as committing suicide, so he crouched and ever so gently pulled back on the handle.

Cesari could barely hear the click of the latch. The guy opened the door a crack and paused, waiting to see what would happen. He wasn't that stupid. He opened the door slightly more, ready to slam it shut if something or somebody came rushing at him.

While he was doing that, Cesari gradually opened his own door half an inch at a time. He kept his eyes on the man's outline at all times. He refused to even blink. The guy had opened the morgue door enough so that he could start to sneak in. Rather than risk turning on the light, he chose to stay in the dark which was smart. He probably assumed that if someone was waiting for him in there, that person might be armed. Better for him not to turn the light on and give him a target. Tough profession.

Cesari stepped out from his room and crept silently across the hallway, crowbar at the ready. The guy was three quarters of the way into the room, and Cesari still had half the width of the corridor to go. His heart was pounding so hard by now he could feel it pulsating into his neck. Another step or two...

The guy had nearly disappeared into the room, and the door was slowly closing behind him. His left hand clung onto the doorjamb for balance. Cesari took a running start, leapt up and kicked the door shut as hard as he could with his right foot. Three of the guy's fingers tumbled to the floor by Cesari's feet, severed by the door as it slammed shut.

There was a muted scream and curse, but the thick metal door provided enough insulation that he barely heard him. Cesari waited as the guy banged on the door futilely from within. Then a popping sound and another muffled scream. He must have shot his gun at the door and the round ricocheted off the steel, possibly hitting him. Okay, Cesari thought, he's not going anywhere.

Cesari then ran to the operating room and quickly found the breaker box. He flipped the switch to the morgue room off. Better to leave the guy in the dark. Nighty night, moron. He returned to Kelly and found her and Cleo in the same position.

"How did it go?" she asked nervously. "You're still alive, so that's good."

He was panting and it took a minute for him to recover. He gave her a thumbs up. "He's locked in the freezer. One down, four to go."

"Only one? Too bad."

"I'm doing the best I can. How's Cleo holding up? Did I make too much noise?"

"No, not really. It just sounded like a door closing forcefully and Cleo did great. She looked up when she heard the sound but I kept petting her and she forgot all about it. She's insatiable for affection."

He checked his watch. "It's almost ten. They're expecting me to arrive any minute. If I don't show, we're back to square one. If this guy doesn't return soon with or without the dog, they're bound to come in here looking for him. I'd say the die is cast unless you want to abort and leave through the other side. We could try making a new life for ourselves somewhere else. I hear Tibet is quite beautiful."

"Not a chance. My people have been running for three hundred years. It's not going to happen tonight."

She stood up and threw her arms around him. She was trembling from head to toe.

He said, "Roger that. Okay boss, we stay and fight. You take the pistol and stay here with Cleo. Hold it with two hands when you fire. Be prepared. You fired it once, so you know how hard it kicks. The other handgun is in the duffel bag if you need it. I'll go out there now. They'll be expecting their friend, so I'll have the element of surprise on my side. Here's my cellphone. If I'm not back in fifteen minutes, assume something bad happened, get out of here and call for help."

"You had better come back, Cesari."

He picked up the shotgun, made sure the safety was off and jammed extra shells into his pockets. He kissed Kelly and headed for the door leading outside. Clutching the pistol grip of the Mossberg with one hand, he took a deep breath and let it out slowly as he reached for the door handle with the other. It was ten o'clock.

And he liked to be punctual.

Chapter 55

"**D**amn Pinky, what a mess."

They stood over Snell's body slumped back in his chair. Pinky said, "That's what happens when you use hollow points, Vito. Cesari needs to be more careful. He shouldn't keep a gun like that lying around fully loaded. Someone could get hurt."

Gianelli had pressed Cesari's weapon up against Snell's right temple when he fired. The round had made a relatively small entrance hole but had left one the size of a half-dollar when it exited the other side, splattering a good amount of gray matter and bone fragments on the painting of Napoleon.

Gianelli considered the bloodstained image of the long-deceased emperor. "What do you think about this guy, Napoleon Bonaparte, Pinky?"

"I don't know too much about stuff like that, Vito. He was king of France or something like that, right?"

"No, he was emperor of France right after the French Revolution. He was a little guy who came from nothing and clawed his way to the top of the food chain. He's one of France's greatest leaders and one of western civilization's greatest generals. And hardly anyone knows the dirty little secret in his closet."

"What's that, Vito?"

"That although he was technically French, he was really Italian."

"What's that supposed to mean?"

"It means he was born on the island of Corsica in 1769, right? Well the island of Corsica belonged to Italy but became officially part of France that same year and just like that, everything and everyone on that island suddenly became French. Before that, everyone there thought they were Italian. His parents didn't get the memo that they were now French, so they named the guy Napoleone Buonaparte, which of course is Italian. Later, he changed it to Napoleon Bonaparte to sound more French. I guess the French kids picked on him in school or something. Ain't that a pisser? It's still quite a sore point with some of the more hardcore types in France. I looked all this shit up last year when Snell got the painting."

"Can I ask you something, Vito?"

"Sure. Go ahead."

"Who gives a shit?"

Gianelli shook his head. "Where's your ethnic pride, Pinky?"

"It's going be in solitary confinement, if we don't get out of here."

"All right, already. Let's clean up. It's almost ten. Cesari should be arriving soon."

He placed Cesari's gun in the dead man's right hand and positioned his index finger within the trigger guard. "See you on the other side, Snell."

They spent a minute to wipe down the room for fingerprints, and as they were leaving, Gianelli stopped at the wall full of Snell's diplomas and awards. He said, "He was a pretty smart guy, Pinky."

"Yeah, he was a real genius."

Chapter 56

Cesari opened the door to the rear of the hospital and was surprised by the sight of Billy Ray Bob about ten feet away, gagged and bound to a wood chair. Momentarily confused, he hesitated trying to understand what that meant. Was this supposed to be bait for him? Billy Ray Bob heard the sound of the door opening and turned toward Cesari. He was a sorry sight for sure with two black eyes and a splinted nose. He looked scared. Cesari was tempted to go over there and kick his ass again for what he'd done to Kelly and was about to do just that but for a new development. A huge guy was hustling toward him from the direction of the parking lot and closing in fast. He was massive, six-feet, six-inches tall and three-hundred-pounds easy and was waving a large handgun in the air, shouting for Cesari to get on the ground.

At just over thirty yards away, the big man finally saw the shotgun Cesari was holding. It was loaded with buckshot and at that range would definitely do some serious damage, but might not necessarily disable or kill the guy on the first shot. The man stopped, aimed his weapon and ordered Cesari to drop the gun. Cesari was at a disadvantage. When he'd come out to the loading dock and saw Billy Ray Bob, the Mossberg was pointing downward in his right hand. His left hand was still on the door which was mostly open, and from the direction he was coming, the guy had a full view of him. Even worse was that Cesari now stood directly beneath one of the overhead lights of the loading dock. It revealed his position clearly and left the man more or less in shadows.

Cesari calculated his situation. If he was really quick and the guy was a really bad shot, he could get off one maybe two rounds safely. If he surrendered, he would be beaten mercilessly, possibly to death and they would have Kelly. He crossed surrender off the list of acceptable options.

His brain ordered the Mossberg into firing position and he felt like he was moving in slow motion as he swung the shotgun upwards. The guy saw it and fired a shot, which took a chunk out of the cement wall next to him. He was about to return fire when a massive explosion rocked the ground beneath his feet.

The second-story windows of the hospital overlooking their position blew straight out, raining glass, metal and human body parts. A bloodied human head hit Gianelli's guy squarely in the chest like a cannon ball, bowling him off his feet and flat on his back. Multiple secondary explosions followed the initial blast and a massive wall of flames erupted from the building above them. The concussive force of the explosion knocked Billy Ray Bob's chair over and he screamed in terror. The heat wave was intense.

Cesari hit the ground rolling and came to a lying down position. He quickly brought the shotgun around and got ready to fire, but when the guy saw the mayhem that had erupted around him, he realized that he was out of his league and bolted for his car. He was running so fast that he almost forgot to drop the head that he had instinctively caught. Cesari watched as he got into a black Cadillac and drove off, tires squealing, almost crashing into another Caddie on the way out. The second Caddie spun around and followed him.

Billy Ray Bob lay on the floor gazing at Cesari helplessly, no doubt wondering what new unpleasantness was about to come his way. Flames and smoke billowed out of the operating room windows above and the temperature on the loading dock was rapidly becoming unbearable.

When she heard the explosion, Kelly had come out from hiding with Cleo docilely by her side. She stood next to him holding the duffel bag with all the weapons. Both she and the dog looked alarmed. Cleo let out a deep-throated growl at the sight of Billy Ray Bob.

"I guess those two have met before," Cesari said.

Kelly nodded, "She's obviously a good judge of character. So what's going on?" She stared up at the disaster taking place above them. "Oh my God, that's OR number 2."

The hospital's emergency alarm system wailed, and sirens screamed in the distance. Soon the hospital would begin a general evacuation of all patients until the threat was contained. All physicians and nurses would be called in to help out.

He said, "We need to move quickly, Kel. We can't be found standing around holding shotguns and a lion-sized dog when the police show up. I'm sure they're only minutes away."

Cesari noticed that Billy Ray Bob was trying to communicate, so he went over to him and pulled the gag from his mouth.

"Please don't leave me here," he pleaded. "I had nothing to do with any of this. You can see I'm as much a victim here as you. They were going to kill me. They told me so. As soon as they had you, they were going to kill me."

Kelly sneered, "We should leave you here on principle. That's what you deserve. I'd love to hear what you would say to your friends when they found you. It would be quite the story in tomorrow's paper, wouldn't it?"

He looked to Cesari for support. "You don't understand. There's a lot more going on here than you know. A lot more, and I can help you. I know everything."

Cesari shook my head. "Your dad told me everything already."

"Not everything. He doesn't know who the Arabs are but I do. I heard Gianelli talking about them to Barazza."

"He's lying. I say we leave him here," Kelly said emphatically and Cleo seemed to agree as she continued to snarl at him.

"Is that your car out there?" Cesari asked, staring at a Buick LaCrosse in the parking lot. It was the only car there.

"Yes, it is. The keys are in my pocket," he said, trying to be as helpful as he could.

Kelly got in Cesari's face. "You're not thinking of letting him go free, are you?"

"No, he's not going free but I sure as heck would like to know exactly what's been going on here and who those Arabs are. We don't have time to play twenty questions right now. Look." He pointed toward the main road leading up to the hospital. Multiple emergency vehicles with their lights flashing were rushing in their direction.

He untied Billy Ray Bob, shoved the gag back in his mouth, and marched him over to the car with the shotgun pressed against the small of his back. He took the keys from Billy Ray Bob's pocket, unlocked the trunk and ordered him to get in.

Glaring at him sternly, Cesari said, "One word out of you and I'll feed you to the dog. Understand?"

He nodded from inside the trunk as Cesari slammed the lid closed, and after he helped Cleo get into the back seat, he walked around to the driver's side. Lying on the pavement next to his door was his friend Alex's bloodied head. Cesari took a deep breath, and gently moved it out of the way with his foot.

As they exited the parking lot, multiple fire engines, police cars, and emergency vehicles swarmed up the entrance to the hospital.

Chapter 57

Kelly and Cesari drove down to the lake, which was deserted at that hour. They needed time to organize their thoughts, so he parked on the beach facing the water almost in the same spot where he had questioned Ozzie. The night air was cool but comfortable.

"Let's take a walk with Cleo while we think this thing through," he said.

"We don't have a leash."

"I'll use my belt."

He looped his belt through her collar and they walked along the beach with Cleo trotting along amiably beside them. She showed not even the slightest inclination to leave their side as they contemplated the extraordinary events that were swirling around them and sucking them in ever deeper.

Kelly asked, "What do you think happened to him?" She nodded in the direction of Billy Ray Bob, who was still in the trunk. "Why was he tied to the chair like that?"

"I'm not sure but I have no doubt that he outlived his usefulness to Gianelli. I doubt he would have volunteered for that. It's possible they put him there on the loading dock either to serve as a distraction for me or to lure me in. Maybe they figured that for your sake I'd lose my head when I saw him because of what he did to you and they would've been right, except things happened too fast. I'll ask him about that later. He's got a lot of explaining to do."

"And what about that explosion?"

"Your guess is as good as mine. Probably a gas line. There's a lot of flammable substances that are used in operating rooms. Hell of a coincidence though to happen tonight. Poor Alex... and whoever else was up there with him."

"It's just awful."

"It is. It's going to throw the town into shock."

She nodded in agreement. "What's going to happen to that guy you left in the morgue? Will he freeze to death in there?"

"I don't know but they say that freezing's not such a bad way to die. You just drift off to sleep. No pain, no anxiety. He's kind of lucky when you think about it that way."

"That's terrible. This is not a joke. He's a human being. Don't you feel sorry for him?"

"I'm not joking and no, I don't feel sorry for him or anyone else who would hurt the innocent for profit."

"You can't be judge and jury, Cesari."

"Sure I can and I don't mean to be insensitive, but if he wasn't trying to kill me, he would be doing just fine right now... Look Kelly, I don't take pleasure in what I did to that guy but I reserve my sympathy for people like Alex and the nurses who died with him in that OR tonight just doing their everyday jobs trying to help someone who was sick. They're real heroes, and you know why?"

"Why?"

"Because even if you had told them ahead of time there was going to be some risk going into that OR, but that it was the only way to help their patient, I'd bet every last cent that they would have gone in there anyway."

She thought it over and said quietly, "I agree... I'm just not used to any of this."

"How could you be? How could anyone be?"

"You seem to be very comfortable with it all."

"Believe me I'm not. In fact, I'm very uncomfortable with all of it but I learned a long time ago that bad people simply don't speak the same language as the rest of us. And there's another thing at play here, Kelly. Unlike Snell, I took that oath and I took it seriously. They weren't just words on a piece of paper for me. My oath was the symbol of the new man I had become. It was my way of promising my mother I would never turn my back on the values she taught me ever again. When I said the words above all else do no harm, I didn't just mean them passively. I meant them proactively as in above all else do not allow harm to come. Physicians have a special place in society. We are respected and looked up to by almost everyone. With that honor comes great responsibility to advise, to treat, to comfort and to protect not just the sick but anyone in need especially the weak and the most vulnerable in our society."

Kelly looked at him for what seemed like a long time and then said, "I think I'm starting to like you, Cesari."

He made a face at her. "Just starting?"

She smiled but didn't say anything. She was exhausted and fading fast. He said, "Kelly, I want you to go home and get some rest while I talk to Billy Ray Bob, man-to-man. I need answers to a lot of questions, and it would be better if you weren't involved. It would make you uncomfortable and possibly an accessory."

"I'm not going anywhere. I'll sleep in the car if I have to."

"Why would you want to do that? The one bit of good news here is that it's probably safe for you to return to your apartment now. I don't think you'll have to worry about anyone else hunting for you tonight. Ozzie's dead and Gianelli is probably on the thruway driving as fast as he can back to New York with his tail between his legs."

"I'm not leaving your side, Cesari."

"I can't do what I have to do with you watching. It would make me... self-conscious."

"You're kidding, right? You have performance anxiety?"

He laughed. "All right, you can come along, but you can't watch. You have to stay in the car."

"Fine. What about Gianelli? Long term, I mean."

"Unfortunately, guys like him have very long memories."

"Great. So we're okay for tonight, but we're going to be sleeping with one eye open for a long time."

"I'm sorry but that about sums it up. I wish I could sugarcoat it. We crossed some very wicked people, and both sides have lived to tell the tale. But let's take it one step at a time, because there's no point in dwelling on the negatives."

"Are we going to be running for the rest of our lives, Cesari?" she persisted.

How do you answer a question like that? He said, "Running is good, Kel. It means you're still breathing. And don't think of it as running so much as getting to see the rest of the country."

Chapter 58

Gianelli rode shotgun while Pinky drove the Cadillac. He was fuming. His army had dwindled down to just two men, Pinky and Mike. Mike had almost crashed into him and Pinky head-on as he fled the hospital following the explosion. Mike was in the back seat now, plucking bits of glass and metal from his face and various other areas of his body. Gianelli had seen the explosion but couldn't imagine what had happened. Of course, with two Arabs running around with four pounds of C4 in each of their abdomens, anything was possible. But what would they have been doing on the second floor of the hospital? He was getting another headache and began massaging his temple.

He turned back to face Mike. He said, "Let's go over it again, Mike. You and Sal tied up Billy Ray Bob. Then Sal went in to get the dog and you went to the car to wait, but Sal never came back out of the hospital. You called him on his cellphone but he didn't answer. As you were going in to see what happened, Cesari came out of the basement with a shotgun and that's when the explosion occurred?"

"That's what happened, Vito."

"You sure about that?"

"I'm sure, Vito."

"This is one hell of a major screw-up Pinky," Gianelli said. "Including Ozzie we've lost three guys now, the Arabs are missing, Cesari's still on the loose and by tomorrow morning this place is going to be headline news. Big Lou is not going to take this well. This wasn't his vision for how things were supposed to take place."

"And Billy Ray Bob may still be alive," Pinky added.

"What about that, Mike?" asked Gianelli. "Is Billy Ray Bob still alive?"

Mike said from the back seat, "I don't know. I was going to pop him the minute I had Cesari, but the blast changed everything. I can't be sure if anybody on the loading dock survived."

Vito sighed, "That's not good enough. Not good enough at all. He's one of the few guys who knows everything."

Mike said, "I'm sorry, Vito."

"It's okay, Mike. I saw the whole thing. You had no choice. If he's alive, we'll catch up with him later. Maybe Cesari will take care of him for us...but we don't even know if *he* made it."

Gianelli brooded for a minute and Pinky said, "What are you thinking, Vito?"

"Turn the car around, Pinky. We're going back. We've got to know for sure if those guys are still alive or not and if they are, we've got to finish this. The more I think about it, the worse it gets. Mike just said Cesari came out of the basement holding a shotgun."

"So?"

Pinky had been driving the big car eastbound on the New York State Thruway at around eighty-five miles an hour. He acknowledged the command by making a sudden U-turn, barely slowing down over the grass divider, and swinging onto the westbound side of the highway heading back to Genesee.

"Don't you get it, Pinky?" Gianelli continued. "Cesari must have known about the basement all along. That means he's the one who probably shot Tony. He might even have the Arabs. He's been playing us since day one... This has been a hostile takeover, Pinky."

"It doesn't get more hostile than this, Vito."

Gianelli pulled out Billy Ray Bob's cellphone and dialed 911.

"I want to report a gunshot," he said when the dispatcher answered the phone.

The dispatcher asked, "What is your name sir, and where are you?"

"The gun shot came from Mr. Snell's office on the first floor of the Genesee General Hospital. I saw a doctor leaving the office. It was Dr. John Cesari. I want to remain anonymous. I'm an employee at the hospital and I don't want to lose my job."

He hung up and threw the phone out the window. Seconds later, a tractor-trailer pulverized it. If he couldn't find Cesari himself, maybe the police could help flush him out.

He said, "Let's think this through, Pinky. One, Cesari died in the blast. Two, he lived through it. If he lived through it, he might have been injured seriously enough to require urgent care, but if he's found on the loading dock with Billy Ray Bob, he'll be implicated when they find the narcotics and all the bodies in the morgue. So if he was strong enough to even crawl away, he would do so and there'd be no way he would seek medical attention even if he was wounded. Does that make sense so far?"

"It does, Vito. And the girl Kelly is a nurse, right? So she could take care of him at home. She could swipe pain-killers, antibiotics and other stuff from the hospital if she had to."

Vito nodded. "Let's start with Cesari's apartment and we'll work our way over to the girl's place. What was the name of Billy Ray Bob's detective friend again, the one he thought might be a player?"

Pinky thought for a second. "Culpepper, I think."

"Yeah, that's it. His name is Dave Culpepper. Goes by Pepper. If he wants in, I'll have him swing by the emergency room to see if Cesari showed up in an ambulance or a body bag."

Chapter 59

Kelly was napping in the car with Cleo when Cesari smacked Billy Ray Bob in the side of the head with the flat side of the shovel. He toppled backwards into the shallow grave. They were behind Billy Ray Bob's barn.

Cesari glared at him. "That was for my friend Alex."

Billy Ray Bob glanced up at him, dazed. "That wasn't my fault. It was Gianelli who brought the Arabs here, not me."

Cesari raised the shovel again. He said, "I swear to God. If you don't start accepting some responsibility for what's been going on, I'm going to cut your head off with a butter knife."

"No, please," he pleaded. "I didn't know anything about it until tonight. I thought they were just mules smuggling drugs for Gianelli."

Cesari smashed the shovel into his leg and he screamed. Cesari said, "That was for Kelly, you son-of-a-bitch."

He paused and leaned against the shovel to catch his breath. Beating a guy like that was hard work. After a minute, he reached into his windbreaker and produced the DVD marked *Kelly*. "Recognize this? I found it in your basement."

Billy Ray Bob gaped at it, his eyes wide with fear and comprehension. He knew what he did. He said, "That was Pepper's idea. He's the one who's into that bondage shit. I only went along for the ride."

"Yeah, I bet." Cesari put the DVD back into his pocket and hit him again with the shovel adding, "And that's for all the aggravation you've caused me this weekend."

Watching him carefully in the moonlight, Cesari sat down on an old wooden bench and leaned back against the barn. He had made Billy Ray Bob dig up Ozzie's grave so he could take a look at the body. He now lay next to his dead friend in the damp muck, panting, covered in dirt, and totally exhausted. As far as Cesari was concerned, Billy Ray Bob was already dead.

Cesari had been curious to see if there were any bullet holes in Ozzie but there weren't. Billy Ray Bob had insisted that Ozzie was already dead when they found him, but Cesari didn't buy it. He inspected the body but didn't find any signs of violence other than the wounds he had inflicted on him. Still, they could have smothered him. Maybe it was a matter of pride, but Cesari didn't like being accused of a murder he didn't commit.

Billy Ray Bob dragged himself to a sitting position. He was cagily eyeing the shotgun lying on the ground near the edge of the grave.

Cesari saw him and said, "Don't do anything stupid Billy Ray Bob. I'm already angry enough to last me two life times."

Billy Ray Bob didn't say anything or do anything stupid.

Cesari went on, "Let's go through this again, and don't leave anything out unless you want to be lying next to your friend permanently, okay?"

It was always a good idea to hear the story twice to see if there were any changes. Billy Ray Bob nodded his head. He'd had enough and decided to bail out with or without a parachute.

He let out a deep breath and said, "I overheard Gianelli talking to Big Lou Barazza. They were talking about the Arabs that escaped. He said they were suicide bombers. Gianelli had arranged to have the bombs surgically placed in their abdomens by the Pakistani surgeons who've been harvesting the organs for us." He took a deep breath and rubbed the side of his face where the shovel had hit him. "There were three guys last week and two this week."

"And where are they supposed to explode?"

"I'm not sure. He said something about a courthouse and a terrorist trial that's supposed to start later this week. But I didn't know what he was talking about. All I know is that Barazza was really upset. That's all I know. I mean it."

Cesari stood up and raised the shovel. "You left something out."

"What? What did I leave out? Please... What? Tell me what. How am I supposed to remember anything if you keep hitting me in the head?"

"I'm running out of patience Billy Ray Bob. For the last time, who are they targeting?"

"Don't... Please don't hit me... I remember now. It's some district attorney named McClellan. I don't know anything else. I swear."

Cesari was taken aback by that and lowered the shovel. "A district attorney named, McClellan?"

"Yes, McClellan. In Manhattan."

"You're sure?"

"As sure as I can be."

Cesari thought he sounded truthful for a change. "All right Billy Ray Bob, I believe you but that's quite a story. Did you really think you were going to get away with this?"

"C'mon Cesari, I heard them talking about you. You were one of them once. You know what these guys are like. Once you're in, you're in all the way. There's no way out with them, and it's not like you're allowed an opinion. You get your call, you're told what to do and that's that. If you don't do it, you're history."

"I almost feel sorry for you, Billy Ray Bob, because I really do know what you mean. But we all have to live by the consequences of the choices we make and you made some really bad choices." Cesari relaxed a little and Billy Ray Bob finally took a deep breath. "Okay Billy Ray Bob, I understand things better now and you've been mostly cooperative, but your treatment of Kelly is unforgiveable."

Billy Ray Bob knew there was no way around this part and looked depressed. Cesari had thought about what his fate should be long and hard and said, "You know Billy Ray Bob, by the time morning comes, everyone's going to know what you and your father have been doing. If I killed you tonight, most people would look at it as a public service. Save everybody a lot of time, you know what I mean? Hell, they wouldn't even have to dig you a grave."

Billy Ray Bob bowed his head and started sobbing. Cesari gave him a moment to consider his crimes before saying, "But I have a better idea."

Chapter 60

It took the better part of an hour for Billy Ray Bob to write out his confession. Cesari made him spell out in great detail both his and his father's complicity with Gianelli, the drugs, the organ harvesting and the latest escalation of their activities with the Arabs. He also confessed to the sexual assault of Kelly with his friends Ozzie and Dave Culpepper. He had him place the confession in an envelope and address it to the editor of the Genesee Times, the local newspaper. He then placed the letter in a plastic bag so Cesari's fingerprints wouldn't be on it. Cesari took the DVD of Kelly from his pocket, wiped it clean and dropped it in the plastic bag with the confession. Then he had Billy Ray Bob call 911 and report a dead body behind his barn.

After he hung up, Cesari said, "One more thing. Write a short note telling them they can find you in the cellar and leave it on the table."

They marched down to the basement and stood there staring at each other. Billy Ray Bob's hands were still free, but Cesari had the shotgun.

Cesari said, "I know what you're thinking. As soon as your pals from the police department get here, you'll smooth things over with them and explain what a maniac I am and how I forced you to write the confession. But it won't work and here's why. There's a dead cop behind your barn with your DNA all over him and the shovel you used to bury him. Your confession details multiple felonies including homicides that took place long before I got up here, things I couldn't possibly have had anything to do with. Your confession contains too many details to have been fabricated and then there are the drugs, bodies, and accounting ledger in the basement of the hospital. In just a few short hours, I would expect that the hospital basement and all its contents will have been discovered by law enforcement.

Denying your guilt simply won't sail. Your best bet is to fully confess and hope to get a reduced sentence or maybe, if you're really lucky and the feds decide they need you to nail Gianelli, you might get yourself into witness protection. Of course, you'll be cringing every time you start your car in the morning, wondering if it's going to blow up, but that's the breaks. On the other hand, as you've already figured out tonight, there's not a chance on earth that Gianelli's going to let you live anyway."

Billy Ray Bob didn't say anything. He stood there waiting for Cesari's next move. Cesari said, "Now lie face down on the floor."

Billy Ray Bob was a bloody mess and Cesari could smell his fear. He found some rope he had lying around and tied his hands and feet much the same way he had tied the guy back in the basement of the hospital. When he was done, he rolled him on his side.

Cesari's gaze drifted to a jar on one of the shelves. It contained two eyes staring at him. "By the way, what's with the anatomy lab down here?" he asked.

Billy Ray Bob said, "Gianelli made me keep them down here as insurance in case I ever got cold feet. He checked on them every time he came up to make sure I didn't get rid of them."

Cesari nodded. That Vito was a regular riot. Then he remembered something he'd been wanting to ask. "Who is Ray Scarborough?"

Billy Ray Bob tilted his head and seemed puzzled and Cesari thought maybe he had hit him one too many times with the shovel. Billy Ray Bob said, "What are you talking about?"

"The Ray in Billy Ray Bob. Kelly told me that your dad named you after his three favorite Yankee players; Billy Martin,

Ray Scarborough, and Bobby Murcer. I've never heard of Ray Scarborough and I grew up a few blocks from Yankee Stadium. I've always been a big fan."

"You're kidding, right?" he asked sarcastically. "You're trying to make small talk with me after all that's just happened?"

Without warning, Cesari kicked him in the side hard and heard a rib crack. Billy Ray Bob gasped, "Goddamn. You didn't have to do that."

"I know but I wanted to. So who was he?"

It took a moment or two for him to collect himself before he murmured, "He was a pitcher in the forties and fifties. He was only with the Yankees one season, but they won the pennant that year. He was one of my grandfather's Army buddies during World War II. He only had a so-so career, but my grandfather worshiped him. My father met him a few times."

Cesari pondered that for a few seconds. "Interesting... I didn't know. Thanks, but now I want you to promise me something."

"What?"

"Let's just say that by some bizarre twist of fate, you don't go to prison for the rest of your life or get a bullet in your head from some mob hit man. I want you to promise me that you will never ever go near Kelly again. Promise me that you will never try to contact her by any method. Promise me, that if you see her walking down one side of the street, you will cross to the other side and run away as fast as you can. Will you promise me that?" Cesari asked seriously and politely.

Billy Ray Bob looked pathetic as he nodded his head. "I promise."

"Do you understand what I will do to you if you break that promise?"

He nodded again.

Cesari picked up the shotgun and slammed the butt end into Billy Ray Bob's head, knocking him unconscious.

He said, "Don't worry. I'll deliver the letter to the newspaper for you."

Chapter 61

He drove by the office building of the Genesee Times in the downtown area of the city and slipped the confession with the DVD under the front door. Kelly was still sleeping in the passenger seat and Cleo was out cold in the back. They arrived at her apartment around 2:00 a.m.

"We're here," he said, gently nudging her.

She didn't answer right away, so he shook her a little harder. Her eyes opened reluctantly and she looked around confused. "Where are we?" she asked groggily, squinting out the window.

He watched her yawn, stretching her arms over her head as she sat upright. He said, "I'm pretty sure this is where you live. I'm sorry for waking you."

"Oh yeah. You're right. Boy, was I asleep. How'd it go with Billy Ray Bob?"

"He was very cooperative."

She gave him a look. "How bad did you hurt him?"

"It wasn't like that. He was very eager to make amends. I really think he's a changed man or at least well on his way."

She shook her head. "Let's go in. I need to lie in a bed."

They helped Cleo out of the car and walked up to the apartment. The dog was even sleepier than they were. Once inside, he got Cleo a bowl of water and made a mental note to get dog food in the morning. Kelly went directly to her bedroom. When she came out, she was wearing fuzzy yellow, one piece pajamas with feet.

He stared at her trying not to laugh. "You've got to be kidding."

"If you don't like my pajamas, you can sleep on the sofa."

"I like them just fine."

"C'mon then, let's go to bed."

"Where's the dog going to sleep?" he asked.

Kelly giggled, "From the size of her, I'd say pretty much wherever she damn well pleases."

She chose to sleep with them in the bedroom.

~~~

"Vito, I got them. They went into the girl's apartment, and you're not going to believe this."

"Spit it out, Pinky. It's been a long night."

"The dog is with them."

"Get the hell out of here. I don't believe it."

"It's the truth. Wagging her tail and the whole nine yards."

"Unbelievable. You can't even trust dogs to be loyal anymore. Okay, I'll be right over. Check out how many ways there are for them to escape the apartment. Mike and I will stop somewhere and get the gasoline."

Chapter 62

Cesari didn't bother to undress. He placed the shotgun on the floor next to him and fell on the bed exhausted. The .357 and the Glock were somewhere in the room, but he was too tired to care.

Kelly was out cold within minutes and he could hear her rhythmic breathing. He stared at the ceiling, still wound up from the day's events. Cleo slept on the floor at the foot of the bed, but only after they convinced her that there was no room for her on the bed between them.

Eventually, he drifted off... And there they were again, Frankie D., his father, the knife, the blood and the baseball. He woke up in a cold sweat as usual. An army of psychiatrists would have had a field day with him. That made him laugh quietly to himself because they already had.

This latest round of dreams was substantially different from the previous ones however. In the past, they had upset him more because of some implied or instinctual threat. Now they were clear and focused. The locations were familiar as well which was also new. His mind was telling him a story that was building up to some unknown climax. Each sojourn into his subconscious seemed to reveal slightly more than the last. In this latest version, Frankie D. took responsibility for his father's death and begged him for forgiveness. But why?

Cesari sniffed the air. What was that? He smelled something pungent. He turned the light on and saw a cloud of smoke wafting around the room, billowing in from under the door. He coughed.

"Kelly, wake up!" he shouted and shoved her. "There's a fire!"

She sprang to attention and Cleo barked excitedly in alarm.

"What's happening?" Kelly exclaimed, jumping out of bed.

"I don't know."

"Let's get out of here."

He stood up and ran to the door. The knob burned his hand when he touched it. Not a good sign. The wood panel of the door was also pretty hot.

"The window. Now!" he coughed again, the acrid air burning his lungs.

Thank God she had a first-floor apartment, he thought. The room was filling up rapidly with smoke and heat. They raced to the window, opened it and helped Cleo out first. This was tricky but Cleo instinctively understood that all hell was breaking loose and cooperated with them. Cesari wrapped his arms around her waist and boosted her over the windowsill. No easy feat but she was smart and knew he was on her side.

In less than a minute, the room had darkened with clouds of smoke and he could barely see or breathe. Kelly gagged and wheezed in front of him trying to climb out through the window when suddenly he felt her body go limp and she slid backward into his arms, unconscious. He grabbed her by the legs and launched her out the window to the grass below. Then he jumped headfirst after her and lay there hacking and gasping.

He thought he heard a shot ring out and Cleo growl. He felt the world swirling around him as if he were at the bottom of a toilet bowl someone had just flushed.

He was in Rome again.

Chapter 63

He woke with an oxygen mask on his face, which he immediately ripped off so he could turn on his side and puke.

"What the hell happened?" he asked of no one in particular.

He was lying on someone's lawn. Fifty yards away, he saw the house in flames and firemen busy doing their thing. There were flashing lights everywhere. Genesee's emergency services were getting a workout tonight. He remembered Kelly had an elderly landlady and he hoped she got out safely.

"You really should keep that on," the young emergency medical technician said when he saw that he had removed the mask.

"Where's Kelly?" he demanded, leaving the mask off.

"Who's Kelly?" the kid asked, placing the mask back on him without permission. He was so young he still had pimples.

"The girl I was with. Is she okay?"

"Oh, the girl. Your friend had to be rushed to the hospital with the other guy. They were both in pretty bad shape when they left here. We were waiting for a second ambulance to take you, but everybody's been real busy because of the explosion at the hospital tonight. Helluva night."

"Bad shape? What do you mean by that and what other guy are you talking about?" Cesari asked, getting agitated. As he started to sit up, he felt a pain in his left arm and realized that he wasn't wearing a shirt.

"Look mister, maybe you should try to relax. You've been through a lot, and I'm sure you'll get filled in on the details once the dust settles." He leaned over to push Cesari back down which was not received well.

Cesari grabbed his wrist and twisted it, causing him to yelp. He said, "I know you mean well buddy, but I asked you what happened to my friend Kelly and the other guy. So I suggest you tell me."

The kid glanced around for help and realized he was all alone. He stammered, "She had to be intubated. When we got here, she still had a pulse, but wasn't breathing too well. Probably has carbon monoxide poisoning. I don't think the guy's going to make it."

He let go of the wrist and asked more politely, "What happened to him?"

"He was attacked by some huge dog that nearly ripped his throat out. He was hemorrhaging bad and was unconscious when we found him. It was pretty gruesome. I think the dog got his carotid. I've never seen anything like it."

"Where's the dog now?" Cesari asked, trying to comprehend what he'd said. Why would Cleo attack anyone?

"I don't know for sure. I think the animal control people took her away. Helluva night."

"Thanks," Cesari said, and rose unsteadily to his feet.

"Not a problem."

"Anybody know who the guy is?"

"We don't. We're hoping he wasn't some neighbor trying to help out."

Cesari was a little shaky and had a bit of a headache but basically felt okay. He felt himself all over instinctively to make sure all the parts were in place. His left arm hurt like hell, and he noticed a bloodstained bandage around his bicep. He reviewed the facts in his mind. A housefire in the middle of the night. EMTs had intubated Kelly and sent her to the hospital with carbon monoxide poisoning. Cleo was in custody because she attacked and may have killed some guy. The kid was right. This was a helluva night.

"I don't think you should leave," the kid said. "You might be in shock. Why don't you lie down and wait for the ambulance? Besides, you've got blood all over you."

Cesari said, "What happened to my shirt?"

"We cut it off so we could bandage your arm. We think that when you jumped out the window, you landed on something sharp like a piece of glass. In the dark and the confusion, we had trouble getting you to stop bleeding. A doctor's going to have to look at that wound at the hospital. Sorry about the shirt."

"Don't be sorry. Thank you for helping me and my friend. I'm sorry I did that thing with the wrist before. I know how dedicated you guys are and what an important service you provide."

The kid watched as Cesari walked away and called out, "Not a problem."

Cesari studied the bandage wrapped around his arm. Some blood had oozed out from beneath it but otherwise he seemed to be coagulating nicely. The wound hurt, but nothing he couldn't stand. He unraveled the dressing to check the injury himself and was surprised to see a small round hole. On the other side of his arm, he found a second hole. He replaced the bandage. Damn, he'd been shot.

Then he remembered the sound of gunfire as he passed out next to Kelly. He also remembered Cleo barking and growling. It was becoming clear to him now what had happened. The fire was set deliberately either to kill them or to flush them out into an ambush. Gianelli and his men were probably waiting by all the exits to finish the job if they made it out alive. Once the shooting started, Cleo realized they were under attack and sprung to their defense, nailing at least one of the bastards.

Good girl.

Walking past the fire engines and police cars to Billy Ray Bob's green Buick, he knew he must have looked quite the sight, barefoot with no shirt and a bloody left arm. It was four in the morning however, and in the confusion no one paid him any attention. He had no weapons, but he had his wallet and the car keys because he had fallen asleep with his clothes on. Thankful for that small iota of good luck, he entered the car and pulled away from the curb.

The gloves were off now.

Chapter 64

Back in his apartment, Cesari took a quick shower and put on a clean pair of jeans. He had some antiseptic in his bathroom and applied it liberally to his wound. It made him wince. Not wasting any further time, he drove to the hospital to see Kelly. He was very worried and tried hard to be positive. He told himself over and over that she was young and healthy and should be fine.

It was very early Monday morning, but the operating room would undoubtedly be closed because of the explosion. It would take days to assess the damage and begin to institute repairs. He assumed all of his patients would be cancelled. Most people would understand the catastrophic nature of what had happened and would agree to reschedule. Some would complain for the sake of complaining. Others would see it as a bad omen, and he'd never hear from them again. Such was human nature.

He parked in the main lot and could see the Porsche two rows over. It was still mostly dark outside, but the sky was starting to lighten up as dawn broke. The fire had been controlled but dark plumes of smoke billowed ominously against the background of the rising sun. A multitude of police cars, news vans, and fire engines clustered toward the rear of the hospital. Cesari waved at the security guard in the lobby as he walked past.

The emergency room was bedlam. He expected a fair amount of activity, but nothing like what he saw. An army of police, SWAT guys, FBI agents and several large German shepherds filled the hallways. They seemed to be focused on one particular room. The other Arab no doubt. As he walked by, he felt the glare of suspicious eyes.

One of the nurses gave him a warm welcome. "Good morning, Dr. Cesari."

"Hi, Nancy," he said. "I heard you guys had quite the night down here."

She was a battle-hardened emergency room nurse who thought she'd seen it all. Nonetheless, she was upset as she filled him in. "You don't know the half of it. There was an explosion in the OR last night and we lost six people in the blast. They told us it was a gas line that may have leaked but no one believes it."

"What do people believe?"

She leaned over in a conspiratorial manner and lowered her voice. "A couple of Arabs came in yesterday. At first we all thought they were smuggling drugs, but most everyone now thinks they're suicide bombers. One of them went up in smoke with our people last night in the OR. The one in that room over there with all the FBI guys probably has a bomb in his abdomen."

She got teary.

"I'm sorry, Nancy. I didn't know until now how many people we lost. I heard about Alex, but that was it. Look, I'd love to chat but one of my endoscopy nurses was in a house fire early this morning. The EMTs brought her in with respiratory failure from smoke inhalation. Is she down here?"

"You mean Kelly? Is she a friend of yours? Poor little thing. They brought her in about an hour ago and hustled her right up to the intensive care unit. They had to intubate her in the field. I heard that her vital signs were stable but that she was still unresponsive. I hope she didn't suffer any brain damage."

Cesari flinched at that. He said, "Me too. Thank you, Nancy. I think I'll go to the ICU and see how she's doing. I hope things settle down around here."

"I hope she'll be okay, I really do."

Cesari turned to leave and got slapped in the face.

"Hello, Cheryl."

Chapter 65

"I deserved that," he said, referring to the slap as he rubbed his stinging face.

"You're welcome. I've been waiting a whole year to do that."

"Who's your friend, Kowalcik?" asked a tall, lanky guy wearing an FBI badge.

"This is the same Dr. John Cesari that I've been telling you about. Cesari, say hello to Special Agent Wilkins of the FBI."

"Hello, Agent Wilkins." They shook hands and Cesari said, "Cheryl, believe it or not I'm glad to see you, but I don't understand. Why are you here?"

"I'm here because of you, Cesari."

"How so?"

"You called in the alarm about a known mobster skulking around a hospital and less than twenty-four hours later, the side of that same hospital blows out, killing seven people. My boss woke me up at 3:00 a.m. and told me to get my ass up here to find you. They had a four seat, single prop plane waiting for me at LaGuardia which brought me to some prehistoric hole in the ground called Penn Yan. I didn't even have a chance to pack and then lo and behold, I practically trip over you the minute I walk through the front door."

"I see. Well I'm sorry about that. Did you say seven dead? I thought there were only six dead."

"The seventh died minutes ago from third-degree burns. We were just informed of that. She was a recovery room nurse and wasn't in the OR proper at the time of the explosion. She had three kids. And now it seems like that guy over there might also be a human bomb, but he won't speak to anyone." She nodded in the direction of the other Arab's room.

"But I thought they started talking last night to the interpreter. At least, that's what someone told me."

"The guy with the stomachache was in so much pain he agreed to the surgery, but that was it. I'd hardly call that talking. We still have no idea what's going on."

"But if you suspect that he might be a suicide bomber, then don't you think you should quarantine him somehow? Personally, I think that would be a good idea."

Cesari wasn't ready to let on how much he knew just yet and they seemed to have things under control. Agent Wilkins stepped in. "We're working on the assumption that he is definitely a human bomb and are in the process of isolating him. I'm glad we ran into you, Dr. Cesari. It saved us the trouble of hunting you down. Now come with us. We have a lot to talk about."

"Sure thing, but I need to check on a friend of mine first. She was in a house fire last night and is up in the ICU. Apparently she's quite ill. I'll only be a few minutes."

Wilkins looked at him up and down. He was about fifty, lean and in pretty good shape. He didn't seem like someone who took a whole lot of shit. He glared at Cesari with sharp gray eyes for a second and then got in his face.

He lowered his voice, "Maybe you didn't hear me the first time, Doctor. When I said that we have a lot to talk about, it wasn't a question. Your friend will still be in the ICU when we're done. Now I want you to be nice and agreeable or I'll cuff you right here in front of all your colleagues and then you won't be going to see anyone today. Understand?"

"Cuff me? Based on what?"

"It's called the Patriot Act, and I don't need a reason. I can I throw you in a cell and leave you there for as long as I like but that aside, you're the number one suspect in a multiple homicide and possibly an act of terrorism. So what's it going to be?"

Cesari thought about that. He wanted to cooperate. He really did. There was a second set of bombers he needed to tell them about but this guy was a little too high strung for his taste and might detain him indefinitely if he knew he had information like that. He had heard horror stories about guys secreted away for months and years under the Patriot Act for less. As much as he wanted to do his civic duty, he had to see Kelly first and that was that, so he decided he would tell them later. Besides, he just wanted to check on her, and then he'd come right back and fill them all in.

Wilkins eyed him with distrust as he hesitated. As if reading his mind, Wilkins said, "Don't get any ideas about bolting, Cesari. You take even one step in the wrong direction and I'll be on you like a spider monkey."

"Spider monkey?"

"They're very agile and wiry."

Cesari sighed in resignation and figured it would be better to submit than get handcuffed. "Will this take very long? My friend in the ICU wasn't doing well when they brought her in."

Wilkins eased up a little. "Hard to say, but not too long would be my guess. There's a lot going on and you're just one part of the puzzle."

They walked together quietly toward the back of the ER where there was a small conference room. He smiled at Cheryl and said, "You look good."

"Shut up, Cesari. I look like crap, and I need a cup of coffee."

He whispered, "So I guess he's in charge."

"Yes Cesari, I'm in charge," answered Agent Wilkins. "And spider monkeys have excellent hearing too."

They entered the conference room and took seats around an oval table. There was a pot of coffee in the center with styrofoam cups and the usual accompaniments. They each poured themselves a cup and waited in silence. Five minutes later, a seventy-year-old man with wispy white hair wearing a rumpled cardigan strolled in. He was short and professorial.

Cheryl stood up and gave him a warm hug. "Hi, Dad."

"Hi, Cheryl. Finally we get to work on a case together. I have to tell you, no one likes being woken up in the middle of the night but when Agent Wilkins called and told me that you were going to be here, I got all excited."

"Thanks, Dad."

"Good morning, Dr. Kowalcik," Agent Wilkins said.

"Good morning, Agent Wilkins."

Cesari stood up and extended his hand. "Hi, Paul. It's been a long time."

He glanced at Cesari and then at Cheryl.

He didn't take the offered hand.

Chapter 66

"It's a bomb, all right," Paul Kowalcik said, addressing the room. "There's no doubt about it."

Somebody had thankfully brought in a couple of boxes of donuts, and Cesari munched on his second glazed donut, contemplating how bad it would look if he grabbed another.

Agent Wilkins responded first. "Could you please explain how you can be sure of that, Dr. Kowalcik?"

Paul was a physicist in the employ of the Department of Defense. He was one of the world's leading experts on improvised explosive devices.

He explained, "I spent the last hour reviewing the CAT scans of our two Middle Eastern friends with the head of the radiology department. It seems that the first time around, they misinterpreted the detonator as an artifact, an imperfection in the image itself. In retrospect, it is clearly an antenna to receive an electronic signal. It's quite small and imbedded in the explosive material which, thanks to the FBI forensics people, we now know is C4. When it receives a signal, it triggers a blasting cap, which in turn causes the device to explode. There are many ways of setting off these bombs, but the simplest way is to program it to receive a phone call or text message. They do this all the time with IEDs in Afghanistan and Iraq."

"What exactly is an IED?" Cheryl asked. "I've heard the term many times but don't know what the technical definition is. Remember I'm a lawyer, so take it easy on me."

He smiled. "It's not really difficult to understand, Cheryl. An IED is an improvised explosive device. Basically, it's any type of homemade bomb. Sometimes they're constructed using conventional military ordinance, such as an artillery round attached to a detonating mechanism. In other cases, they're made of plastic explosives such as C4. Technically, any explosive used in an unconventional manner would fall under the category of IED. So in order to illustrate my point, if you lit a suitcase filled with firecrackers and threw it into a crowd, that would be a type of IED. It may not be very effective, but that's not the point. IEDs in the form of roadside bombs, have been extremely effective at wreaking havoc with our forces in the Middle East because they are very difficult to detect and disarm."

Agent Wilkins, who had been listening carefully to the exchange, asked, "Have you ever heard of anything like this before, suicide bombers with the explosives surgically implanted in their bodies?"

Paul ran his hand through his white hair and frowned. "No, I can't say that I have. And I've been working in this particular area for the last ten years. This is a nasty new development and certainly ups the ante with what our guys are going to have to deal with. The pentagon isn't going to be happy to hear about this."

Cheryl said, "But Dad, the guy who exploded in the OR was heavily sedated, and the other one was under constant observation. How could either one have set off the bomb?"

"That's not that hard to explain. There could have been a third person somewhere who triggered the bomb remotely, or there could have been some type of electrical discharge in the OR itself. Maybe John can shed some light on what goes on in the OR. By the way, I hope the other guy is in isolation."

Wilkins jumped in. "The other guy is restrained and under constant guard. We have him cuffed, hand and foot, to his stretcher. As we speak, he's being placed in the back of an FBI van in the parking lot with a fifty-yard blast perimeter. The van is made of reinforced steel specifically for use by the bomb squad. We have video cameras in the van giving us live feed at all times, and we drained all the gasoline out of the tank, just in case he explodes. He's not going anywhere until we figure out how to safely disarm him."

"Good," Paul replied. "John, what can you tell us about inadvertent electrical discharge in the OR?"

Cesari thought it over for a minute and said, "Well there's lots of electrical activity in the OR, but most of it is deliberate. If this guy went up for a laparotomy, then they were jolting him frequently with electricity. Surgeons use a device called a Bovie. It delivers high-frequency electric current as a means to cut and coagulate tissue. It allows the surgeon to make precise cuts with limited blood loss. In addition, that guy was in pretty bad shape when they took him up last night. He might have went into cardiac arrest, in which case they would have had to shock him with a defibrillator, maybe even multiple times. We'll never know."

Paul nodded. "Well, there you go. The surgeon probably accidentally detonated the bomb last night during what was probably routine medical care." He took a deep breath and a sip of coffee. "Can't blame him, though. He had no way of knowing what he was dealing with."

"No, he didn't," Cesari said. "Everyone, including me, thought these guys were smuggling drugs."

"Is there any way of disarming this type of bomb, Dr. Kowalcik?" Wilkins asked hopefully. He was taking notes on a yellow legal pad in front of him.

The older man took a sip of coffee. "Unfortunately, no. This has been a very frustrating area of investigation for us. The only way of preventing an IED from exploding is to remove the blasting cap from the explosive material. In this case, you would have to perform surgery to remove the bomb from the individual first, and thus expose a whole new set of doctors and nurses to the danger that occurred last night."

"Or," Wilkins suggested, "we could put the scumbag in a hole somewhere and detonate him ourselves."

Paul said, "That would work."

Chapter 67

"**I**f I were twenty years younger," Paul said to me angrily, "I would punch you in the nose for the way you treated my daughter."

He was red in the face, and Cesari hoped he didn't give himself a heart attack or a stroke. Wilkins was off to one side talking on his cellphone.

"Thanks, Dad," Cheryl interjected, "but I think can handle him."

Cesari said, "I'm sorry to both of you. You're right. You're absolutely right to feel the way you do. I have no excuse." He hung his head in shame. This reunion was going badly.

"We're going to have to shelve this discussion for now," said Cheryl. "We have bigger fish to fry. But when we're done, you and I are going to have a long talk."

"Yeah," Paul added, "and in the meantime, I may start taking boxing lessons."

Agent Wilkins finished his call and came over to them. "Okay, Cesari, you're off the hook for now but don't go far. I have more important things to take care of. The ATF and Homeland Security people are waiting for me to bring them up to speed on things. Cheryl, Dr. Kowalcik, I'd like you both to come with me. And Cesari, how about we meet up early afternoon? Let's say about one. Right here would be fine."

"Don't get lost," Cheryl told him, and they all turned to leave together. Paul didn't say goodbye.

Cesari walked out of the emergency room and headed over to the ICU. Law enforcement seemed to have a firm handle on the situation. He'd fill them in later on what he knew. A couple of hours here or there wasn't going to change things.

Standing in front of the entrance to the ICU, he pressed the buzzer and waved at the security camera. Someone inside unlocked the door for him, and he entered. Kelly was in room eight. When he entered, his heart sank even lower. He had hoped that she might have turned the corner in the last hour, but she hadn't and looked pretty bad. She was still intubated, with multiple tubes running into various veins and orifices. He could see urine in a bag dangling off the side of the bed. The sounds of mechanical ventilation hissed eerily in the otherwise quiet room.

He sighed deeply. *Kelly, what have I done?*

Her nurse Patty entered the room. "Hi, Doc. Are you friends with Kelly?"

"Yeah, she works with me in the OR. How's she doing?"

"It's a little hard to say right now. She just got here, but she's holding her own. She's oxygenating well. Blood pressure's fine. She's not responding to stimuli yet, but she was given a shitload of sedatives in the field to keep her quiet. So it's possible that her lack of responsiveness reflects the sedation rather than any permanent anoxic injury. We're not giving her any more sedatives here. She's young and healthy, so they should wash out of her system relatively quickly. I think we'll have a better handle on where she is neurologically in a couple of hours. Do you know if she has any family we should call?"

"I know she has aunts in Ohio, but I don't know their names or how to reach them. I don't know how close they were. I think her employment record might have that information. Sorry I can't be of more help."

"Don't you worry yourself. We'll sort it out."

"Do you mind if I sit with her for a while?"

"Not at all. Make yourself at home."

"Thanks," he said, and sat in a chair next to her bed.

"There's a fresh pot of coffee in the lounge. Help yourself. And try to relax. I really do think she's going to be okay. They always look bad when they first get here."

"Thank you."

He leaned over and held Kelly's hand. She had to come out of this. He'd never forgive himself if she didn't. He pressed her hand against his face and said a silent prayer.

Chapter 68

Pinky drove the big Caddie while Gianelli filled Big Lou in on the weekend's events. They were on the thruway racing toward New York City.

"I know it sounds bad Lou, but there's no way they can link any of this to us, and if Cesari isn't dead already he's going to be facing homicide charges soon enough. No one's going to take anything he says seriously."

"I don't know," said Big Lou in response. "It sounds like a complete disaster, if you ask me. You've lost three guys. One of the bomber teams is gone. Cesari may or not be neutralized. Billy Ray Bob is still alive. Every reporter in the country is on his way to that town as we speak, and you want me to look at the bright side? I'm not sure there is a bright side. I should have taken care of this Cesari kid years ago when I had the chance. That's what I get for being soft. Where are you and Pinky now?"

"We just crossed the Tappan Zee Bridge. Traffic's light, so we should be in lower Manhattan in about an hour."

"All right." Big Lou barked a final command into the receiver, "Get here as soon as you can, and we'll finish this conversation in person."

Gianelli felt Pinky's gaze on him as he hung up. "Don't say it Pinky. Let's keep our fingers crossed and hope the second bomber team gets the job done. It's out of our hands now."

"Maybe the smart move would be to turn the car around and head out west. I hear Vegas is nice this time of year,"

Pinky mused. "Just thinking out loud, Vito. Hope you don't mind."

"Just drive, Pinky."

Chapter 69

By ten o'clock, Kelly had started to wake up and was breathing comfortably. By eleven o'clock, the doctors in the ICU decided that she was improved to the point that it would be safe to extubate her. By eleven thirty, she was demanding to leave, which brought a round of applause from the ICU staff and Cesari. Unfortunately, they advised her to stay overnight for observation, to which she reluctantly agreed. Cesari leaned over and kissed her, which brought another round of handclapping from the nurses.

Patty wrinkled her nose at him and said, "I knew you two were an item." She then turned to another nurse. "I spotted it the minute he walked through the door."

Women always knew. It was one of the great mysteries of life how they were able to divine such things. Cesari and Kelly smiled politely as the staff left them alone.

"I can't believe it," Kelly whispered, her throat a little sore from the breathing tube. "We almost died. Think about it, a few more minutes delay getting out of there and that would have been the end of us. So do they know what happened?"

Cesari glanced around quickly to make sure the nurses were out of earshot and then told her his theory about what happened. She hadn't known that Gianelli's guy was there or that Cleo had mauled him. He told her about the gunshot wound in his arm.

"Are you okay?" she asked worried about him.

"I'm fine. Fortunately, the bullet went clean through without hitting bone or any major blood vessels. It hurts like hell but I'll live. Thankfully, he didn't get to take any more shots at us while we were lying there unconscious."

"Cleo really saved both our lives. Where is she now?"

"The animal control people came and picked her up. Apparently she's okay, but I'm sure they're going to have to put her down after what she did. I'm sorry."

Sadness filled Kelly's face. "Do you think there's anything we can do?"

"You mean like adopt her?"

She nodded. "Yes."

"I don't know, Kel. I like her but that's a big step. That's a monster-sized dog we're talking about. Keeping her in a small apartment might not be fair to her."

"Is letting her be executed because she saved our lives fair?"

"That's a good point... Well, nothing's going to happen immediately, so we'll have time to think it through more carefully while you're recovering. Who knows, we may not have any say in the matter anyway. A judge may order her terminated regardless of our feelings on the matter."

He sat on the side of the bed and put his arm around her for comfort. After a few minutes like that, she lay back on the pillow and closed her eyes. The combination of stress and sleep deprivation had taken their toll.

"It's almost noon," he whispered gently. "I'll let you rest while I go down to the cafeteria to grab a bite. Do you want me to bring you back something?"

She was already asleep.

Chapter 70

He took the elevator down to the basement and when he got off, he glanced down the long corridor. Even at noon with the pharmacy open, the hallway beyond was uninviting. It was a bit surreal to think about the unspeakable horrors that had taken place just a few hundred feet away. He turned and went in the other direction. In the cafeteria, he bought a cheeseburger with a soft drink and carried his tray to a table with several nurses. He nodded hello and sat down to eat.

The place was buzzing about last night's explosion and the tragic deaths of their coworkers. Speculation ran wild through the room. Yet despite the obvious danger, there was no sense of panic, only legitimate concern.

"Isn't that unbelievable what happened?" a nurse said to him.

"Truly," he replied.

"Some people think it was terrorism," she added.

Another nurse declared, "That's what I think. They said on the news this morning that one of the gas lines leaked but I don't believe it. They wouldn't tell us if it was terrorism. I don't mean to be cynical but I don't believe half of what I hear on TV anymore... It's so horrible. They all had such beautiful families."

The first nurse asked, "What do you think, Dr. Cesari?"

"I think that I'm very proud to be working with people like you."

Everyone stopped eating for a second. One of them said, "What do you mean?"

"I mean, look at you. All of you. An explosion took out a whole wing of the hospital. There's a real possibility that we might be under attack and look at how brave you all are. You came to work. You're taking care of your patients and doing your jobs. Sure we're all a little on edge, but that's normal. Any other business would have shut down and sent everybody for counseling. Instead, you guys are sitting here having lunch almost as if nothing had happened."

He gestured around the crowded lunchroom at something that under any other circumstances wouldn't have raised an eyebrow, and that something was business as usual.

"I'm glad we're on the same side," he raised his soda cup to salute them.

They all thanked him and one nurse offered him her curly fries. He was still beaming with pride when two large, uniformed policemen entered the cafeteria with Patty, the ICU nurse. She pointed at Cesari and both cops drew their handguns and aimed them at his chest. Everyone at the table scattered, leaving him all alone.

"Freeze and keep your hands on the table in plain sight," ordered one of the cops.

Cesari gulped the food in his mouth down and sat motionless, his hands resting on the table in front of him. The room went silent as the officers came up behind him quickly. They threw him forward across the table mashing his face into what was left of his cheeseburger. Then they cuffed him none too gently with his hands behind his back as the rest of the cafeteria watched in shock.

"Want to tell me what this is all about, officers?" he asked, as one of them grabbed his crotch in search of a weapon.

"Sure," one of them said. "You're in big trouble."

"That's it? Don't you have to read me my rights or something?"

"We don't have to do shit. Now shut up."

One the officers retrieved his ID from his wallet. "Dr. John Cesari?"

"Yes."

"We've been looking for you."

Chapter 71

At the police station, Cesari was processed and thrown into a holding cell with nine guys who apparently lived on steroids alternating with binges of crack. The place reeked of sweat, urine, and fear. It was going to be a lovely afternoon for sure.

He tried to understand what had gone wrong. Maybe someone had seen him in Billy Ray Bob's Porsche and had reported it stolen. Maybe someone had spotted him fleeing from the back of the hospital after the explosion. Any number of things could have happened.

After about an hour, he was brought into a small interrogation room with a metal table and two folding chairs, one on either side. The officer who brought him there left his hands cuffed behind his back and told him to sit down facing a two-way mirror and the video camera mounted on the wall above it.

Eventually the door opened, and two fat plain clothes detectives came in and introduced themselves. The fat white detective with short blond hair was Reynolds, and the fat black detective was Culpepper. So this was the famous Salt and Pepper. More like Tweedle Dee and Tweedle Dumber. They looked about as smart as wildebeest.

Kelly had told him about these two. Pepper was the one who liked to pretend he was a porn director. Cesari had a bone to pick with him and sized him up. He was about forty, an inch shy of six feet tall, short cropped hair, two hundred and fifty pounds. He might have played ball at one time but now looked like he sat around drinking beer and sucking down hot wings smothered in blue cheese maybe three or four times a week. He was sweating and it wasn't even warm in there.

Salt sat in the chair across from Cesari while Pepper sat on the edge of the table directly in front of him. The table groaned under his weight.

Pepper asked, "So, why'd you do it, Doc?"

"Why did I do what?"

"Why'd you shoot your boss Snell in the head? We found your gun at the scene with your prints on it, so please spare us the denial. Care to enlighten us?"

He grinned from ear to ear as he spoke and Salt snickered in the background. Cesari said, "I don't know what you're talking about. The last time I saw Snell, he looked great. We were planning on going on vacation together."

Pepper laughed. "Hey Reynolds, he thinks he's some sort of tough guy. Do me a favor, turn off the camera for a minute and stand in front of the mirror. I'd like to have a word in private with the doc."

"Sure thing Dave," his partner said and got off his chair. He lumbered over to the mirror, reached up to the video camera above and clicked a button on the side of it. The red light on the camera went off. He then situated his bulk directly in front of the mirror, blocking most of it.

Pepper turned back to Cesari and leaned forward menacingly. "You're a doctor, huh? You probably think that makes you special, don't you? Well think again, college boy. I eat smart guys like you for breakfast. Now, we know you did this and you know you did this, so let's not waste my time and taxpayer money."

Before he could respond, Pepper took his left hand and covered Cesari's mouth so he couldn't make any noise. With his right, he punched Cesari hard in the stomach. It was a solid, nasty blow and he lurched forward, suddenly short of breath and nauseated. Pepper kept his hand tightly over Cesari's mouth, and he had trouble drawing in a breath. From the intense pain he was feeling, Cesari worried that Pepper might have ruptured his spleen. He wanted to throw up but refused to give him the satisfaction.

Pepper leaned his sweaty face next to Cesari and hissed, "Mr. Gianelli says hello, greaseball, and to let you know that you're not leaving here, at least not in one piece. It's nothing personal. I hope you understand that."

Cesari coughed and gasped for air, and finally Pepper took his hand off his mouth. He sucked in oxygen and sat there trying to collect himself wondering if there was anybody in this town not on the take.

Pepper watched him wheeze and said callously, "You're all right. Don't be a baby. That was just a taste of what's to come but if you want more, then go ahead and jerk my chain." He turned back to Tweedle Dee. "You can turn the video back on now."

They both resumed their original positions with Reynolds in the chair and Pepper sitting on the table in front of him. Pepper said as if nothing had happened, "All right, so let's get started."

They went through the usual name, rank and serial number stuff, and eventually he produced a clear plastic evidence bag with his .38 Smith & Wesson in it. He placed it on the table in front of Cesari. "Do you recognize that, Dr. Cesari? I hope so because it's registered in your name, all legal and everything."

Cesari stared at the weapon and his heart sank. He was still recovering from the punch and felt queasy. He asked for the second time that day, "Don't you have to read me my rights?"

"We'll get to that eventually. Right now we're just talking… like old friends. You don't have something to hide, do you?"

"I want to make a phone call."

"You don't get to make a phone call until after you've been charged, and we can hold you for up to forty-eight hours without charging you. Get the picture, college boy?"

Cesari wasn't sure if that was right or not but he was in no position to argue. These guys weren't exactly on the straight and narrow but he blustered with great confidence anyway.

He said, "Depriving me of my right to make a phone call can be interpreted as depriving me of my right to legal counsel. Did you know that?"

They could do whatever they wanted but it never hurt to bluff a little. They didn't buy it and the both of them laughed derisively. Pepper said, "Doc, you're killing me. Where do you hear this stuff?"

Salt added, "They're going to think he's hysterical tonight in the holding cell."

Pepper was starting to get irritated. "Look, these are your choices. If you tell me what I want to hear, then I'll put you in isolation for your own protection. If you don't tell me what I want to hear, then you're going to spend the night with that cage-full of horny crackheads you already met. It's your decision but either way, you're not going anywhere."

Cesari had enough. He said, "Aren't you the guys they call Salt and Pepper?"

They glanced at each other puzzled and Pepper chuckled. "Hey Reynolds, we're famous... Yeah, that's us. Who wants to know?"

"Which one are you?" he asked Pepper.

Pepper looked at his partner, then back at Cesari and laughed. "Which one do you think, moron? I'm Pepper, of course."

"That's not what I meant."

"Then what did you mean?"

"When you two fudge packers are doing it, are you the girl or the boy? I bet you're the girl. I can always tell these things." Cesari winked at him.

Without warning, Pepper backhanded Cesari viciously across the face. The sound of it resounded loudly in the small room. Cesari fell off the chair, landed on the floor and rolled onto his back. He lay there motionless and limp, with his eyes closed, waiting. Another homophobic cop. Did they come in any other flavor?

Reynolds jumped to his feet, alarmed. "Dave, take it easy This is being recorded."

Pepper said, "Shit... Help me get him up."

Salt said, "Why isn't he moving?"

"I don't know. I didn't hit him that hard."

"Jesus, Pepper. He must have hit his head."

"I didn't see him hit his head," Pepper muttered as he straddled Cesari. He was about to bend over and pick him up when Cesari opened his eyes and smiled.

"What the...?"

Cesari kicked him in the testicles as hard as he could. Pepper doubled over, groaning in pain and clutching his groin. He was much closer now, so Cesari curled backwards, cocked both legs and gave him a full throttle kick to the head, which knocked him backwards onto the floor. His head bounced off the hard surface and all hell broke loose. Reynolds came running over from his side of the table to beat the snot out of Cesari. He landed one good shot to Cesari's face and was winding up for a real haymaker when the door burst open and several uniformed officers came charging into the room.

A woman shouted loudly above the fracas, "That's enough, Reynolds! Let go of him and put him back in his chair. Then help your partner get medical attention."

With Pepper moaning in the background, Reynolds grabbed Cesari roughly and hoisted him back into the chair. As he man-handled him, he growled, "Think you're funny wiseguy? I can be funny too."

Cesari said, "If being fat and stupid is funny, then you're hilarious."

His eyes looked like they were going to pop out of his head as his rage nearly overwhelmed his judgment. He cocked his arm back to deliver what surely would have been a fatal blow, but the woman shouted again, "I said enough Reynolds and if I have to say it again, I'll put you in cuffs too."

Chapter 72

A no-nonsense, middle-aged hispanic woman sat down opposite Cesari and glared at him. Tired and rough looking with short hair and dark eyes, she tapped her finger on the metal table. She was irritated and not trying to hide it.

After a while, when she didn't say anything he said, "Hello."

She stopped tapping her finger. "I'm Lieutenant Garcia, and you're a special kind of stupid, aren't you, Doctor? You're the number one suspect in a homicide that was committed last night and you assault the detective questioning you. I don't get it. Are you trying to go to jail for the rest of your life?"

Cesari was pissed, and his face hurt from where Pepper and then Reynolds had hit him. He said, "I'm fine. Thanks for asking."

"Listen up, Cesari. I don't give a crap that my detectives slapped you around. As far as I'm concerned, you deserved it. What I do care about is the dead guy whose office you were seen leaving shortly after you shot him. I have a witness that puts you right there just moments after you blew Snell's head off. They said they saw you leaving his office at 10:00 p.m. about five minutes after they heard a shot fired. But now that you've assaulted one of my men, I have a whole new set of charges we can discuss. You getting the picture? You're not going anywhere, pretty boy. You better start talking and you'd better make a whole lot of sense when you do."

Snell was dead and someone claims they saw him at the scene. Obviously, Gianelli had set him up. He said, "Let me tell you something, Lieutenant. If you review your video recordings carefully, you will see that your detective hit me first and knocked me off my chair. He then stood over me and was about to beat me some more even though I was handcuffed and unable to defend myself. Any jury that sees that tape will fry you and your entire sorry department. If you give me any more grief, my first call will be to the ACLU and my second will be to the New York Times. And another thing, I didn't do it. I was framed and you know it. You're just on a fishing trip."

She watched him for a while and then told the officer behind him, "Take the cuffs off him."

He rubbed his wrists and stretched. His left arm throbbed from the bullet wound. "Thank you," he said. "How about a glass of water? Being tossed around by gorillas makes a guy thirsty."

"Don't push your luck, Cesari. So if you didn't do it how do you explain your gun being at the scene of the crime and an eyewitness placing you there too?"

"My gun was stolen from my apartment. I was out all weekend and was unaware that it was missing until this morning. I was going to file a police report today but I was too busy being framed for a murder I emphatically did not commit."

It sounded plausible.

"And the eyewitness?"

"I haven't a clue. They must be mistaken. I did see Snell earlier in the day yesterday closer to noon, but when I left him he was very much alive."

"Why did you go see him yesterday?"

"I wanted to tell him what a great job he was doing. Guys in his position don't often get positive feedback from their employees. It can be lonely at the top."

She shook her head in disbelief and for a second he thought she might come over to his side of the table and finish what Salt and Pepper had started. She didn't and said, "Okay, let's pretend you're telling the truth and your gun was stolen. Why would anyone want to frame you for murder?"

"I haven't the slightest idea but that's not a crime, is it?"

"You're telling me that you have no idea why the CEO of your hospital was murdered?"

"I didn't say that. I said that I didn't do it. I'm sure there are plenty of people that would like to see him dead, starting with most of the employees at the hospital, his ex-wife and the doctor who brought him into this world."

She grinned wryly. "You're a pretty funny guy."

"I tell it the way I see it."

"You expect me to take your word that you're innocent and let you walk out of here?" she asked rather incredulously.

"That's exactly what I expect and I need to make a phone call."

She frowned. "Lawyer?"

"Something like that."

She reached into her pocket and came out with her cell-phone, which she slid across the table in his direction. "You got one call, so make it good."

He stared at the phone and then at her. "With you sitting right there?"

"With me sitting right here."

He picked up the phone and dialed his friend Mark, the psychiatrist. "Hey Mark, this is Cesari. Got a minute?"

"Of course. By the way, I want to apologize for being a little abrupt the other day. We were all exhausted. I forgot to mention that you're invited to the bris next Sunday at my apartment on the west side. You remember how to get there? I teach part time at Columbia now and have invited two of my senior residents to join us. They're both unattached, sweet as can be and quite attractive. I think you'll like them and vice versa."

"Thanks, Mark. If I can get away, I'd be honored to attend. I'm flattered that you would invite me. I don't know about the girls, though. I'm sort of seeing someone right now. Look Mark, I don't have a lot of time and I wanted to run something by you. I had that dream again last night, only this time there was something about it that made me think it was more than just a dream."

Garcia looked confused and stared at him as if he were crazy. She had assumed he was going to be pleading with some lawyer to come and bail him out.

"Go on," Mark said. "What was different about it?"

"Well first of all, it took place in a school yard, which was new. I looked around and saw the inscription *Holy Rosary* written above the main entrance. Mark, Holy Rosary was the grammar school I attended. There was a little kid there this time, maybe six or seven years old. It was really weird." Cesari felt much calmer than he would have anticipated as he spoke. He went on, "Another thing is that the dream didn't scare me as much as intrigue me, and that's very different. It felt like I was following a news story as it unfolded live on TV. It still provoked a fair amount of anxiety and as always I woke up panting and sweating."

"What do *you* think it means, Cesari?"

"I don't know, but I feel as if my subconscious is trying to tell me something in bits and pieces."

"What about your father? Did you kill him in this dream as well?"

"Yes, I did."

"Well I have to agree. It certainly seems like something is trying to break through to the surface, but what? I wish I could be of more help. Dream analysis was never my strong suit, but I have a friend on the faculty who specializes in it. He went to Harvard and those guys are pretty smart. I was planning to run it by him over cocktails this evening. I'll do that and get back to you, okay?"

Garcia was signaling him to end the call. "I have to run, Mark. Take care."

"Hope to see you this weekend, Cesari. And if you want to bring your girlfriend, she's more than welcome," Mark added.

"Sure and thanks. See you soon." he returned the phone to Garcia.

"Who on earth was that?" she demanded.

"My psychiatrist," he answered and heard the officer behind him chortle.

Garcia scowled at him and said to the officer, "Get this loser out of my sight."

Chapter 73

Back in the holding cell, Cesari kicked himself for not calling Cheryl instead of Mark. With all that had happened, he'd forgotten about the other bombers. He needed to get out of there. According to Billy Ray Bob, the trial wasn't supposed to begin for a few days so there was still time.

He also needed to eat. There were a bunch of small, empty cardboard boxes and water bottles piled in a corner of the cage. Apparently he had missed dinner. He did a quick head count, and there were still nine other guys in the cell with him. He took a seat on the only bench and studied his surroundings. The cage was a twenty-foot square in the center of a much larger room, with steel bars spaced at four-inch intervals. A thick steel door secured the outer room. There were no beds, no phones, no televisions and no guards. The math didn't look good for him if trouble started. He was the smallest guy in the room and the only one without a tattoo running up his neck.

After an hour or so of minding his own business, a very large, friendly-looking African American man sat down next to him. He introduced himself, "They call me Mo. That's short for Mo-reese."

He smiled but Cesari guessed he was just trying to show off his gold teeth. He glanced up at Mo. Even sitting, he was a head taller than him and at least a hundred pounds heavier. Tattoos covered his shaved head and he had a matching gold earring in his right ear. From a fashion point of view, Mo wasn't doing too badly although Cesari thought mouthwash and a little deodorant would go a long way. He extended his hand and said, "Hello, Mr. Mo."

Mo didn't take it.

Instead, he grabbed Cesari's thigh and squeezed. When Cesari looked down, he noticed that Mo's zipper was undone. Mo purred, "Me and the boys, we was thinking."

He nodded in the direction of the other guys as he massaged Cesari's thigh. "What were you thinking, Mr. Mo?" Cesari asked.

Mo was easily the largest guy in the room, and possibly the planet. His biceps were almost as big around as Cesari's waist. He reeked of alcohol, tobacco, pot and sweat.

Mo continued, "It's going to be a long night, and we was thinking about how we could best pass the time. Now the boys over there, they be thinking that maybe you weren't going to be friendly like. But I says no. That's exactly what I says. He seem like a nice fella. I think he be very cooperative."

"Cooperative about what, Mr. Mo?" Cesari asked, glancing quickly at the door and hoping someone would come by and ask him if he wanted to confess again.

"It's like this, little fella. You can either be friends with me, or you can be friends with the eight of them fellas over there. It's one or the other. There ain't no in between on this. Uh-uh. Ain't no in between. We been here befo'. The guards are going to check on us one mo' time 'bout eight and that be it for the rest of the night. You sees my meaning?"

And he gave Cesari's thigh an extra squeeze. Cesari peered over his shoulder and saw the other guys waiting for his decision. He said, "I don't mean any disrespect Mr. Mo, but how can I be sure that if I become your friend, I still won't have to be friends with them too?"

He chuckled. "You sho' is smart. That's exactly what I tells them. He be a smart white boy."

Mo put his massive arm around Cesari and yanked him closer, trapping in him in a vise-like grip. Cesari gagged from his stench, and began to wonder whether he was going to make it through the night in one piece. Mo's hot breath was nauseating and starting to overwhelm him when he heard Lieutenant Garcia yell, "Let go of him, Maurice. Let go now or you know what'll happen."

Garcia and four uniformed officers came rushing into the room. The uniforms were carrying cattle prods, batons and tasers. Right behind them were Cheryl and Special Agent Wilkins. Behind them, another pair of officers led Pepper in, handcuffed. A bloody bandage covered part of the left side of his face. He glowered at Cesari through hate-filled eyes. Billy Ray Bob's confession and the DVD of Kelly must have finally found its way to Garcia. Cesari wondered where Billy Ray Bob was. After the beating he'd given him, he might be in the emergency room.

Lieutenant Garcia opened the cell and ordered, "Maurice, move to the back of the cage now, or I'll put you down like a lame animal. Cesari, get your sorry ass out of my station house and I better not ever see your face again."

Cheryl stepped forward. "I see you've made some new friends, Cesari."

"I'm okay. I really am. Thanks for asking."

"Dr. Cesari, would you mind coming with us?" asked Wilkins. "Like I said earlier, there's still a lot we have to talk about."

"I'm free to leave? Just like that?"

Wilkins said, "Just like that unless you'd like to stay and finish whatever social experiment you were involved in."

"I thought I was being charged with murder," Cesari said as they walked to Wilkin's car.

"You might still be if you don't cooperate, understood? So don't push your luck. There are lot of people very upset right now. The Genesee Police Department is about to take a big hit if half of what I've heard is true. They'd like nothing more than to vent their anger and frustration on someone like you."

Cheryl added, "Look, John, we've all had a long day. We're only trying to get to the bottom of this, and you seem to be at the epicenter of the storm."

Cesari relaxed into a more accommodating posture. "Fine, but I need to call my friend first. The one in the ICU, remember? She's going to be worried sick about me. I just want to let her know everything's okay."

She said, "If you mean Kelly, she's fine. We've been talking to her all afternoon and to be safe, we have someone guarding her room in case Gianelli decides to try something again. She's aware that you're fine and that we were on our way to pick you up. She was nice to us, so why don't you try it as well."

Chapter 74

Wilkins drove them to a dilapidated roadside truck-stop that was barely larger than a doublewide trailer.

"Come on," he said. "I'm starving. It's been a long day."

They picked a lonely booth at the far end of the diner and ordered. Cesari noticed that Cheryl ordered a Greek salad with the dressing on the side per her usual. He hadn't seen in her in more than a year and yet he could have made that request for her it was so ritualistic on her part. It was funny the things you remembered about a person. This diner was classic. The worn-out waitress in the stained yellow uniform swatted a fly on the table right in front of them and then shot them a 'got a problem with that?' look.

After she left, Wilkins pulled out a handheld recorder and turned it on. On his right he placed a legal pad to take notes.

He said, "All right, let's clear the air. Right now everything's off the record, okay? The only reason you're not under arrest is because I find it too hard to believe that you would have called Ms. Kowalcik here for assistance and then gone on a murderous rampage leaving your gun at the scene of the crime. You just don't seem that stupid, but I could be wrong about that. So let's cut the crap." He leaned closer. "Tell me what you know and what you think is going on. You know the players and you've had the longest time to consider things. Everyone seems convinced that you're a smart guy, so I'm sure you have an opinion. By the way, we've already been down to the basement of the hospital, so let's start there."

Cesari liked him. He was a straight shooter, so he thought about it for a while. The trick was to tell him everything without actually admitting anything. He cleared his throat and began, "Snell and his son Billy Ray Bob got involved with Gianelli over gambling debts they incurred at one of Big Lou Barazza's casinos in Atlantic City some time ago, certainly more than a year ago, probably closer to two. They got muscled into participating in a prescription drug-dealing scheme. The drugs were brought to the hospital and stored in the basement, then eventually delivered to the casino for distribution."

Cesari paused to take a breath and choose his words. "Their relationship eventually blossomed into the illegal organ donation business. I can't say for sure whose idea it was but the basement of the hospital was renovated to accommodate their burgeoning business. The 'donor' part is a misnomer, because none of the donors ever made it out alive. They deceived impoverished, homeless people into thinking they were going to get rich quick by donating a duplicate organ such as a kidney, but when they got here, they sliced and diced them. Only God and Gianelli know where they dumped the bodies afterward. Snell used his position to help them find desperate people on the transplant waiting lists and make sure all the paperwork was filled out right."

"Who did the surgery?" Wilkins asked, taking notes feverishly.

"They recruited Pakistani surgeons who did this kind of thing all the time in their own country. Gianelli would fly them in once or twice a month from Islamabad."

Wilkins was stunned. "This is unbelievable, Cesari. What do you mean they did this kind of thing all the time and where are these guys now?"

"I have no idea where they might be at the moment. And what I meant was that Pakistan has one of the highest rates of illegal organ donation in the world. So if you needed surgeons who were experienced and willing to do this kind of thing, then that would be the place to look. How they actually hooked up with these guys is unclear. Who knows? Maybe they just placed an ad on the dark web."

Wilkins continued scribbling. "Keep talking, Cesari. What about these Arab suicide bombers? How do they fit in?"

"Apparently Barazza has been under intense scrutiny by you guys and has been feeling the heat."

Mesmerized, Cheryl finally remembered to blink. She said, "That's true. We were going to ask for an indictment as soon as this terrorist trial in Manhattan was over."

"Well I guess you must be too close for comfort, because Billy Ray Bob told me that Big Lou has decided that your boss McClellan, the DA, has become too much of a pain in the ass and it was time for him to go. These suicide bombers were specifically targeting him for assassination. They were supposed to show up at the terrorist trial in Manhattan this week in time for opening arguments. Then it would be bye-bye McClellan. At least that's what Billy Ray Bob said he overheard."

"Oh my God." Cheryl's mouth hung wide open in shock.

Wilkins stopped writing and put his pen down. His face turned red with outrage. "You have got to be kidding. Please tell me you're kidding. Have these guys lost their minds? Targeting a public official? The D.A. of all people? This isn't the Wild West anymore."

Cesari shrugged and said, "I guess Big Lou didn't get the memo."

Everyone took a deep breath. The waitress came with their food, but no one felt like eating.

Wilkins calmed down. "Okay, where did they find these bomber guys and why would they give a rat's ass about whether Barazza goes to prison or not?"

Cesari picked up his fork. "Billy Ray Bob said Gianelli had a Mideast connection at the casino, some big-shot rich Arab who's a high roller. For a price, this guy supplied the bombers. It gets a little fuzzy at this point because Snell and his son weren't really part of it. Why these guys would do this is anyone's guess, but I don't think you have to be a genius to figure that one out."

"How about revenge as a motive?" Cheryl said. "We're about to fry one of their own in what is undoubtedly going to be a very public spectacle of a trial and possibly a condemnation of Islam."

"That's certainly a possibility," Wilkins added.

Cesari nodded. "You know, when a mob guy goes on trial, that's usually when his life expectancy starts to tank."

"Meaning what?" asked Wilkins.

"Meaning his bosses don't want to take a chance on him spilling his guts."

They thought that over and Cheryl spoke first. "So you're saying it's possible the Arabs want to shut their guy up before he opens his mouth. You know, that makes a lot of sense. I've been working with the attorneys on this case helping them to get ready, and there's been a lot of talk about what a maniac this guy on trial is."

Cesari said, "Aren't all terrorists maniacs?"

"By our standards maybe but usually not by theirs. However, the word on the street is that this guy on trial is a real hardcore, dyed-in-the-wool nutcase, and an outcast even back home. Sort of a loose cannon. His name is Farooq, and he's a distant cousin of the Saudi king. He plotted to blow up Saint Patrick's Cathedral on Easter morning last spring. Apparently this was an unsanctioned hit and the people back home were pissed off about it. They were glad he got caught."

Cesari was puzzled. "I don't get it. Why do they care what he blows up?"

She explained, "It's complicated, but we do a dangerous dance with these guys, Cesari. We try not to cross the lines. They start blowing up our cathedrals during Holy Days, and then we would have every right to start sending cruise missiles into their mosques during Ramadan. Get it?"

He nodded. "Makes sense."

"At any rate, the inside line is that anybody who is anybody in the Islamic world hates him and thinks it's time for him to go away. This guy Farooq however, could give a crap about what anyone thinks. He's a real fanatic, chomping at the bit to take the stand and rail against the United States, and possibly his own people. It seems perfectly reasonable that they would want to shut him up permanently."

Wilkins looked skeptical. "I don't know about this. So he's a tad more extreme than your typical extremist. Extremism isn't exactly a crime in the Middle East, you know. It's more of a hobby. I find this a little farfetched."

Cheryl persisted. "I agree, but Farooq has been bragging about his relationship to the royal family. If he does that on the stand in front of the television cameras, it is undoubtedly going to be very embarrassing to many people in Riyadh."

"You think they would want to kill him just because he's embarrassing them?" Wilkins asked.

Cesari almost snorted coffee out his nose at that. "Are you serious, Wilkins? People die for less all the time."

Wilkins sighed, "Fine, I see your point. All right, so the Saudis want to martyr this guy Farooq rather than let him embarrass them any further, and Big Lou wants to get rid of the D.A., McClellan. They join forces to blow up the courtroom during opening arguments. Everybody dies and everybody's happy." Wilkins frowned as he processed the information and continued, "The Saudis provide the loons willing to sacrifice themselves and Big Lou provides the expertise, the transport, the access. He has these surgeons ready to do his bidding for the right price. They have no scruples to start with, so they don't care. The bombers can easily pass through metal detectors and random pat-downs. All that's left is to get these guys into the courtroom at the appropriate time. Damn, this is bad."

Cesari met Wilkins's eyes. "It gets worse."

Chapter 75

"**A**nd just how does it get worse?" Wilkins asked, taking a sip of coffee.

Cesari squirmed under his gaze. "Billy Ray Bob told me that there are three more bombers out there. Gianelli brought them up last weekend as a backup."

Wilkins slammed his hand angrily on the table and some of his coffee spilled over the side of the cup. "There are three more bombers out there? When were you going to tell us this?"

"Whoa," Cesari said. "First of all, I would have told you this morning, but you were too busy threatening me with the Patriot Act. Besides, I only found out myself last night, so give me a break. I spent most of the night dodging bullets and most of today trying to avoid getting herpes from a guy named Mo."

Wilkins exhaled loudly. "Where are these other three bombers?"

"I don't know, but my guess is they're probably holed up somewhere in Manhattan waiting for the trial to begin."

Cheryl and Wilkins glanced at each other.

She said, "The trial starts Wednesday morning in the federal courthouse in lower Manhattan. That's approximately thirty-six hours from now. The DA and most of his staff, including me, are supposed to be present for opening arguments at 10:00 a.m. The place will be packed. We're expecting it to be a real circus."

Wilkins rubbed his jaw in thought. "I still can't believe this. Barazza would have to be incredibly desperate or incredibly stupid to think he was going to get away with something like this."

"Not necessarily." Cheryl patted the corner of her mouth with a napkin before continuing. "Think about it. The trial itself has nothing to do with Big Lou. On the surface, it would appear that the bombers are Arabs either seeking vengeance for their friend on trial or to silence him before he can open his mouth. Either way, the smart money would have to be on this being an act of terrorism, not a mob hit."

Wilkins's expression changed to frustration. "So these two guys last night weren't meant to blow up this hospital at all, but were supposed to go to New York to target McClellan. Somehow they wound up in the emergency room, and one of them accidentally detonated. Is that it?"

Cesari finished his meal and nudged his plate forward. "That sums it up."

"Why were they restrained after surgery?" asked Cheryl.

He shrugged. "Not sure, but I guess it was to keep them from wandering off in case the sedation prematurely wore off. I doubt they knew where they were and Gianelli probably wanted to keep it that way."

"We still have a big problem. We need to locate these other bombers before the trial starts," Wilkins said. "But there's something I don't understand. Typically these devices are triggered by cellphones, but cellphones and other electronic devices aren't allowed in courthouses."

Cesari said, "There's always the possibility of an accomplice outside the courtroom waiting for the right moment."

"That's right," Cheryl added. "The whole damn thing is going to be televised. Anybody could figure out the right time for detonation just by turning on their TV. The good news at least, is that there are two fewer bombers to worry about. One option would be to delay the trial if we can't find the other bombers, but we'll have to make that decision quickly if we're going to go that route."

Wilkins thought long and hard about that before speaking. "Delaying a major trial like this would be a big deal under any circumstances, and next to impossible based on hearsay evidence. No offense, Cesari, but you're not the most credible person on the planet. Furthermore, if we delay the trial, that still wouldn't get us the remaining bombers and they might detonate somewhere else with equally horrific consequence. I suppose we could always pick them up at the courthouse with bomb-sniffing dogs. But not knowing how they planned to detonate, they might blow up." He glanced at his watch. "It's almost ten. We're running out of time."

Chapter 76

"Okay, Cesari, we need to wrap this up. Cheryl and I searched the basement of the hospital and found some interesting things. Who are the dead guys down there in the freezer? I recognized Frank Dellatesta but not the other stiffs."

"The freezer is actually a morgue that they used to store donor bodies until they were ready to dispose of them. So several of the bodies were persons whose organs were harvested, and obviously they also used it to store certain special people like Mr. Dellatesta."

"Fine, I got that, but what about the frozen gorilla wearing the Calvin Klein suit and missing three fingers?"

"Oh that guy. Well, he might be an associate of Gianelli's. I'm not one hundred percent certain, but he may have been trying to kill me and Kelly last night. It's a shame he wasn't dressed for the weather."

"What about the guy in the recovery room, hogtied with a hole in his ankle?"

"Ditto with the may have been trying to kill me part, but I think Gianelli strangled him."

"Why would he do that?"

"He doesn't take disappointment well?"

Cheryl and Agent Wilkins stared at each other for a moment.

"We're going to put that to the side for the time being," said Wilkins. "Why do you think Snell wound up with a bullet in his head?"

"To be honest, I wasn't that surprised when I heard that. It makes sense when you think about the characters involved. I think Gianelli's probably bailing out. Things are spiraling out of control for him, and he's tying up loose ends."

Wilkins said, "I agree. And now there's the problem of what to do with you, Cesari. You've been running amok up here for the last forty-eight hours, and I'm not sure whether you should get a medal of honor or the electric chair. Let's start with the assault of an off-duty police officer, breaking and entering, possibly a double homicide and let's not forget that it was your weapon found at Snell's murder scene. Give me one good reason why I shouldn't haul your ass back to the Genesee police station."

"Because you don't really believe I murdered anyone."

"No I don't, at least not anyone who wasn't trying to kill you first. I should have mentioned that we traced the 911 call that placed you at the scene of Snell's murder. Apparently it was made from Billy Ray Bob's cellphone somewhere near Syracuse, and not by a hospital employee concerned about losing his job. Obviously, you were set up. Officer Snell is currently in custody. He was found in his own basement tied up by persons unknown. We heard that he is being very cooperative."

Cheryl voiced her own suspicions. "It's interesting that Billy Ray Bob was found hogtied the same way as the guy we found in the basement of the hospital. Would you happen to know anything about that, Cesari?"

"Maybe you should ask Billy Ray Bob."

Wilkins said, "We already did, but he adamantly refused to disclose how he happened to be found in that circumstance. He was too busy begging to enter witness protection. Even more interesting, the Genesee Times received a hand-delivered, detailed confession from him this morning. Among other things, he admitted to stealing your gun from your apartment the night he kidnapped Kelly. Lieutenant Garcia felt very bad about the way she treated you."

"Oh really. She didn't look it."

"Give her a break. She's under a lot stress right now. She just found out half her department is employed by Gianelli."

"I guess that makes it all better."

Cheryl said, "Relax, Cesari. You're off the hook and that's what matters."

He was a little irritated. "You might have mentioned these things sooner but thank you just the same."

"Take it easy," said Wilkins. "We wanted to make sure you were fully cooperative."

"Any idea who the dog belongs to?" asked Cheryl.

"Gianelli brought her up here with his guys. Why?"

"It would be a shame if they had to put her down," Cheryl replied. "She seems nice enough if you've got a bag full of doggy treats and don't wave a gun at her. We heard what she did to Gianelli's guy, so we went to the animal shelter to see her. I didn't know dogs could grow that big."

"How'd she look?"

"She's fine but if no one claims her, I doubt they'll keep her long. She's too big and after what she did, it's unlikely anyone's going to want her."

"I'm thinking about adopting her. She seems to like Kelly and me."

"Well you better make up your minds quick," Wilkins added. "They want her off their hands as soon as possible. She was making them all very nervous. Are you sure you can handle her? I saw what she did. That was no small guy she tore apart. It was pretty bad."

"We got to see a different side of her. She's really very gentle. If you treat her right, she'll do anything for you," Cesari said.

"Women are like that too, Cesari. You should remember that," Cheryl added pointedly.

Wilkins finished his coffee and signaled the waitress for the check. "I guess you're free to go Cesari, but if you think of anything else let us know right away. We've got to figure out a way of getting those bombers with minimal risk of detonation. Then we have to figure out how to remove the explosives from their bodies."

"And would you turn on your cellphone?" Cheryl added. "We could have spared you a lot aggravation if we could have reached you sooner."

"I lost my phone in the fire last night."

"Well get another one in a hurry. I have no doubt that we're going to need to talk to you some more."

They stood up to leave. But Cesari hesitated and sat down again. They both frowned at him.

Cheryl asked, "What's the matter?"

He said, "Look, I have an idea if you wouldn't mind hearing me out."

Chapter 77

"Make it quick, Cesari. The clock is ticking," Wilkins said.

"What have you got on your mind?" asked Cheryl.

"The reality here is that there is no way you are going to be able to find these guys in time. Even if you caught up with Gianelli, he's not going to talk, and his lawyers will have him out in an hour. There's no hard evidence here connecting him with anything. It's all speculation. Like you said before, based on what we have, they probably wouldn't even postpone the trial. Your only option is to screen everybody coming into the courtroom with bomb sniffing dogs, but even then you would take the risk of them detonating."

"You got a better idea?" Wilkins asked.

"Let me talk to him."

"Who, Gianelli?"

"Yes. Let me explain the facts of life to him. That his plan failed and that we know everything he's been up to. I'll offer him immunity if he gives up the bombers and turns on Big Lou."

"Are you crazy, Cesari? I can't offer slime like that immunity."

"You're not offering him anything. I am. I'll make him think that I've been authorized to make the offer. Once he gives up the bombers, who's he going to complain to?"

They sat there quietly, thinking about that.

Eventually Wilkins said, "He'll shoot you on sight, Cesari."

"He'll certainly want to and that's what I'm counting on to get near him. He's been trying to catch me all weekend. He couldn't possibly pass up an opportunity like this."

Wilkins turned to Cheryl. "Do we even know where he is?"

"No, but we know where Big Lou is. He's holed up in his apartment on Mulberry Street in Little Italy. We've had him under constant surveillance for weeks. It's quite possible Gianelli will be heading there."

"It's a good starting point," Cesari said. "Are we eavesdropping on him?"

"No," Cheryl replied. "We couldn't get a judge to authorize a wiretap. Not enough probable cause."

"I'll take care of that," Wilkins said. "We're talking about an imminent terrorist attack now, not just racketeering. I could have long-distance listening devices set up across the street from his apartment in a couple of hours." He signaled the waitress back for another round of coffee for the table. She made a snarky face and he continued, "What are you going to do if he really does decide to shoot you on sight, Cesari?"

"That's a good question. I'll need to convince him of how imprudent that would be. And for that I'll need some weapons of my own."

Wilkins laughed.

Cheryl frowned. "This is not a game, Cesari. You're as bad as they are."

Cesari argued the merit of his idea, "You can't expect me to walk through Barazza's front door unarmed. C'mon, we need to level the playing field or I'll never even get a chance to make the offer."

The waitress poured his coffee. He said to her, "Do you guys ever get French roast in here?"

She glanced at him sideways. "As soon as my shift's over, my boyfriend is going to fly me to Paris in his private jet. I'll bring you back some."

She walked away.

"Was that absolutely necessary, Cesari?" Cheryl asked.

"Relax, she loves me."

"Okay, stop it you two," Wilkins ordered. "What kind of weapons were you thinking of, Cesari?"

He was softening up on the idea of arming him. Cesari said, "A handgun, of course. A taser would be nice, and some plastic wrist restraints."

"What are the wrist restraints for?"

"In case they decide to surrender."

Wilkins chuckled again. "Wouldn't that be nice."

He thought it over and let out a deep breath. "Look Cesari, I see your point but I can't just simply hand you an FBI firearm. However, considering the threat we're under right now, we have to think outside the box a little."

He hesitated and strummed his fingers on the table thinking it over. Then he glanced over his shoulder and lowered his voice. "I may have some personal devices that should meet your needs. I'll arrange to have them delivered to you. They are strictly for self-defense. Understand?"

Cesari nodded. "You're a good man Wilkins, but I don't want to get you in trouble. Can these weapons be traced back to you?"

He glanced furtively at Cheryl and then back at Cesari. With reluctance he said, "Let's just say that I have a few items in my possession that I prefer to keep under the radar. But that doesn't mean I want you blasting up Manhattan with them."

"Understood."

"Anything else, Cesari?"

"Yeah, how about a crowbar?"

Chapter 78

Cesari walked into the ICU shortly after midnight and introduced himself to the policeman outside Kelly's door. He showed him his ID.

He said, "She's going to be checking out."

The officer looked perplexed. "No one told me."

"Sorry about that but she's not a prisoner, right?"

"No, she's not. I'm here for her protection."

"Then thank you for your service."

The officer was silent for a minute and then said, "I'll have to call my supervisor for instructions."

"You can call whoever you want but I'm personal friends with Lieutenant Garcia so make sure you spell my name right."

Cesari walked by him into Kelly's room and found her reading a magazine with headphones on. She was wearing blue surgical scrubs and slippers. She took the headphones off and jumped out of bed when she saw him. They hugged tightly.

She said, "I've been so worried about you."

"Same here. How do you feel?"

"Wired to the max. I've been sleeping all day. I don't know why I agreed to stay overnight. I'm totally fine. I don't even have an IV anymore and I certainly don't need to be in the ICU. I'm not in the least bit sick."

"It was just a precaution, Kel. I'm glad you feel well. Want to leave?"

"Hell yeah. I feel like having a slice of pizza."

"Funny you should say that."

"Why?"

"Because I was thinking of taking you down to Little Italy in Manhattan with me."

"When?"

"Now."

"You're kidding, right?"

"Deadly serious."

"But I don't have any clothes. I lost everything in the fire."

"We'll borrow the scrubs you're wearing and head over to Walmart to get you some jeans and sneakers. They're open all night. Once we're in Manhattan, we'll go shopping on Fifth Avenue."

They waved goodbye to the police officer who was on the phone with Lieutenant Garcia being told to stand down.

~~~

He dozed for the first three hours of the ride while Kelly drove. They switched places when they stopped to gas up and grab some coffee outside of Albany. It was now 4:00 a.m., and he had been driving for the last hour. He estimated that they would arrive at the Blue Moon Hotel around 6:00 a.m.

"So far so good," he said and glanced at her.

She said, "You might want to slow it down. A stolen Porsche going a hundred miles an hour at four in the morning might attract attention."

"It's not stolen. It's commandeered." But she was right otherwise, so he brought the speed down to a reasonable seventy-five miles an hour.

"Either way, it's not your name on the registration or insurance card. If we get pulled over, it will delay us from getting to Saks Fifth Avenue and I want to be there when they open."

Cesari smiled. "Roger that, boss."

Cheryl's cellphone buzzed. He had lost his phone in Kelly's house fire and given the accelerated timetable of their plan, Cheryl had graciously leant him her phone to use. It was now hopping around on the center console vibrating impatiently.

He answered it, "Yes?"

"What's your location?" Agent Wilkins demanded. They were on speakerphone.

"We're about an hour south of Albany on Route 87."

"What do you mean, we? Who's with you?"

"Kelly."

"Are you nuts, Cesari? You can't bring her there. Besides, I thought she was sick in the hospital."

Kelly answered for herself. "I'm fine, Agent Wilkins. Thanks for your concern. I wanted to come. I need new clothes."

"Unbelievable," Wilkins said. "This is what we've got so far. Gianelli's there with another guy called Pinky. They plan to hunker down with Big Lou in the apartment until after the trial begins. As we speak, there are four guys total in the apartment. The three I mentioned and Big Lou's personal bodyguard, Gino. Compared to Big Lou, he's a shrimp, only six foot three and three hundred pounds. But there are two other guards on the street at the entrance to the apartment building. No surveillance cameras that we know of. My guys have set up shop on the other side of Mulberry above a grocery store. Cheryl will call you later after she reviews her Barazza files but she said to tell you that you better not lose her cellphone."

"Roger that and ten four, big daddy."

"This is not a game, Cesari. People's lives are depending on you."

He replied more seriously, "Yes, you're right. I know that, Agent Wilkins."

"Okay, let's synchronize our watches. It's 4:00 a.m., and we have thirty hours until the start of the trial. Remember to keep your phone on at all times. If we find the bombers before you make contact, then you abort. Understood?"

He hung up before Cesari could reply. Kelly said, "He's a pretty serious guy, isn't he?"

"That's what wearing a suit all day does to you."

Chapter 79

The Blue Moon was a beautiful four-star hotel located a few blocks from Little Italy in Manhattan. It had its own garage and valet parking. They checked in shortly after 6:00 a.m. with the weapons concealed in a duffel bag. The spacious room had a great view of the city. Cesari examined the Beretta M9 with the fifteen round clip Wilkins had lent him. It was a nice reliable weapon and the 9mm parabellum rounds would get the job done. The serial number had been scratched off and he wondered where Wilkins had obtained it. He tucked it away with the taser into the room safe. The crowbar was too big for the safe so he left it in the duffel bag which he placed in the closet.

"This room is so beautiful. I want to live here forever." Kelly exclaimed jumping and twirling around on the king-sized bed like a kid. "I feel like I'm in a dream. Make love to me right now. I command you, my prince."

He laughed. "Okay, settle down country girl. Everything in due time. We've got a long day and night ahead of us, so we'll need to pace ourselves."

She leapt off the bed right at him and he caught her instinctively. She wrapped her arms around his neck and her legs around his waist and hung on.

In a husky voice, she whispered, "You cannot believe how horny I am right now."

"How horny are you?"

"I could eat you alive," she said and growled like a tiger, baring her teeth.

"What is it with girls and hotel rooms?" he asked.

"They're exciting." Her cheeks flushed as she unwrapped her legs and let herself down in front of him.

"I thought you wanted to get to Saks Fifth Avenue when it opens... Kelly? What are you doing? Really now. That's inappropriate."

An hour later they lay on the bed, panting and staring at the ceiling. He watched her breathe and said, "All right, can we get serious now?"

"You're starting to sound like Agent Wilkins."

He smiled and glanced at his watch. "It's almost eight-thirty. Let's clean up and get some breakfast. We'll get to Saks by ten, hang out in midtown for a few hours and grab lunch somewhere. Later in the afternoon we'll come back, collect the weapons and scout out the opposition."

"Am I a gangster now too?" she asked playfully.

"Gangsteress, I believe is the proper term. And yes, you're a regular Al Capone."

They left the hotel, grabbed coffee and muffins at a Starbucks down the block and then caught a cab to Saks. As they exited the car, a messenger guy on his bike almost ran them over. The guy flipped them the bird as he sped away but they took it in stride. Welcome to New York.

"This is such a huge city," Kelly said, looking around. "I love it. There are so many people."

"It is pretty amazing, that's for sure."

It was morning in midtown Manhattan. Tourists, office workers, and business people filled the sidewalks and streets. Traffic was heavy as always, and the sounds and smells of a metropolis filled their senses. They walked hand in hand, admiring the window dressings that Saks had on display. Kelly was in absolute awe.

Cesari asked, "Is this your first trip to Manhattan?"

"Yes and no. I came many years ago to see a play on a high school class trip. That was fun but I haven't been back since as an adult. I have been to Chicago a couple of times though, and I've always been told that it's like New York only smaller."

"I've been to Chicago a couple of times too and people told me the same thing, but I disagree. Chicago isn't like New York at all. If it's anything in comparison, then it's more like an echo of New York. Personally, I was disappointed. I don't mean to be a snob, but it was missing something."

"Like what?"

"I'm not sure. Chicago reminded me of a little kid trying to dress up and look like his tougher older brother."

She laughed at the image. "Are you being completely fair?"

"I'm being more than fair. What I really wanted to say was that compared to New York, Chicago has no soul."

"No soul?"

"You heard me."

"That I did. Well c'mon Mr. Soul Man, I'm ready to do some serious shopping."

"And I'm ready to seriously tag along and watch you shop."

"Do you mean that? Most guys don't like to shop."

"Most guys don't have a clue how to make a woman happy."

She smiled. "I'm glad you do."

They navigated their way through the massive store and after about an hour and a half, Cesari was starting to show signs of fatigue. He bought a pair of black leather dress gloves that appealed to him and sat on a cushioned bench watching Kelly. She had picked out a pair of Coach sneakers, a Michael Kors top, a Donna Karan sweater and was now modeling a pair of Ralph Lauren jeans for him.

"How do they look?" she asked, studying herself in the mirror.

"They look about three hundred dollars, but from this angle they're worth every penny."

She liked that. "I thought you said the FBI was picking up the tab for all of our expenses."

"They are, as long as I get the job done."

She bent over in front of him to adjust her sneaker laces, giving him full view.

"Don't do that to me please," he said. "It's not fair."

"I didn't do anything," she said laughing.

Chapter 80

It was a beautiful day in the city. The sun was out, and the air was crisp. They meandered up and down Fifth Avenue for a couple of hours window-shopping and soaking in the sights. At lunchtime they caught a cab to East 33rd Street between Third Avenue and Lexington.

"You're in for a treat now Kelly," he said with excitement as they stepped out of the taxi and stood in front of the Second Avenue Deli.

She looked around and seemed puzzled. "I don't get it. Why do they call it the Second Avenue Deli if we're not on Second Avenue?"

"They used to be on Second Avenue but moved here a few years ago. The name was so iconic they decided to keep it. It's practically synonymous for delicious."

Entering the crowded restaurant, they found themselves third in line to be seated. The place was hot and humid with small tables, narrow aisles and a busy deli-counter for takeout customers. For a few minutes they just stood there, sniffing the air and taking in the robust aromas of a classic Jewish delicatessen. They stared through the glass case of the deli-counter at the brisket, knishes, salamis, gefilte fish, hot dogs and mounds of chopped liver.

Kelly whispered, "It's great in here but are you sure this is the place you've been talking about? It doesn't seem like fine dining to me."

"No one said anything about fine dining. I said delicious dining."

Eventually a short Mexican waiter seated them at a tiny wood table sandwiched between two other tiny tables and handed them menus. To their left was a young tourist couple with their guidebooks out. To their right were two middle-aged bearded men wearing yarmulkes. They were so close Cesari could hear them sweat.

Kelly studied her menu.

"I don't mean to be pushy," he told her, "but on your first trip here, there's really only one thing you can order."

She lowered the menu. "What's that?"

"A hot pastrami sandwich on rye bread with mustard, a dill pickle and cream soda. Mmm, I can taste it already."

She smiled at his enthusiasm. "Sure, I'm game."

The waiter came back, and they ordered two hot pastrami sandwiches. Kelly asked politely, "Can I get Swiss cheese on mine?"

The waiter shook his head. "No cheese."

Then he walked away without explanation. One of the guys to Cesari's right made a snide comment to his friend in Yiddish, and Cesari couldn't believe his ears. Cesari didn't speak Yiddish but he grew up in New York and had spent a lot of time training with guys who did. You can learn a lot by passive diffusion.

Kelly seemed bewildered. "Am I imagining it or was the waiter a little rude?"

"Rude? Maybe a little. Overworked probably. Language barrier possibly. This is a kosher delicatessen Kelly, and kosher law prohibits serving dairy products with meat and vice versa. I should have told you that when we sat down. My guess is the little guy wasn't deliberately trying to be offensive just a little short on social skills. It's a New York thing."

The guy next to him however, was a different story.

She said, "Okay, I can handle that."

The sandwiches came, and they dug in. Kelly was in heaven. "Oh my God," she said. "I can't believe how good this is. It's so moist and tender. This is incredible."

Indeed it was.

"I told you. Eating a pastrami sandwich in a New York deli is one of those things you simply can't explain to people. You have to experience it."

Maybe they were making too much noise, because the guy next to Cesari called someone from behind the counter and said something to him in Yiddish. You didn't have to speak their language to get the gist. He was asking if they could be moved to a different table. Exactly where to, was a good question. The place was packed to capacity. Cesari heard him say a familiar word again under his breath. The man from behind the counter shrugged sympathetically but raised his arms as if to say, 'What do you want me to do?' He went back to work and the guys resumed their meal.

Cesari was getting pissed off and it showed. This wasn't right. It was the twenty-first century for God's sake.

"What's the matter?" Kelly asked, observing his darkening mood.

"Nothing. Just enjoying my lunch. Got a lot on my mind."

"Is everything all right over there?" She used her eyes to point at the two guys.

"I don't know. I don't speak Yiddish." But in his mind, he thought shvatsa was shvatsa in any language.

They finished their lunch, and the waiter brought the check. Cesari paid with his credit card. He said, "C'mon Kel, it's time to pick up a cellphone for you."

They walked out of the restaurant which was still jammed tight like sardines, and now had a dozen people waiting to be seated. Outside on the street, they stretched.

Cesari took out his wallet and feigned concern. "Damn, I forgot my credit card on the table. Wait here for me, Kel. I'll be right back. In fact, why don't you hail us a cab? Look, there's one coming now."

Kelly saw the yellow taxi and waved her hand at it while he went back inside the restaurant. Their waiter saw him and he explained that he'd forgotten something on the table. He let Cesari go right through. He walked up to where they had been sitting, and there was already another couple there. The guy with the yarmulke was still on his right talking to his friend and sipping coffee. He considered Cesari briefly and returned to his conversation. He was leaning back, relaxed on his little wooden chair. There was nothing behind him but the tiled floor. Cesari walked past the table and pretended to scan the floor. He turned back and was now standing in between the two guys.

Keeping the shvatsa guy on his right, he thrust his left hand out suddenly between their two faces, pointing to a far corner of the dining room and yelled hysterically, "Oh my God, there's a rat! It's under that table!"

People screamed and jumped up from their seats. Everybody turned in the direction he was pointing, including the shvatsa guy. Cesari launched a hard right into his left temple, knocking him off his chair to the floor. He then picked up the edge of their table and overturned it.

Cesari screamed again, "It just ran under me!"

He jumped and did a little dance as chaos erupted throughout the deli. Everybody was on their feet dancing, searching for the rat. With all the commotion, it appeared that the shvatsa guy might have tipped his own chair over trying to get a look. His friend had jumped back from the flying table and was frantically scanning all around him. He didn't even notice his unconscious companion on the floor.

Putz.

When the rabbi came out of the kitchen holding a cleaver, Cesari beat a hasty retreat to the front door and found his passage blocked by the little Mexican waiter. He had seen everything and gave Cesari a look of deep disapproval. Cesari took out his wallet and handed him a twenty. He looked at it and rolled his eyes. Cesari took out another twenty and offered the two bills to him for his trouble. He took the money and stepped out of the way.

Cesari spoke a little Spanish and said, "*Muchas gracias.*"

He replied, "*De nada.*"

He flew out the exit and got into the cab with Kelly.

"Everything okay? What's all the fuss about?" She could see the commotion in the restaurant through the large window.

"Oh that," he said. "I forgot to tip the waiter but it's okay now."

She raised her eyebrows in surprise. "Really?"

"They take that kind of stuff very seriously down here, Kelly."

Chapter 81

They napped in the hotel after lunch and around five readied themselves. He wore jeans, black sneakers, a cotton dress shirt and a black windbreaker. Wilkins had provided him with a holster for the Beretta, but he didn't use it and slipped the gun into the back of his jeans. The taser and wrist restraints went into the pockets of the windbreaker. He left the crowbar in the duffel bag.

The cellphone buzzed.

"Hi, Cheryl."

"Where are you?"

"In the hotel. Getting ready to head down to Little Italy."

"Sorry it took so long to get back to you."

"Love means never having to say you're sorry."

"I'm glad you're in a good mood, Cesari. Okay, this is what we know. Lou owns the whole building. It's three stories, and he lives in the five thousand square feet of the second floor. He also conducts all his business from there. The Café Napoli, an Italian trattoria-type place, occupies the street level. Adjacent to the Café Napoli is a doorway that leads up to Big Lou's apartment. There are two guards on the outside at all times. You still listening, Cesari?"

"Yeah, what about the third floor? What's up there?"

"It's his private fitness center where he and his bodyguard work out three or four times a week."

"You're joking. He's a fitness nut? How old is he, anyway?"

"Don't kid yourself, Cesari. They don't call him Big Lou for nothing. He's fifty years old and in great shape. He could easily pass for an NFL lineman. He used to powerlift when he was young and holds several state records in the squat and bench. So be careful, and that's only if you get past Gino his bodyguard, who never leaves his side. He has his own room in the apartment and is with Lou twenty-four-seven."

She paused and he heard her flipping through a notebook. He said, "Any chance I could drop in on them from the roof?"

Kelly was sitting on the edge of the bed, watching television with the sound muted.

Cheryl replied, "Not a chance. We thought about that. He sealed the roof tight. If any work needs to be done, he has them access it from neighboring buildings. No rear entrance or exit either. It's a real fire hazard from that point of view but simplifies his security concerns."

"Tell me about the two guards on the street."

"The front door is guarded around the clock. Two guys rotate every twelve hours. Suffice it to say that they're armed and dangerous. They stand outside a solid steel door that only opens when Lou or Gino press an electronic buzzer located up in the apartment. There is an electronic key pad on the outside, but we don't know the code."

"What do these guys do when they get hungry or need a bathroom break?" he asked.

"The Café Napoli is owned by Big Lou. If the guys need to take a break, they go there one at a time. They're never gone for more than fifteen minutes. The entrance to the restaurant is only twenty feet from Big Lou's front door. Lou hasn't left the apartment in three days. He gets all his meals from the restaurant."

"What, like takeout or does he come and sit down?"

"Neither. There's a dumbwaiter in the kitchen toward the back of the restaurant. He has his meals sent up that way. We know the dumbwaiter is professional grade and was built to support Big Lou's weight in case of an emergency."

"You're kidding."

"No. Remember, there are no exits from the apartment. The windows are all barred up as well. He also uses the dumbwaiter to get rid of trash and get his laundry washed. If an undesirable ever got past his guys at the door, he'd have no other way out in a hurry."

Cesari laughed at that imagery. He said, "So what do you think? This doesn't sound too good."

"You tell me, Cesari. This was your idea, remember? Gianelli's in there with Lou, and they aren't coming out until after the trial starts. We could go in there and grab them but like you said, they're not going to talk and we don't have any real proof of anything." Cheryl sighed. "No one's forcing you to do this."

He said, "I know that. By the way, are there any other houseguests besides Gianelli and his pal Pinky, I might have to concern myself with?"

"What do you mean?"

"Wives, ex-wives, girlfriends, maids, hookers, you know, collateral damage?"

"Not that we know. He's widowed and among other things, we suspect him of having murdered his wife. No children and no romantic entanglements that we are aware of. He's all business. That's all I've got for you, Cesari. Wilkins wants to brief you now. Good luck."

"Thanks and Cheryl, could you do me a favor?"

"What?"

"Could you ask the animal shelter not to make any final decisions on what to do with Cleo until Kelly and I return?"

"I'll see what I can do. Here's Wilkins." He heard her hand off the phone.

"Cesari?"

"I'm still here."

"It's Wilkins. So far, no new players are in the apartment, only the same four we talked about. But the latest is that they're going to watch the Yankee game tonight, which starts at seven. They're having dinner delivered at eight via the dumbwaiter. Right now they're all in the steam room on the third floor. Keep your phone on at all times and be prepared to stand down on my command. Any questions?"

"Yeah. Remember when you said you would pick up all my expenses?"

"I said all reasonable expenses, Cesari. And only if we get the bombers. Yeah, I remember. Why?"

"We probably should have spent more time defining what 'reasonable' meant."

He hung up.

Chapter 82

At six p.m., they sat down at a small table by the window in Umberto's Clam House. Neither of them were hungry but they needed to secure a good vantage point of Big Lou's building before the tourist crowds swarmed all restaurants. It was Tuesday night and still early, so there was plenty of seating when they arrived. He kept his windbreaker on and slid the duffel bag under the table. Glancing out the window, he had an unobstructed view of the Café Napoli across the street. Throngs of people crisscrossed Mulberry Street browsing for a place to eat or buy souvenirs. The guards in front of Big Lou's apartment were smoking and nonchalantly eyeing girls as they walked by.

Kelly looked at her menu. "I'm still full from lunch."

"Me too. I'll order a bottle of wine and we'll nurse it for as long as we can. Maybe in an hour we can get something light, like calamari or clams?"

She scrunched her nose. "I'm not big on seafood."

"Seriously? I love seafood but they have a full menu here, so whatever you want although seafood is good for you. By the way, you look great."

She gave him a big smile. "Thank you. My fat lip's not disturbing you anymore?"

He studied her more carefully. "It's barely noticeable. I think I'll let it go this time," he teased.

She reached across the small table and tapped his left arm close to the bullet hole.

"Ouch. Was that necessary?"

She jumped back. "I'm sorry. I forgot about the bullet."

The waiter came over and asked if they would like something to drink before dinner. His name was Luigi. Cesari inconspicuously handed him a folded twenty-dollar bill and said, "Luigi, bring us a bottle of Pinot Grigio. We're not very hungry at the moment and would just like to enjoy the atmosphere if that's okay? We might order something later but right now all we'd like is some private time."

He discreetly accepted the bribe and replied, "She's a no problem, signore. I bring you the wine immediately."

Kelly was impressed. "You really know your way around this city, don't you?" She looked around and added, "It's cute in here."

"Yeah, I like it. It's not too corny like some of the other places around here. Although you'll get tired of *O Solo Mio* before the night's over," he said, referring to the piped-in Italian classic that they'd already heard twice since entering the restaurant.

"Well I don't go to places like this very often. I think it's romantic."

"Don't misunderstand me. The food here's great but Manhattan's Little Italy has become a massive tourist destination and unfortunately, it's become a little bit like Disneyland. One day I'll take you to Boston's North End. Now that place will knock your socks off. It's very authentic. Almost like being in Italy."

"I don't mean to change the subject, but I overheard part of the conversation you had with Wilkins about expenses. Was he upset?"

"Nah, he was fine. He said not to worry about anything. In fact, he was real friendly."

Luigi brought the wine to the table with warm bread, olive oil and a small plate of marinated olives. He said, "Compliments of a the house."

They thanked him as he filled the glasses and after he left, they toasted each other.

"*Cin cin*," Cesari said.

"Chin chin?" Kelly asked. "What's that mean?"

"It's an Italian salutation like 'cheers' or 'bottoms up'. It may be more Sicilian than Italian. I think it's a derivation of *cento cento*, which means 'one hundred' as in, 'may you live to be one hundred years old' or something to that effect."

He gazed out the window and down the block. "Later, I want you to park the Porsche there at the corner of Mulberry and Hester and wait for my call. Don't come before 10:30 p.m. If you're parked too long in one spot, it'll look suspicious. If I'm still alive, I should be out by 11:00 p.m. Certainly no later than midnight. I realize that an hour of uncertainty is long, but I can't be sure what's going to happen up there. If I'm not out by midnight, I want you to leave immediately and call Wilkins. If I come out on cue, then we head for the highway and back home."

"Why don't we sleep at the Blue Moon tonight and leave in the morning?"

"Not a chance, Kel. Whatever happens in Lou's place tonight, we're going to want to get out of town as fast as possible. I want the car ready and the engine warm. We're going to full-throttle it up the West Side Drive."

"That's too bad. I thought it would be nice to spend the night there," she whined. "That room was so beautiful and romantic and it had a Jacuzzi. You know what I mean?" She smiled seductively and rubbed his leg with her bare foot.

He lifted the table cloth and peeked underneath. "You took your sneaker off to do that?"

"Got a problem with that?"

"It might be hard to run when the shooting starts," he joked.

"You'll protect me."

"You're awfully trusting."

Chapter 83

Kelly returned to the hotel and Cesari walked over to the Café Napoli with the duffel bag. He casually nodded at Barazza's security guards, and they nonchalantly nodded back. Inside the café, he asked for a seat toward the back of the room. Smaller but a smidgeon more upscale than Umberto's, this place was slightly less campy. The music was still Italian, but modern and jazzy with a Tony Bennett flare to it. Cesari suddenly had this image of a silver-haired man in a tuxedo walking around the café singing love songs to the customers. Not a bad idea. He might suggest it to the owner at a future time.

With fifteen minutes to kill, he ordered an espresso and a cannoli to pass the time. The coffee was hot, strong and of very high quality. The crispy cannoli shell held a sweet and delicious filling speckled with candied fruit and chocolate shavings. They knew what they were doing at the Café Napoli. When he finished, he checked his watch and threw some money down on the table to cover the bill.

"Is there a men's room?" he politely asked waiter.

He directed Cesari down a narrow corridor even further to the back of the restaurant and very near the kitchen entrance. Cesari brought the duffel bag with him into the bathroom. He turned the cellphone off and splashed water on his face. Looking in the mirror, he saw grim determination in his reflection. His left arm throbbed from the bullet wound, and he rubbed it. It was a good reminder of why he was here. He took the taser out and inspected it to make sure it was fully charged. It was and he put it back in his pocket. Then he put on the black leather gloves from Saks and slipped the crowbar up the left sleeve of the windbreaker, holding the curved end in his hand. He took a deep breath and let it out slowly.

He left the bathroom and paused. Looking both ways, he didn't see anybody. A picture of Enrico Caruso decorated the wall directly in front of him. The kitchen entrance was a few feet away, and he walked confidently through the swinging doors. Despite a lot of typical kitchen noises, he didn't see anyone, so he made a quick left and headed to the back. He passed a guy chopping onions who didn't even blink when he saw him. Moments later, he found the dumbwaiter where Cheryl said it would be. The buttons to the side of the dumbwaiter were self-explanatory. The green one said *Open* and when he pushed it, the door slid upward revealing an empty steel box, three-feet wide by three-feet high and deep. He had trouble picturing Big Lou curled up in this thing. One could only imagine the kind of emergency it would take to prompt him to do so.

The lower edge of the dumbwaiter was waist high and Cesari curled up into it without too much difficulty although by the time he got his legs in, he was tightly cramped and claustrophobic. After spotting an emergency release switch on the inside, he immediately wondered what it would be like to get stuck in there and didn't like that thought at all. Don't be negative, he told himself.

He stuck his hand out to the control panel but couldn't quite reach it and as he fumbled for the right button, a kitchen worker carrying Big Lou's dinner trays walked in. He wore a dirty apron and sported a Pancho Villa mustache. Unfazed by the sight of Cesari, he walked closer.

"What's for dinner?" Cesari asked.

He spoke with a thick Spanish accent, "Veal Marsala for the two big men, Chicken Parmigiana for the bigger man, and two servings of Osso Buco for the really big man. Penne with vodka sauce on the side for everyone. Who are you?"

"FBI. Would you mind pressing the red button there for me? And if you don't have a green card, this would be a good time to take a cigarette break."

"*Gracias.*"

He pushed the button and as the door closed, Cesari saw him dump the dinners into a nearby garbage can, take off his apron, and walk hurriedly out the door.

Only in New York.

~ ~ ~

Gianelli chanced a glance at Pinky. They had spent most of the day having their ears pinned back by Big Lou, who was only now starting to calm down. Gianelli watched the big man's countenance carefully trying to read his mood. As Lou switched to problem solving and thinking through alternative solutions, Gianelli breathed a sigh of relief. They were now sitting in Big Lou's living room watching the Yankees pummel the Blue Jays.

Gianelli said, "So Lou, you never told me how you know Cesari. If you don't mind my asking?"

"No, I don't mind. It's a lesson to be learned anyway. Never leave loose ends when you do a job, Vito. They always come back to bite you in the ass. Anyway, that's neither here nor there… It was maybe twenty-five years ago. I was just starting out in the business. I got the call to make my stripes up in the Bronx. Some schmuck was making noise and the bosses wanted him to shut up. Cesari was just a kid then. Happy little family and all the usual bullshit."

A bell rang in the kitchen.

Lou interrupted his discourse. "Gino, that's the dumbwaiter. Get our dinners while I finish the story. We'll eat in here. And we'll need another bottle of wine."

"Sure thing, Lou."

Gino left the room and Big Lou continued, "Anyway, as I was saying, Cesari was just a kid playing catch..."

Chapter 84

Cesari had just climbed out of the dumbwaiter and was adjusting the taser as Gino came through the kitchen door and spotted him. Gino's jaw dropped and he stood there gaping in confusion at the sight. He was a no-neck mammoth of a man, but he froze with hesitation trying to understand what was happening. His momentary delay in reacting was a costly error because a moment was all Cesari needed. He raised the taser and shot Gino in the chest. The two prongs pierced his flesh and fifty thousand volts raced through his body, causing him to lurch and rock wildly. He fell to the floor like a rock, hitting the kitchen table and knocking over a chair with a crashing sound.

Big Lou called out, "Hey Gino, what the hell is going on in there? You better not have dropped our dinners."

A second later, Cesari heard loud cheering from the men in the other room as the Yankees did something they approved of, causing them to forget about the noise in the kitchen.

Gino was still twitching as Cesari searched him for a weapon. He found a .45 caliber Springfield tucked away in the small of his back. He checked to make sure it was loaded and then chambered a round. The big man had hit the floor hard and was bleeding profusely from a lacerated lip and his glassy eyes stared blankly at nothing in particular. He clenched and gnashed his teeth, and Cesari couldn't tell if he was conscious or not. He quickly cuffed his hands behind his back with a pair of the plastic restraints, and then did the same to his ankles.

"Gino, are you all right? Where are our dinners, for Chrissake?" Barazza bellowed, and Cesari heard the sounds of the ball game in the background.

"Dinner's going to be late fellas," Cesari said as he walked briskly into the room.

They were facing away from him in a semicircle, staring at a large flat-screen television. Gianelli and Pinky sat on a plush couch, and Barazza was off to one side almost fully reclined in a large black leather chair. The television was quite loud, which had fortunately muffled the sounds he'd made in the kitchen. They turned their heads his way and he waved Gino's gun at them with his right hand as he held the crowbar in his left.

Vito whispered, "Shit..."

"Nobody breathe and put your hands in the air," Cesari commanded.

He stepped quickly around the couch and in front of the television so that he was facing them.

No one moved, but Barazza felt compelled to bluster, "Who the fuck are you?"

He really was a big guy, not an ounce under three-hundred-and-fifty pounds with bulging sinewy muscles everywhere. The description Cheryl had given him didn't do this guy any justice at all. He was twice as big in person. He had wavy black hair that was starting to gray at the temples and Cesari notice perspiration beading on his rugged face. His nose had been broken several times which gave him the appearance of a boxer and he had a gigantic head mounted on a short thick neck. He wore slacks and a turtleneck. His chest and thighs were enormous and Cesari made a mental note not to get too close.

Barazza said, "Are deaf? Who are you?"

Gianelli and Pinky didn't move and remained quiet. Cesari assessed the situation quickly. Pinky was on his right, Gianelli was in the middle and Barazza on the left. It was three against one and all three of them were bigger than him. Barazza was reclined, and a guy his size and age probably wasn't going to be moving too fast. But three against one was three against one and if they rushed him all at once, he'd be in trouble.

He didn't like those odds and looked right at Gianelli, "I said hands in the air and don't make me say it again."

Vito and Pinky slowly raised their hands up followed reluctantly by Big Lou. Vito said, "This is Cesari, Lou. Cesari, meet Big Lou."

Cesari turned to Lou and said, "Nice apartment. Wish I could say it's nice to meet you Lou, but it isn't."

"What do you want, Cesari?" Big Lou demanded.

Cesari ignored him and turned to Pinky. "Who are you?"

He had never met him before and wanted to make sure he had his ducks in a row. The guy squirmed, glanced quickly at Gianelli and said, "They call me Pinky."

Cesari shot him between the eyes. His arms flopped down to his side and his head rocked backward onto the couch. The sudden discharge of the weapon rocked the room causing Big Lou and Vito to flinch. As the smoke cleared, he could see that Pinky was dead before he even knew what happened. Blood oozed down the front of his face from the hole in his forehead, and his lifeless eyes searched for something on the ceiling. The smell of gunpowder wafted around the room as the television announced that someone had struck out.

"Jesus Christ, Cesari," Gianelli exclaimed. "Was that necessary?"

Cesari pointed the gun at him and he shut up. Cesari said, "It was very necessary Vito, because I need you to understand that I'm not fooling around. So unless you want to be the next guy with a hole in his head, you'd better start paying attention."

Chapter 85

"**O**h my God. This can't be happening," Agent Wilkins said as he listened on the phone to his surveillance team in New York. "Don't do anything until you hear from me. Just sit tight. Listen but stop recording, and for God's sake, destroy those tapes. Today never happened, understand?"

He hung up and turned to Cheryl. "Your ex-boyfriend just murdered Pinky in cold blood to make a point."

She was horrified, "Are you sure?"

"I'm sure and it's even worse than that."

"What do you mean?"

"Cesari's on a suicide mission. No one's coming out of that apartment alive if my guys heard right."

"I can't believe it."

"Well believe it. This is an old-fashioned vendetta. He played us good. The only thing we're not sure of right now is whether Barazza's bodyguard Gino is also dead or merely unconscious in the kitchen. Cesari has Big Lou and Gianelli hostage in the living room. I can't believe I trusted that guy to show restraint... And I supplied him with the weapons. Hell, we even told him how he could bypass the security guards on the street with the dumbwaiter. Damn it."

He pounded his fist on the table in frustration. "The FBI armed a maniac with an axe to grind and gave him access to the guy he wanted to grind it on. Do you have any idea what's going to happen if the press catches wind of this?"

"Can we intervene?" Cheryl asked. "We can't let him continue, can we?"

"It'll take time we don't have to assemble a team. All I have in place right now are the two guys listening from across the street and they're not prepared to assault an apartment like that. They have a total of two handguns between them and neither one has ever participated in a takedown like this. They'll never get passed Lou's guards. They might even get killed."

"What about the NYPD?"

"We could call them, but what are we going to tell them? Would you mind going to Little Italy and arrest the guy the FBI personally sent to assassinate Barazza? And by the way, would you please retrieve my handgun for me? That'll go over real well. I'll be on permanent leave pending an investigation before the day is over. Besides, if we rush the place he might start shooting cops. This could turn into a major bloodbath."

She was starting to get very worried. "What are we going to do?"

"I'm not sure. We also have to consider the bigger picture of why we sent him there in the first place. We have to find those bombers before tomorrow's trial starts… I don't think we have a choice but to let it play out a little bit longer and hope he at least gets us the information we need. If we can deliver the bombers, we may have a bargaining chip to use when the shit hits the fan."

His mind racing, Wilkins decided it was time to circle the wagons fast. "Get your stuff, Kowalcik. We're going to Little Italy. I want to be the first one on the scene for damage control."

She grabbed her bag and they ran out to the parking lot. He said, "How fast can you drive?"

"Are you kidding? I'm a Jersey girl. Speeding is what I do."

Chapter 86

"Say it again, Vito. I wasn't sure if I heard you right," Cesari said.

"I understand the gravity of the situation I'm in," Vito repeated.

Cesari looked at Barazza. "And you, Lou?"

Big Lou said defiantly, "Bite me, Cesari. You have no idea what you just got yourself into."

Gianelli turned to Big Lou and cautioned, "I wouldn't if I were you, Lou. He looks pretty serious."

But it was too late. Cesari swung the crowbar like a hammer and brought it down hard on Barazza's left ankle. He screamed in pain. If Big Lou had thought to provoke Cesari, he'd succeeded beyond his wildest expectations.

His ankle wasn't broken or maybe it was, but Cesari wasn't really in a could-give-a-shit mood. Gianelli cringed and Barazza continued to moan in agony. His ankle was already starting to swell.

"Anything else you'd like to say, Lou?" Cesari asked, as if nothing had happened. Lou didn't say anything. "Good, now turn over and stop crying. You're embarrassing yourself."

He lumbered clumsily over onto his stomach still grimacing in pain, and gradually got control of himself. Cesari patted him down quickly for a weapon and didn't find any. Vito sat quietly like a good boy, hands over his head. He was wearing dress pants and shirt without a jacket.

"Vito stand up, turn around and empty your pockets. And do it real slow," Cesari said. He did as he was told. "Now show me your ankles."

Gianelli pulled up his trousers and Cesari asked, "Where's your gun?"

"No one's allowed in here with weapons other than Lou and Gino. We left ours downstairs at the door with the sentries."

Cesari believed him and took a set of plastic restraints from his pocket and tossed them to him. He said, "Put these on the beached whale over there, and keep in mind that I'm already in a bad mood."

Vito took the plastic restraints, pulled Barazza's hands behind his back, and fastened them with the restraints. Cesari watched carefully as he pulled them tight. "I'm sorry Lou," Vito said apologetically.

Barazza remained silent, watching Cesari with pure hatred. He hadn't lost at anything his whole life, and this was an entirely new sensation.

"Tighter," Cesari ordered and Vito pulled on the plastic cuffs so hard they dug into Lou's skin. When he finished, Cesari said, "Thanks. Now it's your turn. Lie face down on the floor and put your hands behind your back. If you so much as sneeze while I'm doing this, I'll put a bullet up your ass. Understand?" He did and was quickly restrained. "Now get up and sit down on the couch next to the dead guy."

"His name was Pinky, asshole," Gianelli hissed as he rocked and struggled to one knee and then onto the sofa.

"You keep it up and your name's going to be corpse number two when they find you. Am I making myself clear?"

"So what do you want, Cesari?" Vito asked.

He walked around the couch to get behind him. Gianelli was a big guy, not as big as Lou, but he didn't want to take any chances. He pressed the barrel of the gun hard into the back of his head and tapped his shoulder with the crowbar.

He said, "I want answers and as you can tell, I've got a short fuse. The game's over for you and there's only one way to come out of this with a pulse. Understood?"

Cesari rapped him with the crowbar a little harder, enough to illicit a grunt. Gianelli said, "You should be talking to Lou, not me. He's the one who's got the answers you want. I wasn't there. I was only a kid like you at the time."

Cesari stepped back from the couch, perplexed by the comment. He looked at an empty wine bottle sitting on the coffee table. "What are you talking about, Vito? How much have you been drinking?"

"Shut up Vito," Barazza shouted. "Don't tell this prick anything. Hear me?"

Cesari stepped over to where Big Lou was and slammed the good ankle with the crowbar. There was a crunching sound this time and he was sure this one had broken.

Lou howled loudly in pain.

Cesari said, "Listen up, Lou. In case you haven't noticed, you are no longer in charge here. The next time you speak without my express permission, I'm going to get nasty. Nod if you understand."

He gritted his teeth and nodded.

Cesari turned back to Gianelli. "Keep talking Vito, and don't leave anything out. If I think you're feeding me a load of bull, I'll assume you'd like your ankles broken too. Okay?"

Cesari held up the crowbar for emphasis. Vito hesitated and glanced over at Barazza, who was now sweating profusely.

Cesari encouraged him and spoke in a reasonable tone, "Look Vito, you fought a good battle but you lost, and there's no point in falling on your sword. Now I promise you that if you tell me what you know, you'll still be around when the sun comes up. But if you make me ask again, I'll be upset and you know how I get when I'm upset. It's your call."

To illustrate the point, Cesari gave him another love-tap with the crowbar. He winced in pain and nodded his surrender.

He said, "Okay already. Enough with the crowbar. At first I thought it was just a coincidence running into you up there in Genesee, but then as things progressed, I thought maybe you were snooping around about Frankie D. Then that thing happened with Billy Ray Bob and I assumed you were trying to muscle your way into our business. It wasn't until tonight that I found out how personal this all was to you."

"Stop talking in riddles, Vito, and tell me why this is personal for me."

From the look on Vito's face, Cesari could tell it had finally penetrated his thick skull that his life had taken a permanent turn for the worse. He gently tapped the crowbar against the side of Vito's head as a reminder of what was to come.

Gianelli said, "Why are you playing games like this, Cesari? We're talking about your father for God's sake."

"My father? What are you babbling about?" Cesari said but even as he did, he felt an unsettling feeling in the back of his brain at the mention of his father.

Vito said, "Why else would you have gone through all this trouble? Nobody does crazy stuff like this unless it's personal. You're trying to figure out what happened to your father and settle an old score but I had nothing to do with any of it. It was all about Big Lou and your old pal Frankie D."

"Vito, if he doesn't kill you, I'm going to," Big Lou growled, forgetting what Cesari had promised to do to him if he spoke without permission.

But something had happened to Cesari by that time. The unsettling feeling had grown and was twisting and turning inside him. He became lightheaded and felt his head swimming. He staggered backward and nearly lost his balance.

"Keep talking Vito," he said.

Chapter 87

Cesari turned the television off, poured himself a glass of bourbon from Big Lou's bar, and sat behind his desk thinking. It was close to eleven, and he had just called Agent Wilkins to tell him where he could find the bombers. Federal agents and the NYPD were heading there now. Once he decided to talk, Gianelli had been a fountain of information and it only took a couple whacks with the crowbar to keep him focused. If Gianelli had lied, Cesari had promised him even more pain but Wilkins had forbid him from killing him or anyone else. He had phoned Kelly to let her know that he was in the process of wrapping things up but still had about an hour to go. She was already downstairs waiting for him in the Porsche with the engine running.

"Nice desk, Lou. Solid mahogany?" he asked. It was ten feet long and the surface was polished to a high-gloss finish.

Big Lou wasn't in the mood for chitchat. "Piss off, Cesari."

"I'm sorry you feel that way. I'm only trying to be pleasant." He opened up the desk drawers one at a time. In one, he found a loaded .44 magnum revolver and a box of shells. He said, "Handguns are illegal within the city limits, Lou. It's mandatory jail time for you."

"Shove it."

Gianelli sat quietly, head bowed. He wanted no part of what Big Lou was having. Another drawer had business records from the restaurant and other various enterprises.

Cesari kept up the banter, "I have to tell you, this has got to be the most comfortable chair that I've ever sat in. I mean it."

"Go to hell."

A third drawer contained one-hundred-thousand dollars in fifty-dollar bills stacked neatly in bundles of twenty next to an ordinary hard-covered notebook, the kind a kid might do his homework in. Its very banality screamed for an inspection. He opened it and found the first page covered with multiple series of numbers and letters. The rest of the book was empty. Passwords, he thought.

Cesari chuckled and held the notebook up for Lou to see. He said, "I found the mother lode here, didn't I?"

In the last of the desk drawers, he found a laptop and smiled. He couldn't wait to find out what secrets it would reveal.

"C'mon Lou, Vito's been cooperative. It's your turn to spill your guts," Cesari said. "It was a great plan. Believe me when I say that I'm impressed but it's over. In about an hour, the bombers will be in custody and the bailiff on your payroll is going to be crapping in his pants when he finds out what he got himself into."

Big Lou had bribed a bailiff at the federal courthouse to reserve seats for the four bombers in specifically designated places at the start of tomorrow's trial. Two would sit directly behind the defense table to assassinate the fanatic Farooq at the behest of the Saudis, and the other two would sit directly behind the prosecution's table to assassinate the D.A. for Barazza. Of course, they were now down to only two bombers, but the effect would be the same if they were successful.

For only ten thousand dollars, the bailiff had agreed to plant a cellphone with a preprogrammed detonation number under each of their seat cushions. In his defense, the bailiff didn't know what the phones were for. He was told that the guys were foreign journalists covering the trial and they just wanted to take a picture or two. What could it hurt? He was also told that two of them had medical conditions requiring them to bring portable oxygen tanks. The Pakistani doctors had written out false documentation of medical necessity for both. The tanks had been drained of their oxygen and filled with ball bearings and gasoline.

Cesari walked over to Baraza and stood there looking down at him, tapping the crowbar in his hand. "All right big boy, if you don't want to talk about the Arabs, that's fine with me. I'll let the federal guys deal with that, but the least you could do is tell me about my father. I'd like to hear it first hand and don't leave anything out. If you're nice, I'll give you some whiskey to drown your sorrows in while you're waiting for the FBI."

He glanced at Cesari with hatred and then at the crowbar. He was angry, really angry. He was angry at Cesari. He was angry at the D.A. He was angry at the FBI. He was angry at the world. But at the moment, he was mostly angry at Vito for telling Cesari everything he knew about the bombers. Lou hadn't personally admitted anything yet, but he was going down with or without a confession and he knew it. He had the look of a man who felt it was time to get things off his chest.

"I'm getting impatient Lou," Cesari said. "Spit it out, and I want the truth."

Chapter 88

Lou began hoarsely, "All right Cesari, I guess it doesn't matter anymore anyway. If you think you can handle it, then I'll tell it to you straight up. But remember, you asked for it."

Cesari said, "Fine, I asked for it."

"It was a long time ago. You were just a kid and I was just starting to make a name for myself on the streets. I was running numbers, breaking legs for the sharks, driving for the bosses and so on. One day, all hell breaks loose down on Mulberry Street and I hear we're in a turf war with some guys from the Bronx."

"What's this got to do with my father? He was never involved."

"Shut up and listen... So we're in a turf war with some ass-wipe named Frank Dellatesta. Your pal Frankie D. was a real hothead back then and causing all sorts of problems. He was trying to muscle his way into the restaurant supply business in Midtown. The bosses warned him to back down, but he flipped them off. Things got out of hand and before you know it, two of our guys turn up in a dumpster. That didn't go over too well, so they sent me up to the Bronx to persuade him to cease and desist."

He paused to search his memory and organize his thoughts. Cesari said, "I want to hear about my father, not Frankie D."

"It's all connected, Cesari. It's all connected. The bosses told me to make an example of Frankie D. to restore discipline. Make it public and make it messy, they said. Send a message. It was my big chance to impress the bosses, so I jumped at it."

Cesari sat down on the edge of the coffee table as he listened. He stared at Big Lou's face and thought the man appeared older than when he'd first entered the room.

"I drove up to the Bronx one afternoon to find him. I had never met Frankie D., but I spread cash around and eventually someone talked. They told me that he was hanging out in a schoolyard conducting business, pressing the flesh with the neighborhood guys, acting like a politician and stuff like that, but that he wouldn't be there for long. I thought a schoolyard would be perfect, so I found the location and drove over there. It was Holy Rosary, a little Catholic grammar school on the corner of Woodhull and Arnow Avenues."

Cesari said, "Holy Rosary? That's where I went to school."

"I know... Well when I arrived, there was a guy standing there all by himself looking like he was getting ready to leave. I hustled out of my car and caught up to him real quick as he was walking away."

Cesari was starting to feel a throbbing in the back of his head. Lou took a deep breath. "Are you sure you want to hear all of it, Cesari? You don't look too good."

He was right. He was feeling queasy. "Keep talking. I'll tell you when to stop."

"When I caught up to the guy, I didn't bother asking him who he was, because I thought I already knew. He fit the general age and physical description I had been given. Besides, I figured he'd try to lie his way out of it anyway. So I didn't waste any time. I grabbed him around the neck from behind and..."

Cesari interrupted him, whispering hoarsely, "And you stabbed him, over...and over...with a butcher's knife."

Cesari stood up in shocked disbelief as the memory of that day flickered and then suddenly came into focus. Closing his eyes, he willed it all to come back and it did, leaving him weak and exhausted. He had retreated back to Lou's desk and propped himself on the edge. He was sweating and having difficulty breathing.

Big Lou continued the story relentlessly, each word like a hammer beating against Cesari's soul. He said, "When I turned around, you were standing there watching the whole thing. Then I laid your father on the ground..."

Cesari nodded as the floodgates opened and long-repressed memories returned. He said, "That's when his baseball glove opened and the ball came rolling toward me."

Stunned, Cesari dropped the crowbar and the gun and felt faint.

"That's right Cesari, and when I saw the ball rolling toward you, I realized I had made a mistake. You just stood there staring, couldn't even speak. You didn't cry or nothing. I knew then your father was just some poor shmuck playing catch with his kid. Wrong place, wrong time."

Cesari trembled and tears streamed down his face. He stared ahead as if no one else was in the room. "I remember now. My father and I had only moments before finished playing catch in the schoolyard. He was tired from work and really didn't want to play that day, but I had begged and whined until he gave in to please me. He always gave in to please me."

He paused to catch his breath. "It was getting late, and we were getting ready to go home. Frankie D. was there with us for a while, talking with my father, but he had left a few minutes earlier. I ran to a water fountain for a quick drink while my dad waited for me and when I returned..."

His father was gone forever in a pool of his own blood. A young boy emotionally traumatized like that, he must have gone into shock and repressed the memory of his father lying there, staring at him. His mother must have known the truth but told him his father had disappeared to protect him from the awful reality. Better to not know some things.

Later the memories manifested as the recurring dream of him stabbing his father. Like any child, he blamed himself for what happened. His subconscious had passed judgment on him. If he had not insisted on playing catch that day, his father would not have been in the wrong place at the wrong time.

"So Frankie D. was there after all, like I was told?" said Lou. "How about that. Well it didn't matter because a week later everyone had made peace again, and it was back to business as usual."

"It didn't matter?" Cesari yelled and stood, furious at his callousness. "It mattered to me then and it still matters to me now." His voice cracked under the strain. "I was only seven years old and you stole my life right out from under me. How could you do that to me? You took my father from me."

His knees buckled under him and he fell to the floor, sobbing. He wanted to let out a primal scream.

"I did you a favor Cesari," Barazza sneered. "I should have killed you too but I didn't have the heart. Maybe it's because you looked so weak and pathetic just like you do now. I kept a close eye on you though. You and your mother were very lucky that you developed amnesia to the whole event."

Drenched with sweat and close to losing it, he said, "You did me a favor? You mean I should say thank you?"

"Enough with the waterworks, Cesari. I told you what you wanted to know. Now where's the whiskey you promised me?"

"Whiskey? You want whiskey?" Cesari was seething. He walked over to the bar and picked up a full bottle of very expensive bourbon. He brought it back to where Lou was, uncorked it and poured it all over his face and head saying, "Here, is this what you want?"

Lou squinted, squirmed, coughed and cursed as he was doused with the entire bottle. When the bourbon ran out,

Cesari tossed the bottle on the floor, searched himself and then asked Gianelli, "You smoke, Vito. Do you have a lighter?"

Vito gasped in disbelief and begged, "Cesari, don't. Please. You start a fire and we'll all die. I was cooperative, remember? I gave you the bombers and everything else you wanted."

Cesari thought about that. He also thought about his promise to Wilkins not to kill either one of them. It was a stupid promise but he was a man of his word.

"Did that make you feel better, Cesari?" Barazza asked mockingly. "Now what? Where do we go from here?"

Through clenched teeth Cesari said, "I go home and you two rot in prison for the rest of your miserable lives."

Suddenly Lou started to laugh. Not an ordinary laugh but a deep-chested, ominous laugh. Eventually he calmed down but still chuckling, he said, "You are one dumb fuck, Cesari. You know that? Listen up. Maybe I get sent away, maybe I don't. I got plenty of get-out-of-jail-free cards that I can and will play with the feds if push comes to shove. I know where all the bodies are buried, and that's why they want me so bad. They don't want me rotting in a cell. They want me to talk."

"Is that what you think?" Cesari said.

"It's what I know. Me and the FBI are about to become great friends. This is the way I see it playing out, Cesari. First, they come here tonight, gather me up and take me to a hospital to fix my ankles. I get out, and there are a few preliminary hearings, depositions and so on where I drop hints about what I really know. The FBI gets wet and make me all sorts of offers. All over lobster and champagne dinners, I might add. This is the federal government we're talking about. But that's not the best part. The best part is that I'm not going to tell them a thing they don't already know unless they meet my demands and you know what I'm going to demand?"

Cesari shook his head. "No."

"I'm going to demand that they make you apologize to me for your bad behavior tonight and you're going to do it."

Cesari said, "You're insane."

Barazza lowered his voice menacingly, "No, I'm not but you are if you think you're going to ride off into the sunset and play house with that girlfriend of yours Vito's been telling me about. You see Cesari, before tonight's over the word is going to be issued on the street that both she and you are personas non grata. There will be no place you can hide. And when we find her, I promise you that we are going to have one helluva party. Hell, we may even let you watch."

Gianelli became alarmed as he watched Cesari's features darken with rage at the threat to harm Kelly. But Lou was oblivious and added, "I hope she likes crack, Cesari... No matter, she will eventually. The great Cesari...in love with a crack-whore."

Cesari picked the crowbar up off the floor. He was shaking. His fury had reached the boiling point. He said, "I promised the FBI that I wouldn't kill you, Lou."

"Yes you did, Cesari. We both heard you. Didn't we, Vito?" He snickered. "And now you know why they made you promise that. It's good to know we're all on the same page. Well Cesari, you know what they say. Don't go away mad... just go away."

Behind Lou's desk was a stereo system with massive speakers in opposing corners of the room. Cesari went over to the radio and tuned in to a rock station playing Guns N' Roses. He turned up the volume so that the room shook and Gianelli watched him wide-eyed, thinking he had gone mad. Then he came back to Lou and stood over him with the crowbar as he calmly listened to the music for a minute.

Welcome to the jungle.

We've got fun 'n' games.

We got everything you want...

Without warning, Cesari raised the crowbar high over his head and unleashed his full wrath on the man who had caused so much pain to a little boy and his mother. With each blow Barazza screamed a hideous blood-curdling shriek, and with each blow Cesari wept uncontrollably. The dam had burst and there was no turning back.

Chapter 89

When he finished, he turned the music off and sat down on the couch next to Vito. He was exhausted, emotionally and physically. Lou had finally stopped screaming and begging for mercy. He most likely would not scream or beg for anything ever again. Cesari's appearance was frightful, his clothes splattered with blood, his eyes vacant and resolute. He was in that zone men entered when they no longer feared consequences. Vito recognized that look and feared for his immediate future as Cesari put his arm around him. Cesari held the crowbar covered with blood, hair and bits of Lou's flesh up to Vito's face and stroked him with it. He could smell Barazza on the metal. Vito burst out in tears. He had just witnessed what Cesari was capable of doing with the crowbar and didn't want to die that way.

"Cesari, please don't. I promise you'll never see or hear from me again. I swear it on my mother's grave."

"You're lucky I'm tired, Vito… and Kelly's waiting for me." He was breathing heavily from his recent exertion.

"That's right, Cesari. Kelly's waiting for you and she's such a nice girl. Don't make her wait."

"But what am I going to do about you, Vito?" he said and slowly ran the bloody crowbar across Vito's lips.

"You don't have to worry about me, Cesari. I'm gone. I'm history. When the feds get here, I'm going to confess to everything. I'm going to get five life sentences easy. You're never going to see me again. If anyone tries to offer me parole, I'll put a bullet in him. No, I'm sorry. I didn't mean that. I meant I'll refuse."

Cesari stood up and looked around. "Where's the bathroom?"

"Over there. Past his desk and to the right down the hallway."

"Don't go anywhere."

Vito shook his head.

In the bathroom, Cesari cleaned his face and clothes as best he could. He left the leather gloves and windbreaker on the floor. He felt disgusting. He scouted around the apartment and found a gym bag, which he filled with the cash from the desk drawer, along with the laptop and notebook. He took Lou's .44 magnum and shoved it into his waistband.

He left the taser, crowbar, Wilkins's Beretta, and Gino's .45 on Lou's desk and then glanced at his cellphone. There were two texts. One from Wilkins saying that they got the bombers and that he would be arriving with Cheryl in an hour, so don't go anywhere. The other was from Kelly telling him to hurry. He ignored the message from Wilkins and walked quickly to the kitchen.

On the way, he paused for a second and said, "Vito?"

Gianelli turned his head. "What?"

"Don't make me come back for you."

"I won't."

He climbed back into the dumbwaiter, finagled the button on the control panel and found himself downstairs in the Café Napoli in less than a minute. It was well after midnight, and the restaurant was dark and quiet. Kelly had pulled up in front with the passenger-side door facing him. She sat behind the wheel with her head cocked in his direction. No more than twenty feet to his right stood Lou's sentries, smoking and yawning.

Cesari pulled Lou's revolver out and cocked it. He called Kelly on the cellphone and told her to get ready. Moving fast, he unlocked the front door to the café and made a beeline to the Porsche at the curb. Kelly had reached over and flung the door open for him. He jumped in with the gym bag in his left hand, pointing the .44 magnum at the two guys with his right. They were speechless at the sight of the large handgun and just stood there paralyzed with indecision. Neither one moved and Kelly hit the gas hard causing the tires to screech as they drove off unscathed.

As the car soared down Mulberry Street, Kell asked, "Where to? I have no idea where the highway is."

"Let's go back to the Blue Moon. I changed my mind. We'll stay the night. I need to get drunk."

Kelly smiled. "Yay."

Chapter 90

The cellphone buzzed, and Cesari accidentally knocked the bottle of Jack Daniel's into the hot tub reaching to answer it. Sitting on his lap, Kelly started to giggle hysterically and then leaned over to save Mr. Daniel's from drowning. They were way past five-o'clock-somewhere. It was after 3:00 a.m., and they were frolicking in the spa on the rooftop of the Blue Moon, well into their second bottle.

Cesari said, "Hello, Agent Wilkins."

"What happened here, Cesari? Kowalcik's in the bathroom throwing up and I thought I told you not to kill anybody else."

"I didn't kill anybody else," he protested.

"The hell you didn't."

"If you're referring to Big Lou, he still had a pulse when I left."

"And he still does…barely. I thought I told you to wait for me here."

"I was pretty upset, and I didn't want to do to Gianelli what I did to Lou. I thought it was best if I just took off."

"Was this really necessary? I mean really? We needed Lou."

"It's not my fault that every time I swung the crowbar, he jumped in front of it."

"This isn't funny, Cesari. How am I supposed to explain this scene to anyone?"

"Well if you use your imagination, it could easily be made to appear that Pinky may have assaulted Big Lou with the crowbar and Gino may have shot him in the head defending his boss.

It was Gino's gun that was fired, not yours. Be creative and try rearranging the furniture a little."

Kelly stuck her tongue into his free ear and he pushed her away. Wilkins was outraged and said, "Then they all handcuffed themselves? I repeat. This isn't funny."

"I know. But look on the bright side, you're a hero. You and Cheryl single-handedly prevented a terrorist attack whose main purpose was to assassinate a United States public official right here in our country's greatest city. This is stuff FBI legends are made of, Wilkins. From this point forward, your name will forever be on the lips of every new recruit at the FBI training academy in Quantico. This will be a case study for counter terrorism tactics for the next hundred years. I don't like to make predictions, but I think you'd have to be on the short list for the Presidential Medal of Freedom. Then there's Big Lou. I saved you guys the trouble and cost of a trial without any real downside, because I'm sure Gianelli knows as much as Big Lou about the people you're interested in. I'd be surprised if he doesn't sing like a canary."

Wilkins snorted. "Well I have to admit, Gianelli does seem awfully cooperative. What did you do to him, anyway? He swears on his mother's grave that you were never here, and we never even asked him. All he would say is that they were minding their own business watching the ball game, when some guy he never saw before came out of nowhere and attacked them. And why does everyone you come into contact with suddenly want to go into witness protection?"

Kelly had turned around and was now straddling him. She giggled into the phone. "Is Agent Wilkins being serious again?"

"Who the hell was that?" Wilkins demanded. "Where are you?"

"Kelly and I are about a half hour south of Albany on the Thruway. We should arrive in Genesee in a couple of hours," he lied.

"Okay. Since we last spoke, did anyone suddenly remember where the last bomber might be?"

"No, Gianelli insisted that the Sheik commandeered him for a different purpose, unknown to them. By the way, now that you got those guys, what is it you plan to do with them?"

"Cesari, kiss me," Kelly whispered.

"It's still up in the air, but Dr. Kowalcik suggested we contact the Pentagon and ask for military surgeons who have worked under combat conditions. Those guys have nerves of steel. We're thinking of setting up an old-fashioned MASH unit. You know, mobile army surgical hospital. We'll set up a tent in a football field or large parking lot away from everything. No electricity, no nothing. Cut those bombs out of them the old fashioned way by candlelight, and keep our fingers crossed."

"Good luck with that. I guess I'll be going then."

"Yeah well, don't go too far, Cesari. We still need to clarify exactly what happened here tonight. Oh, and one more thing..."

"Yes?"

"Thanks."

"No problem."

He put the phone down, uncapped the bottle of whiskey and took another long pull.

"What did the big, important FBI man have to say?" Kelly slurred and grabbed the bottle from him.

"He said he wished he could be here with us."

With her arms around his neck, she regarded him with her drunken green eyes. "I'll bet," she said. "So what's next for us, Cesari? I want answers, and I want them now."

She hiccupped in his face and he smiled. "That was sexy."

"You got a problem with that, buddy?"

He shook his head. "I don't have a problem with anything you do."

She liked that. "Good answer, Cesari."

"So you want to know what's next?"

She took a slug from the bottle, wiped her face with her forearm and nodded. He looked at her very seriously and undid her top. "What's next is that you need to lose the bottoms."

To punctuate that thought, he pulled her close and kissed her first on the nose, then the forehead, then the cheek, then the neck and finally a long passionate one on the lips.

Chapter 91

Toronto

The four Pakistani doctors were sitting in first class on United Emirates Airbus flight 242 to Islamabad, Pakistan with a connecting flight in Dubai. The flight wasn't due to take off until 9:45 p.m., and they had partied hard in the VIP lounge of the Pearson International Airport before boarding and twice as hard after. As the plane taxied on the runway, they ordered another round of gin martinis.

"Blue sapphire shaken not stirred, ho, and don't forget the olives," one of them said, and slapped the flight attendant on her rear end.

This brought a roar of laughter from his colleagues. Equally fired up, they were thoroughly impressed with his command of English vernacular. They were on top of the world and they knew it. With the money they had earned in the last year salvaging human organs for the Americans, and now this latest financial windfall of surgically implanting explosive devices into the martyrs of Allah, they were living large. They would live like princes for the rest of their lives.

Unfortunately for them, the Sheik had decided that their services were no longer required. It would be very embarrassing to the Saudi royal family if they ever let slip what had happened.

Sitting directly behind them was a young man named Sahir. He'd had a rough week. The device in his abdomen had hurt a lot more than he had been told it would, and the narcotics he had been given to dull the pain had dulled his mind and made him constipated. He was eager to get this over with.

He wasn't exactly sure why this particular flight had been chosen, but those more enlightened than he had made that decision. However, after watching the four decadent Pakistani doctors flaunting their sinfulness both in the airport lounge and now right here on the plane, he was glad that they would die with him.

A flight attendant had told him to turn off his cellphone, but he didn't. He fingered it nervously. He had good reception and would continue to do so until the plane reached an altitude of ten thousand feet.

The best time would be a minute or so after takeoff, while the jet was still accelerating upward. With a full load of gas, moving three hundred miles an hour at four or five thousand feet off the ground, carrying six hundred tons of steel and human flesh, there should be no chance of survival for anyone on board.

He gripped the armrests of his chair as the plane surged forward and then upward. A moment later, he felt his ears pop. Be patient, he told himself and said one last prayer. He glanced out the window and saw the ground receding behind him. He clutched his oxygen tank closely to his chest and pressed the *Send* button on his cellphone.

Chapter 92

The bris was late Sunday morning on the Upper West Side.

"Cesari, I'm so glad you could make it. And you too, Kelly. It's a pleasure to meet you." Mark shook his hand and gave Kelly a warm embrace. "You know, Cesari, you could have warned me how beautiful she was."

They were in Mark's apartment on the thirty-fifth floor of a very chic apartment building. He was a thin man in his late fifties, maybe five-feet-eight inches tall. He had a salt-and-pepper beard and a receding hairline. In Cesari's opinion, Mark was a little pale and needed to get out in the sun more.

Kelly said, "Thank you for inviting me, Dr. Greenberg. You have such a lovely home and family. Everyone has made me feel so welcome."

"Please, Kelly, call me Mark. 'Dr. Greenberg' is for the crazies like Cesari here."

Cesari laughed. "Gee thanks, Mark. Mazel tov, again by the way. It was a very nice ceremony. The mohel was hilarious. I haven't been to a bris in a long time. I forgot how funny some of these guys can be."

"Yeah, real funny. That was my brother, Moishe. You wouldn't believe what he wanted to charge me for the ceremony. Now that was funny. Nice suit, Cesari. Where'd you get it, the Salvation Army?"

Cesari laughed again. The trousers and jacket sleeves from the off-the-rack suit he'd bought in a hurry the day before were about two inches too long. He and Kelly had decided to stay at the Blue Moon for the rest of the week and attend the bris. He needed to see Mark, and she had never seen a Jewish circumcision ceremony before.

Kelly saved him. "We had a crazy week, Mark. John didn't have a chance to get it tailored properly. I'm sorry. He's a work in progress for sure. I'm doing the best I can with him."

She wore a stunning blue dress with pearls and matching heels. Mark said, "You keep working on him, Kelly. You on the other hand, are the image of perfection. I hope you're aware of how lucky you are, Cesari?"

"Indeed I am, Mark. I tell myself that every day."

"Thank you," Kelly said, smiling.

Cesari stepped close to Mark. "I hate to take you away from your family on such an important day, but I was wondering if I could have a word with you in private."

"Sure. Why don't we step into my office over here? Kelly, would you mind helping yourself to a bagel and lox? Everything is set up on the table over there in the corner. Make yourself at home."

"Thank you, I will."

She headed away to join a bunch of people at the buffet while Mark led Cesari down a hallway to his office. Cesari had brought a leather briefcase to the apartment which he carried at his side. Mark had noticed the briefcase and also that Cesari hadn't let go of it once since his arrival. Odd behavior for sure at a bris but he figured Cesari would tell him all about it in due time, so he didn't bring it up. Shrinks were like that. The office was a large room with a nice view of the city, wall-to-wall bookshelves and wood paneling. The carpet was faded and worn, like Mark. There was a rosewood desk with a leather chair and of course, a couch. Mark was an avid pipe smoker and the scent of tobacco perfumed the room. A picture of Freud hung on the wall.

Mark closed the door behind them and said, "Have a seat Cesari and take off the damn yarmulke. You look ridiculous. Besides, you have it on upside down."

Cesari unpinned his yarmulke and placed it on the desk, and Mark did the same with his. "I'm sorry to hear about your father, Cesari. That was a tough way to find out, but I do appreciate your calling to tell me. This has been a hell of a week for you and Kelly and I'm sure I only heard the abridged version."

Cesari had given Mark a brief synopsis of all that happened to him and Kelly. Some of it he had learned from the news but he was smart and was able to connect the dots. Cesari nodded in agreement. "Thanks, and yeah, it really was a weak from hell."

"Did you kill the guy who did it?"

"I tried my best but I hear he's clinging to life by a thread. He's in a coma down at New York Hospital." He looked around as if he thought the room might be bugged. "These kinds of conversations are protected, right?"

Mark chuckled. "A little late now, isn't it? But not to worry, as far as I'm concerned you guineas can knock each other off all you want."

Cesari grinned, "Please tell me how you really feel."

Mark turned serious. "I really am sorry John, but I'm glad you finally got resolution after all these years. Maybe you'll finally get a good night's sleep."

He nodded. "I already have."

"Good. Hey, you want to laugh? Not that it matters anymore, but I discussed your dreams with the dream expert at Columbia, right? He's supposed to be the world's leading expert on dream analysis. Chair of the department. The whole nine yards. And you know what he said?"

"No, what?"

"Get this, Cesari. He says you're a homosexual. That's right. He said your dreams represent the inner conflict between your conscious heterosexual self and your latent homosexuality trying to come through to the surface. In your dreams, you're killing off your heterosexual side represented by your father. Is that rich or what? And he trained at Harvard. He must have been one of those legacy kids you hear about. What a loser. I've half a mind to turn him in as a fraud."

"Too funny, but I wouldn't be too hard on him. You're all quacks as far as I'm concerned."

They both laughed.

Mark glanced at his watch and said, "Okay Cesari, so what's in the briefcase you've been guarding with your life and what did you want to talk about? This is a big day for me and I've got my whole family out there waiting for me to say a few words. You know, first grandchild. That kind of stuff."

"I understand and I'll try to be brief. I remembered you were good with computers..."

"I have a master's degree in computer programming and cyber-security from MIT. If I hadn't decided to go to medical school, I'd probably be sitting in the basement of the NSA trying to hack through Russian and Chinese firewalls as we speak. I'd have to agree that I'm pretty good with computers, so what do you got?"

Cesari opened the briefcase and took out the laptop and hardcover notebook he found in Big Lou's apartment. He placed them in front of Mark who eyed them with great interest.

He said, "What are you getting me into, Cesari?"

"Nothing. I just need some advice. That's all."

"Yeah, right." Mark powered up the laptop and while it booted, he opened the notebook, perusing through it for a minute.

"It looks like a list of usernames and passwords. I'm not sure what the series of numbers are."

Cesari offered, "I think they're access codes to offshore bank accounts in the Caymans."

Mark stared at him. "Is this Barazza's laptop?"

"It was. I found it lying around and sort of confiscated it. He won't be using a computer for a while, possibly never again."

"And what exactly do you want from me?"

"I can't get into it. It's password protected and none of those in the notebook worked. I've been trying all week and I can't exactly call the Geek Squad."

"I see."

Mark massaged his beard and started tapping furiously on the keyboard all the while making little noises to himself. Eventually, with his eyes glued to the screen he said, "What's my cut, Cesari? You're making me commit a felony with my entire family in the next room. I think that's worth at least ten percent."

"I was thinking more like a fifty-fifty split, but if ten percent is all you want, then fine."

He smiled. "Why so generous?"

"I'd give it all to you, but I'm going to need something to live on. I don't think I'm going to be employable for a while. I've already been contacted by the Office of Professional Misconduct. They want to meet with me to discuss recent events."

Mark nodded sympathetically. "Ahh, the Office of Professional Misconduct otherwise known as the modern reincarnation of the gestapo. Institutionalized hypocrisy at its finest. I know it well. I've had to counsel many physicians as a result of their unpleasant encounters with those sanctimonious misanthropes but why are they sinking their fangs into you? I didn't know it was against the Hippocratic oath to kill mobsters. I must have missed that part. I thought they only concerned themselves with patient care issues."

"That's what I thought too, but it was explained to me that they have the right to judge a physician's behavior and moral character whether he is in his office or in his swimming pool sipping a piña colada. And that's a direct quote."

Mark looked shocked. "They actually said piña colada?"

Cesari nodded. "I kid you not. Apparently, this happens all the time. Anyway, they caught wind of my activities this week. I don't know how but it's possible somebody reported me."

"Who would have done that?"

"Anybody could have. Complaints against physicians are usually anonymous, so it might have been the CEO, his son, Gianelli or some random guy on the street. There's no way of knowing. Regardless, they're accusing me of conduct unbecoming and beneath the dignity of my profession. Specifically, they're accusing me of being a vigilante and intimated that I could possibly have my license suspended or revoked. They were real worked up about me."

Mark sighed. "Wow Cesari, that really stinks. I'm sorry. If there's any way I can help, let me know but I wouldn't worry too much. They can't prove anything and they're not a court of law."

"That's the problem, Mark. They're not a court of law and don't have to prove anything. It's a bunch of geezers in long white coats sitting around deciding if they like my face or not."

He laughed. "If that's the case, then you're up a creek without a paddle, my friend."

"That's pretty much the way I see it."

"Seriously, Cesari, if you need an alibi tell them you were with me all week. I'm not afraid of them. They can't do squat to me."

"Thanks, I might take you up on that."

"Am I a gangster now?"

Cesari laughed. "Definitely."

"Anyway, back to this laptop and any money it may lead us to, you don't owe me anything."

"The hell I don't. All those years of counseling for some kid without any insurance or money. Your friendship and concern made me feel like a human being, that my life mattered. You're the greatest person I know, Mark. You made a difference in my life that no amount of money could ever repay. The world needs more people like you."

"You're being too kind but thanks for saying so. I appreciate it."

He studied the laptop, scratched his head and opened one of the drawers to his desk. He took out his pipe and lit it while he thought over the problem at hand. "How much do you think we're talking about here, Cesari? Thousands or tens of thousands?"

"More like millions. Maybe tens of millions."

He raised his eyebrows. "Well, this might take a while. Take your jacket off and relax. There's some sherry hidden behind volume 4 of Jung's, *Psychology of the Unconscious*, on the bookcase behind you, if you're interested."

"I'm good, thanks."

Marked worked feverishly for the next few minutes running his hand frequently through his hair and puffing away at his pipe. Soon the room was filled with smoke. He said, "Tens of millions you say?"

"Probably."

The door to the office opened and his wife, Sarah, poked her head in and coughed. "Mark, we have an apartment full of guests out here. They're expecting you to say something."

He looked up and said testily, "Tell them I said to go home. I'm busy."

Chapter 93

Rochester, New York

Cesari's hearing with the Office of Professional Misconduct was six weeks later in downtown Rochester on Allen Street. He stood outside the conference room in the hallway anxiously waiting to be summoned inside. He was accompanied by Mark, his wife Sarah, and Kelly. His attorney, George, was already inside getting briefed on the ground rules of the meeting by the state's lawyers. To say the least, the mood was grim.

"You're going to be fine, Cesari. Take a deep breath, all right?" Mark said as he straightened Cesari's tie and adjusted his lapels for him. He finished the grooming by brushing lint off his shoulders.

Cesari replied, "Thanks for coming up, Mark. It means a lot to me." He turned slightly. "You too, Sarah. Thank you. I know what a long trip it is from Manhattan. I've made it many times."

Mark and Sarah had journeyed the three-hundred-some odd miles from New York for moral support. She said, "Think nothing of it. We're happy to be here with you, John. That's what friends are for and you look very nice. You'll be fine."

The conference room door opened part way and a middle-aged woman came out. "Dr. John Cesari?"

He raised his hand. "That's me."

"Come this way, please."

Kelly stepped forward and gave him one last hug before he went into the chamber. She whispered, "Don't lose your temper in there, Cesari."

"Who me?"

"Just remember, they weren't there. They're just trying to figure things out."

"Thanks Kel, but I doubt that's what this is all about."

"You're too cynical," she said and gave him a quick kiss.

As he turned away to leave them, Mark placed a hand on his shoulder and leaned into him close. "Cesari, keep in mind one thing I learned a long time ago about guys like these."

"What's that?"

Under his breath he said, "They're all assholes. Every last one of them."

Cesari laughed. "Think I should lead off with that or save it for the end?"

"Knock their socks off, Cesari. No survivors."

As he entered the large institutional-style room George stood to shake his hand. "Hey Cesari. Doing okay?"

He'd gone to college with George and they'd maintained a friendship on and off ever since. George was a rough and tumble defense attorney who enjoyed mixing it up once in a while. He also never met an ambulance he didn't like to chase. But Cesari didn't judge people.

He said, "Hi, George. I'm doing okay." He then acknowledged the others in the room. "Good morning, everyone."

George and Cesari sat in the middle of a long oval table. Across from them and to their right were two female attorneys representing New York State. Across and to their left, was the woman who ushered Cesari in, a legal secretary there to record the minutes of the meeting. In the middle of the table and directly opposite Cesari were three older, male physicians with nametags identifying them as employees of New York State's Department of Higher Education. They were the hammer and anvil of Rochester's Office of Professional Misconduct.

In unison the group said, "Good morning, Dr. Cesari."

Cesari glanced around quickly to get a feeling for the place. The walls were a drab green and there was a picture of the president behind the three physicians. They wore white lab coats which he found amusing, since he doubted that any one of them had been in contact with a patient in decades. Guys generally gravitated to bureaucratic positions like this for several reasons. One, they just weren't cut out for patient care. Essentially, they realized too late that going to medical school was a massive mistake and they hated their lives. Two, they were too old for direct patient contact anymore but weren't quite ready to be put out to pasture. And three, deep down they were weak human beings and preferred the security of a cushy, secure, nine-to-five state job with full benefits to the high risk, high pressure conditions of clinical practice.

After a brief preamble, the lead physician wasted no time in tearing into Cesari. Over the next forty minutes, each one took turns telling him that he was an awful person and that it was unclear how anyone could have seen fit to give him a medical license in the first place. It rapidly became clear to Cesari that their job wasn't to find out the truth or to determine a just outcome. Their job was to preserve the appearance of their office and submit a report about what a great job they did in the process. It was their view, that modern physicians shouldn't own guns, beat people up, save the world or do anything but bend over and hand their assailant a jar of lubrication. He had gone rogue, they declared, and they were going to give him an old-fashioned beat down. He needed to be reined in or put down. From their tone, he thought they preferred the latter option.

Cesari felt violated, and the color rose in his cheeks under the verbal onslaught. He tried to imagine a scenario where he could possibly feel more outraged. Perhaps if he had shot some predator he caught in the act of assaulting a child and was then himself sentenced to life in prison for use of excessive force, he might feel more indignant but only by a smidgeon.

As he watched them speak, he couldn't help but think about a scene from the movie *Planet of the Apes*, the original one with Charlton Heston. The scene had three monkeys presiding over a fake trial. One saw no evil, one heard no evil and the other spoke no evil.

He chuckled at the image.

"Excuse me, Dr. Cesari. Do you find something here humorous?" the one in charge said. He had been flipping through the case files and official reports of what had happened and stopped to look over the edge of his glasses at him. Cesari noticed he had a weak chin. He didn't like that.

George whispered, "Keep it together, Cesari, all right?"

Cesari looked around and could see that they all had very bad attitudes, even the legal secretary. It had been clear what was going to happen the minute he stepped into the room. The bureaucracy needed to feed itself every so often, and he was the meal *du jour*. It was good public relations for the medical community to occasionally throw one of its own to the lions. This hearing was a mere formality so they could document how fair they had treated him. The whole thing was a set up. He was getting angry.

The weak chin said, "Well, Dr. Cesari, do you have something you'd like to share with us?"

Cesari wasn't sure if that was a rhetorical question or not. He'd been told that he would be allotted time for a rebuttal but the amount of sarcasm and condescension in the guy's voice made him wonder if they had changed their minds.

"Is it my turn to speak?" he asked politely.

The guy checked with his colleagues and then sat back in his chair. "Yes, I suppose it is. Please, go ahead."

He reminded Cesari of a big-bellied southern judge he had heard about once in a country song. All he needed was a gavel and a big fat cigar to complete the picture. Maybe a rope too.

Before he began, George whispered quietly into his ear, "Choose your words carefully, Cesari, and remember what we talked about. Don't admit that you knowingly participated in any criminal activity. Keep in mind that these guys live for this kind of stuff. They love having power over guys like you, so don't inflame them any more than they already are. Be respectful, civil and most of all, use self-control."

Cesari smiled. He remembered that a long time ago, he owned a crowbar he had dubbed self-control. He then proceeded to completely ignore his lawyer's very expensive advice and glowered directly at the physician in charge. "Yes, I do find something here amusing, even comical to be honest with you," he began softly. "In fact, I think it's hysterical that I have to sit here and defend myself to a group of pencil-necks like you. Who are you anyway but professional bootlickers for the state of New York."

George groaned and the weak chin flared his nostrils. If he had a gavel in his hand, Cesari was sure he would have pounded it on the table and demanded order in the courtroom. He said, "There is no need for insults, Dr. Cesari."

"The hell you say. You and your pals have been flinging them fast and furious in my direction for the better part of an hour, and I took it like a man. Now it's your turn... In regards to the events that took place in the Genesee General Hospital, you may think my actions were deplorable but maybe you didn't get the memo. The FBI, after weeks of deliberation, has cleared me of any and all criminal charges. I don't know this for a fact, but they might even give me a commendation."

George and Cesari had rehearsed his contrite and humble response many times in the days leading up to the hearing, and this wasn't it. He'd gone off script because he realized this trial was just for show and he had nothing to lose. But if they thought they were going to give him a colonoscopy without the benefit of anesthesia, they had made a profound miscalculation. They were on Cesari time now.

The weak chin said, "That's not the point, Dr. Cesari. We as physicians must hold ourselves to a much higher standard."

"If that's the case, then you're not going to mind at all what I'm about to say," he snapped back and George twitched involuntarily. Cesari continued, "I realize that the purpose of this hearing is for me to beg forgiveness for the things I've done in the hopes of salvaging my career. I am also aware of how difficult it is for you to understand the necessity of my actions."

The chin cleared his throat and said, "Dr. Cesari..."

Cesari cut him off sharply, "I thought you said it was my turn to speak."

The rebuke startled him and he let out a deep breath. The legal secretary gave Cesari the hairy eyeball and the chin looked to his colleagues and the lawyers for help. When no one spoke, he said, "And so I did. Please continue."

"That's good because I have a lot to say, and I don't like being interrupted." He paused for effect. "It's like this. I grew up in the streets of the Bronx. Life was cheap and the rules were simple. Everybody did what he or she had to do to survive. Thanks to the love of my mother and the counsel of good friends, I learned not only that there could be a better way but that there had to be a better way.

I went to medical school and spent the next decade learning the art and science of medicine. I sacrificed countless hours every day of every week in anticipation of earning a seat at the table of scholars. When that day finally arrived, do you know what I found out?"

He panned around the room expectantly, and when no one responded to his question, he continued, "I found out that you're all full of shit. Every last one of you. That's what I found out. A typical physician trains for ten grueling years, working a hundred or more hours per week. Everywhere he goes, he's the low man on the totem pole. When he finally starts to see the light at the end of the tunnel, some abusive hospital administrator hires him to make bricks for his pyramid. And if he doesn't do it with a smile, he finds himself in the unemployment line like any other schmuck. As part of his reward for taking endless amounts of crap, he gets to argue all day long with insurance companies whose sole priority is to make sure his patients are denied the care they already paid for. Armies of bureaucrats hound him mercilessly every day to make sure he signs, dates and times every piece of paper he comes into contact with, including his used toilet tissue, as if somehow that will improve quality of care."

He was just warming up.

"But you know something?" he went on. "I didn't give a rat's ass about the bullshit I had to put up with because I believed in what I was doing and that in my own small way, I was helping to make this world a better place. All I ever wanted was for my mom and dad to be proud of me for what I was doing. That's the only thing I ever cared about."

By now he was red in the face and his voice cracked with emotion. He glanced at George, who had turned pale.

He turned back to the group and went on, "Then I came to that cesspool of a hospital, where I discovered that people were being treated like chattel and the guy in charge was committing heinous crimes for profit against his fellow man. But that wasn't the only offense I found there. The real crime I learned, was the breach of trust that had been committed by the medical community itself in embracing a healthcare model that placed the financial well-being of the system above that of the patient. That sniveling runt of a human being, Snell, was the inevitable result of physicians like you allowing bureaucrats and accountants to take over our profession.

Healthcare is about the relationship between physicians and their patients. It's a deeply personal commitment between two human beings that cannot be legislated or managed remotely and it doesn't come with a price tag. It is a bond, a pledge on the part of the doctor to do whatever he can to help someone who is ill or in need. In return, that individual places his trust and confidence in his physician to do the right thing. He literally places his life in the hands of his doctor. Think about that. That's what healthcare is all about. That's where it begins and that's where it ends. Everything else is superfluous.

When was the last time one of you looked into the eyes of an elderly patient and told him or her there was nothing more you could do for them, but everything was going to be all right because you were going to be right there to comfort them at the end? When was the last time one of you told a thirty-year-old mother of two that she had cancer and her insurance didn't cover her treatments? What makes you think you have the right to pass judgment on me?

Your degrees say that you're doctors, but you're not. Not really. You gave up the right to be called physicians long ago. You're nothing but suits now. Even worse, you're the secret police that the state uses to keep guys like me in line. That's what you are. Your job is to protect the status quo and root out nonconformists. You couldn't care less about the right or wrong of any of this. The politicians, the insurance companies, and the pharmaceuticals don't give a crap about the welfare of our patients. And that's who you work for. Don't you even know that? The only reason we're even here now is to make sure that the system comes out of this smelling like a rose, not to determine what is just.

You guys have been sitting behind your desks for so long, you've probably got bedsores. You have no idea what a guy like me goes through on a daily basis to take care of my patients. Every day is an uphill battle, fighting, arguing and wading through mountains of paperwork to get the job done. But you know something...that's my job and I accept it. It's my duty as a physician to make sure that my patients receive the care they need, no matter what obstacles are placed in my way. People rely on me to act on their behalf."

Cesari took a deep breath and let it out slowly as he eyed each and every one of them individually. No one moved and even the legal secretary had stopped typing to stare at him.

After a moment, he said, "You and others like you have shirked your responsibility. You've broken your solemn promise toward your patients. You make me want to puke. You think because you've been given a title, a fat salary and have the authority of the government behind you that somehow you're immune from judgment? Well, think again. No one's immune from judgment."

He was practically shouting now. "Above all else, do no harm. Remember that one? Do no fucking harm. The Hippocratic oath doesn't say, only if it's convenient, or only if Medicare pre-authorizes it, or only if it's an accredited hospital setting. Well they were doing harm and I made it my business to stop them. Our role as physicians is to help people, and it doesn't matter whether it's in our office or in the middle of the damn street. We are the patient's advocate and protector at all times. Even in our sleep. There is no end to that obligation. Now I said what I had to say and I'm going to leave. Try not to take this the wrong way, but you can all kiss my ass."

He stood up and left the room without another word. You could have heard a pin drop. Kelly, Mark, and Sarah were waiting for him in the hallway with solemn expressions. Kelly held his hand as they walked in silence to the exit. He thanked Mark and Sarah again for their support.

"We heard some of it through the door," Kelly said softly. She was concerned. "You were kind of loud. It didn't sound like it went too well."

He gave her a big hug. "Really? I thought it went very well."

"You lost your temper in there, didn't you?"

"No, that's ridiculous."

"What did you say at the end when you were leaving? I couldn't quite catch it all."

"I told them that I hoped we could all be friends one day."

She smiled. "Yeah, right."

The End

Author's Note

Dear Reader,

I hope you enjoyed reading *Hostile Hospital* as much as I enjoyed writing it. Please do me a favor and write a review for me on Amazon. The reviews are important, and your support is greatly appreciated. I can be reached at johnavanzato59@gmail.com or Facebook for further discussion.

Thank you,

John Avanzato MD

About the Author

John Avanzato grew up in the Bronx, New York. After receiving a bachelor's degree in biology from Fordham University, he went on to earn his medical degree at the State University of New York at Buffalo, School of Medicine. He is currently a board-certified gastroenterologist practicing in upstate, New York, where he lives with his wife of thirty years. Dr. Avanzato co-teaches a course on pulp fiction at Hobart and William Smith Colleges in Geneva, New York.

Inspired by authors like Tom Clancy, John Grisham, and Lee Child, Avanzato writes about strong but flawed heroes. His stories are fast-paced thrillers with larger than life characters and tongue-in-cheek humor.

His novels, *Hostile Hospital, Prescription for Disaster, Temperature Rising, Claimed Denied, The Gas Man Cometh, Jailhouse Doc, Sea Sick, Pace Yourself and Night Nurse* are available on amazon and have been well-received.

About the Dog

English Mastiffs are indeed a very large breed of canine but famously gentle in nature, despite their size and often ferocious appearance. The loving, playful personality of the dog once Johnny and Kelly got to know her, was modeled after our family pet, Cleopatra, a black Lab, whom we had the privilege of sharing our lives with for fifteen wonderful years. Late in life, she lay beside me curled up on the rug almost the entire time I was writing this novel. She passed away peacefully in her own bed several weeks following the completion Hostile Hospital. She touched our hearts and souls and we will miss her always.

Prescription for Disaster

Dr. John Cesari is a gastroenterologist employed at Saint Matt's Hospital in Manhattan. He tries to escape his unsavory past on the Bronx streets by settling into a Greenwich Village apartment with his girlfriend, Kelly. After his adventures in Hostile

Hospital, Cesari wants to stay under the radar of his many enemies.

Through no fault of his own, Cesari winds up in the wrong place at the wrong time. A chance encounter with a mugger turns on its head when Cesari watches his assailant get murdered right before his eyes.

After being framed for the crime, he attempts to unravel the mystery, propelling himself deeply into the world of international diamond smuggling. He is surrounded by bad guys at every turn and behind it all are Russian and Italian mobsters determined to ensure Cesari has an untimely and unpleasant demise.

Temperature Rising

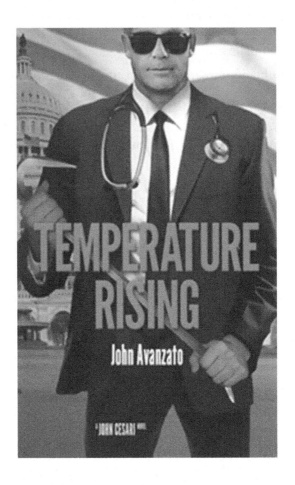

John Cesari is a gangster turned doctor living in Manhattan saving lives one colonoscopy at a time. While on a well-deserved vacation, he stumbles upon a murder scene and becomes embroiled in political intrigue involving the world's oldest profession.

His hot pursuit of the truth leads him to the highest levels of government, where individuals operate above the law. As always, girl trouble hounds him along the way making his already edgy life that much more complex.

The bad guys are ruthless, powerful, and nasty but they are no match for this tough, street-smart doctor from the Bronx who is as comfortable with a crowbar as he is with a stethoscope. Get ready for a wild ride in *Temperature Rising*. The exciting and unexpected conclusion will leave you on the edge of your seat.

Claim Denied

In Manhattan, a cancer ridden patient commits suicide rather than become a financial burden to his family. Accusations of malfeasance are leveled against his caregivers. Rogue gastroenterologist, part-time mobster, John Cesari, is tasked to look into the matter on behalf of St. Matt's hospital.

The chaos and inequities of a healthcare system run amok, driven by corporate greed and endless bureaucratic red tape, become all too apparent to him as his inquiry into this tragedy proceeds. On his way to interview the wife of the dead man, Cesari is the victim of seemingly random gun violence and finds himself on life support.

Recovering from his wounds, he finds that both he and his world are a very different place. His journey back to normalcy rouses in him a burning desire for justice, placing him in constant danger as evil forces conspire to keep him in the dark.

The Gas Man Cometh

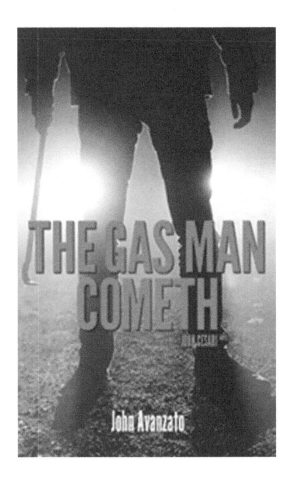

A deranged anesthesiologist with unnatural desires lures innocent women to his brownstone in a swank section of Manhattan. All was going well until John Cesari M.D. came along
becoming a thorn in his side.

Known as The Gas Man, his hatred of Cesari reaches the boiling point. He plots to take him down once and for all turning an ordinary medical conference into a Las Vegas bloodbath.

Hungover and disoriented, Cesari awakens next to a mobster's dead girlfriend in a high-end brothel. Wanted dead or alive by more than a few people, Cesari is on the run with gangsters and the police hot on his trail.

There is never a dull moment in this new thriller as Cesari blazes a trail from Sin City to lower Manhattan desperately trying to stay one step ahead of The Gas Man.

Jailhouse Doc

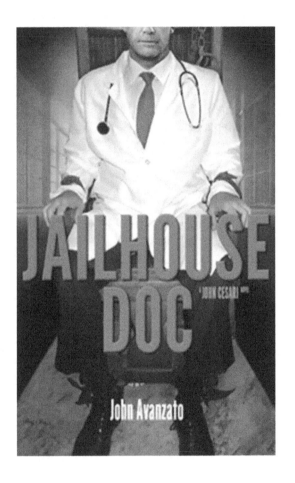

Dr. John Cesari, former mobster turned gastroenterologist, finds himself on the wrong end of the law. A felony conviction lands him in Riker's Island, one of the country's most dangerous correctional facilities, doing community service.

Fighting to survive, he becomes trapped in the web of a vicious criminal gang dealing in drugs and human flesh.

A seemingly unrelated and mysterious death of a college student in Greenwich Village thrusts Cesari into the middle of the action and, forced to take sides, his options are to either cooperate or die.

Sea Sick

Recovering from a broken heart, John Cesari M.D. embarks on a Mediterranean cruise to unwind and clear his head. His goals are to see the sights, eat a lot, and most of all to stay away from women.

A chance encounter in a Venetian Bar with the lusty captain of the Croatian women's national volleyball team just before setting sail turns his plan on its head. When she tells him she is being sold into a forced marriage, he is thrust into the middle of a rollicking, ocean-going adventure to rescue her.

Murder on the high seas wasn't on the itinerary when he purchased his ticket, but in true Cesari fashion, he embraces his fate and dives in.

Pace Yourself

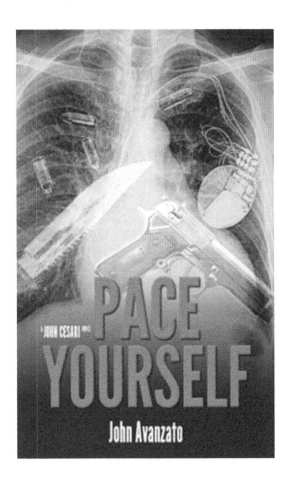

John Cesari's former lover Kelly and her children have gone missing and her husband is found dead in an underground garage. When law enforcement fails to act, Cesari launches his own investigation. He discovers their disappearance is linked to a shady company in Manhattan called EverBeat selling defective pacemakers to hospitals.

EverBeat has ties to both the Chinese military complex in Beijing and to the United States government. Trying to unravel the web of deceit one lie at a time leads to a trail of corpses throughout the city that never sleeps. Hunted by professional killers and thwarted by personal betrayal, his only goal is to save Kelly and her family.

KCM Publishing

a division of KCM Digital Media, LLC

Made in United States
North Haven, CT
21 May 2022

19413056R00251